IF NOT
VICTORY

Novels by Frank O. Hough

RENOWN
IF NOT VICTORY

IF NOT VICTORY

VICTORY

BY FRANK O. HOUGH

CARRICK & EVANS, INC.

NEW YORK

To
Annabel

IF NOT VICTORY

". . . We are at worst
On this side nothing; and by proof we feel
Our power sufficient to disturb his heaven,
And with perpetual inroads to alarm,
Though inaccessible, his fatal throne;
Which, if not victory, is yet revenge."

PARADISE LOST, BOOK II

AUTHOR'S NOTE

The Westchester Guides were real people. Sufficient eye-witness testimony has been preserved in the McDonald Papers to provide the three most prominent with something more than mere names. Thus John Odell and Brom Dyckman play themselves in this book; while the third, Cornelius Oakley, appears thinly fictionized under the name of Abe Kronkhyte. Real, too, were Enoch Crosby, supposed original for J. Fenimore Cooper's "The Spy"; and Elias Cornelius, on whose "Journal" a large portion of Part III is based.

Indeed, aside from Squire Hilton, Molly and the Kronkhyte family, there is not an important character in the book who did not exist either as himself or as a definite, recognizable prototype. Of place names only Hilton Manor and Van Drusen Hall are wholly fictitious, the Powers and Post farms partially so. Most of the major events actually happened approximately as described, although not always at precisely the time and place indicated.

F. O. H.

CONTENTS

PART 1. CLEAVAGE

PART 2. THE NEUTRAL GROUND

PART 3. NOT FOR GLORY

Part 1. Cleavage

Chapter 1

SUNSET

WHEN Abe saw the Young Squire's horse hitched to the post before his father's house, he began to hurry. The green corn, more than knee-high, impeded him as he brushed impatiently between the rows. Even at this distance he could see that the black mare carried full saddlebags and a bulging portmanteau, which meant that the Squire was off on a trip, probably a long one. The prospect of attending him, of getting out of this remote backwater into the world where events were moving so swiftly these days, drove all thoughts of farming from Abe's mind.

He clambered over a stone fence and set off across a sloping pasture. The July sun, close above the western hills, threw his shadow in front of him: the shadow of a lean, wiry youth who walked with the long, knee-bending stride of one accustomed to following the plow. His dark hair and pointed features favored the English rather than the Dutch blood blended in him by three generations in the melting pot that was the Royal Province of New York in the late eighteenth century. Physically Abe Kronkhyte was mature, with the hard, resilient agility which compensates the man of slight build for sheer brute strength. Only his eyes betrayed him: the wide, ingenuous eyes of the back-country rustic.

The black mare nickered companionably at his approach, and he paused to run his hand along her sleek neck. They were old friends, these two. He had groomed her and seen to her wants in many a strange stable: tavern stables and the stables of great estates from one end of the county to the other; on hunting trips where Abe's uncanny nose for game made him well worth his hire; more recently, on business and social journeys where the Young Squire seemed to prefer his company to that of a servant. One of these trips had even taken him to the great city of New York where the houses had to be crowded up against each other to accommodate all the people—more than twenty thousand, someone had told him.

He was too impatient now, however, to waste time on a mere horse. From the open doorway he heard the Young Squire's modulated voice and his father's groping drawl, and he hurried in that direction.

Samuel Hilton, the "Young Squire," was seated in the cottage's tiny living room, facing George Kronkhyte across a narrow table. He acknowledged Abe's arrival with a quick, friendly glance, but his voice continued without a break.

". . . so I'm sure there will be no trouble about the title. If there is anything else you don't entirely understand, please take this opportunity to ask me. I intend to begin my journey immediately upon leaving your house."

"You taking me, Squire?" Abe broke in eagerly. "I can be ready real quick—"

He paused. The Young Squire's face was drawn, his blue eyes dark with trouble.

"Not this time, I'm afraid." His voice sounded natural enough. "Your father needs you here on the farm."

"He can make out, now the hay's in. Can't you, Pa?"

Hilton exchanged a glance with Abe's father, smiled wryly. "I'm afraid I'll be away—quite some little while."

"But he's got along without me other times," Abe protested. He looked from one to the other. Something in their expressions puzzled him; something unfamiliar and vaguely disturbing.

"Get thee outside, Abe," his father said after an instant. "Can't thee see me and Squire's busy?"

He spoke with a heavy finality. Avoiding his eyes, Abe

stared sullenly at the floor, disappointment struggling with a latent antagonism which he had become increasingly aware of during the past few months. But as neither man paid him any further attention, he turned after a moment and slunk out to the kitchen.

His mother was there with his brother Jack, a chunky sixteen-year-old. Heads together, they were bending over a long, closely written paper. They looked up upon his entrance and, in contrast to the worried men in the adjoining room, their faces were beaming.

"Abe!" his mother cried. "Did they tell thee? Did they tell thee what Young Squire's done?"

"All they told me was to get out," Abe said glumly.

"He's sold us the farm!" Jack waved the paper. It looked imposingly legal, with a great red seal in the lower corner beside several scrawled signatures. "Look! It says so right here—well, somewhere in here."

"Sold us the farm?" Abe repeated blankly. "Where did Pa ever get money enough to buy the farm?"

"He paid all he could, and Young Squire fixed it so's he can make up the rest out of crops, just like quitrent," his mother explained. "Leastwise, that's how he told it. Only it ain't quitrent. Thy pa's a real freeholder now!"

Abe was impressed in spite of himself. "You mean he can vote and everything—just like the squire himself?"

"Reckon so. It's all right here in this paper—'deed,' he calls it. He was over to White Plains this morning and entered it in the county records, all legal like. Here, Abe. Do thou read it to us. Jack can't make out some of the words."

Abe took the paper, frowned uncertainly.

> THIS INDENTURE Made this ninth day of July in the year of our Lord one thousand seven hundred and seventy six by and between Samuel Hilton of the town of Bedford in the County of Westchester and Province of New York of the first part and George Kronkhyte farmer of the said Town County and Province aforesaid . . .

He read slowly, screwing up his face with the effort. His unaccustomed tongue stumbled over the strange phraseology.

> . . . absolutely do give grant bargain sell alienate con-
> vey confirm and absolutely make over to him the said
> George Kronkhyte his heirs and assigns . . .

It was only within the past two years that he had learned to read at all—since the Squire had died and the Young Squire, inheriting Hilton Manor, had added to his already heavy responsibilities an unprecedented interest in the welfare of his tenants. He it was who had seen to Abe's schooling, and to Jack's, although the latter had shown no great aptitude or liking for book learning. The Kronkhytes, bound to the soil for generations by the virtually feudal land tenure laws of the region, owed much to the liberalism and generosity of Samuel Hilton. And now—this.

> . . . all that certain parcel or lott of land situate lying
> and being in the above said town bounded as followeth
> beginning at a black oke tree at the North East corner
> of the undivided land and running south by the said
> land one Hundred and Sixty Rods . . .

Abe looked up. "Say! If I got these here boundaries to rights, it ain't only the farm we been working—there's his north pasture and a couple of fields over to the west that always belonged with the Big House. 'Containing ninety acres of land be there more or less,' it says."

Jack slapped his thigh joyously. "Ninety acres! That'll keep us humping! Reckon thee won't have much time to hire out to tend Young Squire and the horses every time he feels like gallivanting all over the county."

Slowly Abe laid down the deed. The brief elation had left his face. "I'll ride with him whenever he wants me, farm or no farm."

His mother's eyes grew shrewd. "He can't make thee, now thy pa's a freeholder."

Abe looked at her, a slow flush creeping up his neck. "He never made me. Anyways, I'd not stand on no such rights, after what he's done for all of us."

"But he don't need thee," his mother protested. "Not really—not with all them black slave men and hired grooms he's got round the Big House and them great stables of his'n!" Her voice took on a whining note. "Goodness knows, he's done harm enough already, taking thee from thy proper work, filling thy head with outlandish notions."

" 'Tis the hire he paid me helped Pa put up cash for the farm," Abe declared hotly. "I'll ride with him any time he wants me."

"Well, I declare! I do believe thee thinks more of Young Squire than of thy own folks."

Abe stared sullenly at the floor. "That ain't true. Only—only—I ain't going to be a slave to no farm!"

"Slave indeed! Thee's been listening to them loafers 'round Hayes's Tavern with their talk of liberty, liberty, liberty. What more liberty does a man want than being free to work his own land?"

Her face, round and red and a little grubby, was intensely earnest. She was a short woman, stockily built and efficient. Although she was much younger than her husband, still in her thirties, years of drudgery had set their mark upon her: the deep furrows etched at the corners of her mouth, the network of tiny lines that crisscrossed under her eyes; the red, rough hands and toil-bent back.

"I don't reckon Young Squire'll take me again, anyhow," Abe said heavily. "So don't you—don't thee go worrying."

He tried to make his tone convincing, but his mother regarded him uncertainly.

"I wouldn't be worrying, 'cepting these times are troublous. I declare to goodness, Abe, it seems sometimes like thee ain't one of us no more since—" She broke off, and her expression became animated once more. "Well, now! All this talk won't get the milking done—nor thy chores either,

Jack. Thy pa will want to have his say, too, so supposing we save it till supper."

Abe grasped a milk pail and hastened to the barn with more alacrity than he had shown in many months. But once inside he did not go immediately to work. At sight of the cows' protruding rumps, all that latent resentment flooded through him again. He turned his back on them and leaned against the wall beside the door, kicking at the jamb with a feeling of frustration.

He was still standing there when his father and the Young Squire came into view around the far corner of the house. He watched them with mingled feelings as they paused for a moment talking together: the tall, lean farmer with his stooped shoulders and seamed, impassive face, looking loutish and uncouth in leather breeches and fustian shirt as he towered above the immaculate young gentleman in cocked hat and shining boots. Then they shook hands briefly, and Samuel Hilton started down the lane alone.

He did not mount at once, but walked along slowly, as though in thought, the black mare's reins looped loosely over his arm. Abe watched him turn toward the west and begin the gradual ascent between the rolling pastures, then ducked out of the barn and set off after him. He moved at an angle that would intercept the lane beyond the first rise, keeping the barn and a few shade trees between himself and the house as long as he could. Once in the open, he began to run.

"Squire! Squire Hilton!"

The man in the lane spun about. One hand flew to his hip. For the first time Abe noticed that he wore both sword and holstered pistols. He drew up short in surprise.

"Oh, it's you!" Hilton's hand fell away from the pistol butt. He looked annoyed for an instant, then grinned wryly. "Well, what's on your mind?"

Abe vaulted the stone fence that separated him from the lane. He was not sure himself what impulse had prompted him to come, and embarrassment clove his tongue to the roof of his mouth.

"About—about the farm. 'Twas real nice of you—"

Hilton shrugged impatiently. "No more thanks, if you please."

He began walking again, the black mare following. Abe fell into step beside him.

"What did you do it for, Squire?"

"What for?" Hilton appeared to consider. "Well, because I like your father, you might say. It gives me pleasure to help him realize the reward he has so honestly earned. It is a theory of mine that worthy, able men should not be denied the opportunity to improve themselves and their position in the world by the operation of arbitrary laws if our country is to benefit from the best that is in her; that every man, regardless of the accident of birth, is entitled to life, liberty and the pursuit of happiness—" He broke off and burst inexplicably into a gale of laughter. "You needn't be frightened," he said quickly, glimpsing Abe's expression. "I'm not going mad. God gave me an ironic sense of humor, that's all."

"What—what's that?" Abe asked uneasily.

"Nothing that need ever trouble you, lad. I was just quoting something I heard at White Plains this morning—some news that decided me to give title to the farm while I still had a chance to."

"You mean about the British soldiers landing on Staten Island?"

Hilton shook his head. "You'll hear soon enough."

He walked on as though engrossed in his thoughts, chin sunk on chest, face troubled. Abe, pacing him in silence, worked himself up to broaching what was really in his mind.

"Squire, you ain't going to stop taking me on your trips, are you?" he blurted.

Hilton looked up. He was smiling; a thin smile, amused,

yet with no mirth in it. "I wouldn't hold my breath till the next trip, Abe," he said drily.

"Where you're going now wouldn't have nothing to do with the war, would it?"

The Young Squire shot him a quick glance. "It's pointless to talk of the war. You know how your father feels."

"He's dead set against any of us taking one side nor t'other."

"Pray God none of you ever has to!"

Abe looked at him doubtfully. "War's against my pa's religion. But being a Quaker never did take with me. If a gentleman like you was to think it's all right to fight—well, I don't want to be stuck way off here with such big doings going on."

Hilton snorted. "Don't be a fool! War's not a game to be played just for the excitement—something to take you briefly out of a way of life that may seem humdrum. Unless a man has ideals worth dying for, he can do nothing more stupid than risk his life—or more criminal than take the lives of others."

He seemed to be speaking more to himself than to Abe, whose forehead was creased with the effort to follow him.

"You've no such ideals. You've no grievance. The underlying causes of the struggle have never affected you in one way or another. The great mass of the people here in Westchester have been isolated from the beginning—more isolated than any in the Province, perhaps in the entire length of the Colonies. We haven't a newspaper in the county, not a city —only scattered farms and a few tiny hamlets scarce worthy to be called villages. With three quarters of our land given over to great manors whose tenants are disenfranchised—why, even the frontier settlements are more alive to political developments than our people! There has been active fighting in New England for over a year. And in Canada. New York City, only a few hours' ride away, has been in turmoil for months. Here? Why, the great majority have been so indifferent, so ignorant of what it's all about, that the Whigs weren't able to establish even a Committee of Correspondence until just recently—and heaven knows, the Tories did little enough to stop 'em." He saw Abe's expression of rustic bewilderment and grinned. "You haven't the faintest idea of what I'm talking about, have you?"

"I—can't rightly say I have," Abe admitted.

"It's no matter. Forgive me for thinking aloud."

They walked on in silence. A short distance ahead the summit of the rising ground loomed black against the sunset sky.

"Do you remember Mr. Tilman who went hunting with us a year ago?" Hilton demanded unexpectedly.

"Why—yes, sir."

"He was my closest friend. Now he's an officer in the Rebel army up north. And Captain Campbell with whom I dined that time you rode to New York with me—he is on Staten Island today, raising a battalion for the King's service. Mr. Bartlet who visited the Manor so often this spring; Mr. Delancey who used to be our High Sheriff—they are with the British, too. General Montgomery, whom you admired so much, died leading the Rebels against Quebec. A hundred conflicting loyalties tug us this way and that—set friend against friend, neighbor against neighbor."

Again he seemed to be thinking aloud. Abe tried to ward off a premonition.

"But you, Squire?" he ventured. "You been a Whig right along, ain't you, even if maybe you didn't holler loud as some?"

"I've disapproved the acts of the Ministry, if that's what you mean. I've supported the Congress and followed its admonitions—drunk no tea in a year, clothed my household in homespun rather than buy imported fabrics. If I have taken no active part, that is because I have been unable to define the issue clearly in my own mind. I've been groping through this maze of ideas, ideals, motives—groping to find the ultimate loyalty that remains when all the superficialities, the plausibilities, are stripped away: that which is so much bigger than any man that he can fight for it with all his power, because he believes in it with his heart as well as his mind. Today a paper was read on the Court House steps at White Plains—" He broke off and a sudden spasm contorted his face. "Oh, my God! A man must have something he can cleave to!"

He came to an abrupt halt. They had topped the rise and stood at the edge of an upland pasture. The wide valley below was patterned with fields and woodland, clear and still. Beyond it the crimson-tinted hills rolled northward, rise on rise, toward the Hudson Highlands, blue with distance. For a long moment Samuel Hilton stood motionless, looking out over the vista he had known since childhood, face pensive, a cloud across his eyes.

Abe broke the leaden silence. "Night will catch you 'fore you can ride far," he said uneasily. "See—the sun's setting already."

"Aye. The sun is setting over all America. Over the America that we know and love."

Abe did not know what moved the Squire. All he knew was that this man who had been so good to him, whom he had looked up to all his life and passionately wished to emulate, was grievously troubled.

"Take me with you, Squire!" he burst out. "Wherever you're going—whatever you're doing—"

Hilton shook his head. "I ride alone. I've asked not even a slave to follow me. Least of all would I influence a lad like you." For a moment longer his eyes clung to the north-rolling hills. Then abruptly he was his familiar self again; brisk, matter-of-fact. "I'll be mounting now, so get along home with you. Here!" He reached into his pocket and drew out a handful of coins. "Here's something to keep life on the farm from becoming too monotonous."

Abe stared at the coins heaped in his hand. "I don't want

your money, Squire," he said miserably. "I want—to go with you."

"Nonsense. Walk over to the village after chores and drink a glass or two to my early return." The Young Squire caught a stirrup and swung up into the saddle. "It might be as well, though," he added, "if you didn't mention to the crowd around the tavern where I'm going—at least, until I'm well away."

"But—but I don't even know where you're going, sir."

Hilton's jaw dropped. "You don't know where—for God's sake, what do you suppose I've been talking about?" He checked himself. That smile came back to his face; that strange, thin smile that had no mirth in it. "I'm going to fight for the British, lad," he said, and jerked the black mare's head around toward the south.

Chapter 2

STRANGERS IN BEDFORD

Abe sensed excitement in the air as soon as he reached Bedford village, even before he saw the crowd collected in front of Hayes's Tavern and heard their clamor. In Westchester, where the Church had never gained any such permeating influence as in New England, the taverns usually served as the real social centers of scattered rural communities. Many had placed bulletin boards beside their doors as a means of serving and attracting customers, and the Whig committees, now virtually the only government the county boasted, took every means to see that news and important notices were posted there as often as possible. What held this crowd was doubtless the news which, heard at White Plains earlier in the day, had affected the Young Squire so profoundly. Abe hurried forward.

A notice was posted, as he had guessed, a large, imposing-looking sheet, but the crowd was so dense that Abe could not get close enough to make out what it said in the uncertain light. A man stood by the board, apparently reading, proclaiming rather, its contents to the others. He was a stranger, a well-to-do farmer to judge by his clothes, tall and angular with an elongated chin and hollow cheeks above which a pair of narrow-set eyes burned with almost disconcerting intensity. He orated to the accompaniment of jerky gestures, but the hodgepodge of unfamiliar words he poured forth only bewildered Abe further.

The man came to the end at last and paused to wipe his

forehead. A few listeners raised a cheer, but most of them looked as puzzled as Abe felt.

"What's it about?" he asked the man nearest him, a neighboring tenant from Hilton Manor.

"Be danged if I can figure. Something the Congress's done down to Philadelphy." He raised his voice. "Say, Mr. Crawford, what's 'the pursuit of happiness' mean?"

The lantern-jawed man brought his head up with a snap. His too-bright eyes ranged over the crowd.

"Must you have an interpreter for these sublime words?" he demanded. "Can it be that the citizens of this prosperous village can fail to grasp the significance of this great human document? Very well! I shall read it again."

"Never mind that. Just tell us what it says."

But Crawford was not to be denied. Evidently he knew its contents by heart, for after a single brief glance at the document he struck an attitude, and his voice boomed out once more, a bit nasally.

"When in the course of human events it becomes necessary for one people to sever the ties . . ."

For all his oratorical gestures, he spoke in a monotone, slurring over words, running others together.

"Reckon I'll wait till I can read it myself," Abe told his neighbor and strolled into the tavern.

The outside attraction had all but emptied the large ordinary. At the farther end a girl with rolled-up sleeves was vigorously wiping the bar with a towel.

"Hello," Abe said shyly.

The girl glanced up. "Well, if it ain't Squire Hilton's little playmate. Does your pa know where you're at?"

Abe shuffled his feet and looked at the floor. His face turned a fiery red.

The girl laughed. "There, lad! Ye needn't be so bashful— I got no designs on ye." She had a ruddy, cheerful face and dancing blue eyes. Jet black hair strayed in lank strands from under her soiled mobcap, but there was a bright, buxom efficiency about her for all her slovenliness. "What'll ye be after drinking—small beer, maybe?"

Abe nodded. As she turned to draw the beer from a barrel spigot, his eyes followed her with diffident admiration.

"W-what's all the shouting for?" he ventured as she set the foaming pewter mug before him. "Seems like nobody can make head nor tail out of what that fellow's saying."

The barmaid nodded toward a nearby table. "Ye might ask them bully boys. They come with the skinny one."

Abe saw two young men not much older than himself debating over a brown bottle that stood on the table between them. The larger he recognized as John Odell from the northern part of Phillipse Manor with whom he had hunted several times among the wooded hills of that region.

"Hullo, John!" he called.

The big man looked up. He seemed to have a little difficulty in focusing his eyes, then he beamed and waved. "Come on over and set!" he invited hospitably. "And bring your own drink," he added.

His companion shook his head. "That's John for you—never taking no chances, not even on having to put out a drink for a friend."

"Well, we ain't got much left," Odell retorted, "and nothing to buy more with. And the rate old blowhard's going, we're like to be on this job all night." He gestured. "Abe, shake hands with Brom Dyckman from down Kingsbridge way. Abe's best rifle shot in the county, Brom, even if he is a Quaker."

"A Quaker?" the stranger repeated. He stared at Abe incredulously. "Well, for Christ's sake!"

Abe stiffened. "What's there to get profane about?" he demanded. He set his beer down on the table. "If you don't like it, you know what you can do."

Dyckman blinked. "Say! What kind of Quaker talk ye call that? Why, John, I do believe the skinny little rooster wants to fight me! *Me!*" He rose to his feet, beaming. His smile held nothing of animosity, only pleased anticipation.

"Aw, sit down," Odell said wearily. "You're like to get a bellyful of fights soon enough without starting none in taverns."

Abe stood his ground. Seated, the stranger had appeared as large as Odell, or nearly so, with wide, lithe shoulders and a thick, short neck. But his bulk was mostly from the waist up. Standing on his bowed legs, he was no taller than Abe, though a good deal heavier.

"Sit down," Odell repeated. His vigorous six-feet-three heaved up out of the chair, towering over his companion. An arm, extraordinarily long even for that great height, shot across the table, and a fist the size and color of a ham gripped Dyckman's shoulder. "He don't mean no harm," Odell explained to Abe. "He likes to fight just for the hell of it."

"And I ain't never fought a Quaker," Dyckman added. He laughed, his teeth flashing white against his swarthy, tanned skin; a quick, easy laugh that had a carelessly infectious quality. "I reckon you might as well set, my boy. You sure can't be no worse company than this big dray horse I been with all afternoon."

"You ain't no more fed up than I am," Odell declared. "You see, Abe, we was detailed by the Committee to ride with Capt'n Crawford out there while he took the Declaration 'round this part of the county—to keep any Tories from knocking him about. Every place we stop, he's got to show folks how important he is by orating, like you see, so Brom and me sits around waiting for him to finish and enjoys what hospitality is provided." He picked up the brown bottle. "Only here seems like the providing ain't up to snuff."

"Have a drink on me," Abe said quickly. "I—that is, I got a little money."

Dyckman brightened. "Have you, now! Ho, Molly! The wench's name's Molly, ain't it? Ho! Fill 'em up!"

The barmaid wiped her hands on her apron and came

over without haste. She ignored the others and addressed Abe. "I heard what they was saying. Don't you let these drunken loafers put on you."

Abe blushed. "It's all right. They—they're friends of mine."

"Ye might choose your friends more careful, seems like."

Abe saw, however, that she was smiling. And not at him. Her gaze passed expertly over John Odell's very masculine bulk and lingered on Dyckman's reckless, laughing eyes. Dyckman, Abe noticed for the first time, was unusually handsome in a rough-cut way.

"What'll you have, boys?" he asked glumly.

Dyckman appeared to consider. "Make mine flip."

"Flip? What's flip?" the girl demanded suspiciously.

"Flip's a New Englander's idea of a drink, sweetheart. You put a gill of rum with a pint of strong beer, then stick in a hot loggerhead. It foams up right pretty."

"New Englanders!" Odell jeered. "That's his way of showing you, miss, he's been down to New York where the army is. I'll have Jersey lightning, and don't spoil it with no beer."

Abe downed the rest of his beer and handed her the empty mug. "I'll try flip," he said bravely. He turned to Dyckman. "I was in New York once."

"Me, I live there," Dyckman declared airily. "Leastwise, I live on York Island," he amended quickly as he saw Odell's mouth open. "Man, I wish I was down there tonight! Most like the Sons of Liberty'll be putting out free liquor for all, now the Declaration's signed."

"The Declaration? That's what I come over to find out. What's this here Declaration, anyways?"

"Why, the Declaration of Independence, of course! That's what old sourface outside's trying to get through them people's heads."

"Independence?" Abe repeated blankly. "You mean they gone and done it—said we—the Colonies, that is—ain't English no more?"

"Well, they used more words, but you covered just about as much ground. The Congress signed it last week, and the York Convention proclaimed it today over to White Plains where they been meeting since the British fleet scared 'em out of the city. Reckon they mean business this time."

"Oh," Abe said. To avoid his companions' eyes, he gripped the hot mug the barmaid had set before him and buried his face in the pungent steam. The concoction had a queer burned taste, like liquid leather, he thought.

"There won't be no backing down now," Odell was saying. "Look you, Abe. There's a company forming over to White Plains, figuring to go down and join the army right off, 'thout waiting regular militia call. Volunteers, that's what—all young fellows like us. Why'n't you join us?"

"Me? Why, I—"

"Sure, come on!" Dyckman put in. "We elect our own officers, so we won't have to take orders from none of them damn New Englanders—nor from windbags like big-jaw Crawford out there, neither."

"And we'll draw full pay and rations like the Continental regulars," the practical Odell added, "only we won't be under Continental regulations, which they tell me's something fierce. You like hunting, don't you? Well, this ought to beat the best ever."

Abe looked from one to the other. A prickling, exuberant expectancy bubbled up inside of him, filling the emptiness that had been there an instant before. "You think they'd take me? I mean, I only just turned nineteen—"

"A fellow can shoot like you can? Hell, Abe! We ain't much older ourselves."

" 'Twill be a fine donnybrook, me lads, and no foolin'!" Molly the barmaid cried unexpectedly. She had lingered by the table waiting to be paid for the drinks, but that object seemed forgotten for the instant. Her rosy face had turned a deeper red, and her Irish eyes were alight with excitement.

"What I wouldn't give for a swing at them lobsterbacks my own self!"

Dyckman laughed uproariously. "Come along with us, sister!" He caught her around the waist and pulled her over to him. "We'll find a berth for you—eh, lads?"

"You keep your big hands off of me!" she cried indignantly. She pushed him away, but Abe saw that she was still smiling; at him this time. To cover his confusion, he downed what remained of his flip at a gulp, oblivious to its heat.

"Fill 'em up again!" he ordered. He pulled some coins from his pocket. Suddenly they felt icy in his hand. He stared at them for an instant, bewildered. The money the Young Squire had given him; Samuel Hilton, who had been his friend, his family's benefactor; who had ridden away from his home a scant hour ago, not knowing when he would return. He held the coins there in a hand gone nerveless until Molly snatched them up with a laugh and bustled back to the bar with the empty mugs.

"What ails ye?" Dyckman demanded. "You look kind of sick."

"Must be that damn flip," Odell suggested. "I always said it ain't no drink for a white man."

"It—it ain't the flip," Abe said. He rubbed a puzzled hand across his forehead. It came away clammy.

In the momentary lull the clamor of the crowd in front of the tavern sounded very loud all at once. Crawford had stopped orating at long last. He stood beside the notice board in what he must have imagined a striking attitude, viewing the effect of his efforts with eminent self-satisfaction. Awareness of the full significance of the Declaration appeared to have penetrated his auditors simultaneously. The din of cheers and shouts swept upward to a crescendo; not sporadic now, but frantic and excited. Then suddenly, with the same mass unanimity, the whole pack burst through the door and swept like a tidal wave toward the bar where Ben Hayes, with the foresight of long experience, had already reinforced Molly.

The ordinary became a bedlam. Everybody seemed to be talking at once at the top of his voice, slapping the back of the man nearest him. Abe viewed the extraordinary scene in amazement, but his companions' expressions showed tolerant boredom.

"We seen this a dozen times already today," Odell explained. "Better look to your musket, Brom. We'll be leaving soon."

For the first time Abe observed that his companions were armed. There was nothing unusual about that, for many travelers took their guns along in the hope of knocking over small game along their way. But now the sight of those long brown barrels had a new and faintly sinister implication.

"Neighbors! Friends! Hear me!"

The voice, repeating the words, penetrated the din by degrees. A man, his back against the bar, was facing the crowd, trying to make himself heard.

"This Declaration—it ain't right, neighbors!"

Briefly the words sounded clear; then a chorus of catcalls drowned them out.

"Who's that?" inquired Dyckman with reawakening interest.

By climbing on a chair, Abe was able to see over the heads of the crowd. The man at the bar was stooped, with big, gnarled hands and a seamed face burned dark by the summer sun.

"It's old Seth Wiggin—works a small freehold out along the Poundridge Road," he reported.

" 'Tain't right, I tell ye!" the farmer shouted. "Our Congress delegates been agin it right along. The general—General Washington himself—he's been agin it, too. It's them consarned New Englanders put this over on us!"

The crowd gave back a little, and for an instant the clamor died down.

"That was long ago!" someone yelled. "That was before we'd been fighting the scoundrels for a year!"

"Shut up, ye old bastard!"

"Treason! Treason!"

Again the din rose, but Abe saw that here and there men with faces gone thoughtful did not join in.

"Neighbors, listen to me! This means the end of hopes to get our troubles settled peaceful-like. There won't be no stopping 'em now. They'll ride over us roughshod, crush us—"

"We'll stop 'em our own selves!"

"Us—stop the regulars? Why, they got a whole fleet off New York right now. They've already drove our people out of Canada, and they'll be coming down the lakes any day— thousands on 'em! We'll be smashed like between the hammer and the anvil."

Crawford, the man who had posted the Declaration, cleared a passage through the crowd and confronted the speaker.

"You mean to say the regulars will overcome us now that the Colonies are united?" he demanded.

"I sure do!"

"You're a liar!"

"Ye say that, I reckon, because you never seen no regulars," the old man returned tolerantly. "Me, I seen aplenty. I fought side by side with 'em back in the French War. I don't like 'em no better'n you do. But we ain't a-going to whip 'em—not with troops that turns tail first time they hear volley fire, headed by officers don't know their arse from their elbow!"

Crawford's face was convulsed. "Arrest that man!" he shouted.

In an instant the room went deathly silent.

"Arrest me?" Wiggin cried, aghast. "In God's name, what for?"

"As an enemy to the United States of America!"

The old man scratched his head. "I never heard of these here United States till you just now read that damn Declaration," he said. "But I ain't no more an enemy to America than you be. I been for the rights of America all along, like my neighbors here'll tell ye. Only the rights of America won't be served by—"

"Arrest this Tory, I tell you!" Crawford spun about furiously. "Who's on your Committee here? Who's head of your militia?"

An embarrassed man stepped forward. "I be—Ebenezer Lockwood, at your service." He eyed the stranger doubtfully. "You reckon it's really bad's all that, Capt'n Crawford? Seth Wiggin here, he's one of our most respected citizens—"

"Crawford, huh!" Wiggin interrupted. "I know ye now! Ye're Sam'l Crawford from down Scarsdale way—the feller been ranting round the county hollering 'Tory' at all them as don't see eye to eye with ye." His arm shot out, shook a knobby finger under the thin man's nose. "Here's something else I learned a-fighting the French: loud-mouthed fellers with big outsticking chins like yourn is either dumb brave like a bulldog or ain't got the guts of a louse. If ye want to prove which you be, then try standing up to those there regulars ye belittle and leave honester folks alone!"

Someone laughed. The sound seemed to bring Crawford to himself. His face, livid an instant before, darkened with returning color. Turning his back on Wiggin, he addressed the crowd, his criticized jaw thrust forward still farther.

"Fellow citizens," he began, "this is no time to indulge in personalities." His voice was controlled, dangerously calm. "I appear before you this evening as special emissary of the Convention of the State of New York and the Westchester County Committee of Safety. By the rulings of both these bodies the words you heard spoken a moment ago constitute treason and render the speaker subject to instant arrest. I bear no personal ill will toward your Tory neighbor, but—"

"I'm no more Tory than you be!" Wiggin protested indignantly.

Crawford ignored the interruption. "This Tory has damned the Declaration of Independence proclaimed by your own duly elected delegates. He has belittled our soldiers, criticized our officers, declared our sacred cause to be hopeless. If such talk does not brand him an enemy to America, what in heaven's name does?"

"If this here's a free country like your Declaration says, why ain't a man free to speak his mind?" Wiggin demanded.

But the crowd's attention was on Crawford now. The old man seemed to sense the shift, and for the first time a troubled expression crossed his face. The emissary sensed it too, and his posture became more dramatic.

"We are confronting a desperate struggle. A life and death struggle. To that extent what this Tory says is true. A determined enemy is moving against us on two fronts—hired mercenaries, paid to kill! Can our brave soldiers face those enemies with confidence, knowing that other enemies lurk behind them—crawling snakes in the grass, seeking to thwart them at every turn?"

He paused, and his fanatic eyes swept the faces of his audience. "There are those of you right in this room who belong to the militia. Soon you will be called out—not just for monthly muster, but to offer your very lives on the altar of freedom! How will *you* feel if there are skulking traitors waiting only a safe opportunity to slip a knife into your backs? When you march away to defend your homes and firesides from the brutal enemy in front, will you leave your loved ones at the mercy of these enemies in the rear? No, I say to you! A thousand times no! These traitors must be stamped out! Now is the time, before—"

A hoarse rumble drowned his voice; an ominous mutter, rising like the voice of an angry sea. It sent a chill upward along Abe's spine, set the hair roots on the back of his neck atingle. From his vantage point on the chair he looked down at his companions. Odell's face was troubled, but Dyckman suppressed a yawn.

"The Capt'n's sure in top form tonight," he observed.

Wiggin had reeled back against the bar. His face, gone pale under its tan, looked drawn and sallow.

"Neighbors!" he croaked. "Friends—" For the first time the quaver of age sounded in his voice.

Crawford pointed dramatically. "Seize that traitor!"

Half a dozen men sprang forward. But Lockwood, the local militia captain, interposed. He was a short, stocky man with an earnest, honest face.

"Hold hard, Capt'n Crawford! Seth Wiggin, he's just an old man. He won't do none of those things—"

"He'll weave a whole tissue of lies out of one thread of truth. You heard him! And because he's been respected, folks'll believe what he says." Crawford thrust his face within inches of the old man's. "Will you sign the Articles of Association?" he demanded.

Wiggin steadied himself. "Like hell I will!"

A burly youth brushed both Lockwood and Crawford aside. "Swear the oath, ye son of a bitch!"

Wiggin shook his head. A swinging fist caught him flush on the mouth, knocked him sprawling half across the bar.

"Take the oath, Seth!" Lockwood urged. "Take it, man, and they'll leave you be!"

The old man drew himself erect. He spat out a couple of yellowed teeth. Scorn burned the brief glaze from his eyes. "So ye'd have me a damn coward like the rest," he mumbled.

"Douse him in the creek!"

"Where's tar and feathers?"

"String up the Tory bastard!"

Now the mob was in full cry. The old man, struggling futilely, was half carried, half dragged, to the door. Here there was a moment of confusion as everybody tried to get out at once. Then the taproom was empty and seemingly silent, for all the din outside.

The terrified numbness snapped in Abe. He leaped down from the chair. "He's a friend of my pa's! I got to—"

Dyckman's long arm pulled him back. "Sit down, you fool. Try and stop 'em, and you're like to get a dose of the same."

"I don't like this kind of business," Odell said uneasily. "If a fellow's honest in being Tory, seems like they could leave him be—leastwise, a harmless old man like that."

Dyckman shrugged. "Oh, let 'em have their fun. They ain't going to do him no real hurt. Hell! Down in the city things like this been happening every day almost."

Abe stared at him. "You mean the Whigs do this to any Tories got the courage to stand up to 'em?"

"Sure—if there's enough of 'em and the Tories ain't armed. There's a war going on, in case you hadn't heard, and in a war lots of folks get hurt one way or another." He rose and reached for his musket. "Hist, John! Here comes old big-mouth."

Crawford had reappeared in the tavern doorway. Frozen, Abe stared at him with a sort of horrified fascination. He appeared harmless enough now. What he conceived as his duty finished, his big jaw hung slack with weariness, and his too-bright eyes had dulled to a satiated glow.

"Come along, lads," he said matter-of-factly. "The crowd'll take care of him now, and we must carry the Declaration on to Salem."

Odell rose, too; hiked up his breeches. His big hand fell on Abe's back with hearty friendliness. "See you at White Plains soon. Come quick's you can, 'cause we're for the army most any day."

Abe heard himself mumble a reply; he never knew exactly what. He watched them go out, Crawford looking slight and ineffectual between his husky escorts: a yapping terrier, safe between two impassive mastiffs. Then he was alone at the table, alone amid the eerie shadows cast by the flickering candles that emphasized the emptiness of the suddenly silent taproom. He raised his mug with an unsteady hand. Neglected during the commotion, the flip had become tepid. The acrid, leathery taste of the burnt beer gagged him.

Molly was still at her post, the only other person left in the room, leaning nerveless against the bar. He went over and laid money for the last drinks at her elbow. She looked up, and there were unexpected tearstains on her cheeks.

"Poor Mr. Wiggin! And him always such a nice old man. Tory or not, I'm right glad you and your friends took no part, Abe."

She had called him by name for the first time; him, the impecunious son of a small tenant farmer. She seemed very close, all at once, her blue eyes soft and friendly.

"You heard what those fellows was saying to me," he blurted. "You think I ought to go off with 'em?"

"Go off and fight? Why, sure!"

"To fight for folks who pick on helpless neighbors—them who's been their friends?" He saw her puzzled expression. "I don't know nothing about this war only what I seen hereabouts. I—Pa and me—we got no grievance 'gainst nobody." What remained of the Young Squire's money pressed against his thigh in a small, knotty lump. "You reckon it's right to take arms against people—kill 'em maybe—not knowing what for?"

Her expression changed. "Why we got Congress delegates, 'cept to figure out 'what for' for us? You're a man, ain't ye?"

He gulped but could not speak. The tears had vanished from her eyes, the momentary softness with them. After a few seconds she turned away. He watched her pick up his money, watched her lips move mechanically as she counted it, then laid change disdainfully on the bar in front of him.

He was not a man as he slunk from the tavern, turned in the direction away from the mob that howled on the village green. He was only a back-country farm boy, tongue-tied, frightened, lonelier than he had been in all his life.

Chapter 3

THE TRANSIENT PERSON

Abe met the stranger first one afternoon in late September while he and his father were mowing in the field that lay along the main road. The man sat his horse by the stone fence for several minutes while Abe cut a swath toward him. When they were within easy speaking distance, the stranger inquired how much farther it was to the village. There was nothing unusual in such an inquiry. The county was full of strangers these days: militia officers from other parts, members of the State Convention, Whig refugees from Long Island, Sons of Liberty and other of that ilk who had been obliged to flee New York upon its recent occupation by the British. Abe replied readily enough, but the stranger showed a disposition to chat.

"Maybe you can tell me what's the best tavern," he suggested. "I'm like to stop over several days. Interested in a deal in livestock," he added, smiling for no apparent reason.

"Try Ben Hayes's, mister. It's across from the church, hard by the green."

"Thanks, I will. Stop by some evening and I'll buy you a drink in return for your help. Miller's the name."

"That's right kind of you, mister. Don't mind if I do."

The stranger still lingered. He was a florid man, strongly built, with nothing distinctive about his appearance unless it were his eyes: quick, keen, with a shrewd, appraising look to them. His clothes were of good quality but lacked the finishing touches that proclaimed the gentry.

"You folks are tenants of Squire Hilton, ain't you?" he asked. "I heard tell he'd gone Tory."

"What's that to thee?" George Kronkhyte demanded. He had thrown down his scythe and come up quickly behind his son. His lean, weathered face was hard, his eyes hostile.

"Why, I was just passing the time of day," the stranger protested, surprised.

"Then pass it and leave folks to their work!" The elder Kronkhyte turned to Abe. "Get on with thy mowing," he ordered curtly, and strode back to his own swath.

Abe reddened in mortification. Since the Tory mobbing, more than two months before, he had been at pains to avoid the village, with the result that he had had small opportunity to talk with anyone but his own family and the nearest neighbors. If he had been restless under restriction before, he was doubly so now.

"You go getting many more folks down on us, and we're like to end up in Peekskill jail right quick!" Abe declared later, as he and his father were returning to the house, the day's work finished. "We been suspect enough on Young Squire's account and because of you refusing all truck with the Committee."

George Kronkhyte grunted. "It ain't keeping a tight mouth gets a fellow in trouble, Abe. It's talking free and easy with every transient person comes along."

"Keeping a civil tongue's never done no harm I heard of!"

The stranger, however, appeared to have taken no offense. He rode by again the following day when Abe was working alone and repeated his invitation to have a drink with him at Hayes's.

"Your pa's right, lad," he shrugged when Abe attempted to apologize. " 'Twas my fault for mentioning politics."

"Pa's so dead set on keeping clear of both parties, he won't talk to nobody hardly."

"I reckon that's about the only way it can be done. Up this

way it seems like everybody who ain't an out-and-out Whig's counted a Tory. Now, out to Long Island it's t'other way about. Guess it's a matter of which army's closest, which party's top dog."

"Oh, you come from Long Island?"

"Aye—and I come fast as hell, once them redcoats landed!" He laughed at what he appeared to consider a rare joke. "Well, I'll be looking for you at the ordinary this evening."

Abe thought that over, and the more he thought, the more tempted he was. This was a Saturday, and there would be a crowd in the village during the evening, eager for news and gossip and congenial companionship. Restlessness overcame his reluctance as the afternoon wore on. After supper he arranged with Jack to do his share of the chores, then ducked off down the road without telling anyone where he was going.

By the time he reached the outskirts of the village, he realized that this was an extraordinary Saturday evening, even for these troubled times. The single street was so crowded that at first glance it reminded him of his one short visit to New York. Saddle horses were tied to every hitching post on either side, lined two deep in front of the taverns, occasional carts and wagons showing among them. A few tents were pitched haphazardly on the green.

"Militia from Dutchess County," explained a passer-by in response to Abe's question.

"What they doing here?"

"On their way to Kingsbridge. Ain't ye heard?"

"What for?"

"I don't know. Go ask Eb Lockwood. He's over to Hayes's."

The captain of the local militia company was standing beside the bulletin board in front of the tavern, hemmed in by a crowd of men, all of whom appeared to be talking at once. He looked harried and sweaty, and was gesticulating with his big farmer's hands in an effort to dominate the situation.

" 'Tain't what you fellows like or don't like," he shouted above the clamor. "We're called out, and by God, we're a-going!"

"I tell ye, I can't, Eb," one man cried. "My grain ain't in yet."

"Mine neither. How's my kids going to eat if my crops are ruined?"

"Let somebody else go! We was out last June when them frigates come up-river."

"Aye—ye was out," retorted Lockwood bitterly. "For four days ye was out, then the whole pack of ye begun sneaking off home. 'Twas the hay ye had to get in then. Ye think more of yer crops and cattle than ye do of yer country."

Briefly the clamor subsided. Lockwood mopped his brow.

"It ain't only us fellows," he continued. "All the milishy in the county's called, and them in Dutchess and Orange and Ulster, too. If men that far off's willing to go, what right you got to complain? They got crops, too, ain't they?"

"Listen, Eb," someone suggested. "Why don't ye take them as can be spared to home and let the rest stay. There'd be enough."

Lockwood looked dubious. "Well, how many of ye allow ye can be spared? Let's see ye raise yer hands."

A few hands went up here and there; then, reluctantly, a few more—perhaps a dozen altogether. Lockwood shook his head.

" 'Twon't do. Reg'lations say fifty privates to the company; three corporals, three sergeants, two lieutenants and me—not counting fife and drum which we never did have."

"Oh, you ain't doing so bad!" called the Dutchess County captain who had been watching sympathetically. "I only had 'bout twenty to start, and a couple of them's gone home already."

"Try beating for volunteers, Eb. There's plenty of men hereabouts who ain't enrolled for one reason or another who're better off to go than most of us."

The crowd caught up the idea eagerly.

"That's it—drum 'em up!"

"Make 'em show their colors!"

Someone grasped Abe's arm. "How 'bout you, young fellow?"

"Hey!" cried Abe, startled. "Leggo o' me!"

"It's young Kronkhyte."

"His pa's a Tory."

Strong hands hustled him through the crowd. He had a bewildered impression of a sea of faces, open mouths. Everybody seemed to be shouting now.

"My pa's no Tory," he protested. "He needs me on the farm—"

"Yah! Needs three to work that scrubby little rock pile!"

By now Abe could not have made himself heard, even had he been able to think of anything to say. Memory of what had happened to old Seth Wiggin came over him, and he paled.

Lockwood placed a protective arm about his shoulders. "I won't let 'em touch ye, Abe," he said quietly, lips close to Abe's ear. "Ye needn't come 'less ye want to. But why don't ye, lad? 'Twould mean an end to folks making trouble for yer pa."

Anger burned away Abe's confusion. "I ain't taking arms just to save trouble for nobody—nor for the threat of trouble, neither."

"Now, now!" Lockwood soothed. "I ain't trying to threaten ye." He grinned faintly. "Just thought you might like it better'n working on the farm, that's all. Supposing ye slip into the ordinary and think over that side of it."

He edged over to the tavern's open doorway and, when Abe had dodged hurriedly inside, interposed his reassuring bulk. But none of the crowd attempted to follow. The militiamen were disgruntled rather than angry and had already found a new subject.

Most of the tavern's patrons had been drawn to the door

and windows by the commotion. They made way for Abe with the amused tolerance of onlookers privileged to see a compatriot in trouble without being involved themselves.

"Well, well! It's my young Quaker friend."

Abe winced and sprang nervously aside as a heavy hand slapped down upon his back.

"Oh! It's you, Mr.—Mr. Miller."

"And ready to buy you that drink," agreed the transient person heartily. "What'll it be?"

"Why—beer, I guess."

The stranger snorted. "You need something stronger 'n beer after what you just been through. Why, look at yourself!"

Abe became aware that he was trembling. "They can't bully me!"

"Sure not!" Miller laughed and guided him toward the bar. "Them super-patriots is brave as all get-out, ain't they, when they're fifty 'gainst one—specially if that one ain't armed!"

"You think they'll make trouble for Pa? By God! If they do, I'll—"

"You'll what, son?"

Abe gulped. There was nothing he could do, and he knew it. Miller watched him curiously for a moment longer, then shouted for a bottle of the best rum in the house. Molly the barmaid set it in front of him, together with two pewter mugs. Miserably Abe avoided her eyes.

"Here, lad. Drink deep and you'll feel better."

Abe tossed off the fiery liquor neat with what he tried to make appear an experienced gesture. It burned his throat and set him sputtering and brought tears to his eyes, but he contrived to swallow quite a bit. He could feel it sinking down inside of him like a tangible weight, spreading a pleasant warmth. Miller promptly replenished his mug.

"Take it slower this time," he advised with a grin. "So you figure farming's a better life than soldiering, huh?"

"I didn't say nothing of the sort," Abe protested. "Capt'n Lockwood knows I got no love for the farm. That's what made him say what he did."

"Then I'd think you'd jump at the chance to be a red-hot patriot, despite your pa."

Abe blinked. "Hell, mister! I don't know nothing about being a patriot. I can't make no more head nor tail out of what them Whig orators shout about than—than most of them militia can, if you was to pin 'em down." He gulped some more rum, and his jaw set stubbornly. "I got my own reasons for not taking up arms, and I ain't a-going to be bullied into it, that's all."

Miller grinned. "I don't blame you, lad. Still, soldiering can be a real good life. You ought to try it sometime."

"Say!" Suspicion filled Abe's eyes. "You ain't trying to talk me around to the militia?"

The stranger shook his head slowly, deliberately. "I said 'soldiering,' " he corrected.

Abe became conscious again of sound and movement elsewhere in the room. The patrons who had gathered to watch the excitement were beginning to drift back to their tables and toward the bar. Outside, Captain Lockwood still argued with his recalcitrant company, but less emphatically now.

"He'll be coming in presently to ask you yes or no." Miller's grin had vanished. "Him and his men behind him, all shouting you down. Suppose we go up to my room where they won't think to look for you." He caught up the bottle and turned toward the stairs. "Grab them mugs and come along."

As Abe started mechanically to obey, Molly grasped his arm across the bar. "Don't you go with him!" she whispered urgently.

"Huh?"

"I been listening. That fellow's a recruiter, I tell ye! There

was three of 'em through last month—'listing men for the
Continentals. Have a care!"

Abe stared at her open-mouthed for an instant. Then resentment flamed in his cheeks. "So you reckon I ain't able
to take care of myself, huh?"

"Ye little fool! 'Tis drunk ye are already."

Abe snatched his hand away furiously. At the door Miller
had turned to look back for him. He seized the mugs and
crossed the room walking straight as a die.

He did not feel drunk in the least as he followed his new
friend up the inn's narrow staircase—only self-sufficient, ad-
venturous. Strong drink was no novelty to youths in this region. Cider and home-brewed beer were available on every
farm, often to children barely able to walk. And for those
desiring something more robust, there was applejack and its
first cousins, peachy and pearry; also metheglin, made from
honey, and a distillate of grains known as whiskey. But rum
was something new to Abe, and compared to New England's
famous tipple the homely concoctions with which he was
acquainted appeared crude and feeble. He had had enough
by now to stimulate his mental processes for the moment,
however it might affect them subsequently. By the time they
reached the top of the stairs, Molly's words had taken effect,
and the instant they were in Miller's room he leveled an
accusing finger.

"You can't fool me," he declared. "You're a recruiter!"

"Hush!" Miller closed the door hurriedly. "Now sit down,
lad, and help yourself out of the bottle."

Abe did not stir. "You'll not sign me up for your damn
Continentals!"

The man studied him for an instant from eyes gone suddenly hard and appraising. "All right. If you'd rather talk
to them militiamen than hear what I got to say, go on downstairs."

Abe hesitated, then subsided into a chair. The stranger
laughed shortly, but his eyes lost none of their wariness.

"I'm recruiting, like you guessed," he said. "Only it ain't for the Continentals. It's for the Provincials. Here. Hold out your mug and let me pour you a drink."

"The Provincials?" Abe repeated blankly, watching the liquor splash into the mug. "What's the Provincials? Why, ain't that what the militia was called back in the French War?"

The stranger nodded. "That's right—American troops serving with the British. Only, you see, this ain't the French War."

Abe's face was a picture of bewilderment. Mechanically he downed a slug of rum. Miller was smiling again, a small, twisted smile that made his lips seem thin and bloodless.

"By God! You're a Tory!"

Abe half rose. The stranger, he saw, had moved with apparent aimlessness to the far side of the room. He was still smiling that narrow smile. His hand rested negligently on a chairback across which his saddlebags had been hung. One of these had been moved aside just far enough to disclose a holster hanging beneath it, from which protruded the butt of a heavy horse pistol.

"A Loyalist," he corrected with a slight shake of the head. "And what the hell do you think you are, son?"

Abe sank back into his chair. His eyes clung in fascination to the pistol butt. In the silence the din from the taproom below carried to them faintly.

"Listen to 'em!" Miller said softly. "Your Patriot friends down there. A-scared to face the British themselves, but with plenty of courage to bully helpless folks. A few minutes ago you was wondering what you could do if they made trouble for your pa. Well, I'm giving you a chance to do a-plenty— and get paid for it."

Abe finished the rum in his mug. He could think of nothing else to do. Now his brain was really reeling.

"God, mister! I couldn't do that."

"Why not? What you got to love the Rebels for? Not

their politics—you say yourself you don't know nothing about them nor give a damn. The sweet, kind treatment they give you tonight, maybe?"

"I—I don't love 'em, mister. But—I don't want to fight 'em."

"You don't want to fight with 'em and you don't want to fight against 'em. What do you aim to do, son—work your back off on a rocky little farm while others reap the glory and rewards, and you get nothing but trouble and abuse whichever side wins?"

He saw Abe's eyes waver and pressed on. "You got more ambition than that, for certain. And you ain't no coward—I could see by the way you stood up to them yelling militia. In the Provincials you'd be a man among men—a soldier in an elegant uniform fit to knock the wenches' eyes out, and money in your pocket to loosen their heartstrings. You'd have a chance to travel about, see new places, win glory for yourself, with no worries only how fast you can win promotion. Why, a smart lad like you might even get to be an officer—an officer and a gentleman! I ask you—will you pass up a chance like that to sit like a bump on a log, doing just what you done all your life, and your pa before you, and his pa before him? Or will you make a place for yourself in the world?"

Abe's head was swimming. He scarcely noticed the stranger refilling his mug. "I—I couldn't go Tory. The Rebels would ruin Pa for certain then. He's worked real hard for what he's got. They'd take all that and jail him and—"

"They won't have no chance, son. The British army'll be moving up-county any day, now they've took the city. Heroes like them downstairs ain't going to stop the regulars for a second—not fellows won't turn out for fear of losing their crops. And them Continentals they boast about—our people chased 'em off Long Island easy as herding so many cattle. Why, lad, the whole war's like to be over in a couple of months. And where'll your precious Rebels be then? I'll tell you where: them not important enough to hang'll be in jail, their lands turned over to good Loyalists!"

He had been fumbling in his saddlebags as he spoke. Now he drew out a small sack that clinked musically. "Hold out your hand," he ordered.

Abe obeyed mechanically. His eyes popped as a stream of glittering coins cascaded into his palm.

"Gold!"

"Count it."

"Ten pounds!" It was more hard money than he had seen at one time in his life.

"That's bounty money, lad. That's what you get the minute you pass muster, over and above regular pay." He took the coins from Abe's unresisting hand and stowed the little sack back in his saddlebag. "Pay starts at two shilling-six a day and gets higher as you're promoted. And that ain't all. The Provincials figure to do most of the foraging for the army, which means there'll be lots of prize money for all and first pick of the swag."

"Prize money?" Abe repeated vaguely. "Swag?"

"Sure. We get a share of enemy supplies we capture. And in enemy territory we pick up what we want for ourselves before the rest of the army gets a chance at it. See? To the victor belongs the spoils. Why, with a little luck a man can get rich in no time! Because you don't have to buy nothing for yourself. Government takes care of all, from your small clothes to your rations—even has doctors to look to you when you're sick. They feed you, clothe you and house you—even give you a regular rum ration. What more can you ask?"

"I tell you, I can't go Tory—"

"Why can't you? Plenty of good men have. More every day—hundreds, thousands of 'em." The recruiter paused and his eyes narrowed. "You set great store by Squire Hilton, don't you? You think he'd do anything wasn't right? Well, maybe you don't know it, but he's a captain in the Provincials right now!"

"You—you know Young Squire?"

"Of course I do! Why do you reckon I sought you out of all the others soon's I come here?"

"Young Squire—sent you—after me?"

"Sure, sure! He's got to raise his own company, you see, and naturally he wants fellows he knows are brave and dependable."

"But when he went away, he told me—"

"Think it over, son. Only think fast. Here's another drink to help you."

The last thing Abe needed was another drink. His tongue was thick, and there was a singing inside his head. He leaned back and tried to focus his eyes on the opposite wall. A framed worsted sampler hung there. He tried to make out the lettering on it, but the vivid colors danced about like a kaleidoscope. He downed another snort of rum. It went easily this time without choking or gagging him. Briefly his eyes focused. "Matilda Hayes—Her Work—A.D. 1771," the sampler said. His lips moved as he spelled out the words.

"Well?"

The recruiter's voice jarred him back to reality.

"I—I reckon I better talk to my pa, mister."

"Your pa! Good God! Are you a man or ain't ye?"

Abe winced. Who had said that to him before? He felt hot blood in his cheeks. The sampler across the room blurred. The whole wall faded. He seemed to be looking out across a vast expanse of countryside as though he stood on a high hill. It was dotted with farms and villages, and there were strange cities in the distance. He saw the little farm on the edge of Hilton Manor that had been home to him since he could remember. All at once it was shabby and forlorn, very small and very far away. Then it was obscured by a long column of soldiers marching behind Young Squire through a street lined with cheering multitudes; men in brilliant regimentals from which an intensely golden sun struck shafts of vivid color. The man at Young Squire's side looked vaguely familiar. He peered more closely and saw without surprise that it was himself.

Miller was talking again. Gradually the crazy phantasma faded out. The wall was there again, and the little worsted sampler. "Matilda Hayes—Her Work . . ." Abe jerked his head sharply in an effort to clear it. Words reached him, but for the life of him he could not make sense of them. Unsteadily he rose to his feet.

"Gimme another drink," he said thickly. . . .

Chapter 4

THE RECRUITS

Abe's first waking sensation was that his head was about to burst. He kept his eyes tightly closed for fear they would pop out the instant he removed the pressure on their lids. His mouth tasted as though somebody had crammed it with soiled woolen stockings.

Someone was shaking him. Every jerk sent a fresh stab of pain through his head.

"Don't, Pa," he protested. "I'm acoming."

"I ain't yer pa," retorted a strange voice. "Git up and come below. The capt'n's here."

Abe opened his eyes with some effort. A man he had never seen before was bending over him; a stringy, middle-aged man with a thin nose that looked as though it had been pressed between pincers and twisted to the left, and a squint that was almost ludicrous.

"What the—where—"

Abe sat up and looked about. Every movement of his eyeballs made him wince. This was not the familiar garret at home where he slept with his brother Jack, but a strange hayloft.

"Git up," repeated the stringy man, "and hurry up about it. We aim to be marching right soon."

He moved across to the other side of the loft where Abe heard him rousing another sleeper. Two more, already up, were sleepily brushing wisps of hay from their hair. As far as he could tell in the half light, Abe had never seen either of them before. He put his head in his hands and groaned.

Memories of the previous evening were beginning to come back. They still did not make much sense, but for the moment he felt too wretched to care.

From below someone shouted impatiently. Abe followed the others down the ladder, urged along by the stringy man. Several other men were already there, gathered about an individual with an authoritative air who was seated on a chopping block in front of a crude table made by a plank laid across a couple of trestles.

"Reckon this is all of 'em, Capt'n," reported the stringy man.

The man at the table looked up. For all his military title and air of authority, he might have been any plain farmer from his appearance. He wore a rusty homespun coat above leather breeches, and his unpowdered hair, clubbed in an eelskin, had a greasy appearance. From the partly opened door, morning sunlight, heavily dust-moted, slanted across a coarse-featured but intelligent face.

"Check 'em over, Miller," he said shortly.

Abe's companion of the night before emerged from the deeper shadows of the big barn. "Eight altogether. That's right." He turned to Abe, grinning. "How do you feel, son?"

Abe tried to speak, but all that came was an inarticulate croak. The man addressed as captain gave him a sharp glance.

"For Christ's sake! Another drunk!"

"Oh, he'll be carrying it like a dragoon in a month," Miller declared airily. He turned to the others. "Boys," he announced, "this here is Captain Palmer, your commanding officer. See you treat him respectful."

The captain ignored him. "Come over here, you," he ordered, leveling a finger at Abe. "Now then. You know where you are?"

Abe wove an unsteady course across to the trestle. He ran a thick tongue futilely over dry lips. He had a vague recollection of leaving the tavern mounted on a horse behind Miller, but that was all.

"N-no, sir."

"Know why you're here?"

"N-n—yes, sir. To be a soldier."

"What kind of a soldier?"

"A T-t-tory soldier, I guess."

" 'Tory! You guess!' " The captain whirled on Miller. "What the hell sort of men are you bringing me?" he demanded furiously. "You expect me to pay you for a lout who doesn't know—"

"You're damn right I do!" Miller retorted. "You hired me to help you raise men enough for a company so's you could get a captain's commission—two shillings-six a day and four rations. You didn't say nothing about how much brains they got to have. Anyways, this here young feller's one of the best you got. You ought to of seen him stand up to them Rebel militia."

"Oh. Had trouble with the Rebels, eh?" The captain turned back to Abe, and his whole expression softened. "I guess those bastards have made life pretty miserable for all of us. Sorry I misjudged you, lad. Only don't be referring to 'Tories' hereafter, understand. That's a dirty Rebel word. We're King's friends, here—Loyalists—and that's what you are."

"Yes, sir," Abe muttered miserably, staring at the hard-beaten earth floor. "It sure appears like I am."

"There's a well out in the yard. Go souse your head in the bucket and maybe you'll feel better."

This was good advice and Abe obeyed it literally. Then he drew a second bucket and drank about half of it. Thus revived, he looked at his surroundings with awakening interest. From the general lie of the land he deduced that they were somewhere above North Castle Church—just where, he could not tell for all his familiarity with the region. The farm itself was entirely strange, as was its proprietor who emerged presently from the house bearing a large iron pot in one hand and an earthenware jug in the other.

Breakfast consisted of corn-meal mush washed down with weak cider. Abe approached it with some qualms and had to hold his nose to get it down at first. Once it was settled, however, he felt a little better, though his head still ached fit to split. At the trestle-table the captain and Miller were conferring in low tones. There was a clink of coins changing hands.

"Well, good luck," Miller said. He glanced indifferently at the eight men squatting around the pot and strode out.

"Golly," Abe muttered. "He's sold us at so much a head—like so many cattle."

"Wassat?" inquired the man next him through a mouthful of mush.

"Nothing," Abe said quickly. "Just my belly grunting, I guess."

The captain rapped on the plank for attention. "Any of you men familiar with the county south of here?" he asked. "How about you, Swane?"

"Not me," said the stringy man. "Us Cortlandt Manor folks don't get down that way real often."

Several of the others nodded. The captain frowned.

"Where you want to get to?" Abe inquired warily.

"Think you can get these fellows to White Plains without having to ask directions?"

"I reckon."

"Well, the town's full of Rebel committeemen and militia, so you better not try to go through it. Skirt around and hit the Old York Road below. After a couple of miles there's a road to the left that brings you to a big estate. You can't miss it even in the dark."

"You—mean Van Drusen Hall?"

"You been there?"

"Yes, but I didn't know the Van Drusens was—uh—"

"Never mind what the Van Drusens are," the captain said sharply. "You aren't to approach the big house, understand?

Just you take these men in sight of it, and Swane here will
do the rest."

The stringy man nodded. "Leave it to me, Capt'n."

"Then you better be getting ready to start. Remember: no
loose talking. Don't attract attention to yourselves. Give a
wide berth to any militia you see—they've all been called out,
but some are still on the march. If anybody questions you,
tell him you're on your way to join the army." He grinned.
"No need to say what army. You'll find it easier to get by
without lying—until you have to."

The captain, it appeared, was headed on a recruiting expedition of his own in his home district—back of Peekskill and
up near the Dutchess County line. As soon as they were ready
to leave, he turned the command over to Swane, briefly
wished them luck, and set off on horseback in the opposite
direction.

The morning was clear and pleasantly cool, the air bracing
with the tang of early fall. It acted like a tonic on Abe. His
headache began to subside, his nerves to cease their jangling.
His first sensation at the prospect of tramping close to
twenty miles in his wretched morning-after condition had
been one of dismay. Now, as the cobwebs cleared in his brain
and saliva washed away the dark-brown taste in his mouth, a
sense of exhilaration began to take possession of him. For
better or worse, he had severed his connections with the
farm. Of that, at least, he was free; of all the narrowness,
drudgery, frustration, that it implied. Even the familiar road
they followed seemed all at once endowed with a new mysterious quality that drew him onward eagerly. Cheerfully he
began to whistle as he swung along, until Swane at the head
of the party told him sourly to quit.

He fell to studying his companions. They were all
strangers; from the north, Cortlandt Manor, Crompond,
Salem—the part of the county with which he was least familiar. They were not a very prepossessing crowd: laborers
and sons of small farmers like himself, he judged. Except for

Swane, none appeared older than his early twenties. They were uncommunicative, suspicious, meeting his tentative advances with blank stares or monosyllabic evasions until, abashed, he ceased making them. From their conversation among themselves he gathered that several had been friends before enlisting; that all had felt in some degree the lash of Whig persecution. Perhaps this would account for their reticence toward strangers; perhaps their suspicion arose from instinctive sensing of his lack of the common tie. An oppressive loneliness commenced to weigh upon his rising spirits.

They stopped for lunch in a field near Wright's Mills. The other men had all contrived to bring off a few possessions from home, bundles of spare clothing and whatnot, which they carried in their hands or slung on sticks across their shoulders. These came open now to reveal small stocks of food: cheese, slabs of bread, cold salt pork, bottles of beer and cider. Empty-handed, Abe stood about uneasily. The supply, he saw, was scanty. When no one volunteered to share with him, he tramped off down the road to a farm where he was slightly known and begged milk and pie from the farmer's wife. While he was wolfing this in the kitchen, the Bedford militia company slogged by, a scant dozen men strung out behind Eb Lockwood, dusty and red of face. Fortunately they did not stop.

When he returned to the pasture, he found his new companions greatly perturbed. They had sighted the column in time to avoid detection by taking cover behind stone fences, but the experience had given them a bad moment.

"We got to get off this road," Swane declared. "White Plains will be full of the bastards, and some of the Rebel committee's there, to boot. You, Kronk—whatever your name is! You seem to know this region. How you figure is the best way to skirt it?"

Abe considered. "Well, you can swing west by way of Young's Corners, re-fording the Bronx below Chatterton's Hill."

"Seems like I recall a road forking east below Wright's Mills. Where's that go?"

"It rambles all over hell and gone."

"Figure we can reach the Sound that way without hitting the Old York Road again?"

"Sure, but not tonight you won't."

"Don't aim to. We're to jine another crowd down Scarsdale way. You march up ahead side of me. Come on, lads! On yer feet!"

They proceeded more warily now, relaxing their vigilance only when they had turned off the main road on to the fork the leader had spoken of. This road was narrower and less traveled, but no less dusty for that. The midday sun was high and hot. Rivulets of sweat traced muddy courses across flushed faces, trickled down necks and over chests and backs. Abe plodded doggedly, head bent. The effects of last night's liquor had worn off long since. In its place waves of tiredness engulfed him. After all, he had not had a great deal of sleep and more excitement and nerve strain than he was accustomed to. He wilted steadily as the afternoon wore on. Swane had to prod him sharply several times to keep up the pace.

The leader himself seemed tireless. His stringy frame swung along as vigorously at five in the afternoon as it had at nine that morning. "The sooner we git there, the sooner we eat," he protested whenever others demanded a halt. "T'other crowd's supposed to have vittles ready for us. Want 'em to get all cold?"

The cool of sunset made Swane positively garrulous. The country they were passing through interested him increasingly. His pinched nose swung left and right like the beak of a questing hawk, and his squint eye appraised standing crops, pasturage, gleaned fields. "Nice bit of forage yonder," he would remark; or, "Reckon they got enough grain off o' that there patch to be worth carryin' off." "Jist look at them fat cattle, will ye! Say, boys! We'll be coming this way agin right soon, I'm thinkin'. Remember the road, some of ye."

"Would that be Sam Crawford's place?" he asked Abe on one of the rare halts, pointing to an unusually prosperous-looking white house some distance off the road.

Abe nodded wearily. "He's captain of the Rebel militia hereabouts."

"Don't I know!" put in one of the others. "He's the son of a bitch that led the mob tarred old Seth Wiggin!"

Swane studied the house. " 'Twill make a right nice blaze one of these nights," he declared. "A house the like of that ought to have real silver plate inside of it. And maybe jewels!"

"Shouldn't wonder."

"And them outbuildings means plenty of hogs and fowl. And will ye look at them cows yonder! I'm a-telling ye—there's a mint of prize money right here, even if nothin' better."

Abe shook off a little of his weariness. "You fellows enlist to make war on the Rebels or on their livestock?" he asked uneasily.

They looked at him. "Both, I reckon," someone said. "What about you?"

"Well, I don't rightly know as robbing people's my idea of being a soldier."

"Maybe you ain't been robbed by the bastards yourself, huh? If they'd of had ye in Peekskill jail for two months like they had me, maybe ye wouldn't be so damn finicky!"

"I bet Squire Hilton won't go in for that sort of business," Abe declared.

"What's Squire Hilton got to do with it?"

"Seems like he'd have a whole lot since he's commanding us."

Swane snorted. "The hell you say! Squire Hilton ain't even in this regiment, far's I know. That Capt'n Palmer we seen back there—he's the fellow we 'listed under."

Abe's jaw dropped. "But that recruiter told me—"

"That son of a bitch'd say anything so's to get his bounty money! . . . Well, come on! We must be pretty close by now."

Mechanically Abe resumed the march. Coming on top of his utter weariness, this latest revelation left him shaken. Gone was all trace of the exhilaration he had felt that morning. So preoccupied was he that he missed a turn and had to make the whole party retrace their steps for a quarter of a mile, to their outspoken disgust. Dusk was beginning to settle when at last they sighted Van Drusen Hall, sprawling comfortably on its hilltop.

Swane halted his men and studied the terrain for several minutes, now and again consulting a slip of paper on which a crude plan was drawn. Orientated at last, he led the way up the road for a short distance, then took a path that angled off into a patch of woods on the left. After half a mile or so they emerged into cleared land, still well below the main house and so far behind it as to be out of sight. Here the path joined a lane skirting the wood, debouching presently before a small, seemingly isolated barn. Abe knew the place. It had belonged to a tenant cottage that had burned to the ground the previous winter. He could glimpse the ruins beyond the far corner of the barn, the stone chimney still standing forlornly. To his astonishment a curl of smoke was emerging from its top.

Swane strode up to the barn door and knocked: two quick taps followed by two slow ones. The mutter of voices, clearly audible an instant before, ceased abruptly. After an interval Swane repeated the signal. This time the doors opened a crack.

"Eight for Capt'n Palmer," he announced. With a rude jerk he pulled the doors wide. "If you fellers think you're hiding from anybody, don't make so damn much noise!"

In the middle of the floor four or five men squatted on a blanket, playing cards in their hands, startled eyes round in the gleam of a lantern slung from a beam overhead. Another was hurrying forward tardily, fumbling with a musket. The man who had started to open the door had a drawn sword in his hand. He dropped its point sheepishly.

"Christ almighty! What ye want to scare folks to death for?" he demanded.

"Better to be scared by us than shot by the militia, mister."

"Hell! There ain't no Rebels to fear nearer than White Plains." The man held out his hand. "Davenport's the name —John Davenport. I got the boats over to Mamaroneck to take us across to Long Island."

Swane grunted. "Good. But what us boys want to know right now is—when do we eat?"

"Any time ye say. We been waiting for ye."

The new arrivals stacked their bundles along the barn walls, then followed the others outside. Three more men were gathered amid the ruins of the burnt cottage. Debris had been cleared away from in front of the kitchen fireplace where a large stew pot hung from the crane over a bed of coals. Inexperienced as he was in such matters, Abe sensed something incongruous in men who felt it necessary to hide away in a barn casually cooking their meals in the open where any passer-by might see them, even though the isolation of the spot minimized the chance.

His curiosity overcame his weariness briefly as he watched the men gathered about the hearth where the stew was being ladled from the big pot. It was nearly dark by now, and he saw them only as the red firelight fell across them. There was little to distinguish the majority from the men he had been with all day and with whom they were beginning to fraternize. But two stood a little apart, sullen and uncommunicative; older men, as tough-looking customers as Abe had ever seen.

"Couple o' jailbirds," he heard Davenport inform Swane, aside. "The Rebels turned them and the paupers loose when they quit the city. They been a real pest in the lower county. Ought to make good soldiers, though, handled right."

Abe was watching them in fascination when a man he had not seen as yet stepped across his line of vision and approached the hearth. He stood well above medium height, strongly built, with wide, sloping shoulders and a round, taciturn face: the first familiar face Abe had seen since setting out on this adventure. As soon as he had had his own plate filled, Abe went over to where the man had seated himself alone at the edge of the crescent of firelight.

"Ain't you Enoch Crosby, the cobbler?" he asked. He paused in surprise, for the man had looked up sharply, dark eyes gone suddenly alert. "Why—why, you remember me, don't you? You was at our house over to Hilton Manor last year when—"

The man glanced over him. "Abe Kronkhyte, ain't ye?" He indicated the ground beside him. "Set if ye like."

Abe seated himself gingerly. The man addressed himself to his stew. He ate in silence, quickly, efficiently. Abe, unable to think of anything further to say, followed suit.

"What—what you doing here?" he inquired at last.

"Same's you, I reckon."

Crosby wiped his mouth on the back of his hand and reached for his pack which Abe observed he had kept half slung to one shoulder even while he was eating. Unlike the makeshift bundles of the other men, this was big, bulky and well-constructed: the complete kit of an itinerant shoemaker. From it he extracted a large brown bottle. He drew the cork, took a deep swig and passed it to Abe.

"Cider," he said tersely.

It was good and it was potent. Abe tossed a second drink after his first and watched with disappointment as the recorked bottle disappeared once more into the cobbler's pack. He felt less tired now but no less uneasy as the silence between them protracted itself.

"I don't know why I come here!" he burst out miserably. He felt those sharp, dark eyes on him again.

"Plenty of men had change of heart lately," Crosby said after a moment.

"I ain't had no change of heart. I didn't have my heart in nothing, really. That recruiter said Young Squire sent him, and he got me drunk and—and—"

"Scared?" The cobbler's voice had no particular inflection either of contempt or curiosity.

"No, I ain't scared—leastwise, not like I was scared to fight. But these fellers—it don't seem like they aim to fight. All they talk about's plundering folks and burning their houses. I don't want to make that kind of war on poor folks. Why, some of 'em's friends and neighbors. I—I—"

He paused. In the firelight Crosby's eyes were inscrutable. For an instant Abe thought that he was about to say something, but instead he turned again toward the hearth.

"Oh, God, Enoch! What—what am I going to do?"

Crosby did not look up. "You've made your bed," he said harshly. "Quit whimpering and lay in it like a man!"

Chapter 5

ENOCH CROSBY

For the second successive morning Abe awakened in a strange hayloft. Someone had opened the door through which the hay was hoisted in, admitting a gray, uncertain light. For several moments he lay on his side staring out at the early morning sky, dyed faintly with the glow of approaching sunrise. All about him was the stir of waking men, closely packed in the constricted area. The tireless Swane moved among them, prodding, shaking, kicking.

"Git up! Git up!"

The man beside Abe rolled over. "What the hell's the matter with ye?" he demanded. "All night ye was tossing and muttering. Can't ye let a body sleep?"

Abe made no reply. His every muscle ached, and his brain was sodden with lingering fragments of troubled dreams. As he climbed down the ladder, he realized that his feet were still sore from yesterday's long tramp.

Crosby lay asleep beside the big barn door, his head pillowed on the big cobbler's pack. Davenport began shaking him.

"Hey! Wake up, damn ye! Anybody come by during the night?"

Crosby opened his eyes and sat up. "Huh?"

"I said, did you hear anything during the night?"

"I didn't hear nothing." The cobbler rubbed his eyes sheepishly. "Reckon I must of fell asleep."

"You're a hell of a lookout!"

"Well, I didn't catch none of you fellows volunteering for the job—nor coming down to spell me, neither."

They set out after a scanty breakfast, just as the sun was topping a low hill to the east. The combined party totaled twenty-one. Davenport led the way with his drawn sword. This was an old brass-hilted navy cutlass, its scabbard so battered and bent as to make sheathing all but impossible, but after the general confiscation of arms of all Tory suspects, he was lucky to have any weapon at all. Swane marched at the rear beside the man with the lone musket. The rest were strung out between, carrying only their little bundles, save for Crosby, stooped under his cobbler's pack. Abe stayed close beside him, but his efforts at conversation elicited only grunts.

Heading toward the southeast, they had the morning sun squarely in their eyes. The weather was unseasonably warm for late September. Sweat-blinded, sun-blinded men began to grumble, but from the rear of the column Swane urged them on pitilessly.

"Keep going! Keep going! It ain't far now!"

Keep going they did, to such purpose that within a couple of hours Abe began recognizing landmarks that indicated they were nearing Mamaroneck. Soon Davenport turned off on a lane to the right, and in a few minutes they glimpsed the Sound ahead and on their left. After perhaps a mile they made their first halt of the morning in the lee of a low hill.

"The boats are in a creek over yonder," Davenport announced. "Wait here till I make sure all's clear."

He set off alone up the slope while the others sank gratefully into the tall grass that bordered the lane.

"How far to Long Island hereabouts?" someone asked.

" 'Bout ten mile. Maybe more, maybe less."

"Hell! I hope them boats got sails to 'em. That's a damn long ways to row—"

The speaker broke off short. A shout carried from the direction of the hill. Davenport was running back toward the

lane. As they turned to look, he jerked sharply to a halt and
shouted again. His cutlass flashed in the sunlight as though
he were pointing.

"Jesus! Look!"

From a clump of woods some two hundred yards inland
burst a company of mounted men, heading for the lane at a
gallop. The sun struck sparks from heavy dragoon sabers,
brandished wildly.

"It's Townsend's Rangers!"

"Run for your lives!" Swane shouted. "Scatter! Every man
for himself!"

For an instant they were too stunned to move. The two
ex-jailbirds, quickest to react, streaked off down the lane in
the direction of a swamp a short distance ahead, whither
Davenport had already turned after his shout of warning.
In another instant pandemonium broke loose among the
rest.

Abe's first instinct was to flee directly away from the
enemy. Before he had taken a dozen steps, however, a band
of militiamen on foot crested the hill. These were the ones
who had first alarmed Davenport. Blindly he darted back to
the lane, now choked with milling Tories. Men trying to flee
in one direction collided with others fleeing in the opposite
one, knocked each other down, clawed their way through the
mob.

Abe fought his way clear and sprinted toward the rear. At
that instant another half-dozen armed men leaped into the
lane, cutting off escape that way, too. He doubled back frantically. But the horsemen were closing in fast, and the Rebels
on foot were bounding down the hillside.

"Surrender, ye bastards!"

"Quarter! Quarter!"

Abe dodged past a couple of men with their hands in the
air. Before he could take two more steps a clubbed musket
smacked him between the shoulders and sent him sprawling.

"Got him!" somebody shouted.

Rough hands jerked him to his feet, pinioned his arms. In the lane Enoch Crosby was still fighting. He had unslung his heavy pack and was laying about him with it, bowling over assailants right and left. One of these lunged forward and grasped his knees. Down he went, lost to sight under an avalanche of flailing arms and kicking legs. Panting, the Rebels looked around for more fighting. There was none to be seen.

The leader of the mounted rangers swung down from his horse and made his way along the lane. He was tall and rawboned, with a rough, weathered face. A dilapidated captain's epaulette was stitched to one shoulder of his homespun coat.

"Line 'em up!" he shouted. "Line 'em up, boys, and let's see what kind of fish we've netted!"

The men holding Abe hauled him over with the other captives. Those on top of Crosby began unpiling themselves. They hoisted him to his feet and stood him up beside Abe where he teetered uncertainly. His face was bleeding in a dozen places and one eye was closed.

The captain halted before him, staring incredulously.

"Holy Jesus!" he gasped. "How did you get here?"

"How the hell do ye think?" Crosby mumbled through puffed lips.

"Who's he, Captain Townsend?" inquired a shorter man in a plain coat who had been trotting along behind.

"By God, Mr. Duer! It's Enoch the patriarch! I swear, he vanishes out of our hands as mysteriously as his ancient namesake vanished from the earth. I had him in Fishkill Jail a week ago—and in the stone church a month before that."

The man addressed as Duer peered at the cobbler out of nearsighted eyes. He was slight of build, with a thin face and pursed lips. "My, my!" he said nervously. "Well, I suppose we can hardly blame the poor fellow for consulting his own safety."

"Poor!" shouted the captain. "If he's poor, it's because the British have been holding out on him. If spying merits promotion, King George owes this bastard a dukedom!"

"And the Congress owes him a halter!" put in one of the other rangers. "What ye say we pay off right now, Capt'n?"

"May I never live to be a major if we don't!" the captain cried. "Ho! Some of you get rope!"

"Now, now, boys!" remonstrated the thin man uneasily. "Don't go killing any of these misbegotten swine yourselves —we pay a hangman to do that."

Despite his unprepossessing appearance, his words seemed to carry weight, for the captain stepped back crossly. His glance traveled along the sullen, bewildered line.

"Which of you's in command here?" he demanded.

There was no answer.

"How about this weasel-faced shitepoke?"

He grabbed Swane and yanked him out in front of the line. Whether he merited this honor because he was the oldest among them or because his previous activities were known was not clear. He certainly looked anything but a leader at the moment. His greasy hair had become unclubbed in the struggle and hung in a ragged fringe over his eyes, giving him the appearance of an emaciated sheep dog. Blood from a broken nose smeared the lower part of his face and dripped from his receding chin on his filthy coat which had been torn in several new places.

"Speak up! Are you the chief cutthroat of this gang?"

Swane stared sullenly at the ground. The rest of the rangers had dismounted and gathered behind their leader, faces dark with anger.

"Answer, goddamn ye! Where were ye taking these men?"

Swane's lips only closed tighter.

"By Christ, I'll make him talk!"

A big man with a shock of bright red hair stepped forward. He shifted his musket to his left hand and swung his right in a sweeping arc. A great hairy fist crashed against Swane's mouth. He reeled into the man behind him, and the two of them went down like pins in a game of bowls.

"Come on—speak up!"

Swane sat up slowly. He spat blood into the road and ran a dazed hand over his jaw. "Go to hell, ye lousy bastard!" he mumbled.

The red-haired man kicked him in the stomach. Others closed in, pummeling and shouting curses. The Tories looked on in horror. At the far end of the line a man, watching his opportunity, turned suddenly and sprinted off down the lane.

"Hey!" the captain yelled.

A couple of startled muskets slammed. But the fleeing man did not break his stride. Before the rangers could get to their horses, he was plunging into the swamp.

"Ye damn fools!" shouted Townsend. "There's another got away. After him, a couple of ye!"

"Tut, tut!" clucked Duer reprovingly. "Unless you start back soon, Captain, it begins to look as though you'll not have much to show the other committee members for this day's work."

The attackers, sobered, stopped battering their victim. Swane got slowly to his feet. His bloodshot eyes glinted balefully.

"Ye'll pay for this, ye goddamn traitors!"

"Shut up! Tie him, boys. Gag him if you want to. Tie up the pack of 'em."

Each prisoner's hands were bound behind him with rope obtained from a fisherman's hut on the shore near by. Then they were herded back up the lane to the road, cursed and kicked the while, prodded along by the bayonets of the few militiamen who had them. Here Captain Townsend turned them over to the foot militia, with strict admonitions to permit no more escapes, and rode off with his rangers and the important Mr. Duer. Battered and footsore, the hopeless captives commenced the weary return journey toward White Plains.

They did not take the most direct route. Those left in charge were local men, and much too proud of their accom-

plishment to pass up any opportunity to exhibit its results
to admiring neighbors. First they marched into Mamaroneck
for a few drinks, then detoured all the way to New Rochelle
for the edification of that village. Farm people along the
road ran out to enjoy the show. At every tavern where they
halted, crowds collected to cheer and jeer—and set up drinks
for the victors. By midafternoon many were half drunk and
all a little weary, so they called a halt at a convenient ordinary and ordered up a meal. No one suggested feeding the
prisoners. They were driven into the stable yard like so
many cattle and left there under guard.

Not until he was able to sit down did Abe begin to realize
how tired he was. Since the capture he had moved like one
in a trance, oblivious to pain and abuse, his mind mercifully
dulled to full realization of his predicament. Instinctively he
edged closer to Crosby, the only man in the whole crowd
whom he knew even casually. The cobbler was as impassive
as ever, as reticent.

After a while, noting the guards' relaxed vigilance, Swane
came over and crouched beside him.

"You been taken before, huh?" he began. "Then maybe
you'll agree with what I'm thinking—that it wasn't no accident, them Rebels laying for us right where we was going.
We was betrayed, that's what!"

Crosby grunted. "Take ye till now to figure that out?"

Irritation clouded Swane's discolored face. "All right, wise
fellow! Only you was the one went to sleep on watch last
night—and 'twasn't till then we could have been betrayed
'cause things was kept so secret there wasn't none of us knew
where we was headed till then."

"Davenport knew. Whyn't ye ask him?"

"Ye damn fool! Davenport's one of them that got away!"

"Aye. And wasn't it funny as hell how quick he got away—
him and those two jailbirds of his."

Swane stared for an instant, then his face paled. "The
son of a bitch! If I ever get my hands on him—"

"Silence, there!" barked one of the sentries. "You Tories is to be seen and not heard."

When the militiamen had eaten and drunk their fill, the weary march was resumed. All afternoon they plodded northward under the blazing sun, many of them hatless, all bruised and footsore. Several collapsed and were dragged to the side of the road, left to the tender mercies of local Whigs. Abe scarcely noticed. His body ached and his eyes ached. His mouth was parched, his nose clogged with dust. The ropes chafed his wrists, restricted circulation until his hands felt like ice. The journey took on the aspects of a nightmare: marching and halting, staring faces, voices shouting epithets. White Plains differed from other stops along the way only because there were more faces and louder voices.

"Committee's busy right now. Put 'em in the jail."

A man in a blue coat with the epaulettes of a militia colonel was talking with the leader of their captors. Abe noted that the sun had set and dusk was closing in. A sea of featureless faces swam across his blurred vision. Suddenly one stood out: young Isaac Oakley, his own cousin, gaping at him incredulously. Miserable, heartsick, he dropped his eyes.

He was dimly aware of crossing the common, halting before the big courthouse; of the blue-coated officer issuing orders and directions. Another man passed along the line of prisoners. Abe winced as cold steel touched his wrists. Then the slashed ropes fell away. Mechanically he moved his hands, brought them around in front of him, looked at them in wonder, as though he had never seen them before.

"Come along, ye bastards!"

Keys jangled. The jail was in the basement of the courthouse. As he stumbled down the steps, a hand gripped his arm.

"Stay close to me," Crosby's voice whispered.

Their footfalls echoed in the narrow corridor. An iron door clanged. "First eight of ye get in this cell." Another door; another command; another group of disheveled figures, dim in the half light, were shoved unceremoniously out of the corridor.

"We still got two left, Colonel."

"Put 'em in the small cell around the corner."

Again Abe felt Crosby's hand on his arm. A narrow door opened in the wall before him, and he was pushed through it so violently that he sprawled headlong, skinning his knees on the stone floor. Crosby tripped over him, and the iron door clanged shut.

He heard the cobbler scramble to his feet, but for another moment he lay where he had fallen. Only when his companion bent over to help him up did he stir to help himself.

The last dregs of daylight found their way through a barred window high up in the farther wall. They revealed a narrow cell, shut off from the corridor by a grilled door. The furniture consisted of a shelf-like wooden bunk built against either wall and a single backless chair. The air was stale and dank.

Suddenly pandemonium broke loose throughout the entire basement. It was as though all the prisoners found their voices at the same instant. All the day's pent-up emotions found expression in a sort of mass hysteria now that the men were crowded together with no enemies among them. They screamed and yelled and beat impotently upon the clanging doors. They cursed the Rebels and the Congress and the militia until the whole jail and the courthouse overhead seemed to shake from the intensity of their hatred.

But Abe hardly heard them. His own emotions, too, had broken. He threw himself face downward on the nearest bunk, buried his head in his arms, and cried like a baby.

Chapter 6

COMMITTEE OF CONSPIRACIES

How long Abe lay there he did not know. Gradually his sobbing weakened and he sank into a coma. He was dimly aware of a rattling at the door; of the turnkey's strident voice and of Crosby cursing him in unemotional monosyllables; of a lantern's brief gleam before the door clanged shut again. It seemed remote, with no bearing on himself. Then he felt an arm about his shoulders, half raising him.

"Water," Crosby's voice said. "Make ye feel better."

His hands found an earthenware jug, raised it to his fumbling lips. The water had a stale smell, but its coolness was delicious. It revived him, but it did not make him feel better. Instead it brought realization to him in a dismaying flood.

"Enoch, you—you figure they aim to hang us?"

"Not us, I reckon. Swane, maybe, and the recruiters if they can catch 'em. Simsbury Mines for the rest of us, most like."

"Oh, God! I'd as lief hang!"

His brain seemed clearer now that he had control of himself again. He saw that the cell had become completely dark, that the din in the jail had died away. Crosby was a disembodied voice, speaking softly in the black stillness.

"Call me a coward if you want to, Enoch," he continued after a moment. "Only 'twasn't just fear made me whimper. It's—it's being took with these people. Maybe you had some good reason for joining 'em, but me—hell! First off when the militia jumped us, I was glad, forgetting I was tarred with the same brush. And when I seen all them folks staring at me —hating me—folks like myself, even some that I knowed!"

74

He paused, swallowed hard. "If I was facing what—what we got to face with other fellows like myself—for something that I felt was right—then maybe I could take it like a man."

His voice trailed off. Crosby made no reply. Abe seemed to feel his unspoken contempt bearing down upon him through the heavy stillness. He lay back limply, staring upward into the darkness, lonely, lost.

"Get up and come over here." Crosby's voice was low, uninflected. Bewildered, Abe raised himself to a sitting posture. There came a faint scraping sound, as though a piece of furniture were being dragged across the stone floor. Looking upward, he could make out the dim gray oblong of the barred window. As he watched, Crosby's head and shoulders made a dark blur against it.

"Come over here," the flat voice repeated. "Don't say nothing."

More bewildered than ever, Abe groped toward him. The cobbler was standing on the backless chair. He drew a deep breath, grunted as though from physical effort. The grating gave forth a faint metallic sound.

"Reach up. Here." Abe's fingers closed on cold iron. "Easy. She's heavy."

Abe braced himself. The cell window was lowered to him, frame, bars and all. Its weight threw him off balance. One corner struck the stone paving with a clang that sounded deafening.

Crosby cursed under his breath. For a long moment they stood motionless, not breathing. A couple of voices muttered in the next cell, died away. The chair creaked under the cobbler's feet. Then his bulk loomed in the empty window.

"Follow me."

Abe's foot found the chair. He mounted. He groped for the sill. A hand, reaching down, closed about one of his wrists. Then he was up, squeezing through the narrow aperture. Cool night air fanned his clammy face.

There was no moon, only the bright points of the stars.

Against them the courthouse bulked black. Abe, orientating himself, saw that they had emerged at the rear of the building. Crosby led the way off to the left, staying close in the shadow. At the corner he paused, staring off toward where a line of tall trees was silhouetted against the night sky. Scattered lights showed in windows along the road a short distance beyond, and from Oakley's Tavern, directly across the green.

Suddenly a spark showed among the trees. It was weak and faint, and vanished so swiftly that it might have been an illusion. Then, after a moment, it showed again at the same spot.

"Stay close," Crosby whispered.

He left the shadow and started across the sward, swiftly, effortlessly, flitting like a ghost. Within a few yards he seemed to merge with the darkness. Too dazed to move at once, Abe stared after him. Then he followed, heart in mouth, expecting every instant a challenge or a shot. He moved clumsily, panting with the effort. Once he stumbled, leaped up in panic.

"Don't run!" Crosby's hand was like iron on his arm. Together they slipped into the shadow of the trees just as the light showed again, very close.

"That you, Crosby?"

"Here, sir."

The light brightened. It came from a shrouded lantern held high by a tall man in a blue coat. A random beam glinted on the gold of epaulettes. Abe, jaw agape, stared into the face of the Rebel militia colonel who had ordered them into the jail. He had a heavy pistol in his other hand, gestured with it.

"This the lad you spoke of last night?"

"Aye."

"Follow me."

Veiling the lantern cautiously, the officer picked his way back to the road. At its edge he paused to make certain no

one was in sight in either direction, then scurried across and
turned into a lane on the opposite side. Abe, completely at
sea, felt a wild impulse to run, to lose himself in the darkness
and take his own chances. The officer beckoned with the
lantern, but he held back.

"Who—who—what—"

"Be still, ye fool!"

Crosby caught him by the coat collar and pushed him into
the road, propelled him across it. They followed the officer
up the lane, turned left and arrived presently in the rear of
Oakley's Tavern. A militia sentry challenged in a high,
scared voice, then stood aside and opened the back door.

"Committee's upstairs, Colonel."

"Yes, yes. I know."

He unshrouded the lantern and led them up the back
stairs. Bright candlelight showed under the crack of a door
on the second floor, and from behind it came the indistinguishable grumble of voices. He paused before it, listening,
then knocked.

"Come in."

Three men were seated about a large table strewn with
papers. They were gentlemen; even as he blinked in the
glare, Abe sensed that from their clothes and their bearing.
Puzzled, aghast, he recognized the thin face of Mr. Duer
who had been with Captain Townsend at their capture that
morning, the pursed mouth now smiling affably. One of the
others was an officer, stout, rather short, wearing a powdered
wig, neatly queued, and resplendent in the epaulettes of a
Continental major general. But it was the third who riveted
Abe's attention with a sort of horrified fascination, though
he had only seen him once before: John Jay, Congress dele-
gate and head of the Committee of Conspiracies, probably
the individual in the state most to be dreaded by any whose
politics were even faintly suspect.

There was nothing very terrifying in his aspect at the
moment, however. He leaped to his feet, a vigorous, keen-

looking man in his thirties, and a broad smile of contagious enthusiasm spread over his whole face.

"By heaven, Crosby, you've done it again!" he cried. "Let me shake your hand, sir!" He paused, staring at the cobbler's battered countenance. "Good Lord! Did the militia do all that to you?"

Crosby grinned. "Reckon I gave 'em too convincing an argument, sir."

"Convincing enough so that I had all I could do to keep Townsend from hanging him on the spot," Duer corroborated drily. He turned to the officer. "General Heath, this is the man we spoke of earlier—the most dependable spy in our service—indeed, virtually the only one we can really rely upon."

The general bowed somewhat stiffly. He studied the cobbler from shrewd, appraising eyes. "Commendable work, sir. I congratulate you."

A flicker of expression crossed Crosby's impassive features. "I don't like the word 'spy' no better'n you do, sir."

"Oh." Heath's brows went up. "No offense intended, I assure you."

"I served an enlistment in the Northern Army, sir. I was on my way to join up again when I stumbled into this work by pure chance. They—these gentlemen and the rest of the Committee—told me my duty lay in keeping at it. By choice I'd be in the ranks today."

"But you can't do that," Jay interposed quickly. "Why, in your present capacity you're worth a hundred soldiers—a thousand!"

Crosby shrugged. "Aye. So I must keep on being hunted like a beast in the forest—beaten and jailed by my own people—till one party or the other hangs me."

Heath cleared his throat with an embarrassed rasp, breaking the brief, uncomfortable silence. "And who is this young man?" he asked.

The others' heads turned sharply. For the first time their

eyes came to rest on Abe. He had been keeping behind
Crosby as well as he could, trying to make himself as incon-
spicuous as possible. Jaw gaping, his face a study in rustic
bewilderment, he shrank back against the wall.

"What's this?" Jay demanded. His angry eyes shifted from
Abe to the militia officer. "Colonel Malcolm, you are per-
fectly well aware that none but the Committee and yourself
are to know Crosby's true identity. What do you mean by
bringing—"

"He's one of the captured party, sir," the colonel broke in
hastily. "Crosby particularly asked that I arrange his escape
and bring him."

"A Tory—here! Are you mad?"

"He ain't a real Tory," Crosby said. "Knowing how he felt,
I couldn't turn him in along with them others."

Duer glared at Abe. "If you're not a Tory, what were you
doing with those scoundrels? Speak up!"

Abe licked dry lips. "I—I—"

"A recruiter got him drunk and lied to him, sir," Crosby
explained patiently. "A recruiter I ain't come across yet. He's
seen the man higher up, too, the real boss—Capt'n Palmer,
he calls himself. More than that, he knows this county like
the palm of his hand—better'n I do, even. I figured he might
come in real handy helping lay 'em by the heels."

Abe found his voice at last. "I'll do anything, sir! I—I made
a mistake. I'll do anything I can to—to make up for it."

Jay's glance shifted to the cobbler. "Mistake or not, would
you trust him, Crosby? Would you put your life in the hands
of a man capable of doing what he has done?"

"I reckon the truest friends are them as has reason to be
grateful, sir—if they're honest fellows at bottom, of course."

"I fail to see it in that light!" Duer snapped. "There's
more than just your life involved, Crosby; there's the success
of our whole enterprise, to a great extent. I'll have no proven
traitor connected with it!"

Jay nodded. "I'm inclined to agree. But what are we going

to do with the lad? We can't simply turn him loose, knowing what he has learned tonight."

"Put him back in jail, and I join the army tomorrow," Crosby said without emotion.

There was a short silence. Again it was General Heath who broke it.

"Perhaps I can solve this deadlock, gentlemen." He turned to Crosby. "You say this lad is familiar with Westchester County?"

"None more so, sir. There's few had his chances to get around."

"Then perhaps he is just the man I am looking for. It was my intention, gentlemen, when we had finished other business, to ask you to recommend me a man competent to act as my guide. As you well know, this county with whose defense I have been entrusted has never been mapped—is *terra incognita* to myself and virtually the entire army. I have been observing this lad while you talked, and I am inclined to believe he will serve our purposes admirably."

"A traitor!"

The general smiled. "I flatter myself that I understand human nature, gentlemen, though perhaps not so well as Mr. Crosby here. In any event, surrounded by my staff he would be under constant surveillance—and I'll warrant to keep him so busy that he will have small time or opportunity for dubious activities. If, after a probationary period, we find that a mistake has been made—well, military law provides swift and sure means for rectifying it." He turned to Abe. "What say you, young man? Will you undertake the service I have described?"

"You—you mean I should join the army?" Abe stammered.

"Joining two opposing armies on the same day is a good deal to ask of any man," Heath said drily. "No, you will simply guide me where I want to go and show me what I want to see, and hold yourself available on an instant's notice to conduct other officers and portions of the army to such points as may be designated. Well?"

Abe's tired brain was reeling. "Why, sir, I—there ain't nothing I'd rather do!"

The general cut him short. "Prove that with actions, not words!" He turned to the militia officer. "Colonel, be so good as to see that this man has a place to sleep and some food. He appears exhausted, and I want him fit for the road by sunrise. Keep him out of sight lest he be recognized by any who saw the prisoners brought in."

Abe was barely conscious of leaving the room. His feet seemed to belong to one person, his head to another, his body to a total stranger. The door closed behind him, and he was following Colonel Malcolm along the dark hall.

"You're lucky, son," the latter observed. "I wonder if you'll ever realize how lucky you've been tonight."

Abe wondered, too, but he was too dazed to wonder for long. The instant he lay down, sleep claimed him; the dreamless sleep of utter weariness. It held him until a hand shook his shoulder, and he opened his eyes to see pale dawn spreading grayly over a new world.

Chapter 7

THE WESTCHESTER GUIDES

"Where did you get that horse?" Brom Dyckman demanded.

John Odell leaned forward and stroked the neck of the big, sleek gray. "You'll not believe it," he said, "but he was given to me."

"Oh, sure. Some Tory give him to you, huh? 'Take the horse, my fine lad,' says he, 'and for God's sake stop pointing that big pistol at my head!' " Dyckman stepped back and observed the gray appraisingly. "How do I know he's a Tory horse? By using my eyes and using my head, like the general tells Abe you got to do to be a good scout. That there horse has been fed regular and groomed regular. He's a gentry horse and ain't never had to pull a plow. Well, all the gentry's Tories, ain't they?"

"No," Odell returned imperturbably, "so happens they ain't. 'Twas General Van Cortlandt give me this horse himself."

"Huh?"

"He just now sees me riding by on that nag the Committee give me, my feet dragging the ground, and he says that fellows picked to guide the army ought to be mounted decent, and that a big, brave fellow like me ought to have a horse likewise. So he give me this one."

"Since when you been hobnobbing with the Van Cortlandts?"

"Why, the general's known me since I was knee-high. Him and my pa—"

"If he knows you that well, then most like he give you that horse figuring a big, brave fellow like you couldn't run away quick enough on t'other, like you done over to Long Island!"

"If I hadn't run that time, and picked the right place to run to," retorted the practical Odell, "a couple of them Hessians would of seen we never needed horses again."

"Listen," Abe interposed uneasily. "Don't you reckon we ought to be starting? General Heath said we was to hurry."

Dyckman saluted with exaggerated deference. "Aye, aye, sir! At your service, Colonel, your Excellency! Lead on!"

"Oh, shut up!" Abe said crossly. "This ain't nothing to joke about."

Never before had he been placed in a position of telling persons older than himself what to do, and it made him ill at ease. To cover his lack of assurance, he turned his horse about and put it to a brisk trot. He was anxious to get out of White Plains as quickly as he could, in any event. This was the first time he had been in the town since his "escape" from the jail a month before, and he did not like to chance anyone's recognizing him as a member of that party of Tory recruits. He had a paper with him to prove his present status against just such an emergency, but suspicious militiamen were likely to shoot first and ask questions afterward. Everybody was nervous in White Plains just then, what with the British eight miles away and the Continentals God only knew where.

A busy month that had been for Abe; a month of movement and clamor, with new experiences crowding upon each other so fast that they left him confused. He had ridden south with Heath the morning following the Committee meeting, and he had been at the stout general's side constantly ever since. Heath's task was to defend the county against the enemy invasion that everybody knew was coming. In preparing for it, he had been in the saddle continually, studying the lie of the land with special regard to the natural strategic features of the terrain and the location of roads. He visited personally all of the most obvious danger points, personally saw to the disposition of the troops supposed to guard them. A stranger to the region himself, with no map to aid him, he found Abe's knowledge invaluable.

For the first week or so, awed and grateful, Abe confined himself to answering questions and guiding the general wherever he wanted to go. He was acutely conscious of being there on a sort of probation and was zealous to please. But as familiarity with his new position overcame his shyness, as the general's attitude toward him became less stiff and speculative, his natural inquisitiveness got the better of him. He began listening to discussions between Heath and his staff. What he heard did not make much sense to him, ignorant as he was of military terminology—indeed, of all things military. But the general chanced to note his obvious interest on one such occasion and voluntarily undertook to enlighten him.

"You're a bright lad, Kronkhyte," he declared. "Perhaps if you understand the reasons back of some of the things we do, you will be able to use your own knowledge of the territory to better advantage."

Heath was garrulous by nature and inclined to be somewhat pompous, but at bottom he was a simple, friendly man. He had gained most of his own military knowledge from books, recently enough so that he still delighted in displaying it. His own staff had come to regard him as a pedant and something of a bore, to yawn off his frequent dicta, sensible and sound though most of them were. Abe, therefore, was virgin territory: a pupil on whom exposition of the most elementary principles was not wasted, and a fine sounding board when the general wished to expound higher tactical and strategic theories.

He followed no logical sequence in these little lectures. While Abe was digesting a homely explanation of why it was desirable to fight with a river in front of you rather than behind, the general was likely as not to launch into an esoteric discourse on the strategic significance of the encircling movement the British had in contemplation, or the value of artillery fire as a preliminary to assault upon a fortified position. Abe's ability to listen with interest, whether he comprehended or not, won him the warm affection of his new mentor and killed any lingering suspicions of his attachment the general might have retained, but the net result of this sketchy yet concentrated military education was to throw his mind into a state of utter confusion. Later he was surprised to discover how many salient facts he had absorbed. That these were of any use to him in performing the duties of the moment, however, was highly doubtful, though he contrived to function well enough so that, when the invasion actually materialized and the need for swift action became urgent, the general had dispatched his protégé back at once to obtain other qualified volunteers for similar service.

Abe had been lucky. The Committee of Safety, to whom he had been told to report, had recommended Odell and Dyckman, among others, both of whom were already in the village. The volunteer company which they had joined had been dispersed at the Battle of Long Island and, as was the case with many such loosely organized units, its members had made their way home without bothering to reassemble. Not being enrolled in the regular militia, they were unattached, and Abe had little trouble convincing them that serving as guides for the army offered better chances for excitement than anything else in the immediate offing.

"What're we going this way for?" Odell inquired as, instead of taking the York Road, Abe led the way toward the bridge that crossed the Bronx at the foot of Chatterton's Hill.

"The army's coming up this side. We're to meet 'em and bring 'em to White Plains by the shortest road."

"The York Road's shortest, and better traveling, too."

"Sure, but the idea is to keep the river between us and them. That way the Bronx covers our open flank, see?" Their blank expressions gave him a new feeling of importance.

"The general tells it like this. Our army's been on York Island all this time, like you know. They're leaving now and heading for White Plains, but on account of Kingsbridge being so narrow and them not having enough wagons and the like of that, it's going to take time to get 'em all off safe and sound. Well, the British aim to cut 'cross county and get in front of us so's we'll be caught like in a pocket. Either that or catch our boys on the march, all strung out so's they can't fight together. Only to do either they got to get over the Bronx, and even a little river like that ain't easy to cross if there's fellows with guns on the other side don't want you to. The general figured maybe this way we can hold 'em off long enough to get the army clear, see?"

He paused to let his erudition make its proper effect upon their minds. He was a little surprised himself at how well he had grasped the situation.

"Now ain't that just fine," Dyckman said. "Only it so happens the British ain't heading for the Bronx at all, but t'other way."

"Huh?"

"Sure. They was in New Rochelle this morning, and a fellow rode in while you was talking to the Committee saying the Hessians has pushed on beyond and are going into camp."

Abe's importance collapsed. "What—what they doing that for?" he asked weakly.

"You tell us, Colonel. We're just a couple of farm boys who ain't been around much."

"There ain't no doubt about it, Abe," Odell said. "Folks from that region been straggling into White Plains since dawn, bringing off what they could of their stuff, and all of 'em tells the same story, just about. Them troops ain't marching. Most of 'em's on the loose, raising merry hell, seems like."

Dyckman laughed. "And the funny part is the Tories are catching it bad's our people. Remember that stubborn old goat Caleb Tompkins the Committee's had all the trouble

with? Well, I was talking with a couple of his neighbors this
noon. Seems they was getting ready to pull out of there when
this here Caleb comes strutting over to see 'em off. He's all
tricked out in his best Sunday-go-to-meeting ready to welcome the 'liberators,' as he calls 'em. He jeers at these poor
folks who got to run for it, cursing and insulting 'em, but
they're too busy to pay no 'tention. Just about then, along
comes the 'liberators' theirselves, so old Tompkins runs to
meet 'em, waving his hat and whooping for joy.

"Well, sir, 'pears like these partic'lar 'liberators' happens
to be Hessians. Maybe they don't understand what he's saying or something. Anyhow, first anybody knows one of 'em's
rammed him in the belly with a musket butt, and the whole
pack of 'em's turned into his yard. His wife comes to the
door, all smiles, only I guess they didn't understand her
neither, because they grabs her and shoves her out of the
way. Then they all stacks their muskets against the wall and
goes to work. Some goes into the house and begins hauling
stuff out while the rest runs after the pigs and fowl with
them big swords they carry, all jabbering in their heathen
lingo and laughing and having a hell of a time with theirselves. Seems they don't bother the old folks none only to
kick 'em out of the way when they try to stop 'em.

"After a while along comes a British officer with gold and
stuff all over him, riding on a horse. Tompkins runs up to
him, waving his arms and yelling. Well, before you can say
'God-save-King-George-III-the-dirty-bastard' the bloody-back
claps him under arrest and orders him hustled off to jail as
a goddam Rebel!" Dyckman slapped his thigh and roared.
"The fellow who told us 'bout it hung around watching so
long that he had to leave his stock to 'em and ride like hell
to get away himself. But he says 'twas worth it—just to see
them 'liberators' do a job on their friends!"

Odell smiled wryly. "I reckon them Hessians'll be making
Rebels out of good Tories most as fast as the Sons of Liberty
made Tories out of them as might of been good Whigs had
they been given half a chance. Still and all, it seems some-

times like this war's harder on the poor folks in between than on them turns out to do the fighting."

Abe scarcely heard them. His mind was trying to grapple with this utterly unexpected development. To launch this invasion the British had come up the Sound in transports, landing their troops unopposed at Throgg's Neck. Their first thrust had been checked by judicious defense of a natural bottleneck through which they had to pass to advance inland. But two nights ago they had shifted their base a few miles farther east to Pell's Point, and from there had fought their way against stubborn resistance as far as Eastchester Church, where their advance patrols had been reported at today's dawn. Definitely, they had broken through this time. No organized troops remained between them and the Bronx. A couple of hours' forced march would place them squarely on the flank of the American line of retreat from New York, once sufficient troops could be brought up. That they should fail to pursue the advantage gained with such great difficulty seemed incredible. Abe suspected dark motives.

"The general ought to know about this right away," he declared with concern.

"Don't you reckon he's heard by now?"

"Maybe, and maybe not. 'Twould surprise you what these folks don't know once things start happening fast."

"Come on, then!" Dyckman cried. "John, stick a spur into General Van there and let's see can he run."

"Who?"

"That broken-winded hay-burner you got between your legs. Ain't you going to name him in honor of the high-falutin' friend who give him to ye?"

"Well—I don't know as General Van Cortlandt would like—"

Dyckman leaned over and fetched the big gray a lusty clout across the rump, and in another instant the two of them were racing down the road in a cloud of dust, whooping like wild Indians. Abe followed at a leisurely canter to save his own horse which had been ridden twenty miles that day already, and found them waiting for him a mile or so farther on.

"Listen, fellows," he began. "Supposing we work it this way: you two go with any troops we come on and I'll push ahead and report to the general. That all right?"

"This here's your party, Abe. We'll do what you say."

The sun was low in the west by now, and a chill was creeping into the crisp, late October air. They continued southward at a trot and came at last upon the head of the retreating American column piled up at the crossroads beyond Tuckahoe.

This might have been an army in a hurry, but at the moment it looked anything but the part. Except for their muskets, these men might have been any band of particularly shabby farmers; ragged, dusty without a semblance of uniform among them. Most of them lay sprawled by the road side in attitudes of dejected weariness, while a few more energetic souls prowled a near-by farmyard from which a chorus of cackling and squealing gave evidence of their purpose. Before the gate of the house a mounted officer in a blue coat was arguing impatiently with a man who was apparently the owner.

"I'm as good a Whig's any!" the latter whined as the three horsemen approached. "Your men got no right robbing my hencoop."

"I don't give a damn about your hens," cried the officer in exasperation. "All I want to know is which of these roads leads to a place called White Plains!"

"There's two ways you can get there," Dyckman called, pushing forward.

The officer turned. "There are, eh? Which is best?"

"Well, now, that depends on—"

"For Christ's sake! Can't one of you thick-headed Dutchmen give a man a straight answer?"

Dyckman bridled. "Who ye calling a thick-headed Dutch-man?"

Abe caught at his arm. "Brom!" he cried in alarm. "Hold on! He's an officer!"

Dyckman shook him off. He thrust his head forward between his big shoulders like an angry turtle. "Take that back, ye Yankee bastard, or I'll break your head!"

For an instant the officer was too dumfounded to speak. That he was of high rank was evidenced not only by his epaulettes but the fact that he was mounted. Probably it had been a long, long time indeed since he had been addressed in any such manner.

"Treason!" he gasped. "Treason!" He raised his voice. "You men! Arrest this scoundrel!"

The men in the road gaped up at him. None of them moved. The officer tugged at his sword. He shouted the order again, his voice rising in fury, and this time a couple of the men scrambled reluctantly to their feet. Abe and Odell grabbed Dyckman on either side as he made to lunge forward.

At this critical moment, however, an interruption occurred. A second officer galloped up from the rear, his face mottled with anger.

"What's the meaning of this?" he demanded. His voice had a hard, metallic quality, but lacked the nasal twang of the New Englander. "Can't you see you're holding up the whole army?"

The first officer whirled. "Who the hell might you be?"

"Colonel Haslet of the Delaware Line! If you don't—"

"I'll take no orders from you! My colonel's commission's dated—"

"I don't give a goddamn when your commission's dated! You get your men moving, or I'm going to march my regiment through you—at bayonet's point if I have to!"

The three guides observed this strange scene in astonishment.

Abe saw that several officers of the New England regiment

were running up to their chief's support, but the latter's eyes
had already fallen before the cold rage of the Delaware
colonel.

"I can't help it if I've slowed up the retreat!" he growled.
"How's a man to find his way in this accursed country? The
confounded natives are too stupid to tell you anything, and
then along comes this pack of insolent Tories to lead us into
a trap!"

Anger overcome Abe's awe of his superiors' presence. "We
ain't Tories!" he cried. "We're guides sent by General
Heath!"

He felt Colonel Haslet's cold eyes upon him.

"Why didn't you say so?"

"We didn't get no chance! The colonel here—" He broke
off, fumbled a paper from his coat pocket. "Here, sir. This
says—"

Haslet leaned forward and snatched the paper from his
hand. " 'To whom it May Consarn,' " he read aloud.
" 'Abraham Kronkhyte bearer Hereof is Volunter employ'd
to guide the Army and enlist Others for s'd Service and is to
Be Treated accordingly by All Committees and all Officers
and Men of the Continental service and melitia. Signed
W. Heath, M. Gen.' "

He thrust the note back at Abe and turned to the other
officer. "If you still fear a trap, Colonel, get your men out of
the road, and I'll assume responsibility for the advance
guard."

"You can go to hell!" snapped the New Englander. He
turned. "You rascals say you're guides, eh! Well, lead the
way and make it fast!"

"Not me!" Dyckman retorted. "I'll guide anybody else,
but this son of a—"

Odell, bulking huge on his big gray horse, shouldered him
aside. "I'm at your service, sir," he said quietly.

Abe breathed a sigh of relief. Colonel Haslet's stiffness
relaxed a trifle.

"Good lad!" he said to Odell, ignoring the other colonel.

"Set a brisk pace. Any Yankees who can't keep up will find Delaware bayonets jabbing 'em in the arse!"

He pulled his horse's head around and trotted off the way he had come without another glance at any of them. Dyckman was still glaring at the New Englander, but he followed without protest when Abe tugged at his arm.

"Say! I know that fellow Haslet," he remarked, his ill nature evaporating. "He put up one hell of a fight over to Long Island—him and them Marylanders was about the only ones did. 'S wonder he's got any regiment left!"

They came upon the Delaware men presently. To the casual eye there was nothing to distinguish them from the New Englanders ahead of them, but Abe noticed that the moment their colonel shouted to them they leaped up, weary as they were, and fell into ranks with little fuss or confusion, even those at the rear who had been engaged in acriminious bickering with a New Jersey regiment that followed them. The Jerseymen, in turn, were exchanging compliments with the regiment following them, men who spoke in the soft drawling accents of Virginia. Tempers reached the boiling point as the two guides approached. A fist swung wide, thudded, and in a flash the road was a tangle of grappling bodies and flailing arms.

Dyckman whooped joyfully. "Hey!" he yelled. "Is this here a private fight, or can anybody get in?"

"For God's sake, Brom, come on!" Abe pleaded. "This ain't none of our business."

Dyckman followed him, chuckling. "What an army! If these here United States was as keen on fighting the British as they are on fighting each other, we'd whup 'em overnight, b'Jesus!"

A mile farther on they came upon the baggage train. Although the road was dry and free from mire, the leading wagon, topheavy from overloading, had contrived to overturn in the deep ruts. Sacks and barrels of flour, casks of pork and gunpowder, spare clothing, cooking utensils, officers' baggage and a weird miscellany of field equipment were strewn for dozens of yards in every direction, while the upset wagon itself blocked traffic as effectively as a log palisade. The sprawled horses, struggling in a tangle of traces, lashed wildly with their hoofs at the teamsters trying to get them loose. To add to the general uproar, a score of slatternly women camp followers ran about amid the scattered load, snatching up whatever plunder pleased their fancy and screaming happily to each other in strident voices.

As Abe and Brom picked their gingerly way around the obstruction, they encountered a mounted officer galloping up from the rear; a fresh-faced young man clad in the natty, somewhat dandified uniform affected by aides-de-camp and staff officers generally.

"Get that goddam wagon out of the road!" he shouted. "You're holding up all the troops behind you!"

One of the teamsters looked up. He was a thin, leathery man, his face grimed with dust through which sweat traced muddy rivulets. "What ye think we're trying to do?" he snarled. "Look at them horses, will ye!"

"Shoot the beasts and drag 'em aside! Get that wagon out of the way if you have to hack it apart with axes!"

"The hell you say!" the teamster retorted hotly. "Them horses and that wagon belongs to me!"

"I don't give a damn whose property they are! We're not going to jeopardize the army on account of—"

"The hell with the army! I'm a good citizen, I am, hauling on contract, and there ain't you nor nobody else shooting my horses!"

There was a growl of assent. With one accord the other teamsters abandoned their efforts and lined up beside their companion, a threatening knot of hard-bitten men. The officer checked whatever he was about to say and glared back at them, his face a study in impatience and bafflement.

Abe rode to his side. "Begging your pardon, Major," he began diffidently. "If you was to turn the whole train around, there's a fork to the west about a quarter mile back that'll get 'em to White Plains by another road 'most as quick. Then the army can have this road clear for theirselves—and still be betwixt the wagons and the British."

The major clutched at the straw. "Come with me," he ordered, and turned back toward where they saw a group of mounted men in uniform sitting their horses in a field, apart from the confusion in the road. This was obviously the staff of a high officer, a general at least. They had no difficulty picking him out, for he was posted a little in advance of the others, a florid, rather handsome man upon whom sat immense dignity.

The major rode up to him and saluted. "These natives, General, say there's a parallel road to the west where we could route the baggage and thus keep this road clear for the foot troops."

"Hmmm," said the general. "Ah, yes. Hmmm."

He turned slowly and peered at the two guides from eyes that did not appear quite to focus. Abe, anticipating the inevitable question, promptly handed him his paper of identification.

The general squinted at the signature, forehead wrinkled. "Ah, yes, Heath. Able fellow, Heath, for a Massachusetts man." He returned the paper and gazed out over the landscape with an expression of deep thought.

"It strikes me the idea has merit, m'lord," the major ventured after a moment.

The general withdrew his gaze from the scenery and thrust his face close to Abe's. "A trustworthy young fellow, I'm sure," he decided. He paused to belch. The power of his breath made Abe blink, but the principal effect of the liquor seemed to be to heighten his almost overpowering dignity. "Yes, yes, a splendid suggestion. See to it at once, Major, there's a good chap."

"Say," Dyckman asked in a low voice as they turned back toward the road, "what's all this 'm'lord' stuff about?"

"Why, that's Lord Stirling," the major returned in some surprise.

"Huh? What's he lord of?"

"I don't know that," the major said drily. "As long as General Washington doesn't care, why should you?"

He rode ahead and began issuing orders for the new movement.

"You know, Abe," Dyckman chuckled, "I was just thinking, back there where them fellows was cursing and slugging each other—all this army needed to be a sure enough madhouse was a drunk at the head of it. I reckon this here war's like to be real int'resting!"

Turning the bulky wagons around in the narrow road promised to be quite a job. Not without misgivings, Abe left Dyckman with the major to guide the baggage train on their new route and pushed forward in search of Heath. At the general's former headquarters on Valentine's Hill he was informed that his chief had been called away a short time before to confer with the Commander-in-Chief somewhere in the neighborhood of Kingsbridge. That meant another five or six miles. By following a more circuitous route he was able to avoid the troop-congested road and thus make better time, but the swift October dusk had closed in before he reached the Harlem. The narrow bridge itself was packed from rail to rail with men, edging their way as best they could around the limber of a field gun which had chosen this strategic position to break an axle. Infantry officers were heaping abuse upon the luckless artilleryman in charge who cursed back at them, and it wasn't until they decided belatedly to co-operate and manhandle limber and gun across that Abe was able to force his way through the congestion.

He had no difficulty picking the house where the Commander-in-Chief had established temporary headquarters. Light blazed from every window, and the yard was crowded with tethered horses. In front of the gate a sentry paced a short beat. No dusty scarecrow from the marching regiments, this, but a smartly uniformed soldier who moved with the stiff precision of an automaton. At Abe's approach he faced about, clicked his heels, snapped his musket to the port and demanded the countersign.

"Get down off of that horse," he ordered disdainfully when Abe confessed his complete ignorance.

Abe obeyed. To avoid involved explanations, he drew out his paper of identification and waved it under the sentry's nose. The man peered at it suspiciously, squinting in the dim light. From his over-portentous frown, Abe guessed that he had never learned to read, but apparently he recognized Heath's signature because after a moment he stepped aside and indicated with a curt gesture that Abe might enter.

The house was not over-large, and Abe's first impression was that the living room was packed to the walls with officers. Feeling small and furtive, he stole in as unobtrusively as possible.

"You—countryman there! What's your business?"

Blinking in the glare of a score of candles, Abe saw that the speaker was seated at a paper-strewn table beside another door at the opposite end of the room. He fumbled off his hat in acute embarrassment and made his way thither.

"I—I want to see General Heath," he stammered.

"Heath!" cried the officer indignantly. "Don't you know that this is his Excellency's headquarters?"

"Huh?"

"His Excellency General Washington, you oaf! What do you mean by intruding here?"

"They—they told me the general was—was—" He held out the paper that worked so well all afternoon. But this officer did not appear to be impressed.

"Go outside and wait in the yard," he ordered. "Get out of here now!"

Abe's eyes had accustomed themselves to the light by this time. The officer, he saw, was no older than he, a pink-cheeked, supercilious youth with unshaven down on his upper lip. Despite his embarrassment he felt his gorge rising.

"I got word of the enemy movements maybe the general'd like to hear about," he persisted stubbornly.

"Oh! You got word of the enemy movements!" the officer

mimicked. "Well, you can take it and yourself out of here!"

Abe stood his ground. "Listen. I been riding all day, and I—"

The door of the adjoining room opened and the head and shoulders of another officer popped into sight.

"Who's got news of enemy movements?" he demanded.

The youth at the table indicated Abe with a gesture of distaste. "This filthy yokel just blundered in and—"

"You half-baked little fool!" The older officer turned to Abe. "Come in here!" he snapped.

Abe followed him into a smaller room. Three men were seated at a table and he was aware of several others hovering in the background. He glimpsed Heath's kindly face, drawn and haggard with care and weariness, his blue coat loosely wrinkled over his ample paunch. But it was the man facing him who caught and held his gaze: a man as big as John Odell, and as powerful, whose grim face might have been chiseled from granite. Tongue-tied, Abe could only stare at him in awe.

"Well? Well? The cat got your tongue?" demanded a high-pitched, querulous voice.

Still dazed, Abe turned toward the officer on the right of the Commander-in-Chief. His momentary impression was of two unblinking eyes, close set on either side of a long, pointed nose that overhung an insignificant chin and a thin-lipped mouth which looked like a particularly unpleasant slash across the narrow face. More striking than his face, however, was the uniform that covered his angular torso: well cut, richly laced with gold, it was so filthy as to do discredit to a militiaman. Abe, unable to speak, stared in a sort of awful fascination at a particularly large blot of what might once have been soup.

"Give the lad a chance, General Lee," interposed the big man quietly.

His voice was low-pitched, unexcited. His grim lips did not relax, but there was something in the level eyes that brought confidence, reassurance. Before he was well aware of it, Abe found himself stammering out what Odell and Dyckman had told him of the British occupation of New Rochelle. Washington heard him through without interruption, merely nodding at the end.

"Thank you, lad." He turned to the others. "Well, gentlemen, this appears to bear out earlier reports. There can be little doubt now: instead of marching to intercept us, the British are extending their flank eastward. What do you make of it, General?"

The man addressed as Lee shook his head vigorously. "That doesn't sound like Billy Howe!" His accent and diction stamped him an Englishman even to Abe who had never seen one this close before. "By heaven, no! I've served with him, sir—and I know him. Lazy he may be and given to dallying with the ladies a bit too much, perhaps. But he's a consummate tactician, sir—one of the finest in the army, by gad! This rustic is either ignorant or a liar."

Abe felt blood tingling in his cheeks, at the roots of his hair. The Commander-in-Chief's level eyes appraised him briefly, turned to Heath.

"I take it you have confidence in this young man, General?"

"Perfect confidence, your Excellency." Heath's face was an angry red. He glared across the table. "A lot more confidence than I have in certain higher-placed persons I might mention," he added.

Lee laughed unpleasantly. "Nothing like forty years on a farm for developing one's military judgment, eh, General?"

Washington's fist banged down on the table. "That will do—both of you!" He glared from one to the other. "I fear the strain has made us all irritable, gentlemen," he said, calm again. "For the love of heaven, let us set aside our petty differences and strive for the common good!"

Lee smiled, pleased by the neatness of his thrust. "By all

means, General," he said blandly. "Let me be the first to agree."

Heath was less easily mollified. It was obvious that his wit was no match for the Englishman's, and for several seconds his face reflected the struggle going on inside him. Then the angry blood began to subside, and he turned to Abe.

"You obtained the guides I sent you for?"

"Yes, sir, General. Two of the best men—"

"What! Only two?"

Abe shifted uncomfortably. "They was all I could get hold of right quick. I figured time was important."

"How far was the head of our column from White Plains?"

"John Odell can get 'em there by midnight, sir, if they keep marching." He hesitated. "Brom Dyckman's leading the baggage wagons to the west by the Sawmill River so's to keep the short road clear for the troops. A—a gentleman they called Lord something-or-other seemed to think 'twas a good idea."

Lee sniggered. "My word! First time I ever knew of that self-made peer being able to think after drinking his dinner!"

Muscles knotted briefly at the corners of the Commander-in-Chief's square jaw, but he gave no other sign of hearing. "Well, gentlemen," he said quietly, "if the enemy chooses to give us breathing space, that is our good fortune. We will carry out our own movement as originally planned."

His voice continued in the same level tone, reviewing the situation, repeating instructions previously given. Ill at ease, Abe shifted his weight from one foot to the other. They had obviously forgotten his presence; yet he feared to leave until they should dismiss him. The accumulated weariness of the long day, forgotten while movement and responsibility had occupied his mind, swept over him now like a great wave. But he saw that these haggard generals were weary, too. Even Lee, for all his superciliousness, had that pinched, drawn look about him.

He had heard much of this Charles Lee during his brief

month with the army. All manner of wild rumors about the man were in circulation: that he had held high command with the Poles, the Russians, the Turks, the Portuguese and other vague nationalities; and it was pretty well established that he had achieved a certain rank and distinction in the British army before resigning, for reasons variously given. There were those who held him to be a rare military genius, the real brains behind Washington, whose second-in-command he was, outranking all the other generals in the army. Watching the two men at the table, Abe wondered glumly about that.

It was a movement by Lee that brought him out of his abstraction at last. The thin man had risen and was bidding the Commander-in-Chief good night. He bowed to Heath with elaborate irony and strode out of the room, calling to his staff much as a hunter might whistle up his dogs. Heath heaved himself up ponderously to follow, but Washington raised a restraining hand.

"One moment, General. I'd like a word with your young friend here."

Abe braced himself as those level eyes sought him again, tried to brush away the tired fog from his brain.

"Tell me, lad," the deep voice said. "Have you heard aught in your journeying of the activities of an enemy regiment known as the Queen's Rangers—or Rogers' Rangers?"

Abe could only shake his head.

"It's a regiment made up of Americans—Tories, or Loyalists—what the enemy call the Provincial Line. Shortly before you arrived a deserter brought in a tale, unsubstantiated as yet, that they were afield and planning a raid on a place called Mamaroneck. Do you know where that is?"

"It's—it's on the Sound, sir. Maybe five miles beyond New Rochelle and this side of Rye."

"That would be farther out than any other troops have been reported, would it not?"

"From all I heard, yes, sir. Quite a ways."

The Commander-in-Chief drummed on the table with his fingers.

"If those rascals actually take the field and place themselves in such an exposed position as this would appear to be, I propose to teach 'em a lesson they'll not forget! I'll make an example that will cause the deepest-dyed Tory to think twice before taking the King's shilling! Our raw Continentals may not be able to stand up against the regulars on even terms this early in the game, but, by heaven, we can whip the tar out of any gang of renegades that scoundrel Rogers can muster!"

Heath's tired face brightened. "Splendid, your Excellency! We'll scotch this threat at the very outset!"

The Commander-in-Chief turned to Abe. "Young man, do you think that you and your friends can find out what we want to know and guide an attacking force to the scene should that appear advisable?"

"Why—why, sure, sir. That is—"

"Good! I am leaving for White Plains in a few moments with my staff. With you to guide us, we should join the advance division there by midnight."

"Tonight?" Abe gasped in dismay.

The tall general smiled faintly. "You're tired, I see. I'm sorry, lad, but you'll find that in a war nearly everybody is tired nearly all of the time. I'll see you have a fresh horse, anyway." He became brisk again. "I'll need as many scouts and guides as you can get on short notice—but they're to be dependable men, mind you, and fearless ones. Those not properly armed may draw what they need from the army stores."

Abe kept his eyes on the floor. "I—I ain't in the army, sir. I kind of figured I oughtn't to go armed."

"Not armed?" cried the Commander-in-Chief in astonishment. "Good heavens! Don't you realize this is war?"

Abe shuffled his feet without looking up.

"His family are Quakers, your Excellency," Heath explained. "As there has been no necessity for his carrying arms heretofore, I have never pressed him to do so."

"I see." Washington's voice was gentler. "Look you, lad. General Greene, one of my ablest officers, comes of a Quaker family. There are others among us, convinced that in serving our righteous cause they are obeying the true will of their Creator."

Slowly Abe raised his eyes. "I won't lie to you, sir," he said unhappily. "I don't hold by my pa's beliefs. It ain't that." He hesitated, swallowed hard. "I know what some Tories are, but there's them among the Tories that's folks about like us—who think they're doing what's right just like we do. There's a—there's them among 'em that's been friends to me."

There was an instant's silence when he stopped speaking. Half fearfully, half defiantly, he looked at the Commander-in-Chief. But the latter was not looking at him. There was a cloud across his eyes, and his big shoulders drooped a little.

"Aye," he said heavily, "I've friends among them, too—those who have been friends since boyhood; men at whose board I've dined, and they at mine. Most of us have. We call each other 'traitor' and drench our country with the blood of neighbors—brothers' blood! This freedom we seek is not cheaply bought. Pray God those who come after us may find a joy in it some of us can never have."

He stopped speaking, moody eyes on the table before him. Heath looked from one to the other, his tired face a study in bewilderment. In his native Massachusetts, lines of cleavage had been sharply drawn by years of contention. One knew who one's enemies were and could fight them with singleness of purpose. He cleared his throat, shattering the brief silence.

"I don't know what ails the boy, your Excellency," he said, "but I'll vouch for his sincerity and ability. Furthermore, he is the only one familiar with the territory whom I've had time to teach even the rudiments of scouting. We have plenty of men to fight, after all. It is no new thing for armies to employ non-combatants as guides."

Washington shrugged. "I'll press the lad no further. Heaven knows, we've enough half-hearted patriots as it is!" He rose to his feet. "Reed!" he called. "Colonel Reed!" An officer appeared in the open doorway. "Be so good as to inform the staff that we are riding for White Plains at once."

"The horses are ready saddled, your Excellency."

"Splendid!" He grasped Heath's hand. "I count on you to keep 'em off our backs, General. The rear guard could be in no abler hands!" He turned to Abe. "Your country's thanks, young man, for your service this day. If you will but guide us to White Plains now, I'll ask no more of you."

"I—I'll guide you anywhere, sir!" Abe cried. He checked himself. Before the Commander-in-Chief's searching eyes his own dropped.

For the second time the tall general smiled: a faint smile without much mirth in it. He spun on his heel. "Come along then."

He strode through the anteroom and out into the dark yard. An orderly with a lantern held his horse in readiness at the doorstep.

"Mount, gentlemen!"

Accouterments rattled, leather creaked. The Commander-in-Chief swung into the saddle, motioned Abe to his side at the head of the little cavalcade. Outside the gate they turned northward. Their hoofs echoed hollowly on the planks of the bridge, settled to a rhythmic trot on the road beyond. The sky was overcast, starless; so dark that Abe could scarcely distinguish the great, rugged bulk of the man who rode so close beside him. Yet tired as he was in mind and body, shivering in the sharp autumn air, there was not a moment during that long night ride when he was not aware of that man's presence.

.

Chapter 8

FIRST FIRE

It was nearly midnight the following day when Abe rode in with the final report on the Mamaroneck situation. All day long the footsore Continental regiments had been coming in, taking post on the hills to the north and west of White Plains. The last of their campfires had died out long since. Tentless, they bivouacked in the open, weary men sleeping on their arms. But there was no rest for those at the Miller House, a short distance in the rear. Candlelight blazed from every window, aides came and went; there was the confused drone of many voices—all the bustle of a Commander-in-Chief's headquarters in the field.

Abe left the other guides in the yard and went to report with the captain who had been with him most of the afternoon: a tall, hard-bitten man named Pope from one of the Virginia regiments. There was no wrangling with officious aides this time. They were ushered at once into a spacious room where Washington himself was seated in conference with a general and two field officers.

Abe recognized Haslet, the Delaware colonel, who had told off the New Englanders so emphatically on the road the previous afternoon. The other general was the immensely dignified Lord Stirling, his breath comparatively mild tonight. The third officer, a major, he had never seen before.

Captain Pope made his report without hesitation or excess verbiage. He was an experienced officer in whose company Abe had learned more of the practical aspects of scouting an enemy position than he could have from a month of Heath's theorizing.

"The Rangers raided Mamaroneck at sunrise, as you have already been informed," Pope began. "They drove off what militia there were with no difficulty and seized all the stores laid up in the mills and houses along the Mamaroneck River —mostly rum and molasses, far as we can learn, with some flour and pork. They later took post on what the guides tell me is Heathcote's Hill, a little behind the village. Rogers took over the school there as headquarters after sending the children home. His command is close by, bivouacked around large fires of fence rails or whatever else in the way of fuel they could steal."

"Could you discover anything of their number?"

"Persons we questioned estimated it variously from four hundred to seven hundred. From what little I could observe myself, I'd place it lower, sir."

"Then you did get a look at them yourself? Good! What manner of men do they appear?"

"About like our own, offhand, sir. The officers wear green coats ornamented with silver, but the rank and file are not uniformed as yet."

"Good Lord!" groaned Colonel Haslet. "One band of un-uniformed men attacking another band of ununiformed men in pitch darkness!"

"If any soldiers can be depended upon under such diffi-culties, Colonel, they are those you'll lead this night," Wash-ington declared. "Don't you agree, Lord Stirling?"

"Eh?" The man addressed blinked a couple of times. "Ah, yes. Yes, indeed! Picked 'em myself—Delaware men, Mary-landers and Virginians. Cream of my division—cream of the whole army, I daresay."

Captain Pope gave a brief description of the enemy's dis-positions. The hill on which they were camped provided a fairly good defensive position, but far from invulnerable against surprise attack. Strong outposts had been placed to cover the approaches from three directions: toward Rye, Harrison and White Plains itself.

"But their inside flank is wide open, sir. Toward New Rochelle they have only one picket—one lone sentry below the hill, a good quarter-mile out."

"Doesn't the main body of the British lie in that direction?"

"Yes, sir." Pope paused, grinned faintly. "Only they're not in direct contact. We scouted the entire distance between—two miles by the lowest estimate!"

"Good heavens!"

"That doesn't sound like Rogers," Haslet said after an instant. "He may be a scoundrel, but there is no precedent in his record during the last war for such carelessness."

Washington shook his head. "Rogers isn't the man he was, Colonel. If he were, I'd have found use for him in some capacity when he importuned me a year ago, even though I never fully trusted him. He's been thrown in jail, virtually cashiered from the British service—couldn't get a command till he recruited this one himself. If he's stone sober tonight, 'twill be the first time in years."

Colonel Haslet turned to Abe. There was recognition in his eyes, but he gave no other sign of recalling their previous meeting. "How about it, young man? Think you can take us between them and the main army without alarming either?"

"Easy, sir. Me and Captain Pope and the others we just come in that way."

"Good. Then prepare to move at once. I'll join you presently."

Abe returned to the yard where the rest of the guides stood at the heads of their restless horses. John Odell and Brom Dyckman were there, and the others they had recruited hurriedly for this special occasion: Brom's older brother, Mike; Abe's cousin, Isaac Oakley, whose father's farm lay a short distance west of the village, and young John

McChain from near Mamaroneck, whom they had drafted that afternoon because of his special knowledge of the region. Except for Abe, they were all armed. In addition to his musket Brom Dyckman wore a dragoon's saber he had picked up somewhere, a great curved cutting sword that slapped awkwardly at his legs when he walked. Colonel Haslet emerged after a moment, followed by Pope and the strange major. At a word they all mounted and followed him toward the center of the village.

Before the courthouse they halted. Other officers came up about them. There were low-voiced orders. Sergeants went among the soldiers scattered thickly on the green: veterans snatching what sleep they could.

"Get up! Get up! Fall in! We're marching!"

The strange major halted beside Abe. "I'm Green, First Virginia Line Regiment. You and Captain Pope are to ride with my advance guard."

He led the way down the road for a short distance to where four small companies, apart from the rest, were forming under the urging of their officers, perhaps a hundred and fifty men. Wheeled into column, they formed a dense, compact mass. Although there was no apparent need for quietness here, some instinct caused everyone to keep his voice low, giving a tense, furtive air to the business.

A squad detached itself from the column and trotted down the road at the double, halting after they had gone about two hundred yards. They were followed by a larger detachment, a platoon, which halted about midway between them and the rest of the battalion. At the major's direction Abe rode forward and posted himself a short distance in advance of the foremost unit. He took Jack McChain with him, since he was even more familiar with this particular route than Abe was. The rest of the guides were stationed elsewhere, either with the larger main body where Colonel Haslet rode, or acting as connecting files to maintain contact between the extended elements of this advance guard formation.

"Forward—*march!*"

Accouterments rattled. Feet shuffled in the dusty road.

"March at ease, men. But no talking, mind you."

For some distance they moved down the Mamaroneck road. The night was clear but moonless, and a light mist in the upper sky dimmed the star points which provided their only light. Despite the darkness they made good time for the first hour, for the way lay straight and fairly broad. At Cornell's fork, however, they turned on to the New Rochelle crossroad, and the going became much slower. Not only was this road narrow and rough, but it was taking them toward the right flank of the British main body. Frequent halts were called to feel out the ground ahead, to keep the rearmost elements from straggling, to maintain the advance guard formation intact.

"Silence, there! Silence in the ranks!" The whispered admonition ran the length of the column. "Pass the word— silence!"

"Close up! Close up!"

Starting and stopping, expanding and contracting like a giant accordion, the column crept forward through the night. At the outset Abe had felt a strange sense of unreality, as though the whole adventure were something conjured out of the night by his weary brain. "In war," Washington had said, "nearly everybody is dead tired nearly all of the time." And he had been in the saddle two days and most of two nights with only a briefly snatched sleep between. Now, however, as the slow hours dragged by and the climax drew closer, he felt that sense of unreality giving way to something very different: an acute alertness, an indefinable awareness, not quite like any feeling he had ever known before. With no volition of his, he found his eyes turning ceaselessly to left and right, trying to penetrate the darkness; his ears straining to catch every alien sound. Protracted suspense drew his nerves tighter and tighter.

"Ever hear musketry fire, Jack?" he whispered to the new guide riding beside him. "I mean, volley fire?"

"Sure," McChain said. "When the British was fighting over to Pell's Point, there was a-plenty of it."

"Oh. Was you there?"

"No, but we could hear it, all right."

"What I mean's musketry fire that's being aimed at you. Don't you reckon you'll be scared?"

"Hell!" McChain's voice was puzzled. "How can a fellow tell whether's going to be scared or not till he's found out?"

They halted again at the crossroad just below the Quaker Meeting House. They were dangerously close to the British posts now, but there was no challenge, no sign that they had been discovered.

"We turn left here and head for the Sound," Abe informed Major Green, who had ridden up to the advance.

The major held his watch close in front of his eyes and peered at it intently. "It's past three o'clock already. How much farther?"

"Not more'n a couple miles."

The column moved forward.

"Silence in the ranks! . . . Close up! . . ."

A half mile short of the Boston Post Road Abe signaled for the column to halt. There was no special landmark here; no house, no crossroad, only open pasture land stretching on either hand, losing itself in the dim starlight.

"Is this the spot?" The major was still at his side.

"Yes, sir." Abe spoke tersely to keep his teeth from chattering.

"Guides this way!" the major called softly. "Pass the word— all guides to the head. . . . Close up the column on the advance guard."

John Odell rode up from the rear, looking enormous atop his big gray horse, his face, strangely pale, swimming like a detached cloud out of the darkness. Abe heard Brom Dyckman's laugh, light, eager; then Colonel Haslet's deep growl telling him to shut up. More riders . . . the shuffle of many feet as the rearward units halted directly behind the advance. Major Green had dismounted and was conferring in a low voice with Captain Pope, who was pointing across the fields to the left.

"You know the plan, gentlemen," Haslet said quietly. "We leave the horses here and cross the fields on foot. Major Green will command the advance, directly behind the guides who are to act as pioneers—not only showing the way, but clearing aside fence rails and other obstructions in our path. I will bring up the main body in support and attempt to encircle from the left once contact is made. All clear?"

Voices muttered assent. There was the sound of men dismounting. Abe felt his knees trembling as his feet touched the ground, but to his relief they supported him.

"Get going, guides! Spread out as widely as you can and still keep in touch with the men next you. You two big fellows"—he singled out Odell and Dyckman—"I'm depending on you to overpower that sentry without giving the alarm."

Abe walked gingerly toward the stone fence that separated the pasture from the road. Two guides were already lifting aside the rails that formed a gate near by. Suddenly a hand gripped his shoulder.

"Here, you!" It was Major Green. "Where's your musket?"

"I—I don't aim to use one," Abe stammered. "I ain't a soldier. I'm a civilian—a noncombatant—"

"You mightn't have time to tell 'em that," the major interrupted drily. "To go into a scrimmage like this unarmed is like committing suicide." He turned and snatched a gun from one of the soldiers detailed to hold the horses. "Here! Take this whether you use it or not."

This was no place to argue. Besides, Abe was afraid his teeth would start chattering if he tried. His fingers froze around the stock, and in another moment he was in the field.

They crossed the pasture, treading lightly. The close-cropped grass made a cushion under their feet so that they seemed to move like ghosts, flitting without sound. As they paused to remove more rails from the fence at the farther side, Abe saw the Continentals come up and halt a short distance behind them, a long line of shadows merging into the night. A small plowed field succeeded the pasture, then a meadow where knee-high grass clutched at their legs. Beyond this the hill that was their objective loomed black against the faint stars.

Abe crept up to the fence. A lane passed here, angling toward the Sound, and it was upon this that they had located the lone sentry that evening. After an instant Abe's curiously attuned ear caught the sound of the man's slow steps, receding to the left. He raised his head but was unable to see that far. Even as he tried, the man next him rose, crossed the fence and stepped noiselessly into the lane, disappeared as the darkness swallowed him.

"Ga-a-h!"

The sound was choked off so swiftly that it might not have been a sound. Without conscious volition Abe leaped into the lane and ran in that direction. John Odell had both huge hands around the sentry's neck from behind, had lifted him clear of the ground, but the man was struggling like a fury. Then there was another shadow in the lane. It lunged with a low grunt, and the sentry's struggles ceased. Odell let the nerveless body drop to the ground as Abe came up. It gave off a curious odor, sweetish, half rancid.

"For Christ's sake! An Indian!" Dyckman was wiping off his bayonet.

"Hush, you fool!"

A new sound rooted them. It came from the field on the lower slope of the hill beyond the lane: a man's cough sounding in the tense silence loud as a gunshot. For an instant they stared at each other, dumfounded. Then their now keyed-up senses caught another sound: a low, uneven buzzing, such as might be made by a number of men snoring in their sleep a short distance away.

Abe ran back to the fence and climbed it hastily. The Continentals were approaching cautiously behind Major Green, a drawn sword in his hand.

"There's something wrong, sir! There's men in the field beyond!"

"What's that!"

"We got the sentry, sir, but there's others! And we're still a quarter-mile from their camp!"

The major threw down his sword in rage. "What kind of scouting do you call this? What kind of—"

"They weren't there this evening!" Captain Pope had hastened up. "I scouted the ground myself. I told you it was too good to be true. Rogers must have posted 'em there after dark!"

The major's rage gave way. He stooped to retrieve his sword. "Hold the troops here!" He pushed Abe forward. "Show me!"

Odell and Dyckman were crouched behind the fence across the lane. They pointed in silence. After a few seconds, night-accustomed eyes discerned darker shadows in the field, a great number of scattered shadows that might have been clumps of low bushes, a hundred yards away.

"Wake up, Captain!" A voice, tense with urgency, carried across the intervening space. "There's somebody out there! I heard—"

The shadows that might have been bushes began to stir. "Rouse! Rouse!"

"Bring the men up," the major ordered quietly.

He rose to his feet and peered into the field where the shadows moved, changed shape. A muffled clank of accouterments sounded in the lane behind. A man slipped up to the fence beside him, bayoneted musket silhouetted against the night sky. There were others to right and left.

"Rouse! Rouse!"

Shadows in the field were changing shape. A few moved forward. Any instant now they would be discovered. Any instant the night would explode in fire and din and sudden death. Abe's face felt stiff, his knees like jelly. His mouth hung half open and his eyes were dilated. He did not know whether he was breathing or not. He looked at the major beside him. Green was watching the field, his jaws moving without haste, as though engaged with a chew of tobacco. His head turned coolly right and left where his men were taking their positions. Then he was on the fence with one bound.

"Up, boys!" After the suppressed whispers of the past hours, his voice slashed the night like the crack of a whip-lash. "Up! Charge the Tory scoundrels!"

There was a startled shout from the field. A musket slammed. Another. A mightly yell went up from the men along the fence. A man close to Abe scrambled over. Everywhere men were climbing over, running forward.

"Up and at 'em! Up and at 'em!"

The major was still on top of the fence, waving his sword in great circles. More men were racing across the lane, jumping down into the field. Abe crouched where he was, unable to move. A ragged volley from up ahead rocked his numbed brain. Major Green gave a sharp cry, spun halfway around and crashed down on him.

"Where'd it get ye?" Abe extricated himself somehow and bent over the stricken officer.

"Shoulder . . . The sons of bitches . . . Oh, Christ!"

He subsided and lay groaning, his breath coming in short, puffing gasps. Abe took hold of him with the vague idea of trying to carry him off to the rear, but the major's yell of pain stopped him.

"Never mind me . . . Get in there and fight!"

Abe raised his head gingerly above the fence. The field, lighted eerily by scattered flashes of musket or pistol, had become one great appalling tangle of milling, yelling men, locked in the viciousness of hand-to-hand combat. The night, so still a moment before, was hideous with din: curses, groans, screams; snarling voices, hoarse and savage, high-pitched and nerve-jarring. Abe had been in a few rough-and-tumbles himself. He had seen tavern brawls, young as he was. But these men were fighting to kill. Nerveless, ill, he reeled against the fence.

"Rangers! Rally, Rangers! Never yield to Rebels!"

Briefly the voice sounded clear above the din. That voice he knew so well. His stomach seemed to turn over inside of him. Then his numbed brain was alive again. But he did not realize that. He had forgotten his terror, forgotten himself. There was not a conscious thought in his mind as he leaped the fence; only sensations, impulses.

He ran toward the melee, toward where that voice still shouted the rallying cry. He detoured a knot of men clubbing blindly at one another with musket butts, hurdled a snarling pair grappling on the ground. A man rushed at him with leveled bayonet, but he leaped aside with the agility of a rabbit and ran on.

At the far edge of the struggle a compact wedge of men were fighting shoulder to shoulder, holding off a disorganized spray of assailants behind a serried hedge of bayonets. The spray receded, gathered in a black wave.

"All together, boys! Charge the Tory dogs!"

Abe recognized Captain Pope's voice. The wave rolled forward, surged against the barrier with a crash that sounded above the confused uproar. The wedge recoiled, bent. Steel struck sparks from steel, wood thudded.

"Rally, Rangers! Rally!"

Watching his chance, Abe dodged around the flank of the turmoil, cut in behind toward the disembodied voice.

"Squire! Squire Hilton! It's me! It's Abe!"

He caromed off a locked pair of stabbing, gouging men. In the flash of a musket discharge he glimpsed a green coat, silver-laced. A face, powder-blackened and scarcely recognizable, was thrust toward his. He side-stepped mechanically as a clubbed musket flailed past his ear from behind, clutched at the green coat to keep his balance.

"Go back, Squire!" he panted. "There's more of 'em! They're circling to cut you off! They're coming that way!"

He sensed rather than saw the clubbed musket swinging again. Frantically he threw up the arm with which he had been trying to point. . . .

The next thing he saw was the gray of dawn across the upper sky, dimming the scattered stars.

His arm ached where that descending musket butt had struck it. But that was nothing compared to the ache in his head. There was a bump on the back of it that felt as big as an egg. At least his head was all there. He had broken the force of the blow enough to keep from being brained.

Awareness began to return to him. Up the hill, some distance away, muskets still thudded sporadically. He sat up dazedly and looked about. In the leaden half-light the scene had a weird, unearthly quality. Near at hand lay what might have been a bundle of old clothes. Peering more closely, he saw that it was a man, lying face downward, blood oozing from a hole in his back. He had never seen a dead man before. Sick and weak he turned away. But similar bundles were strewn haphazardly everywhere he looked, some stirring, some inert.

"Hey!" called a voice. "Lend me a hand, can't you!"

Some distance to his left a man was sitting up, barely visible in the gray light. Abe got to his feet with a prodigious effort and reeled over to him. It was Captain Pope.

"Some bastard ran a bagnet through my leg, and I can't walk," he explained. "If we don't get out of here pretty damn quick, we're like to be left behind."

"I ain't sure I can walk much myself," Abe mumbled. His head was ringing like a gong.

The captain peered at him. "Oh, it's you. I thought you were the fellow who wasn't going to fight!"

Abe said nothing. He got both hands under the captain's armpits and heaved with what strength he could muster.

"Jesus! Go easy!"

Pope got his one good foot under him somehow, one arm about Abe's neck. Clinging to each other, they set a wavering course back across the trampled pasture.

A squad of men with slung muskets loomed out of the dimness ahead of them, a detail sent out to bring in any wounded they could find. One of them supported Captain Pope on the other side, and after that they made better progress. A pitiful moaning and groaning, punctuated by screams of pain, guided them unerringly to the other wounded. They had been gathered on the sward beside the lane where the surgeon and his mate moved among them, working swiftly, deftly. Abe counted more than a dozen, some writhing on the ground, some lying inert, a few sitting up weakly, propped against the fence from which the charge had started. Major Green, very white of face, sat a little apart. The entire right side of his coat had been cut away, and blood was already staining the mass of fresh bandages that swathed his shoulder.

"That you, Pope?" he called. "Man, I thought you were a goner for certain!"

"What happened?" the captain asked.

"Probably nobody knows—or ever will. It seems everybody was yelling, 'Kill the Tories!' and 'Get that traitor Rogers!' and the Tories, seeing how things were going, took up the cry themselves till nobody knew who was fighting whom. Then part of Haslet's men got mixed up in our fight instead of pushing on against the hill, and by the time he could untangle 'em, Rogers had his whole force on the alert and firing by volley. God, what a madhouse!"

"Guides! Guides this way! Where're those damn guides?"

The call came from the meadow beyond the lane. Abe left Captain Pope to the care of the surgeon and hastened in that direction. He walked more steadily now, though his brain still reeled.

The attacking column was re-forming. Following the

voice, Abe descried presently a small group of men beside the fence some distance farther along. He recognized the backs of his fellow guides and edged in among them as inconspicuously as possible.

Colonel Haslet faced them, his eyes blazing. "The failure of this operation rests mainly with you men!" he declared furiously. "If you'd been where you were wanted when you were wanted, we'd have taken the hill on the flank and not a one of 'em would have escaped!" He singled out Dyckman. "Where were you when the main body came up?"

"Why, I was fighting, of course!" Dyckman said in surprise. "I did in three of the bastards—"

"Oh! You were fighting, eh! Who told you you were to fight? Who gave you authority to risk your life?"

Dyckman blinked. "For Christ's sake, Colonel! It's my own life, ain't it?"

"No, it isn't your own! Your life belongs to your country! The lives of all of us belong— Well, what is it?"

An officer had hastened up from behind. He saluted.

"Report on casualties, sir. Only three known dead and fifteen wounded, maybe a few missing. Haven't checked on theirs, sir. The field seems littered with 'em."

"Yes, yes?"

"We took sixty stands of arms, a pair of colors and thirty-six prisoners. All sorts of camp equipment there's been no time to sort out."

Haslet frowned. "Hmmm. Might be worse."

He turned back to the guides. "I don't mean to be too hard on you lads," he said more calmly. "You can't be expected to know everything after only a couple of days with the army. But get this through your heads right now: the result of an expedition like this rests largely in your hands—not only its success or failure, but the fate of the men concerned. With such responsibilities on your shoulders you've no right to take any more risks than you absolutely have to! Understand?"

He glared from face to face of the little group. It was John Odell who broke the brief silence.

"Begging the colonel's pardon," he said imperturbably, "but if you're finished giving us hell, supposing we get started out of here. There'll be British swarming all over us soon's there's light enough for 'em to find their way."

"All right. Go to your posts. If you get us back as efficiently as you brought us down, I'll see that you're commended for that much, at any rate."

The colonel turned on his heel and strode off, shouting orders. Dyckman expelled his breath gustily.

"I'll be goddamned! What kind of a war's this, where a fellow gets dressed down for fighting?"

The group was already breaking up. Abe slunk away without answering the questions several of them flung at him. He did not know the answers, and the last thing he wanted to do was talk. All he knew was that his head ached fit to split, that a cloud seemed to have settled on his brain. He walked slowly through an unreal world, the meadow grass swishing about his knees like water. A short distance to his left, half seen in the lightening dawn, men were being herded into formation; laughing, exultant men, calling to each other in excited voices, still keyed up for the fight they had won.

It was the contrast presented by another group farther on that caused him to pause, come nearer. These were not laughing or cheering. They stood huddled together, staring sullenly at the ground. It was only when he saw that they were unarmed that his dulled mind grasped the fact that these were the prisoners. His eyes ranged over them with awakening curiosity, half fearful: men like himself, ordinary men in shabby, nondescript clothing, with only their bearing to distinguish them from the captors who stood guard over them. Nowhere was the silver-laced green coat of an officer to be seen.

He walked over to them. "Who's your captain?" he asked.

A face, half sullen, half defiant, glared back at him. "Captain Hilton! And you bastards didn't get him, neither!"

"Oh," Abe said. He hesitated for an instant, then resumed his heavy-footed course toward the head of the column. For the first time he knew that what had happened out there in the hideous darkness had not been a dream. But he still did not know the answer, or whether there was any answer. And he did not want to think. . . .

Even later, when the cloud had left his brain, he did not want to think of the implications of that incident. He never spoke of it to anyone, and more than a year was to pass before anyone spoke of it to him.

Chapter 9

A HERO COMES HOME

When they reached the outskirts of Bedford, Abe put his horse to a trot, and his companions followed suit. Hoofs spurned hard clods from the packed snow of the narrow roadway. Their voices shouted cheerily in the crisp, frosty air. Three months had passed since Abe had been in the village, and he had a special reason for wanting to make his return as impressive as possible. Odell and Dyckman had volunteered to come along and help. As they slithered to a halt before Hayes's Tavern, he was glad they had, though he would not have admitted that to himself. Here, among people who had known him since childhood, it might not have been so easy to remember his new position in the world.

Attracted by the din, the landlord had hurried to the door while they were tying their horses at the hitching rail. Abe greeted him with an airy wave of the hand.

"Hi, Ben! Butter some rum for us—best in the house—and stick a good hot loggerhead in it!"

Hayes's jaw dropped briefly. To the best of his knowledge this was the first time young Kronkhyte had ever addressed him by his first name or ordered rum, let alone hot buttered rum. Mechanically he mustered his host's smile.

"So you're the famous Westchester Guides? It's an honor, lads."

Brom Dyckman laughed. "We're part of 'em, anyhow. I reckoned you'd have heard of us."

The taverner had heard enough of them to guess that whatever drinks they consumed in his establishment would not be paid for, at least, by them. He stood aside without enthusiasm as they swaggered past him and slammed the door behind them to shut out the biting winter air.

It was late afternoon of the day before Christmas. Half a dozen men lounged about the large ordinary, filling the air with the blue smoke from their clay pipes and the pleasant steam from their hot drinks. A few called greetings which Abe acknowledged with an all-embracing gesture. Their eyes too blinded from the outside glare to recognize anyone in this subdued light, the Guides headed straight for the roaring hearth fire, stamping the powdery snow from their boots and chafing the cold from their hands.

"We've rode all the way from Peekskill today," Abe explained. "You can't dish up that there rum too quick to suit us."

He glanced impulsively toward the bar. Molly was in the process of reaching a large brown bottle down from the shelves behind. Although her back was toward him and he was still unable to see very well, he turned away more quickly than he had intended to.

"Well, what bad news you boys brung from the army?" inquired one of the other customers.

Odell peered in that direction. "What makes you think the news is bad?"

"There ain't been no other kind, has there?"

"You fellows ain't leading no forage party, be ye?" inquired another in some apprehension.

Odell blinked. "What the hell ails you folks?" he demanded. "Foraging is right by law. Everything taken for the army's paid for."

"Sure—in Congress paper! And what loot them thieving Continentals snatch up for theirselves that's got nothing to do with no army—that ain't paid for at all!"

"There's punishments for soldiers caught plundering outside the enemy lines. All you got to do to get your stuff back is report to an officer."

"Like John Martine done over to Greensburgh, huh? By the time he got through arguing with a pack of them damn Yankees, the loot had been shipped clear up to New England by pack horses!"

"Oh, leave be, John," Abe interposed. He could recognize the speakers now. "Them fireside generals was complaining about everything even before there was a war."

Molly bustled from behind the bar with their order: a large pitcher of sweetened rum and water with great gobs of golden butter floating on top. She placed it on a near-by table with a flourish and stooped for one of the loggerheads, large-headed pokers, that were heating on the grate.

"Hey!" cried Dyckman. "Something to warm our breeches, boys." Struggling with temptation, he viewed the barmaid's upraised posterior. His hand came down with a resounding smack. "And the same to you, sister!"

Molly straightened up with a yell, brandishing the glowing loggerhead. "I'll warm you, ye—"

"Brom!" Abe cried sharply. "You quit that!"

"Huh?"

Dyckman and the barmaid were both staring at him. It was hard to tell which was more surprised. Abe felt his cheeks turning red.

"That—that ain't no way to do to a girl!" he ended lamely.

"That ain't—what?"

"Why, Abe!" Molly exclaimed. She lowered the threatening loggerhead. "Was it pertecting my honor ye was?" She laughed. "Why, I don't need no help handling the likes o' him!" She stepped forward and plunged the hot iron into the pitcher with a great hissing and foaming. But she smiled at him sidewise through the pungent steam, and he saw with a start that her blue eyes were soft and friendly.

"Listen, Abe," Odell advised. "If you're going to stick your chin out every time Brom lays hand on a wench, you ain't going to have time left to get on with the war."

" 'Sall right, lad!" Dyckman was choking with laughter.

"Didn't know I was poaching your private preserve. I'm right sorry."

"But it ain't—she ain't—"

"Come on," Odell interrupted. "Let's finish up Abe's business so's we can get down to serious drinking."

Molly was stirring the concoction in the pitcher with the sizzling loggerhead. When the lumps of butter had melted to form a thick, rich scum across the surface, she decanted the still-bubbling liquor into pewter mugs. She did not look at Abe again as they drew up their chairs but hastened back to the bar to tend the wants of a new customer who had just come in, bringing an icy gust with him.

"Eb Lockwood!" Abe cried. "Just the man I want to see!"

The new arrival squinted uncertainly in that direction, blinking glare-blinded eyes. "Who's it wants to see me?"

"It's me—Abe Kronkhyte. I got something here I want you should know—and the rest hereabouts, too. Come on over and set."

He introduced his companions. The militia captain nodded to each, but his quizzical eyes turned back to Abe. A great deal had happened since that September evening when he had befriended a bewildered rustic youth in front of this same tavern.

Abe drew a paper from his pocket. "I want you should read this here so's you'll know what it says and can tell the Committee and others."

Lockwood looked closely at the paper, handed it back. "I reckon you better read it out loud, Abe. My eyes ain't used to this light yet."

Abe cleared his throat. "It's dated: 'Camp at Peeks Kill, Dec. 23, 1776'—that's yesterday." He raised his voice so that it would carry to the others in the room, now listening curiously. " 'To Whom It May Consarn. All Patriotick citizens are hereby Warned under civil and Military law to respect the Person and Property of George Kronkhyte, farmer, living at or near Hilton Manor formerly so called, in the Town of

Bedford and County of Westchester, State of New York, as a person not disaffected to the Congress of the United States.' " He paused for emphasis. "It's signed by Major General Heath himself, commander of the army in this county. See— right here!" He laid the paper on the table and glared belligerently about. "What the hell you folks hereabouts been doing to my pa?" he demanded.

Lockwood did not reply directly. "You must stand in real strong with the general for him to take all this trouble for ye," he observed.

"We stand in strong as anybody in the army!" Dyckman bristled.

Lockwood turned toward him. "For a fact, now?" he said mildly. "This here's the first I knew you fellows was even in the army."

"In the army? Why, sure we are—that is, we are and we ain't, kind of."

Their precise status defied accurate definition. At the conclusion of the White Plains campaign Heath, left in command of the region, had asked them to stay on as a more or less permanent group of volunteers to continue the services at which, in his opinion, they had proved of great value: guiding detachments and foraging parties, scouting, riding express with official messages and orders. They were attached to the army for pay and rations, yet not duly enlisted in it nor under its regulations to any greater extent than implied by their promise to hold themselves available at all times for such duties as might be assigned them. To make this position more confusing, they were often called upon to serve under both the State Convention and the Committee of Conspiracies, although they had not been officially enrolled in the militia, either.

"That ain't the point," Abe interrupted. "What about my pa?"

"Now don't go getting your hair up," Lockwood soothed.

"Nobody's harmed your pa. A delegation from the Committee just called on him, that's all."

"I know how them delegations call on folks! I don't want to hear of nothing like that happening again."

Lockwood raised his brows. "Kind of full of yourself, ain't ye?" he observed. He paused, forehead wrinkled. "I know your pa's all right, Abe, and I reckon with this paper in his hands he'll be let alone by the rest. Only you been busy with the military so long I reckon you don't realize what us folks is up against. There's Tories all about us—recruiters, spies, robbers who steal our cattle by night and sneak 'em off to New York. Now, you can figure easy enough they couldn't do all that 'less they had friends among us to harbor 'em. Folks refusing to sign the Articles of Association are naturally the first ones suspect—"

"My pa's a Quaker! Them Articles oughtn't apply to him!"

Lockwood appeared to consider. "Maybe not. Anyways, I'll see he ain't bothered from now on. But listen, Abe. Since you're such an important fellow now, supposing you tell General Heath how things stand with us and talk him into moving the army down-country where it can be some protection to folks. For all the good he does us up there in Peekskill, he might as well be scampering around Jersey with the rest."

In the background someone sniggered. Abe looked about in bewilderment. Several of the other patrons, he noticed, had left their tables and gathered to listen to the conversation. There was little of friendliness in their faces, much of bitterness, discouragement.

"I'll tell you how it is, Capt'n," Odell's dry voice cut in. "Us fellows and the general we made an agreement. He don't tell us how to get around Westchester, and we don't tell him how to run the army. See?"

There was a mutter from the ring of uninvited listeners.

" 'Bout time somebody told them fine generals how to run things!"

"What's any of 'em done, 'cept seize our forage and plunder our houses and run like hell every time they see the regulars?"

Lockwood turned in his chair. "Hold hard, folks!" he said sharply. "Whatever the army's done or ain't done, these lads have played their part right well. So supposing you mind your own business and leave 'em drink their drinks in peace." He raised the mug Molly had filled for him. "Well, boys—confusion to the Tories!"

They sipped the hot stuff gingerly, inhaling the pungent steam, feeling its warmth seep through their chilled bodies.

Dyckman smacked his lips. "There's one thing you got to give them New Englanders credit for, Capt'n. This here drink's their invention."

Their spirits were rebounding quickly. But the rum that so stimulated them served only to plunge Abe into deeper gloom. This was not the sort of reception he had expected after three arduous months in the field. Just what he had expected, he was not quite certain, but it wasn't that the reputation of the Westchester Guides would need defense by a militia captain in his own town. He caught snatches of their talk and laughter, amiable now that the tension had been relieved, but he did not listen. His mind was elsewhere; not anywhere in particular, just casting about.

He knew in a general way what ailed these people. The White Plains campaign had left a bitter aftertaste in Westchester: a taste compounded of defeat and disillusionment. It was not the failure of the campaign that bore on them so heavily, for in a broad sense the campaign had not failed. Washington had withdrawn his army intact. Although the British had stormed his right on Chatterton's Hill with almost absurd ease, they had declined to attack his main position; after a few days of futile gesturing they had withdrawn in a body and shortly thereafter had transferred the theater of war to New Jersey. Except for the outworks above the Harlem, the entire county was clear of enemy troops.

But it was clear of American troops, too, save for the few hundred Heath held at Peekskill at the county's opposite extreme; held close for reasons which it was obvious these people refused to comprehend.

The deeper trouble lay in the dismal wake of devastation left by the two campaigning armies. The region below White Plains was virtually prostrate. Part of White Plains itself lay in ruins, pillaged and burned, not by the British but by New England Continentals. The courthouse where the State Convention itself had met; Oakley's Tavern which had been the traditional gathering place for the Whigs, whose proprietor had held a Continental commission in the first Northern Campaign; a dozen private homes and farms, all destroyed without regard to their occupants' political sentiments, by a few irresponsible officers under the unfounded impression that some military advantage was to be gained thereby. In return for this the army had only defeat to show: Fort Washington taken by storm, Fort Lee surprised, Washington himself harried all the way across the Jerseys to the far side of the Delaware; General Lee, that great genius who was supposed to be his military brains, captured asleep in a tavern and hauled off to New York in his nightshirt. Small wonder morale everywhere had reached a low ebb.

But the army, or what was left of it, was still in the field. Ragged, hungry men, shivering in the bitter cold, hung on, grimly confident that the tide would turn. That those who were supposed to be behind them, well-fed men in a snug tavern, could find nothing better to do than complain was doubly disheartening to one just come from camp.

Abe finished his drink and rose. "Reckon I'd best be getting home 'fore my horse freezes."

Dusk was closing as he left the tavern and took the ascending road; the swift, early dusk of December. Candles were beginning to appear in windows throughout the little village, glowing softly in the clear, crisp air. He breathed deeply and felt his spirits reviving, his punctured ego inflating again. A hero might be without honor in his own town, but now he was going home; home for Christmas. All that had happened made the months since he had been there last seem like years. When he reached the top of the rising ground, he put his horse to a canter.

Somehow the house looked smaller than he had remembered it. But light showed within, warm and cosy, and from the chimney a plume of blue wood smoke reached toward the brightening stars, to lose itself in the windless night. He headed for the barn to stable his horse before going in. Jack was there, milking by lantern light. At Abe's hail he looked up, eyes popping with surprise.

"Abe! What brings thee here?"

"Brings me? Why, I've come home. The general gave me leave for Christmas."

"The—general?"

"Sure—General Heath. He's give me a paper for Pa, so's the Committee won't make him no more trouble."

Jack was unimpressed. "Thee's going to catch it nonetheless," he declared.

"What for? Didn't Pa get that letter I wrote him?"

"He got it, all right. But what does thee expect—walking out without so much as a by-thy-leave with the harvest coming on?"

"Good God! There's a war going on! Or ain't Pa found out about that yet?"

He turned abruptly and made his way to the house. But in spite of himself he felt more a prodigal than a returning hero as he let himself in. Nor was his greeting reassuring. His father looked him over coldly for a full minute before he spoke.

"So thee came sneaking back!" was all he said.

"I didn't come sneaking! I come because you're my folks and—and—" He snatched out the order General Heath had signed. "Here, I brung you this."

His father read through the paper, his lips moving me-

chanically. He stood frowning for several seconds after he
had finished, then turned deliberately and to Abe's astonishment laid the paper on the fire.

"I need no such protection."

"For Christ's sake, Pa! The general signed that himself—"

"Silence! Has the army made thee a blasphemer as well as
a murderer?"

"Murderer!" Abe cried, aghast. "What the—why, I—"

"War is nought but murder. Soldiers are no better than
common murderers."

Abe gulped. "But, Pa, I ain't a soldier. Us guides—well,
some of the boys fight when they got to, but me—I been what
they call a noncombatant all along!"

"Is that why thee carries that musket?"

Abe looked blankly at the long brown weapon in his hand.
Since Mamaroneck he had become so accustomed to having
it with him at all times that he took it for granted, now.

"I never used this," he protested earnestly. "I swear I
ain't! I just carry it because—well, some of the places we
have to go folks would make a peck of trouble for us if they
didn't see we was armed."

"Oh, have done, Pa!" his mother interposed. "'Tis Christmas Eve when all of us ought to be happy. Ain't it enough
for tonight that our boy's come home unharmed?"

Slowly his father's sternness relaxed. He held out a gnarled
hand. "I'll take thy word, Abe, now that thee has seen fit to
mend thy ways and come home."

"But—but I got to go back, Pa!"

His father's face stiffened again. "Back to the army?"

"I got to. I promised General Heath. I—he needs me—"

His mother gave a choked cry. "But we need thee here!
Thee can't go back—not back to the war!"

At sight of her pleading eyes, Abe bit off the protest that
was on his tongue. Silent, unhappy, he stared at the floor.

"There is no need to tell thee where thy duty lies," his
father said heavily. "War is an evil thing—man's greatest sin

against Almighty God! I'd not willingly have the blot of it on thy soul for a hundred farms the size of this one. If thee has any gratitude toward thy family, thee will respect my wishes. Write the general tomorrow saying I forbid thy return."

"You forbid—"

"Aye! I forbid, and there's an end to it!"

Abe made no reply. He had learned to speak easily and thoughtfully when generals consulted him, asked his advice. But when a stern Quaker farmer spoke, he could think of nothing to say.

Supper was a homely meal, but there was plenty of it; better and more ample than the food to which the army had accustomed him. He ate slowly, trying to enjoy it. Jack asked him a few questions regarding his adventures, and he brightened in the recounting until his parents' cold, heavy silence bore down on him. After that talk turned to the farm: last year's crop and the plans for next spring's planting; the reallotment of chores now that there were to be three men on the place instead of two. His father had thought everything out carefully and explained in meticulous detail. Across the table Jack's round farmer's face was alight as he followed mechanically. Although his mind was a million miles away, Abe felt the old restricting walls closing invisibly about him.

The only drink was weak home-brewed beer, sour and musty; and, unlike the plentiful food, this was rationed sparingly. Afterward in celebration of the holiday George Kronkhyte served them each a small glass of peachy—a cordial made from fermented peaches, locally distilled. It was sweet and heavy, but there was warmth to it and a heady aroma. Abe sipped it slowly, trying to make it last because he knew there would be no more. They told him what local news there was and such gossip as had managed to penetrate their isolated lives. He tried to appear interested, as though this meant something to him, but gradually they lapsed into silence. When all had finished their peachy and were yawning openly, George Kronkhyte ordered them off to bed, admonishing them to be up long before the sun if they were to finish the chores in time to get to meeting and enjoy the rest of Christmas day in comparative leisure. . . .

Evenings at camp were not like this. There the boys would be gathered around the fire in their little log hut, perhaps playing at cards, perhaps just sitting over such drink as one of them had managed somehow to come by, talking among themselves until, one by one, they rolled into their bunks: Brom Dyckman, who laughed so easily; John Odell, quiet and cautious; quick-tempered Isaac Oakley, a bundle of nerves; perpetually puzzled Jack McChain, so stolid that Big John appeared vivacious in comparison; Mike Dyckman, slow-thinking, sure-acting, so different from his headstrong younger brother. Or perhaps they would be abroad, one or two or three of them: scouting, foraging or riding express through the night, stopping to beg hospitality at a house known to be friendly and whose owner would be happy to offer his best to the Westchester Guides. If it were pay day, he and Brom might go over to the fort to try their luck at dice against the Continentals stationed there, or they might stop in at a tavern. . . . Brom and Big John would be at Hayes's right now. They had planned to spend the night there, where Abe was to pick them up in the morning and bring them home for Christmas dinner, after which they would ride back to Peekskill together. Abe had not mentioned this to his family and did not intend to, now. . . .

The familiar garret where he had slept since he could remember seemed close and stuffy, redolent of burned tallow candles and sweat-stained clothing. Once they were alone, Jack bubbled over with questions, but there was little Abe could talk about to his brother now. He turned his face to the wall, and at last oblivion found him.

How long he slept he did not know. Tired though he was, fragmentary dreams impinged to trouble him. He was conscious of tossing for what seemed hours in the restless borderland between sleep and waking. Then he lay still on his back, eyes wide in the darkness. Apart from Jack's heavy breathing, the little house was silent.

After a while he rose, taking care to make no sound, and dressed quickly. Through the habit of months he had placed his thin saddlebags, unpacked as yet, within easy reach. He found them without striking a light, and the tall musket that stood beside them. At the trap he paused for an instant, his ears attuned, then let himself carefully down.

He unbolted the kitchen door, latched it gently behind him, and crossed the hard-packed farmyard. The moon had risen, a lopsided three-quarters moon, that made the snow-covered world nearly as bright as day. He led his horse from the barn and saddled her by its light. The snow muffled her hoofbeats as he turned her down the lane, into the Bedford road.

The village was dark, but a dim light still showed in Hayes's taproom. The hour must be well past midnight, for the last of the Christmas Eve celebrants had staggered their homeward ways. Molly was there alone, just finishing tidying up. She turned at his entrance, and he saw that her normally rosy cheeks were pale with weariness.

"Can't serve no more tonight." Her voice, like her face, was tired. "I was just after closing up."

"I—I don't want nothing. I—"

"Oh, 'tis you, Abe." She smiled faintly. "I should of thought you'd been safe in your little bed long since."

"I'm looking for Brom and John."

She shook her head. "They ain't here. Capt'n Lockwood took 'em home with him."

"Oh," he said. He stood uncertainly for an instant, then slumped into the nearest chair.

"Why, lad, what ails ye?" She was scrutinizing him closely. "Why, ye look a wreck! I'll fix ye a drink. I was only fooling when I said—"

"I don't want no drink."

After a moment she came out from behind the bar, wiping her hands on her apron. "Tell me about it. You went home like ye planned?"

"Aye. I went home." He looked up at her, standing beside him. Some of the tiredness had left her face, and her blue eyes were soft and deep. "I went home, but I couldn't stay. It seemed like the folks was strangers—and me, too. Like I was a stranger in my own home."

"Didn't you expect something of the sort?"

"I don't rightly know what I expected."

He felt her fingers running through his hair. "Poor lad!"

He jerked away. "Don't do that!" he cried. Then before he could control himself, he buried his face in his arms and began to sob.

"Go ahead and cry if it pleasures you, darlin'," she said quietly; " 'cause if I figure things rightly, 'tis the last time ever you're a-going to."

He looked up, surprise choking off his sobs. There was no contempt in her voice as there had been on that other night when he had shown weakness; only sympathy, an intuitive understanding.

"I—I reckon I got no home no more," he blurted. "And I'm only just finding it out."

She shook her head. "You got a home, Abe. The army's your home, as it's been to many a stout fellow before ye!" She was smiling, and the color had returned to her cheeks. " 'Tis homesick ye are for it, that's all ails ye—homesick for to be with men who act like men—for the bully boys ye ride with!"

He eyed her doubtfully, unsure whether she was serious. "I don't just know as—"

"You don't know now, but you will—just like I knew the minute you walked in this afternoon with them two other fellows. You ain't the same clumsy, scared boy that went away three months ago."

"You can say that—after I been bawling like a baby?"

Her fingers were stroking his hair again. "Ties you had all your life ain't easy broken, Abe. 'Twas the jolt made you bawl—the jolt of discovering all of a sudden you ain't a boy no more and not knowing quite what you are or how you got that way. So don't be after feeling sorry for yourself, 'cause I don't feel sorry for you—not no more."

She was still smiling. Slowly he rose and faced her, his uncertainty slipping away before the warm, friendly glow in her blue eyes.

"Molly," he began, "one time you asked me was I a man or not. Do you think—well, do you think maybe now I am?"

For a long moment she stood there, very close to him, as though waiting. Then, when he did not move, she turned and picked up the lone candle from the table.

"Come," she said softly, slipping her hand into his. "There's no time like the present to be finding out."

Part 2. The Neutral Ground

Chapter 1

MAJOR GENERAL HEATH

MAJOR GENERAL WILLIAM HEATH sat in his office at headquarters behind a desk that was piled high with papers, staring morosely out a window at the Hudson. It was a blustery morning in early March, 1777, and the ice had not yet begun to break up. It showed in ugly gray patches where the wind had swept the surface bare of snow, a mile-wide, mottled stretch that ended abruptly at the foot of the rugged West Shore highlands whose summits were hidden in lowering clouds. There was the smell of more snow in the raw air. Born and raised in Massachusetts, the general had never thought much about snow until this winter; he was used to it. Now he was responsible for the welfare of some hundreds of men, most of whom lacked decent shoes or adequate clothing, and for whom he had been unable to obtain pay or a full ration issue for more months than he cared to remember. Ignoring the cluttered desk, he continued to stare out the window, his soul as bleak as the wintry landscape.

William Heath was forty, of medium height, stout and ruddy-faced, though considerably less stout and ruddy than he had been the previous fall. Slack flesh was beginning to bag along his jowls, and a network of sharp lines were etching themselves at the corners of his mouth and around his harassed eyes.

William Heath had not known a great deal about being a general when he was pitchforked into this war, but he flattered himself that he knew more now. He had set about

learning with a plodding thoroughness that was characteristic. Everything that could be gained from books had been
stowed away in his commodious if not over-critical brain. His
military library was a compendium of the best authorities of
the past quarter century, who waged war according to the
precepts of Frederick the Great and the cult of the battle
line, and he kept a journal of his own experiences for further study. He had proved himself an able division commander and so thoroughly gained Washington's confidence
as to be entrusted with the most important command apart
from the main army itself.

But nothing he had read in all those treatises on the "sublime art" of formal warfare, as its devotees liked to call it, was
much help to him here. The great Frederick, apparently, had
never been obliged to cope with anything like what people
were beginning to refer to as the "Neutral Ground"; and it
was becoming evident to students on this side of the water
that no tactitian in Europe had had an original idea since
that versatile Prussian had laid aside the sword in favor of
the flute.

The stout general withdrew his eyes from the river and
observed the litter on his desk. With obvious distaste he
picked up the first paper that came to hand and commenced
to read:

> We your Honours Petioners the Committee of Bedford
> Humbly Sheweth that Bedford is now Becom a frontier
> against the Enemy in Said County toward New York
> and toward the North Rivers and the Drafts from the
> Mellitia that you ordered out for wise Ends are Sta-
> tioned Sixteen Miles below us and not Being now
> Likely to be Numerous Enough to Stretch from River
> to River the Enemies are Masters, and there being a Ser-
> tain Company of Robers, otherwise Called Rogers
> Rangers, that keep Conseald in Parts of North Castle &
> Cortlandt Maner; Hardly a Night Passes but there is
> Some Roberies Comitted or Some of our Good men

Captivated and Draged in a most Barberous maner to the Enemy; our Remaining Mellitia has Been Obliged for Some time to watch Every Night of which, Considering the Season of the year they are much fetigued with s'd Dutty; therefore, and for the Safty of the town and the Good People which have taken Refuge here, we, your Petioners, humbly Pray that a Number of the Late Drafts of about forty men, Including a Non Commissioner Commanded by two Viglant officers Be Stationed in and about Bedford to Gaurd this Place and Detect those Robers; and in the mean time, Your Petioners will Ever Pray for your Honour in the Execution of the Great and Difficult task Comitted to your Care.

    Signed by Order of the Comittee

                EBEN'R WARD, Chairman.

This touching document was addressed "To the Hon'le B. General Georg Clinton Commander in Chief of the Melitia of Westchester County, &c., &c.," who had sent it along with a notation that he had no militia to spare for such duty. And Heath would be double-damned if he was going to send out any of his half-starved, half-naked Continentals on such an assignment. He was not quite certain where Bedford was, but if it were sixteen miles above the outposts . . . Good God! Had the trouble spread that far already?

Heretofore such activities had been confined to the region below the lines: the Neutral Ground proper, where no law existed nor the means of enforcing any. The British had abandoned this section following the White Plains campaign, and the Americans had never reoccupied it, at least in force.

The next paper was a report from one of his agents deep in the affected section. "The recent failure of our arms has emboldened the Tories beyond description and so discouraged our own people that many until now staunch in the Cause are becoming disaffected. . . ."

Heath winced. What people chose to consider the "recent failure of our arms" actually had been nothing more than a demonstration in force made at the express orders of General Washington to relieve pressure on the main army in New Jersey. Unfortunately, it had relieved nothing but British minds, though Heath had made as fine a job of it as lay within his power. The splendid work of the Westchester Guides had enabled him to converge three columns on Fort Independence (which the British had re-christened Fort Number Eight) with such secrecy and good timing that it had been almost a complete surprise. But the fort's commander, knowing that the militia which made up a large part of Heath's force would never storm the place, had laughed at the demand for immediate surrender; and, after a few futile gestures with inadequate artillery, Heath had been obliged to withdraw without accomplishing anything.

"Shameful. . . . Cowardly!" Washington had termed it. "You have exposed the army to humiliation and ridicule!" The stout general's ears still burned when he thought of that letter. For the hundredth time he persuaded himself that the Commander-in-Chief had been tried almost beyond endurance when he had written it, and resolutely turned his attention to the report in his hand.

A dismal catalogue of depredations: cattle and horses stolen, houses looted, here and there a burning. Instances of personal violence were rare and for the most part only rumored; but Heath, remembering the French and Indian Wars, knew that these would be more frequent soon, and better authenticated.

". . . John Delancey is cutting down Gen. Morris's fine woods and selling it at 5 or 6 £ per cord. He and his Brother James are the two greatest Cow Jockeys in His Majesty's Service."

A fine occupation, that, for scions of one of the most distinguished families in the whole length of the Colonies! The James Delancey mentioned had been High Sheriff of Westchester County under the Crown. Now people were crediting him with all manner of lawless doings.

The attempt to blockade New York by land, the report continued, had become a joke. Not only was stock from near-by farms being stolen for sale in the city, but farmers upstate and in adjacent Connecticut were passing their produce through the lines at will: sleighs loaded with provisions and forage, droves of "fatt cattle" moved through the Neutral Ground escorted by armed guards. There was good authority for the estimate that five hundred cattle had reached the British over the Boston Post Road alone during the past fortnight—for the British paid in gold, whereas the starving Americans could offer only Continental paper.

"Come in!" Heath called in answer to a knock on the door.

An aide entered, a worried-looking young man in a faded captain's uniform. "There's a deputation from Rye in the anteroom, sir. More complaints, I don't doubt."

The general sighed resignedly. "Very well. Show 'em in."

His aide hesitated. "There's someone ahead of them, sir—a filthy old tramp."

"What does he want?"

"He won't state his business—just mumbles that he must see you."

"He can state it or get out!" Heath snapped. "Tell the others that I'll see them now."

The deputation filed in, half a dozen men in shabby homespun. They clustered around the desk, hats in hand, shuffling with rustic self-consciousness. Heath rose courteously.

"How may I serve you, gentlemen?"

The leader drew a paper from his pocket and began to read in a flat, uninflected voice. Heath sank back into his chair. This might have been the Bedford petition all over again, or any of a dozen he had been obliged to read or listen to during the past month. The familiar phrases droned on. ". . . Loyal citizens . . . humbly ask protection . . . cruel and merciless outrages . . . vindictive enemy . . ." The

general looked up with a start. The man had finished reading and was looking at him expectantly.

Heath cleared his throat. "I sympathize with you deeply,
gentlemen," he began. "I would be happy indeed were it in
my power to help you. As it is, I can only urge that you bear
your trials with fortitude, confident that the early victory of
our glorious cause will bring the blessings of liberty to all,
and to you particular satisfaction in consciousness of the
heroic sacrifices you have made."

The pompous words had a hollow sound, even in his own
ears. The farmers looked at each other nervously.

"I reckon you don't understand quite how things is with
us, General," the spokesman said. "Last fall, you recall, we
was ordered to thresh all our grain so's to have straw for the
army—our army—and the army come and took it, and the
grain, too, off those that hadn't had time to thresh. Then
the British come and the Hessians, and they plundered our
houses and slaughtered our stock. Now hardly a night passes
without a party of them cowboy scoundrels prowling the
countryside to rob us of what little any of us managed to
save from the others. Some of us are destitute, sir. There's
none but knows our turn's like to be next—our wives and
children left to starve. We want the blessings of liberty, sure,
but unless this thievery's stopped, there ain't many going to
live to enjoy 'em."

"I can only repeat, gentlemen, that I wish it were in my
power to help you."

"You—you mean, then, you wash your hands of us?"

"I wish to heaven I could!" Heath muttered under his
breath. Aloud he said, "I simply mean that under the circumstances I can do nothing."

"But you command the army hereabouts. What we got an
army for if not to protect citizens?"

"I might counter by asking what you have a militia for,"
Heath retorted tartly. "The purpose of the army is to combat
the enemy; that of the militia to defend their own localities—

as they have been at pains to tell us whenever we have asked them to co-operate elsewhere. If you gentlemen chance to be members, you should be quite as aware of that fact as I am."

He saw them exchange glances and resumed more coolly. "Let me explain the situation. As commanding officer in this region, my principal responsibility is to prevent the enemy from marching northward in force and effecting a junction with the army invading from Canada, thus cutting our country in two along the line of the Hudson and the lakes. To do this I have less than a thousand Continental soldiers, the only men kept constantly under arms. I have posted these here at Peekskill to guard the passes of the Hudson Highlands where the nature of the ground favors defense. Here, too, is being collected a great military depot containing the sinews of war necessary to carrying on our glorious struggle. What would happen to these were my little force to be overpowered? Frankly, gentlemen, I dare not take post farther south lest precisely this should happen. The enemy can put ten or fifteen men in the field to my one, and I must be distant enough from their base so that I can take measures to cope with such odds before they have time to fall upon me."

This military logic, he perceived, made no impression whatever upon his listeners. He could feel their antagonism hardening: the distrust of the "foreigner" from New England.

"It ain't only what we suffer from the enemy," one of the others said. "With our own army impressing our teams and forage—"

Heath's fist crashed down on the desk. "Enough of that!" His face flamed angrily. "The governing body of your own state passed the law authorizing such warrants when the army is distressed for subsistence. The pity is that it should prove necessary to issue them. If such of the inhabitants as can spare what we need to keep alive will not cheerfully sell it for what we can pay—then they do not deserve to be free!"

He shook a pudgy finger under the speaker's nose. "You'll not take Continental paper unless we force you by impressment, though your army be starving, but there are those among you who will go to no end of trouble and risk to get your hands on a little hard money. I have here a report of five hundred beef cattle reaching the British in New York over the Boston Post Road during a single fortnight. Over the road that passes straight through your town! What have you to say to that?"

"Good God, General! Them wasn't our cattle! Why, there ain't that many cows left in the whole township. The drovers said they was for General Washington. We couldn't have stopped 'em anyway, guarded like they was."

Although the room was chilly, Heath mopped his moist forehead. "I spoke hastily, gentlemen. I trust you will pardon me. I fear an accumulation of petty vexations has made me irritable." He paused, choosing his words. "The army is the servant of the people; that is the impression I am anxious to leave with you. But you must realize that this refers not merely to the people of Westchester County or even of New York State, but to the people of all the states, now happily united in a great cause. We will do all we can to aid you, but we cannot jeopardize the interests of the rest of the country in doing so. For protection of your homes you must rely on yourselves—upon your own militia, over whom I have no authority save that specially delegated to me in cases of emergency. Let us understand our respective responsibilities clearly, so that there may be more of co-operation between us and less of recrimination."

From their expressions he gathered that they got the point. He would have had his own misgivings were he obliged to trust the safety of his home to such protection.

"Now, here is a bit of news that may be welcome," he resumed, simulating an air of great optimism. "General Clinton, commander of the militia of the four lower counties, is planning an operation in force on your behalf. I can tell you no more, as the nature of the enterprise must be kept secret, but we are convinced—" in spite of himself he gagged a little on the "we"—"General Clinton and the Committee are convinced," he amended quickly, "that this will put an end once and for all to the enemy depredations of which you complain. So be of good cheer, and let us all play our parts manfully in this glorious struggle."

When at last they took their departure, he sat back in his chair and cursed until the sight of his aide's astonished face in the doorway brought him up in some confusion. Neighbors back in Roxbury had been accustomed to regard William Heath as a substantial, God-fearing citizen. The thought of how some of them might look were they in his aide's shoes at this moment made him smile.

"Well, now what?" he inquired more cheerfully.

"That old tramp, sir. He still won't state his business, but he said to tell you that his name's James Smith."

"Smith?" Heath repeated. "James Smi—" He leaped to his feet. "Show him in at once!"

At first sight the man fitted the aide's description aptly enough. His clothing in rags, his unclubbed hair filthy and matted, a week's stubble of beard on his dirt-streaked face, he slunk into the room like a furtive animal. He closed the door carefully behind him, and in an instant his whole aspect changed. The sag of age vanished from his shoulders as he straightened. He seemed to grow inches in height, to take on power, vigor.

Heath grasped his hand. "Crosby! By heaven, man, you're a genius!" He laughed. "I'd not have known you myself, I swear."

"Well, I hope the same goes for the others hereabouts," the cobbler said gloomily.

"Oh, you need have no concern for them. Even should you be recognized, you can trust to the discretion of my household."

Crosby grunted. "After some things I seen, I ain't trusting nobody."

Heath sat down again and gestured hospitably toward a near-by chair. Crosby, however, ignored the invitation and remained standing, holding a battered hat in his square hand.

"I been down to Morrisania like you wanted, General," he said.

"Then you've prepared a report?"

"I ain't written it out—don't do to carry papers, not in the Neutral Ground. But I can tell you what the stir's about. This fellow Delancey—James it is, the one lives over to Westchester Village—he's gathering all the Tories who got nothing better to do and settling 'em thereabouts, with himself as head man, you might say."

"Can you make out what his object is?"

"Well, to hear him tell it, he's just a big-hearted gentleman feeling responsible for poor folks who got nobody else to look out for 'em. Some's local people, of course—tenants on his land or workers in his mills. But the most's from elsewhere—up-county, up-state, even some from Connecticut—who've been run out of their own homes so's they can't make a living for theirselves nor their families. This Delancey's settling 'em on farms in that region out of which he's run folks he thinks is Whigs—see? But there ain't farms enough for he's moving in over to Morrisania, just north of where the Harlem runs into the East River. Got 'em building a regular village—log huts going up for a couple of hundred already, I reckon. They aim to live on what they can plunder in the Neutral Ground or smuggle in from outside. Cattle's easiest, of course, because they travel on their own legs and because fresh meat's selling sky-high in New York."

"Then these are the notorious 'cowboys,' as people call them?"

Crosby's brow wrinkled. "I don't rightly know about that, General. 'Cowboys' is kind of a loose term hung on to anybody stealing cows. That would cover these fellows, of course, but I reckon it'd cover some others, too. The 'Westchester Refugees' is what Delancey's gang's called officially—far as anything about 'em's official."

Heath's fist clenched. "The scoundrels! I thought these depredations were the work of Rogers' Rangers. I received a complaint just this morning to that effect from a place called Bedford."

Crosby shook his head. "Rogers' men's in winter quarters—ain't been nowhere near Bedford. Folks has got the habit of blaming everything on them Rangers—'Queen's Rangers' is what the British call 'em—because they was in the field first and because cowboys getting taken always claims to be rangers so's they'll be treated as prisoners of war rather'n plain thieves. The real Rangers is duly mustered as a Provincial Line regiment, and as such it ain't their business to be lurking sixteen miles back of our posts driving off farmers' cows."

Heath's fingers drummed on the desk. "But these Refugees—don't they rate as Provincials? If not, what the devil are they?"

"A sort of militia, far's I can make out—and maybe not a whole lot different from our militia, at that. They ain't right under the British to hear 'em tell it, but under some sort of higher-up Tory government. A fellow named Maxwell Bartlet from over Throgg's Neck way, he's recruiting a couple of companies of light horse on a major's commission, and they aim to have foot troops, too. Delancey calls himself a colonel."

"Who'd imagine a man of his standing would stoop so low as to organize a pack of confounded bandits!"

"War does funny things to folks," Crosby said soberly. "It's made a general out of you and a dirty spy out of me." He paused. "If you're thinking of scotching 'em, the time'd be right now. 'Tis said they're getting sergeants out of the regulars to drill that light horse."

"What do you suggest I use for men?" Heath demanded bitterly.

Crosby's face was expressionless. "Maybe you could talk General Clinton into lending you all them militia he's going to call out."

Heath frowned with the effort of rapid thought. "'Twouldn't do. I know that region. The Harlem angles almost due south beyond Kingsbridge. Morrisania's close to eight miles below Fort Number Eight and the other outworks. We'd have regulars on our flank and rear before—" He broke off short, and his jaw dropped. "In God's name, man! Where did you learn the militia was to be called out?"

"Down to Morrisania," Crosby said imperturbably.

"But how—why, only a few know—"

"Wasn't you just telling them fellows from Rye?"

"Why, I—I told them nothing exact. They're reputable citizens—representatives of their town Committee."

Crosby made a contemptuous gesture. "This accursed region's full of reputable citizens ready to run off below with the littlest crumb of information they can pick up they think the British would pay for. And most like come back with some enemy information worth selling to you! I tell ye, General, it ain't only the walls got ears hereabouts but the trees and stones to boot. In the Neutral Ground I wouldn't trust my own brother no farther than I could throw a yoke of oxen."

"This operation was planned to surprise them while their troops are still in winter quarters save for the outpost garrisons," Heath said thoughtfully. "If they have time to put an adequate force in the field, God help us! Do they know our plan?"

"Not yet, General. It's no more'n a rumor hardly, and they done nothing about it that I heard of."

"Well, then I'm not going to tell even you. I'll pass along what you've told me, of course, but I fear we'll get small thanks for our pains. Thank God I've managed to keep my men out of the whole stupid business." He dismissed the subject brusquely. "Did you find out the reason for the sudden increase in Tory recruiting that's been reported?"

Crosby nodded. "There's been commissions issued for some new regiments."

"You don't mean besides the ones already organized?"

"Aye—four I know of for sure, and others there's talk about. Biggest they call the Prince of Wales American Regiment under General Montford Browne—ten companies if he can raise 'em. Then Mr. Beverly Robinson that took over the Phillipse's Highland Manor a little north of here, he's got a commission as colonel to raise what they're going to call the Loyal Americans. And there's the King's American Regiment, near half-strength already I hear, and there's recruiters out across the river for another gang of rangers to be raised in Orange County—King's Orange Rangers. I reckon they figure Tory bastards under them fancy names won't smell so rank."

Heath counted on his fingers. "That makes eight that we know about, either mustered or forming. And we can't keep the Continental Line half filled!"

"The Congress don't offer pay and bounty in hard money," Crosby pointed out.

"Money!" Heath cried bitterly. "England isn't fighting us— she's buying us! Hired regulars, hired Hessians—and now Americans bribed with gold to murder their own countrymen. War used to be considered an honorable profession. By heaven, it's no better than speculation in livestock, with the eagles of victory riding the heaviest moneybags! Honor! Patriotism! Freedom! Oh, hell!"

"Begging your pardon, General," Crosby said after a moment, "but there's quite a few of us who ain't been paid in some little time—and who ain't gone over to the enemy, neither."

"That's true," Heath said gravely. "A handful of brave, devoted fellows—half starved and nearly naked. A pitiful handful to fight the battles of a nation. A nation that repays them with abuse and neglect!"

For some moments after Crosby had gone his furtive way, Heath sat there alone, lost in the gloom of his thoughts. Was it a nation, this conglomeration of peoples scattered between the seaboard and the mountains? Would it ever be a nation? Did it deserve to be?

He heaved his ponderous bulk out of his chair and strode to the window. The cheerless vista brought little light to his spirit. Before the house a sentry was pacing his post, shivering in the raw March wind, a ragged, emaciated fellow, his feet bound in filthy rags. . . . Yet it had been with soldiers like this that Washington had whipped the Hessians at Trenton and the British at Princeton a scant two months before. Soldiers like this had saved Jersey after it had been lost and turned the tide when the ebb was at its lowest. . . .

The stout general turned abruptly and went back to his desk.

"A soldier has no business philosophizing," he informed his astonished aide sternly as the latter responded to his summons. "Leave that to politicians, and let's get on with this confounded war!"

Chapter 2

THE GRAND FORAGE

Spring was in the air, or the first forerunner of spring, swept in from the south on the breath of a soft March wind. There was still snow in the mountains, but in the lowlands the ground lay bare, rich and dark in the plowed fields with long lagoons of silty water lying in last year's crumbling furrows. The Guides, standing in a restless half circle in front of headquarters in Peekskill, felt the sun's warmth gratefully through their torn, mud-spattered clothes.

There were nine of them now. The half dozen who had volunteered for the Mamaroneck expedition had been with the army ever since, and three newcomers had been taken for the Fort Number Eight affair: David Hunt of West-chester Village, Peter Pine from north of the Croton, and Big John's cousin, "Uk" Odell, from the section of Phillipse Manor known as Lower Yonkers, deep in the Neutral Ground. Holding their horses' heads, they looked up at the stout general on the steps with eager young faces reddened and roughened from a winter out of doors.

"I've no orders for you, lads," Heath said. He spoke heavily, without enthusiasm. "You will report to Colonel Thomas, who will assign your duties. I wish only to caution you. You will be dangerously close to the enemy outposts. And you will be serving with the militia—not Continentals. Never relax your vigilance for an instant. In case of emergency—" He hesitated. "Well, I can only say this: I want you back here—all of you—so watch out for yourselves."

The Guides looked at each other, shifting their feet in the gluey surface mud where the sun had thawed the frost.

"Maybe 'twould help, General, if you was to tell us what this here Grand Forage, or whatever they call it, is aiming to do," Abe said at length.

"The object is to strip bare all the country within easy reach of the enemy. That is, below the Phillipseburgh-Eastchester Road. All that we can't carry off is to be destroyed, and all the boats in the Sound below New Rochelle are to be burned." The general hesitated. "It is believed that this will serve to check the enemy's raids by leaving them nothing worth the trouble of carrying off."

Brom Dyckman coughed. "What the hell, General! Won't that just make 'em raid farther afield, like they started doing already?"

"It's not for you to question orders," Heath said sternly. "Or me either, for that matter. These orders come direct from the State Convention. Well, good luck, lads—and look alive!"

"The general don't like this for a damn," John Odell observed when they were mounted and trotting southward over the Albany Post Road. "What you figure he meant by that 'look out for yourselves' business?"

"That the militia ain't likely to be much good in a pinch, I reckon."

"Hell! He don't have to tell us that after what happened at Number Eight."

"Well, whatever he was driving at, I'm taking him literal-like," Odell declared. He leaned forward to pat the neck of his gray horse. "Me and General Van's lighting out for Peekskill at the first show of trouble, and the hell with the State Convention."

Brom Dyckman laughed. "Be damned if I see why you hang around the army, John. Here we been rotting in this dump for weeks, and the first thing you think of when we get out is how quick you can get back! You might better of stayed on the farm for all the fun you're getting out of life!"

"Wish I had," Odell said lugubriously.

But it was hard to be downcast for long on a day like this. They were young and high-spirited. Boredom lay behind, adventure ahead. The restlessness of the changing season quickened their blood, swept away the brief depression the general's strange indirections had brought them.

They found Colonel Thomas below White Plains where his militia were still in the process of assembling. These, too, were in high spirits. Winters were dreary on back-country farms; lonely, uneventful. One saw the same people, did the same chores, was concerned with only his own small affairs. Militia duty right now came as a welcome release, for it was not time yet to worry about the spring plowing, and they knew that they had not been called out to fight. Foraging was fun; a chance to see old friends again, roam the countryside with a lot of congenial fellows and, with luck, perhaps pick up a little something for themselves.

Their numbers gave them a feeling of security, a sense of their own importance. They cooked their suppers around cheery campfires, while the more enterprising spirits visited neighboring chicken coops and pigpens, laughing at the protests of the hapless owners. Tired from their march to the place of assembly, they slept the sleep of the just, in haylofts, sheds, houses, or under the mild March stars. Two more days passed before the last of the units put in a leisurely appearance, and local inhabitants breathed a collective sigh of relief when the colonel announced that finally they were ready to begin operations.

As they moved southward, the companies spread out fanwise to sweep across every inch of the area that was their objective. Wagons followed them, great vans and wains and smaller carts. Grunting horses, phlegmatic oxen, made slow going over muddy, rutted roads and lanes, but no one was in a hurry.

Abe was assigned to guide the so-called Upper Regiment

and attached himself to the company of Captain Noah Bouton, whom he knew slightly. Bouton came from Salem, up near the Dutchess County line, and was entirely unfamiliar with this region. Abe tried to describe the lie of the land to him and point out the best routes for falling back, for orders were that the forage parties should retire a safe distance for the night, but like the rest of his command the captain was too interested in the work at hand to look that far ahead.

"Well, boys, I guess this is where we begin," he announced when they reached what Abe indicated was the Phillipseburgh-Eastchester Road.

He led the way up a lane and arrived presently before a small clapboard farmhouse. The men with one accord headed for the barns and outbuildings, from which arose a great squealing and cackling that brought the owner on the run.

"You can't do this to me! I—I—"

"Sorry, mister. Orders of the Committee of Safety."

"But I'm a good Whig! I've signed the Articles of Association!"

"Then you ought to be right glad it's us and not them cowboys."

The farmer started to say something more, stopped with his mouth still open. Over Bouton's shoulder he saw that men were already loading sacks of grain into a cart drawn up before his barn. Others led out his last two cows; indifferent men, laughing among themselves. On his face indignation gave way to glum despair.

"I got a family. How we going to live?"

A forage commissioner bustled up, a self-important little man with a sheaf of papers. "You'll be paid for everything we take. I'll make a careful tally."

"Paid in Continental dollars?"

"In the rightful money of your country—of course."

The farmer's face turned a slow red. "The British pay in gold. By God! If I'd a-thought my own people—"

Abe touched his arm. "If you're wise, mister, have a care what you say."

The man looked at him from blank, stricken eyes. Abe turned away and followed the captain over to the barn where the commissioner had begun listing the confiscated supplies. This did not take long. When they returned to the house they found that the farmer's family had joined him, a woman and several half-grown children huddled in a forlorn group before the door of their home, watching with eyes that did not quite comprehend.

"Here's your receipt," said the commissioner. "Present it at headquarters. Then my advice would be to find safe refuge somewhere behind our lines."

The man took the paper mechanically. He did not speak. His eyes had lost their bewildered look, and his face was stony. Glancing backward as they moved down the lane, Abe saw him rip the receipt lengthwise with a jerk of his calloused hands.

The same scene was repeated, with variations, at every occupied farm they visited. The owners all declared themselves good Whigs when the foragers arrived, and most of them gave evidence of being something quite different by the time the party left. But many of the farms they came upon were unoccupied. Here the foragers were entirely uninhibited, taking it for granted that these were the homes of avowed Tories. They broke into the houses with joyful whoops and ransacked them from garret to cellar before turning their attention to what stock and forage might remain in the barns and granaries.

As each wagon was filled, its driver turned back the way they had come and lurched off northward through the mud. Drovers followed, driving their herds of accumulated livestock. It was slow business, for most of the farms were small and many had been visited before by parties of one faction or the other. Before noon Abe was thoroughly bored. In his capacity he was not expected to take part in the actual work, and the detachment clearly had little need of a guide at this stage. He was becoming uneasy, too. He had been on foraging expeditions before, but these had always left their victims at least one horse, one cow and sufficient fodder to see them through till harvest, this being specifically stipulated American policy. The people here were being stripped of everything, and he did not like the reaction he saw taking place before his eyes. There was something else that troubled him, too; something less definite that he was unable to put a finger on.

Leaving the detachment to its own devices, he mounted and rode forward. He scouted nearly to the Harlem, turned north and west to within sight of the enemy's most forward outworks without noting any signs of unwonted activity. With the militia sweeping behind him like a veritable plague of locusts, the normal quiet of the countryside ahead had a quality that was almost ominous.

Feeling hungry at last, he turned back. He did not head the way he had come, however, but bore off more to the west with the idea of finding John Odell, who had been assigned to that sector, and of doing a little private foraging for their own lunch. Here he soon came upon two situations which brought Heath's warning to the front of his mind: a party of militia, posted in advance to intercept anyone approaching from below, were so intent on ransacking an abandoned house that he rode right by them without being challenged; and the first foraging detachment he met was so scattered and out of touch that they could give him only the vaguest idea where he might find the companies supposed to be in contact with them on either flank.

He found Odell at last engaged in a heated argument with a militia officer amid a scene of confusion which was remarkable even for that confused day. Sacks of grain, heaps of hay and straw, miscellaneous boxes, bags and bales were littered all over the yard of a farm somewhat larger than most in this region, while the men supposed to be handling them stood in a knot about the disputants, injecting comments of their own, and two milk cows and a small herd of beef cattle added their disconsolate lowing to the din. The only men engaged in any activity were industriously looting the house, throwing the plunder on the ground before another man who was tabulating the items on a sheet of paper. And this house, Abe saw, had not been abandoned. Beside the doorway a girl of about fourteen was sobbing into the apron of a woman with scornful eyes who patted her absently on the back and surveyed the despoilers of her home with haughty disdain.

"I'll not have any lout like you telling me what I can or can't do!" the officer shouted.

Abe halted in his tracks. The man's back was toward him, but he recognized that voice. He felt again that same chill of revulsion he had felt the first time he had heard it: that night in Hayes's Tavern in Bedford when Captain Samuel Crawford had set the mob on old Seth Wiggin.

" 'Tain't right, I tell you!" Odell declared. "I know these people. Mr. Walton ain't no spying, thieving turncoat. He never made no bones about being for the British. Shoot him on sight if you get the chance, but you got no right robbing his helpless women-folk like you was a bunch of them damn cowboys!"

This fine point of ethics brought forth a chorus of hoots and jeers.

"The son of a bitch's a Tory, ain't he?"

"The hell with him! This here's lawful prize money for us!"

"Goddamn traitor!"

In a brief lull the woman's voice carried clear. "He's an officer in the Provincials, you cowardly scum!"

"Strip the wenches!" somebody yelled. "Maybe they got jewels on 'em!"

"Make 'em show where the silver's hid!"

Odell's deep bellow cut through the din. "I'll break the first bastard's head who tries it!" He mopped his brow and addressed Crawford again. "You know the law on this well's I do, Capt'n! If General Heath was here, he'd—"

"The hell with Heath!" Crawford retorted. "He wouldn't venture his precious Continentals on this business, so he can damn well keep out of it himself. And the same goes for you!"

"The law says," Odell persisted, "that we can't do no plundering outside the enemy lines, Tories or no Tories!"

Crawford laughed unpleasantly. "If that's what's bothering you, you can shut up. Because here we're below the enemy lines!"

Odell's jaw dropped. "Huh?"

"There's a British sloop of war lying off Dobbs Ferry. Saw her myself last evening. I suppose you're going to tell me we aren't below Dobbs Ferry?"

This bit of rationalization took Odell aback. He blinked a couple of times and began to stammer indignantly. Abe turned away from the sight of Crawford's triumphant leer. Wanting no part in this scene, he dismounted and went over to where the loot from the house was being sorted. The man tabulating the items was evidently a forage commissioner, for a separate list of the commandeered supplies lay on the ground beside him. Abe glanced at it curiously:

> "11 Bags with Rye & Buck wheat
> 2 Bags with Oats
> 6 Faggots of steel
> 7 Barrs of Iron
> Parcels of Carriage Wheels
> Boxes of bands, Bolts &c.
> 4 large Staks with Hay
> 10 Bails with straw
> 2 Milk cows
> 9 fatt Cattle."

The list in his hand was infinitely more varied. By looking over his shoulder, Abe could make it out easily, written painstakingly with a soft lead bullet.

"Certificat of a Large Bootey taken from a Person went to N. Y. of a commission to wit—1 white Coverled, 2 Fether bedds, 4 Matrass, 3 Calico gowns, 4 white Pettycoates, 2 Brass Kittels, 6 Puter Platters, 1 Puter Cover, 4 Shetts, 4 pillow Cases, 1 Gauz Hankerchef, 2 pr. wosted mittens, 1 womans Housewife, 1 Large Pair Shears, 18 Puter Plates, 1 small Chist with a Picter Papers &c., 1 Toaster Iron, 1 Coarce Apron, 1 cotton Mantel, 4 Smoothing Irons, 14 forks, 11 Knives, 2 tin Candel Stands, 1 bunch Twine, 6 Blanketts, 4 Shirts, 1 Nail Hammer, 4 Puter Cups, 2 pr. Womens Shoes, 1 paper Pins, 1 Bunch calimass, 1 pr. saddlebaggs, 1 pr. Mens Shoes and Buckels . . ."

"Come on, Abe. Let's us get out of here."

John Odell had come up behind him, leading his gray horse. From his red, annoyed face, Abe had no difficulty in telling how the argument had come out.

"And you can stay out of here!" Crawford called after him. "I know these parts a sight better than any guide among ye."

Odell mounted without replying, and Abe followed suit.

"Reckon we ought to post forward, John. If somebody don't keep watch, them heroes of yourn are like to get an unpleasant surprise."

"Serve 'em right if they do," Odell said sourly. Thought creased his forehead. "I swear, Abe, I don't know how to figure out fellows like that. Them militia—they're folks about like us—farmers, mechanics and so on. Back home in peace times they wouldn't no more think of robbing their neighbors than we would, but turn 'em loose where they can smell plunder and they run hog-wild. You hear a lot of talk about the 'brutal soldiery' and the thieving cowboys, but I don't see as we're a hell of a lot better ourselves."

Abe shrugged. "That ain't for us to worry about. Our job's to keep 'em out of trouble."

They rode forward about a mile through the ominously quiet countryside. It was in their minds to beg a meal at some farm as yet unvisited by the foragers. But the first few they came to had been abandoned, and at length, rather than venture too far, they broke into one of these, salving their consciences with the knowledge that the militia would reach it in a couple of hours, anyway. A glance showed that little of value had been left behind for the looters, but in the cellar they found a ham and a barrel of cider that served their purpose admirably. They gulped their food in silence, constrained in the quiet emptiness of the strange house, watching the surrounding country through south-facing windows.

"I been feeling kind of funny for the last couple of hours," Abe said at last. "Maybe it's seeing so many places like this—places where the folks has moved out within the last day or two and taken time enough to carry off their stock and valuables with 'em. You know, John, it looks to me like certain folks was warned we was coming—and 'twasn't them as claims to be Whigs, neither."

Odell's worried expression deepened. "If they'd known we was coming so close to the lines, you'd think we'd of seen signs of it before now."

"Let's go have another look."

They scouted southward again, riding across the whole front of the Grand Forage. It was inconceivable that the alarm had not reached the British posts by now, yet nowhere did they see anything to indicate that countermeasures were under way. This was understandable on the face of it, for the normal outpost garrisons would be helpless to cope with an incursion in such force, and the organized units—British, Hessians and Provincials alike—were scattered in winter quarters. Time would be required to assemble any considerable force at the scene of action; time enough to allow the foragers to complete their work and retire a safe distance, provided the enemy had not had reason to prepare in advance for such a contingency. Reassured at last, they abandoned the effort and returned to their own lines.

By then it was late afternoon and officers were beginning the colossal task of reassembling their scattered commands.

Chapter 3

"KILL EVERY DAMN REBEL YOU CAN!"

Abe rejoined Captain Bouton's company which had been augmented by stragglers from several others who had lost touch with their own commands. By this time the entire foraging force had become so scattered and disorganized that Abe soon abandoned hope of withdrawing the regiment as a unit and set out with this group along the York Road, detaching men at every crossroads with instructions for any others who might follow.

Orders had been to retire for the night to a safe distance; which, under the circumstances, he interpreted as meaning as great a distance as possible. He set such a brisk pace that the men began to protest. They were still in good spirits but tired from their exertions, and the day-long absence of all signs of enemy activity had heightened that feeling of security which Abe found himself still unable to share. He got them past Morrel's Tavern by dint of much persuasion, but when they came upon a couple of loaded forage wagons parked in the yard of the Ward house a mile farther along, Captain Bouton himself called a halt.

"We can't keep a-going forever with dark coming on," he declared, silencing Abe's protests. "These folks of our party?"

"Much as anybody can be, living in the Neutral Ground."

Bouton strode into the house without knocking, followed by several other officers and as many of the men as could crowd in behind them. They had entered so many strange houses that day that this procedure seemed only natural.

The owner fell back before them. "I'm a good Whig. I

signed the Articles . . ." Mechanically he voiced the same routine protestations they had heard a score of times since morning.

"We ain't foraging this far up, mister. All we want's to camp the night here."

The teamsters from the two wagons were in the kitchen, lolling at their ease and being waited on by Ward's wife and a couple of half-grown children. The new arrivals brightened at the smell of cooking.

"We'll feed many's we can," Ward said resignedly. "We ain't got much, though. The cowboys paid us a call a while back."

Bouton decided that the officers should eat in the house and ordered the rest outside to cook their own meals. This precipitated a long argument as to why the officers regarded themselves as better than anybody else, which was interrupted finally by the sound of squawking and squealing from the direction of the outhouses.

Ward exchanged a despairing glance with his wife. "I'm a good Whig. You fellows oughtn't to—"

"They won't kill no more of your fowl and pigs than they need for their dinners," Bouton cut in. He was a farmer himself, and embarrassment made his voice gruff.

"You'll give me a receipt?"

"Well, now, I reckon you'll have to see a forage commissioner."

Several of the men, deciding that they might fare better if they picked their own victuals, acceded to their captain's order and joined their comrades in the yard. The rest clustered around the kitchen table and took what the harried housewife put before them. Abe ate in silence. Before the others were half through, he rose and wandered outside. Several fires had been kindled in the yard, and the smell of roasting fresh-killed meat was strong on the still air of early evening. Knots of men crouched about the fires, their faces high-lighted ruddily in the gathering dusk.

Abe seated himself on the front steps alone. But he found it hard to sit still. To keep his mind occupied, he listened to snatches of conversation that floated to him. The men's voices sounded tired yet contented. They were discussing the day's events.

A sound from far off to the southwest jerked him suddenly to his feet. It was as though he had been anticipating this all day, had had his ears attuned to catch it: musketry, faint with distance but unmistakable. He saw that the men in the yard had heard, too; had fallen silent. But the single short burst was not repeated, and presently they resumed their talk. Just a nervous outpost firing at shadows, probably. But Abe could not relax the strange inner tension that had gripped him.

Restlessly he left the steps and made his way to the barn. His horse nuzzled him with a friendly nose, and he shook down some more hay for her. He debated an impulse to re-saddle and ride out in an effort to establish contact with some of the other parties, but before he could come to a decision a chorus of shouts from the men in the yard brought him outside again.

A short column of militia, fifteen or twenty men, had turned off the road toward the house. The man at their head, although no more uniformed than the rest, carried a sword instead of a musket, which established him as an officer. Abe recognized him as the lieutenant left in command of the detachment Bouton had posted a mile down the road to cover the main approach.

"Capt'n Bouton inside?" he demanded.

Abe led him to the kitchen. The captain looked up, his mouth open as he chewed the last of his supper.

"There was firing off to the west, Noah," the lieutenant reported. "I figured we'd ought to come in and tell ye about it."

Bouton wiped his mouth with the sleeve of his coat. "Why, sure, Charley. We heard it, but thanks anyhow. You et yet?" He paused. His face reflected the slow working of his mind.

"You mean ye brought in the whole detail? You didn't leave nobody on outpost?"

"Well, I thought we'd ought to tell you about the firing."

There was an awkward silence. Bouton passed a hand across his wrinkled brow. "It don't seem like you needed the whole outpost to do it," he said slowly.

He glanced toward Abe as though for confirmation. But Abe was no longer there. He was in the hallway, re-priming his musket. "Look out for yourselves," General Heath had said.

He stepped out of the front doorway, treading instinctively on the balls of his feet, as though stealth were vital. The men from the outpost detachment had scattered among their comrades at the fires who were sharing the remains of their suppers with them. If anyone was keeping watch, that fact was not apparent from where Abe stood. He hurried down the lane, but before he could reach its foot, he was brought up short, every hair on end. A hundred yards away the York Road was choked by a compact column of men. They were coming from the south and coming fast.

Abe spun about and began to run. His first blind impulse was to make for the house. But the house would be a trap.

"The British!" he shouted, and swerved sharply to the left where a stone fence offered temporary cover.

"Halt!" yelled a dozen voices.

Abe only ran the faster. Several muskets slammed behind him. He heard a soft lead ball splash against the fence. He hurdled it at a bound, threw himself prone, as more balls whined overhead.

He was in a plowed field. Beyond it loomed a small wood-lot. It looked very far away across the open ground. Frantically he began to crawl along the fence away from the spot where the soldiers had seen him jump it, pressing his body into the half-frozen mud.

But no one paid him any further attention. Either they thought he had been hit or were too busy elsewhere to bother

with one man. Officers were bellowing orders, muskets were
going off at random. Assured at length that they were not
firing in his direction, he ventured his head above the fence.

The farmyard had become a bedlam. Militiamen milled
about in utter confusion, falling into the fires in their panic,
knocking each other down. A few fired blindly, then threw
away their arms and screamed for quarter. Others were bolting off in all directions, crossing the cleared land in grotesque leaps and bounds.

Abe tried to gauge the distance to the barn in a mad hope
of recovering his still-unsaddled horse. But already detachments of the enemy were racing across the lower fields to
close in from behind, cutting off escape in both directions.
Even in the uncertain light he could distinguish their uni-
forms: red, green, blue—regulars, Tories and Hessians, a
heterogeneous detachment. Beyond them a mounted company circled widely to the east at full gallop. In a matter
of minutes the whole place would be surrounded, as the
house itself already was.

"Quarter! Quarter! We surrender!" Captain Bouton
shouted. He pushed open the front door and stood in plain
sight, arms raised above his head.

A Provincial officer strode forward, a burly, florid man.
Abe recognized Archibald Campbell who had been a friend
of the Young Squire's.

"Fire away, boys!" he shouted, brandishing his sword at
the militia captain. "Kill every damn Rebel you can!"

A spattering of shots ripped into the clapboards. Bouton
wavered. His head turned left and right like that of a cornered animal. Then with a clutching motion he jerked a
pistol from his belt and fired pointblank. The Loyalist officer went down like a clubbed steer.

Abe ducked back behind the fence, his stomach contracted
into a small, hard knot. When he looked out again, Bouton
had disappeared under a wave of vari-colored coats. A dozen
Tories were battering down the door with their gun butts

while others fired in through the windows. In the yard, lit by the remains of the cooking fires, a score of militiamen, arms raised, were being prodded into line by British and Hessian bayonets. Everyone in sight appeared intent on what he was doing.

Abe got his feet under him. Feeling dangerously exposed as he left the cover of the fence, he turned and started across the plowed field. He went at a stumbling run, bent nearly double, making heavy going in the muddy footing. Every instant he expected a challenge or a shot. None came. Lungs bursting, he fell panting among the trees at the edge of the woodlot.

After a moment he rose again. His brain told him that he was in little danger now, but his instincts urged him to get away from there as quickly as he could. He plunged into the woods, groping his way blindly, colliding with tree trunks. Underbrush clutched at his legs like nightmare hands. He was breathless again by the time he reached the road. But incipient panic drove him on, and he broke into a dogtrot, staggering from exhaustion.

A crashing in the underbrush brought him up short before he had gone twenty yards. Half a dozen men burst from the woods and leaped into the road some distance ahead, staring about wildly in all directions. Abe froze in his tracks, his knees turned to jelly. But even in the near-darkness he could tell that these men were not the enemy but fellow fugitives.

"Hey!" he panted.

The men gave a terror-stricken howl and scattered. Some dodged back into the woods, others darted up the road as though the devil himself were on their tails. One snapped his musket blindly. Abe saw the powder flash in the pan, but either the gun misfired or the man had been too frenzied to do more than prime it after the last discharge, for there was no report.

"You fools!" Abe panted. "You—you damn cowards!" He laughed shakily. "By God! There's fellows more scared than me!"

The sound of his own voice sobered him a little. By this time, he realized, he should be well beyond the cordon he had seen the enemy throwing around the Ward place. Those at the house itself would be so busy with the prisoners they already had that they would be unlikely to waste time trying to run down the stampeded wretches who had escaped. More calmly he set off up the road, walking without haste in order to catch his breath and assemble his wits.

"Halt!"

He had forgotten those mounted men he had glimpsed circling more widely beyond the foot troops. One of them loomed directly ahead of him, horse and rider monstrous in the dusk.

The panic of a moment before swept over him again. He leaped for the side of the road, scrambled over a fence and began to run with all his might. He ran blindly. Terror made him oblivious to the pounding of his heart, the gasping of his lungs.

He had passed beyond the farther edge of the woodlot and found himself now in an open pasture. There was no cover anywhere. His feet slithered on the soggy turf. He heard the clatter of accouterments as the dragoon's horse cleared the fence, the thud of hoofbeats riding him down.

"Quarter!" he screamed. He threw down his musket. "Quarter! Quarter!"

"I'll quarter ye, ye bastard!" the dragoon yelled.

His saber was upraised. Abe saw it start its downward stroke and sprang frantically to one side. The blade caught the upturned brim of his hat, sent it spinning a dozen yards as horse and rider careered past him.

He doubled back toward the only cover he could reach: the stone fence he had just left. He was halfway there before the dragoon could check his headlong impetus and wheel his horse around. Then Abe heard something else that made him catch his breath in a gasping sob: the hoofbeats of another horse coming up the road at full gallop.

This would be the end. Exhausted as he was, two of them

would ride him down without trouble, saber him at leisure. Despair swept aside his terror. The hopeless fury of the cornered animal cleared his brain in a split second. Again he doubled back, this time toward where he had dropped his musket.

He dodged again as the dragoon shot past him, and the saber swished down harmlessly. Then he had his hand on the musket. He spun about. The horse, pulled up short, was rearing, pawing the air, dancing on its hind legs, as the cursing rider fought it with both hands.

Abe raised the musket to his shoulder. With the icy calm of the skilled marksman who has nothing to lose, he sighted along the brown barrel. The dragoon's face made a gray, featureless blur in the dusk. Then powder smoke blotted it out, and the musket butt kicked back against Abe's shoulder.

The dragoon's saber flew in one direction, his hat in another. The horse gave a high-pitched scream and bolted. The rider's body slipped backward over its rump and thudded limply on the ground.

Abe threw aside his now useless musket and sprang for the saber just as the second horseman sailed over the fence.

"Stand!" he croaked with what breath he could muster.

"It's all right, friend! I'm a guide!"

"John!"

"Is that you, Abe? My God! I thought he had you!"

Abe's knees began to buckle. Blackness deeper than the March dusk rose up before his eyes. "I'm just—wore out," he gasped, and let himself slump to the ground.

For several moments he lay limp while colored lights danced crazily before his eyes and his lungs threatened to burst. It was Odell's urgent voice that brought him at last to himself. The big guide was bending over him, shaking him.

"Get a-hold of yourself, Abe! Mount up behind me and let's be getting out of here. There's more of the bastards about."

Abe sat up. Now his brain felt clearer than it had all day. The dragoon's saber, he noticed, was still clutched in his hand.

"Wait a minute," he said.

He rose and walked over to where his enemy had fallen. It was hard to believe that that grotesque heap of clothes had been a man a few moments before. He looked down at it indifferently, then with quiet deliberation unstrapped the wide sword belt, adjusted it around his own waist and slid the saber back into its scabbard.

"Well," Odell observed sardonically, "I reckon our Quaker lad don't aim to call himself a noncombatant no more."

"The son of a bitch would of killed me, John. I ain't aiming to ask for quarter again."

This was the first shot he had ever fired in anger, and it had killed a man. The three-quarters-inch slug had caught the dragoon squarely between the eyes and blown off half the top of his head, leaving exposed a bloody mass of mangled brains.

Odell turned away. "Come on," he urged, "before I lose my lunch."

"Wait a minute," Abe repeated. He reloaded his musket, priming carefully. Then he searched around until he found the dragoon's helmet. It was made of stiff, heavy leather, with a horsehair crest running across its top like a mane. "This ought to come in right handy," he said, clapping it on his head. It was a little large, but the chin strap held it in place comfortably enough.

Odell gave him a hand to swing up behind on the big gray horse. "Hang on," he warned. "General Heath he says to look out for ourselves, and that's what we're doing from now on."

They went for a good two miles at full gallop. Several times they came upon parties of fleeing militia who ran for cover at their approach, and twice they were fired upon by fugitives. But of the enemy they saw no further sign, and at last Odell slowed down sufficiently to make conversation practicable.

"We was the first party they jumped, I reckon, and I tried to get warning to you," he explained. "But hell! They had the business too well planned. They must of had spies watching us all afternoon, and soon's we're settled and off guard they come right where each detachment was and jumped us all at once. I figure we was first only because we was closest, Capt'n Crawford figuring it's damn foolishness for a brave fellow like him to waste time falling back."

"I'm beginning to see this now," Abe said thoughtfully. "That's why we didn't see none of 'em during the day. They was laying low, letting us do the work so's they could come out and take the forage we'd collected—and most of us along with it."

"Sure. Folks'll blame us for robbing 'em while the Tories and the rest collect prize money on the loot."

"What happened to your people, John?"

Odell did not speak for a moment. Abe, holding on behind him, could not see his face.

"Well," he said finally, "it was kind of funny in a way, only maybe 'funny' ain't quite the right word. We was eating in a house over near Valentine's, and Crawford was accusing the folks of being Tories to show what an important fellow he is and raising hell generally. He hadn't bothered to post no guards, of course. First we knew they was there was when they let go a volley in the yard, and somebody busts in the door with a musket butt.

"Well, our hero goes green around the gills and reaches for the ceiling. 'We surrender!' he squeals. 'Please, dear Tories, have mercy on us!' or something like that. Then the room's full of 'em. They're all laughing fit to bust—it's been that easy they feel fine. But all of a sudden one of 'em sights Capt'n Crawford, and his face turns purple. He lets out a yell, and before nobody can stop him, he dives for him, bagnet first."

Odell paused. He did not turn his head. "'Twas Will Wiggin, son of old Seth Wiggin they tarred that time over to Bedford, remember? Jesus, Abe! That bagnet went clear through Crawford and come six inches out his back!"

"How did you get away, John?" Abe asked after a moment.

"Cut my way out," Odell said simply. "They was all looking at Crawford and Wiggin, so I grabbed a sword off of the nearest officer and jumped out the window. On a hunch I'd left good old General Van tethered in the woodlot 'stead of the barn. There was more of 'em in the yard, of course, but I only had to cut down three—they was surprised, I guess—so I got to the horse all right and come right over to warn you—too late, just like everything's been today."

They rode in silence for a while, engrossed with their own thoughts.

"Capt'n Bouton tried to surrender, too," Abe said at length. "Anyhow, he got the bastards' commander before they got him."

Odell shuddered. "You know, Abe, there's more to this here war than maybe some of us have thought. Christ! After tonight I'll never hear a musket fired without soiling my breeches. I'll never ride into the Neutral Ground again without feeling goose pimples along my back and the blood like ice inside of me."

"You aiming to quit the Guides, John?"

"Quit the Guides?" Odell half turned in surprise. "Hell, no! Are you?"

Abe shook his head. "It's different with me. I don't feel like you do. It's like something happened to me, out there in that field." He hesitated, frowning. "I don't know as I can say what I mean, and most like it'll sound pretty silly. But there's one thing I do know, as sure as I know you and me's riding this here horse of yourn: I ain't never going to be scared of nothing again—not nothing, long as I live."

Chapter 4

THE MILITIA

They rode to White Plains and spent the night in a barn on the outskirts of the village. Abe was asleep the instant he fell into the hay, but Odell tossed restlessly until dawn. His eyes were bloodshot, with dark circles under them, when he roused Abe an hour later.

"We better ride on," he announced. "There ain't nothing to eat hereabouts."

"What's the matter?"

Odell shrugged. "Militia been coming through, I reckon. Folks are getting ready to run."

In the barnyard the farmer and his sons were herding their livestock together, while the women were hurriedly loading their more valuable belongings into a cart drawn up before the house. They had no time to prepare food for hungry men, and turned deaf ears to the guides' assurances that there was no imminent danger of an attack this far up-county.

"Guess we might as well help ourselves to anything that's left," Abe said at last.

None of the people of the household tried to stop them, and by dint of ransacking kitchen and cellar they managed to find a little salt pork that had been overlooked in the confusion of packing. They ate this cold, the hearth fire having been extinguished, washed it down with hard cider, and set off feeling a bit queasy.

Once in the village itself, they could comprehend better the panic that was sweeping the countryside. All night the scattered militia had been trickling in. The green in front

of the ruined courthouse was littered with the sprawled forms
of sleeping men who had fallen there from sheer exhaustion.
Others were still drifting up the York Road and from the
direction of New Rochelle: men with frightened eyes, staggering with weariness, many of whom had thrown away their
arms in flight.

Beside the debris-filled cellar hole of Oakley's Tavern a
major in a soiled uniform was arguing with a knot of fifteen
or twenty men; armed men who still appeared in fairly good
condition.

"You ain't going to run off and leave the folks here to the
scoundrels' mercy, be ye?" he shouted. "You'll stay! You got
to stay!"

"Well, we ain't a-going to," one of the men retorted. "We
got folks of our own to look out for."

"But listen, fellows! If we don't make a try at stopping
'em here, the whole county's going to be open to their raids.
That means your homes, too."

"We'll mind our own when that time comes."

Odell nudged Abe, mounted behind him. "Let's us get
going, too, before he sees us."

Abe shook his head. "That's Eb Lockwood, John. Wonder
since when they made him a major?"

In desperation the officer tried a new approach. "A fine
pack of soldiers!" he cried scornfully. "There's some excuse
for them that's been whipped and scared half out of their
wits. But you—why, none of ye's seen hide nor hair of the
enemy."

" 'Twasn't no fault of yours or the colonel's we come off
safe," the spokesman retorted bitterly. "The way this here
business was handled, it's only the grace of God all of us
wasn't cut down where we sat or herded off to New York like
so many cattle. We got our bellyful of taking orders from
them what calls theirselves officers!"

The major winced. "Your enlistments ain't up! If ye go
now 'twill be desertion!"

"Call it what ye damn please. Come on, boys!"

Lockwood watched them shuffle off up the road, his face a study of conflicting mortification and despair. Abe slid over the horse's flank and walked up to him.

"Got any use for a couple of guides, Eb?"

Lockwood looked up slowly. "Oh, that you, Abe?" He spoke without surprise. "A couple of men! Last night there was a couple of thousand of us."

"Where's the colonel? Seems like this'd be his job."

The major shrugged. "Where's the lieutenant colonel and the rest of the majors? Where the hell's anybody? Off home counting their cows, I reckon! Anyways, they ain't here, and I wish to God I wasn't." He looked at Abe more closely. "Say! Where'd ye get that dragoon helmet?"

"I got it off of a dragoon."

"Ye don't say!" The major brightened a little. "Well, seeing as there's a couple around ain't had the breeches scared off 'em, I'd take it kindly if you'd scout to south'rd and see what the enemy's up to. If they ain't too close on to us, maybe I can hold a few of these heroes, after all."

"Sure, Eb. Only we got but one horse between us."

"There's a few of them we collected yesterday still over to Hatfield's. Just help yourself. The drovers has run off like everybody else."

Abe made the best of a sorry selection and appropriated a saddle he found in the tavern stable. They turned down the York Road toward where they had last seen the enemy. A few militia stragglers still plodded back along it, and here and there appeared the loaded wagons and herds of local people fleeing their homes. Others, determined to stay, stood glumly by their houses, watching the road with apprehensive eyes. This traffic thinned as they proceeded, but still they encountered no signs of the enemy. Persons they questioned, while furnishing all manner of conflicting rumors, could give no definite information.

Some distance above the Ward house they took to the

fields, moving cautiously until they gained the woods through which Abe had escaped the night before. From the edge of these the scene of the attack could be observed from cover. After watching for ten minutes without seeing anything astir, they rode boldly up to the house.

The smashed-in door was so much kindling strewn on the stoop, and the shattered windows gaped emptily. A few bedraggled fowl scattered squawking at their approach, but nowhere else about the place was there a sign of life. All the stock had been driven off and the house itself looted: furniture broken, mattresses and upholstery ripped open with bayonets in search of hidden valuables. The bodies of six dead militiamen had been thrown into the yard, and they found another wedged under the kitchen table. What had become of Ward and his family they could only speculate, and they wasted little time on that. The important thing was that the enemy had obviously departed the way they had come, taking plunder and prisoners with them.

Much the same condition obtained at the house where Crawford had been murdered, and they came across several other houses that had been looted, two of them burned. They pushed forward to the edge of the territory swept by the Grand Forage and scouted widely through it without catching sight of hostile troops. Indeed, they caught sight of scarcely anyone. The region was like a country of the dead: empty, silent, ominous.

It was late afternoon when they got back to White Plains with their reassuring report. Conditions there were not much improved. Major Lockwood had managed to collect a few militia, perhaps two hundred, but even these were standing by with great reluctance. It was possible now to piece together most of what had happened the previous night. Several other detachments had been dispersed by attacks similar to those visited on Crawford and Bouton, but with much smaller losses. Most of the parties, however, had not been attacked at all, and a few which had been out of earshot of the firing had been on their way to resume foraging before news of the debacle reached them.

On the whole, the losses were absurdly disproportionate to the demoralization they had caused. The trouble was that the wild tales of the victims, magnified in the retelling, had spread far and wide, bringing alarm to those unaffected. While the panic of the night and early morning had subsided, the atmosphere was tense with apprehension, compounded of fear, disgust with the dismal mismanagement, and distrust of leadership proved so flagrantly incompetent. Although Lockwood had been able to hold these few men as long as he could keep them all together, he had soon discovered that detachments he posted forward to guard the approaches simply set off for home as soon as they were out of his sight.

Brom Dyckman rode in at dusk with his brother Mike and Isaac Oakley. They had been assigned to guide the Connecticut militia who were supposed to be co-operating in the Grand Forage, and their report deepened the gloom. Although they had not been attacked themselves, it appeared that these gentry had turned tail and scurried off the instant they heard what had happened to the west of them.

"We went along and tried to talk to 'em," Brom declared. "They got to defend their own state, says General Wooster, the damn old she horse! They didn't even slow down till they was over Byram Bridge, and then they told us to go to hell."

So the entire southeastern part of the county was undefended, wide open to the enemy. Brom reported bands of cowboys aprowl along the Boston Post Road. Twice they had been fired upon.

Word of that got abroad, and during the night a dozen more militiamen stole away. In the morning two captains from the affected region waited on the major and announced bluntly that they were going home and taking what was left of their companies with them. Lockwood cajoled and threat-

ened for an hour. But he had no new arguments to advance,
and the old ones sounded half-hearted even to him.

It rained all that day; a cold dismal rain, hard-driven by
intermittent gusts of a bitter March wind. The miserable
militiamen huddled around their cooking fires. They break-
fasted on supplies impressed from the local populace, foraging parties refusing flatly to venture out of the village, and
afterward crawled into what shelter they could find—in
houses, sheds and barns—to feel sorry for themselves. There
was certainly nobody else to feel sorry for them. The villagers, disgruntled by the burden of supporting this mob and
skeptical of what protection it could hope for from them,
protested to the harried major without avail and gathered to
talk apprehensively among themselves, falling silent with
suspicious quickness on the approach of anything resembling
a soldier.

"The pack of 'em'd go Tory at the drop of a hat, if they
thought the Tories would have any part of 'em," John Odell
observed. "I bet a dozen has sneaked off already to take word
to the British of what shape we're in."

There was no keeping out of the wet for the guides that
day. Immediately after breakfast they headed south again.
Nobody ordered them out, but they knew that they were the
only ones who would leave the main body with any intention of returning. And somebody had to patrol below. They
kept together in order to present as formidable an appearance as possible, which was not very formidable since there
were only five of them. Whether the rest of the guides had
returned to Peekskill or simply vanished into thin air like
the detachments to which they had been assigned, no one
knew. Prepared to ride for their lives on an instant's warning,
they pushed onward over roads which the heavy rain had
converted into quagmires.

"I don't reckon there'll be no troops moving with such
going underfoot," Abe speculated.

"Maybe not. But this won't keep them cowboys from raiding no more'n it'll keep the militia from deserting."

They encountered no signs of new depredations, however, and were reassuring themselves that enemy spies had not yet learned the true numbers and morale of the militia when, in midafternoon, they heard news at Dobbs Ferry that sent them back to White Plains posthaste: a powerful fleet of British transports had been sighted heading up the Hudson.

The news had preceded them by an hour, and they found the last of the up-county companies just marching off. Major Lockwood, red of face, was surrounded by a gesticulating crowd of villagers.

"We can't stay no longer, I tell ye!" he protested. "They'll land troops in our rear, cut us off—"

"Them troops ain't after us, Major," Abe declared, pushing his way through the throng. "Sure as shooting, they're aiming to raid the supplies at Peekskill." His mind was working rapidly. "Look. General Heath he's been watching out for this all along. What they done is wait till the militia's scattered all over hell and gone so's they can't help the general, figuring they can swamp his Continentals with numbers. Don't you see?"

The major eyed him dubiously. "Well, ye may be right—"

"Makes sense, don't it? You ain't going to let them men go and leave the whole county open?"

Lockwood glanced up the road at the column straggling out of sight around a curve. "They gone already, Abe," he said morosely. "God himself couldn't get 'em back now. I done all I can."

That was true. He had done his best, and if it had proved hopelessly inadequate, that was hardly his fault. He was not an experienced soldier; just a farmer like the rest of them with a home of his own to look out for. He had never commanded anything larger than a militia company until the disappearance of his superiors had left a situation on his hands that might have baffled a genius.

"Oh, let 'em go!" said a scornful voice from the crowd. "The lot of 'em would run anyhow, first time somebody took a pot shot at 'em!" It was Captain Anderson of the local company, a scant score of scared wretches who were still there because they had nowhere to flee. He turned to the guides. "You young fellows been more use than the whole kit and caboodle of 'em. If you'll stay and help us, maybe we can still make shift for ourselves."

The guides looked at each other.

"Well, I don't know," Odell began. "General Heath he was right anxious to have us back to Peekskill—"

Lockwood paused in the act of mounting his horse. "Why, Heath ain't at Peekskill no more," he said. "Didn't ye know? Orders come for him to go to Boston day the Grand Forage started. General McDougall was left in command."

"The general—gone—"

Abe saw the stunned expression in his companions' eyes. But they looked no more stunned than he felt.

"Wonder what that makes us?" he said at last. "General Heath it was who got us together and give us our orders and all."

"I don't know about that neither," Brom Dyckman cut in. "But I know that old goat McDougall, all right! He'd have the whole army digging necessary-vaults twenty-four hours a day before he'd let 'em risk their hides in a fight. You fellows can do what you want, but I'm for staying where we can be of some use."

"How about it, Abe?"

Abe realized that they had all turned to him. For an instant he felt self-conscious, abashed. Puzzled, too, for he was the youngest among them. Then that feeling passed.

"We stay till further orders," he declared decisively, and an unfamiliar sense of pleasure warmed him as he realized that every one of them would do exactly what he said.

Chapter 5

THE SKINNERS

A hand was shaking Abe's shoulder. In spite of his weariness, of the depth of his slumber, he sat up and reached for his musket with a single movement, blinking in the glare of a lantern held close to his eyes. Five nights in the Neutral Ground had taught him to awaken that way. He could see Brom Dyckman's face, caricatured by the up-thrown shadows. John Odell, who had been sleeping next him, had already swung both feet to the floor over the opposite side of the big bed.

"Come below quick as you can," Brom said. "I reckon it's finally started."

They had gone to bed in one of the upper rooms of Hatfield's Tavern. Mike Dyckman and Isaac Oakley had preceded them down to the taproom where Captain Anderson and half a dozen sleepy militiamen were gathered. In their midst stood a bedraggled boy of about fifteen, wild-eyed and soaked to the skin.

"Sam Jones here thinks something's going on over to the Powers farm," Anderson explained. "That's northeast of here—little place, off by itself. Sounds kind of funny to me. How many shots you think you heard, son?"

The boy stammered in his excitement. "I d-d-didn't c-c-count 'em, mister. Five—s-s-six maybe."

"It's sure they wasn't shooting crows out of the corn this time of year," Brom said impatiently. "What we waiting for?"

"How long ago was that?"

"I d-don't know. Half an hour—maybe l-l-less. Pa f-figured we'd be next, s-s-so I rode here fast's I c-could."

One of the militiamen spat into the fire. "Them Powerses is Tories."

Anderson shook his head. "We don't know that for a fact. Anyways, them goddamn cowboys ain't particular who they rob."

"I ain't going out on a night like this to help no Tories," the man declared sullenly.

Abe looked from face to face. What he read there was fear.

"If there's a raid on, 'tain't likely they'll stop with one place," Anderson said quickly. "Now, here's what we'll do. Us fellows with horses will ride straight to Powers'. The rest of you cut over to Rye Road—that's how they're most like to fall back if they're driving off cattle—and lay for 'em in ambush. You'll do that much, won't ye?"

There was no answer.

Mike Dyckman pushed his hat back and scratched his head perplexedly. "I ain't been around this here war long's some," he observed, "but it comes on me to wonder what you fellows turned out with muskets for, 'less you aim to use 'em."

"We don't need no help from them as won't help their neighbors," Brom said. "Let's go, and the hell with 'em!"

"There's only five of us," Odell said dubiously. "Six, counting the captain."

"Who said we wasn't going?" the militia spokesman demanded. "We'll ambush 'em like you say, Capt'n. Only we ain't helping no—"

"Then gather as many more as you can and hurry!" Anderson interrupted. He turned to the guides. "Come on, boys!"

They ran out to the stable where the taverner and a couple of his men were saddling their horses by lantern light.

"Follow me," Anderson directed when they were mounted.

They rode past the ruins of the courthouse and turned off presently on a narrower road that angled more to the east. The night was intensely dark, with a misty drizzle falling. Moving at a cautious trot, the horses literally felt their way along the muddy ruts. Abe, riding beside young Sam Jones, heard the chatter of teeth although even that close he could not see the boy.

"Steady, son," he said in a low voice.

Behind him he heard Odell chuckle. It was funny in a way: Abe Kronkhyte, not yet twenty, addressing anyone as "son." Yet tonight it seemed the most natural thing in the world. It seemed natural to be riding out in the blackness and rain, with the mutter of men's voices around him sounding above the muffled rattle of accouterments; riding toward none of them knew what. He might have done this a hundred times before. "I'll never be scared again," he had told Odell a few minutes after he had killed that dragoon. There was no fear in him now, only a subdued expectancy that left his mind clear and keyed-up, his body relaxed.

When they reached the Jones farm, the captain called a halt. The house was unlighted, the windows shuttered. His knock on the door brought no response.

"It's me—Sam!" the boy called. "I've brung the militia."

The house remained silent.

"Don't go calling us militia, ye little squirt!" Brom muttered under his breath.

"It's George Anderson, folks," the captain put in. "You heard anything more over Powers' way?"

There was the sound of a bolt being drawn. Hinges creaked as the door swung outward a little way, but still no light showed.

"There ain't been no more shooting," a man's voice said hoarsely. "We was hoping they'd went."

"Get your musket and we'll go see."

"Me?" the man cried. "Like hell I will!"

The door closed with a slam and the bolt shot home.

"Pa!" wailed the frightened boy. "Pa! Let me in, Pa!"

Anderson caught him by the arm. "You stay with us, Sam, since your pa's like that. I ain't sure as I can find their lane in the dark."

"Oh, no! Please—no—" The boy's voice was pitiful.

Abe and big John Odell moved up close on either side of him.

"Come on, son. We won't let 'em hurt ye."

He made no resistance, and they rode on another quarter mile. Here a lane angled off to the left into a patch of woods, narrow and dark and lonely.

"P-p-powers' is just up t-there a piece."

"Let him go," Brom urged disgustedly. "Them chattering teeth of his is enough to alarm every cowboy this side of Morrisania."

They felt their way cautiously along the lane. There was no talk now. The misty drizzle, collecting on the branches that arched overhead, trickled down upon them. Invisible tree limbs lashed wetly in their faces, but they did not even curse.

At the far edge of the woods Anderson halted. "They're still there, right enough," he said grimly.

The house, some two hundred yards away across rolling land, seemed to their night-accustomed eyes a veritable blaze of light. The glow from the open doorway threw a yellow patch on the wet ground outside, and the windows made bright oblongs against the night. As they paused to observe the intervening terrain, a shadow moved across them. Then, suddenly, a woman screamed; shrill, eerie, terrible in the stillness.

"Christ!" Odell gasped.

Abe heard a saber grate in its scabbard. He grasped the bridle of Brom's horse just as it gathered to bound forward.

"Leggo!" Brom cried furiously.

Abe's voice was sharp, incisive, though the short hair on his neck was crawling. "Stay where ye are!" He turned to the others. "Most like they got a man on watch. Maybe there's a lot of 'em. We got to count on surprise. Leave the horses here and sneak up afoot."

It did not seem strange that he should be giving orders. He swung to the ground and groped for a tree to tether his horse. The rest followed suit without a word. That they should obey his orders did not surprise him, either. It had not occurred to him that they might not.

"Brom, you stay with me. The rest of you spread out wide and close in around the house. If any of you's hailed, shoot and we'll all rush the place together."

They crossed the open land swiftly, yet without haste, every sensitized nerve alert. The soggy footing muffled their steps. They were not challenged. The only sound that came to them was a confused murmur of voices from within the house. Just beyond range of the light, Abe paused to give his companions time to come up on the farther sides, then crept to the window nearest the open door. It had been shuttered, he saw, but the shutter had been splintered, the whole window frame smashed away. Cautiously he inched upward until his eyes were level with the sill.

The interior of the cottage looked like something out of a nightmare. Broken furniture was littered everywhere. Draperies had been pulled down, upholstery ripped open. An unconscious woman, her clothing torn to shreds, lay half across what was left of a bed, purple bruises showing vivid against her white skin. A half-grown girl with frenzied animal eyes, crouched in a corner by the fireplace, gripping a large kitchen knife.

But no one was paying either of them any attention. The men in the room—at first glance it seemed crowded with them—were intent on other business. Two were pulling the stuffing out of a slashed mattress with searching hands. Another was stowing miscellaneous loot in a pillowcase. The rest moved back and forth, bringing plunder in from other rooms or picking through that already heaped on the floor. To heighten the nightmare illusion, their faces were smeared with lampblack. They might have been wild Indians or visitors straight out of hell.

But what riveted the observers' gaze in horror was a grotesque, dangling figure at the farther end of the room: an old man hung by the thumbs to ropes thrown over a rafter.

As they watched, one of the intruders paused in passing to fetch him a clout across the face.

"Come on—where's the money hid?"

The old man was suspended so that his toes just touched the floor. The force of the blow knocked out this precarious underpinning, set him to swaying. He gave a single gasping groan, and his head lolled forward limply. His assailant shrugged and walked away.

The instant he was beyond reach, the girl in the corner sprang forward. Before anyone realized what she was up to, she had leaped upon a chair and slashed the ropes with her big knife. The old man crumpled on the floor.

The man nearest gave a startled yell and grabbed for the girl. She jumped back and made a wild slash at him. But another man, coming up behind, knocked the knife spinning with a blow of a heavy pistol barrel.

"Get the little bitch!"

He had her arms pinioned in a trice. But she could still kick and bite and scream. In another second the two of them were a clawing, grappling tangle on the floor.

"Tie her up!" the first man ordered. "And for Christ's sake gag her! Knock her on the head and get it over with!"

Brom bounded toward the doorway, saber in hand.

"One second!" Abe called imperatively.

He rested the muzzle of his musket on the window sill, sighted along the unwavering barrel. The range was no more than twenty feet. Deliberately he waited until the assailant had the girl pinned down, had raised himself clear to strike; then he let him have it.

The explosion rocked the house. Brom plunged through the doorway. His swinging saber split one man's head. It stuck there. After a futile tug he dropped it and yanked out a pistol.

"Surrender, ye bastards!" he yelled.

Abe was already beside him. Their companions were scrambling in through other windows. Stunned by the concussion, the raiders could only stare at them, jaws gaping.

"Stand over against that blank wall!" Abe ordered.

For another instant they stood frozen. He jabbed the point of his sword half an inch into the rump of the man nearest him. The latter's yelp of pain broke the daze that held them. With one voice they began yammering for mercy.

"Get over there! Get over! Face the wall and keep your hands in the air. Ike, hold your musket on 'em. Blow daylight through the first one moves."

He slid his saber back into its scabbard and went over to the man he had shot. He was dead; very unpleasantly dead. Under his inert weight the girl was struggling feebly. Abe dragged the body aside. Her dilated eyes stared at him from a paper-white face; terrified, uncomprehending.

"You're all right, sister." Embarrassment made his voice sound harsh. "Go tend your ma."

"Hey!" John Odell called. "Take a look at this, will ye!"

He and Mike Dyckman had lifted the body of the unconscious old man. Both his thumbs were dislocated, one nearly torn from his hand, and as they turned him over they saw that the seat of his breeches was a mass of charred rags through which angry red flesh showed.

"B'Jesus! They give him the hot seat!" Anderson exclaimed.

"What's the hell's that?"

"A way them cowboys has for getting folks to tell where their valuables is hid. They knock out the seat of a chair, sit a fellow on it, and build a fire under him."

"Say!" Brom cried. He had finally freed his saber and was wiping it on his victim's shirt. "That's an idea! Let's us see what a cowboy looks like on the hot seat!"

"Cowboys!" cried one of the prisoners. "Good God! We ain't cowboys! We thought you was cowboys."

"Huh?"

In their amazement they let the old man slip to the floor.

"Sure!" one of the others added eagerly. "We're all of us as good Whigs's anybody! These folks here is Tories. They been selling cattle in New York, so we come to get the—"

"Turn 'em around!" Abe interrupted. "Let's have a look at 'em."

There were eight prisoners, nondescript men in rough country clothes. Whatever expressions they might have worn were hidden by the lampblack that disguised their faces.

"You know me, Capt'n Anderson," one of them whined. "Sure ye know me—Caleb Stebbins from over to Tuckahoe."

Anderson came forward and peered at the man intently, then picked up a piece of torn sheet and rubbed off the lampblack. The prisoner's face emerged streaked but recognizable. The captain turned.

"Skinners!" He spat the word.

No one spoke. The guides stared at their prisoners with a mixture of repugnance and curiosity. The so-called "skinners" were a recent development in the Neutral Ground: armed bands claiming Patriot allegiance who prowled by night, preying on those they chose to brand Tories. Rumors of them had been circulating of late, but until now none had been caught red-handed. Most people, indeed, were inclined to doubt their existence, attributing the outrages laid at their door to the ubiquitous cowboys whose counterparts they were and whose methods they imitated. There was no arm of law enforcement to cope with them, in any case.

Anderson addressed the girl. "How's it your pa ain't home?"

She was busy wrapping the older woman in a torn blanket. At his words she looked up. Her mouth came open, but she could not speak. Terror was in her eyes again.

"Don't be afraid," Odell urged gently. "Tell us what happened."

The girl swallowed convulsively. "There was just the three of us. They come and knocked. They said they was friends. But Grampa wouldn't open." She swallowed again, and her voice steadied. "One of 'em tried to come down the chimney, only I threw a feather pillow on the fire and smoked him out. Then they tried to pull off a shutter, and Grampa shot at 'em. 'Fore he could load again, they fired through the windows and broke in. They—they hurt my ma."

Odell held her trembling hand. "Did they hurt you?"

She shook her head. "I got a knife. I cut Grampa down. They wanted money. They wouldn't believe when we said Pa had it with him."

"Where's your pa?" Anderson persisted.

She did not reply. Her mouth, tightly closed, made a thin, hard line across her colorless face.

"I'll tell ye where her pa is!" the man named Stebbins declared. "He's snuck off to Kingsbridge to tell 'em the militia's gone and it's safe to raid us. He's a dirty spy, that's what!"

Anderson looked from him to the girl. "I reckon maybe he's right," he said uncertainly.

"Leave be!" Odell interposed. "What difference does Whig or Tory make with helpless folks in the shape these are?"

He turned his back on the others and bent over the still unconscious woman. With that characteristic gentleness, so incongruous in one of his bulk and appearance, he began chafing her wrists. She stirred and groaned, but did not open her eyes.

"Of course I'm right!" Stebbins declared. His courage was flooding back as he sensed his captors' indecision. "Here we are doing our patriotic duty, and you fellows come in and shoot us!" His voice became indignant. "Shoot your own people, you do! By God, there's going to be hell to pay for this! Them two you killed was militia in Colonel Drake's regiment. When we tell him what—"

"You ain't going to tell nobody nothing!" Brom Dyckman cut in savagely. "You ain't going to live long enough!"

The man's indignation collapsed. His face turned pasty. "You—you ain't—going to—"

His voice trailed off. The sudden, heavy silence was broken only by the girl's low sobs.

"Well," Anderson said at last, "I reckon we might as well wipe off the rest and see does we know any more of 'em."

With the lampblack removed, the prisoners appeared less than formidable; a frightened, hangdog crew. Except for Stebbins, all were strangers to their captors. But Abe paused before the largest of them, the man who had ordered the girl hit over the head.

"Where've I seen you before?" he demanded.

The man glared back at him. He had a low forehead that beetled above narrow, shifty eyes, and a livid scar ran diagonally across one pock-marked cheek.

"Jesus!" breathed Isaac Oakley. "You'd never forget that face had you ever seen it before!"

"You the leader of this gang? Speak up!"

The man's lip snarled back. "Go to hell!"

Abe turned away, bewildered. Then he remembered. . . . A hearth fire in the open; a man named Davenport pointing ". . . couple of jailbirds . . . make good soldiers . . ."

He turned to Anderson. "There's one Tory among 'em, anyhow. This son of a bitch got away when that recruit party was took over to Mamaroneck last fall. I bet they're all—"

"No, no!" cried the frightened Stebbins. "He deserted from the Tories! He—"

"Like you deserted from the militia, ye rat!" Anderson interrupted. "Deserters—that's what the pack of ye are, from one army or t'other!" He turned to Abe. "What the hell are we going to do with 'em?"

Abe frowned and looked away. It was customary to bring captured cowboys to Peekskill to be dealt with by the military authorities. But there was no precedent for dealing with skinners. And Peekskill was twenty-five miles away.

He felt his companions' eyes upon him, hanging upon his decision. A few moments ago when there had been fighting to do, he had assumed command by instinct, and they had followed him without hesitation or question. But now no instinct told him what to do. He walked across to the other side of the room, away from them. His eyes saw the details of the scene with extraordinary clearness, but his mind refused to focus. John Odell had left the unconscious woman to her daughter and was kneeling beside the mutilated old man. He glanced up as Abe paused above him.

"For God's sake, do something with 'em, and do it quick!" he urged. "These folks are like to die if we don't get 'em to a doctor."

"Why not just hang 'em and have done with it?" Brom suggested.

Abe shook his head. "We ain't the law. 'Twould be murder."

"Killing a dog ain't murder!"

"No. Reckon we better take 'em to White Plains and hold 'em till we can figure out."

"On a night like this half of 'em'd get away," Anderson said dubiously. "We can't risk letting the likes o' them loose on defenseless folks again."

"Say!" Brom Dyckman brightened. "You got an idea there, Capt'n! 'Twould surprise ye how many prisoners gets shot trying to escape. Only why take all that trouble when they can try here just as well?"

There was an instant of stunned silence. Abe saw comprehension dawning on his companions' faces; hesitation hardening into determination. But it was the prisoners who grasped the full significance first.

"Jesus! You can't do that!"

"Don't kill us! Don't kill us, friends! We'll—"

"Mercy! For the love of God—mercy!"

They were all yammering at once; gasping, shrieking. The sheer terror in their voices turned Abe's blood cold.

"Mercy!" Brom shouted. "Mercy, ye say—ye thieving, murdering bastards!" He gestured toward the half-dead victims. At sight of them his face crimsoned with renewed fury. "Get outside! Get outside, the pack of you, before we shoot ye where ye stand!"

His brother laid a hand on his arm. "There's eight of

'em, Brom, and only six of us. Wait till we load a couple of extra muskets."

Abe looked about. He saw Odell's face, stamped with horror; Isaac Oakley's, angry and frightened at the same time; Anderson's white and grim. In numbed fascination he watched the Dyckmans coolly loading the extra muskets.

"Outside!"

Slapping with the flat of his saber, Brom herded them through the doorway. Whimpering, half paralyzed now, they were as powerless to resist the doom they saw as so many sheep. Abe followed, scarcely conscious that he did so. He was no longer in command of the little troop, or even in command of himself.

"Run!" somebody shouted.

He had a confused impression of screaming men scattering in all directions; of muskets thudding.

There was a man in front of him; a whining, cringing man. "Ye'll not kill a comrade in cold blood?"

Abe recognized the Tory deserter. He gestured with the musket he had raised without knowing he had done so.

"Run! Run for your life!"

The man did not move. "Mercy!" he screamed. "In God's name, don't shoot!"

Abe felt cold and ill inside. This man was a criminal, a murderer; a menace to the whole countryside. But he knew that he could not shoot him. Not like this. Nerveless, he lowered his musket.

"Get out! But if I ever lay eyes on you again—"

He glimpsed the man's swift movement. In the split second that his brain functioned, he remembered that they had neglected to search the prisoners. . . .

He saw the pistol. Flame leaped at him, not ten feet away. A thousand multi-colored lights flashed before his eyes.

Then darkness shut them out. A darkness that was not the night.

Chapter 6

LOW EBB

Twilight succeeded the darkness; a lingering twilight through which people moved dimly and nothing about him had substance or reality. His head, swathed in bandages, did not feel like his. Even after the pain had died to a dull throb, it was some time before he could focus his eyes without concentrated effort.

He was at the Oakley farm, a couple of miles west of White Plains and a short distance above. The Guides had left him there and gone away. He grasped these facts slowly. Ben Oakley, Isaac's father and his mother's cousin, repeated them patiently, but Abe found difficulty keeping one thought in his mind long enough to digest it. Memories were elusive, too, like flour sifting through a sieve. A lethargic incuriosity held him as the days dragged by, each about like every other.

Then one morning when the pain had subsided enough to permit him to sit up, he became aware of some familiar objects placed near his bedside: a dragoon's crested helmet and heavy saber, a tall brown musket. He looked at them for a long time, and when Mrs. Oakley brought his dinner, he said suddenly: "Where did the boys go, Cousin Kate?"

She nearly dropped the tray. "Land sakes, Abe! Ben's told you a dozen times. They was called back to Peekskill."

He thought that over a moment. "Oh," he said simply as the thought slipped away. But from then on the twilight lessened.

The next day he got out of bed and sat in front of the house in the warm spring sunlight. It was now mid-April.

192

For nearly a month he had been in that hazy borderland of consciousness, but once he was in the open again his physical recovery was rapid. His wound was not serious in that respect. The skinner's bullet had creased his scalp diagonally above the left eye, leaving a scar that he would carry for life, but apparently doing no major damage. The concussion, however, seemed to have scrambled his brains. Putting two and two together remained a colossal task long after awareness livened in him again.

The British had raided Peekskill on the very day he had been wounded. They had timed the stroke shrewdly to coincide with the wholesale dispersal of the militia following the Grand Forage, when no reinforcements would be available to the small Continental garrison. They had sailed up the Hudson in transports and landed an overwhelming force below the village. General McDougall, who had succeeded Heath in command of that post, had withdrawn to a stronger position without attempting to oppose them. They had not bothered to attack him or to storm Fort Independence which commanded the Highland passes. But all the materials gathered so laboriously against the coming campaign had been carried off or destroyed, the troop barracks and many private homes burned.

" 'Tis said they used regulars and a couple of them Tory regiments they call Provincials," Ben Oakley said. "I reckon that's why we ain't been troubled with no troop foraging hereabouts. That's God's own mercy! The Continentals done little enough for us folks, and they'll be scarier than ever after this. And with the militia all chased home, there ain't nothing to stop 'em short of the Croton, as I can see."

So the Grand Forage had had precisely the effect a few of the more foresighted authorities had predicted: far from acting as a check on enemy raids, it had opened virtually the entire county to them. Thus far the eastern section, over toward the Connecticut line, had suffered most, that being most accessible to the British base of operations growing up at Morrisania; but roving bands of doubtful composition had been reported above Bedford and even within a few miles of Peekskill. For the most part such gentry contented themselves with carrying off a few cattle and horses here and there by night, lying low by day in the houses of confederates. As yet they were more a nuisance than a major menace, but success was increasing their boldness. Should the British move any considerable body of organized troops into the lower county, there would be no restraining them.

This perpetually impending peril acted like a creeping paralysis upon the entire lower portion of the county. Farmers who should have been busy with spring planting put in just enough to cover their families' bare necessities and spent the rest of their time hanging around taverns, miserably clinging to each other's miserable company.

"Why should we work our hands to the bone making a crop?" they said, "when one army or the other is bound to impress it? Why lay up fodder to winter our stock when them damn Tory robbers are dead certain to drive the cattle off?"

Any effort appeared futile. Houses and barns began falling into disrepair. Materials for their upkeep were hard to come by, and, besides, what was the use of expending money and labor on buildings that were likely as not to be burned to the ground the next time a raiding party chose to move in that direction?

This pervasive defeatism had a depressing effect on Abe. The first day he felt well enough he strolled a mile down the road to Acker's Tavern in quest of such news and gossip as he knew were customarily dispensed in such places. But there was no news worthy of the name, and the gossip consisted of rumors, seldom substantiated, of cow raids and burnings. That was just about all the conversation there was, and that ceased instantly upon the appearance of a stranger, for it was known that all manner of spies and agents of one sort or another were roaming at large. Few of these hangdog men

drank much; they just sat around feeling sorry for themselves
while their lives went to pot.

Now and again it would be reported that some family in
the vicinity had disappeared, and they would know that another hopeless wretch had abandoned his home and stolen
off to New York to make his peace with King George and
obtain for his family the sanctuary that he despaired of his
own people ever providing. They would curse him, but
often there would be envy mingled with their bitterness.
All that prevented many more from doing the same thing
was the knowledge that victims of their own earlier political
activities had gone before them and would see that they were
made less than welcome. They were between the devil and
the deep blue sea. But when militia officers tried to call them
out for some concerted effort in their own behalf, they were
always too busy and temporized by drawing up long-winded
petitions to helpless committees and harassed officials higher
up.

A year of defeat and impotence had reduced the general
morale disastrously. In the southern third of Westchester
County, at least, the sacred flame of liberty, as the orators
liked to call it, was guttering out in its own grease.

Not all of the farmers, fortunately, reacted so abjectly.
Ben Oakley, with a scattering of others, went ahead with
their business as usual.

"You're tempting fate," neighbors told him. "Long as you
got nothing worth their taking, maybe they'll leave you be."

"Maybe," Oakley agreed. "I got no delusion I'm going to
enjoy the fruits of this here toil of mine; only long as I'm
busy all day, I got no time to worry about that, and I'm
too tired to worry at night. Worry's killed a lot more folks
than hard work ever done."

This excellent philosophy was lost on most of them, but
Abe grasped at it and asked to help around the place.

Oakley was dubious. "If you're well enough to work a

farm, don't you reckon you ought to go back with the other boys?"

"I—I don't know as I'm going back."

"Not going back! You mean you aim to quit the Guides?"

"I don't know," Abe repeated dully. "Put me to work here, will you, Cousin Ben?"

It was still hard to think. Thoughts that intruded themselves troubled him. He stubbornly evaded Oakley's questions, and the latter finally acceded to his request. With Isaac away, he had only his wife and three little girls, and he was hard put to work the farm properly alone. Then, too, he was glad to have another man about the place. He started Abe off with lighter chores, but within a few days they were sharing the heavy work between them. It did Abe more good than anything a doctor might have prescribed. He had the inner satisfaction that he was repaying in some part the Oakleys' kindness to him. And the long, strenuous hours out of doors tuned up his physical well-being, crowded out those uncertainties that troubled him.

Early in May John Odell rode in from the north with Isaac Oakley on what they described as a recruiting expedition. General McDougall, they said, was too busy building a new camp on the strong hill behind Fort Independence to do much else, and with the militia dispersed there was little guiding to be done. So they had joined up for the time being with Captain Townsend's company of mounted rangers. These men, although rating technically as militia and drawing pay and rations accordingly, comprised in effect an independent unit of individual volunteers, on more or less permanent duty and functioning directly under the orders of the County Committee of Safety. Together with a couple of other similar companies, they were virtually the only troops that harassed body could depend on, and the Committee was making an effort to build them up.

"A lot of 'em's fellows got nothing else to do," young

Oakley explained. "Fellows that's been cleaned out of all they got or drove from their homes so's they can't make a living. Well, we figured the closer we got to New York, the more such there'd be, so we come down to see could we find a few among the neighbors."

"I wish you luck," his father said sardonically. "You're sure going to need it."

"It's nice work," John Odell put in. "On top of regular pay, we get prize money on all the cattle we take when we lay a pack of cow jockeys by the heels. Reckon we've gathered in a couple dozen already. You'll like it fine, Abe."

Abe looked away. "Ain't this Captain Townsend the fellow used to run down Tory recruit parties?" he asked.

"Aye—still does. And they're coming through thicker'n ever, and from farther off. Why, we took one batch from Livingston Manor, and 'tis said over across the river they took some from clear up Albany County."

"Oh. Then folks all over feel like—like they do hereabouts?"

Odell's face was puzzled. "I don't know what the hell you're talking about, Abe. There's some Tory regiments forming, sure, and they got recruiters out offering cash bounties to fill 'em. Seems like since the regulars and Hessians ain't been able to whip us, they figure to skim off the scum of our own people and fight us with them. If some I've seen are fair samples, they can have 'em and welcome! Anyways, there's a new law saying anybody taken recruiting behind the lines is to be treated like a spy. I reckon hanging a few will put an end to this right quick!"

After supper they proposed visiting the tavern to begin their own recruiting activities, and Abe accompanied them. He had been silent through most of the meal, and several times he noticed them observing him curiously. But apparently they attributed his reticence to the aftereffects of his wound, for they did not question him further.

The usual crowd was congregated at the tavern. Isaac

Oakley knew them all personally as friends and neighbors. They greeted him cordially enough and demanded news, but when Odell backed up against the bar to address them, Abe sensed suspicion in the way they drew back to give him space, latent hostility in the sudden silence that descended on the crowded room.

"Friends," Big John began, "we come to you in the name of the Committee of Safety, asking the help of the bravest among you."

Probably this was the first time he had ever made anything resembling a public speech in his life. It was obvious that he had memorized the words, and he began to sweat with the effort of keeping them straight in his mind. He described the situation up county; how, because of the recalcitrance of regular militia drafts, the Committee was obliged to rely upon volunteer companies to cope with cow raids and recruit parties. He pointed out what they had accomplished and hoped to accomplish, outlined the nature of such service and the inducements it offered, and asked for volunteers. The words boomed out unnecessarily loud, sank dully into the all-enveloping silence until at last he stumbled to a halt and glanced about expectantly at the faces of his audience.

These were sitting or standing about as they had been at the beginning, in what might have been listening attitudes. For a long moment no one spoke.

"Where's this here Committee of Safety hanging out these days?" inquired a man seated at a near-by table nursing a mug of small beer.

"Why, at Crompond. They've took over the Presbyterian parsonage and—"

" 'Committee of Safety's' right! Their own safety is what they think about!"

"What have they done way up there in Crompond, most out of the county, for us folks who're in real danger?" demanded a man leaning on the bar.

Odell blinked. "Why, I was just telling you what they're trying to do! If enough fellows like you join up with us, we can—"

"They left us to our fate, that's what they done! Them and the army too. Let 'em catch their own cow jockeys!"

Isaac Oakley, who had been mingling with the crowd, came forward and took post beside his companion. His face was flushed.

" 'Twasn't the Committee let you down," he declared. " 'Twas the militia—and that means yourselves, since most of you are in it! It's because you militia won't turn out that—"

"The militia was betrayed! Sending us so far down we fell prey to them troops coming out of Kingsbridge!"

"Nobody'd of fallen prey if they'd kept decent watch. Or if they'd had the bowels to fight like men when they was surpriscd!"

"How they expect us to stand up to regulars when the Continentals theirselves turn tail, like they done every chance they got?"

Oakley started a hot retort, but John Odell interposed quickly.

"Now listen, friends, that ain't true—that we can't stand up to troops." He still looked bewildered, but his voice became persuasive. "You heard what happened when the British raided the stores over to Danbury just last week, ain't you?"

"We heard they burned it without no trouble, like they done Peekskill."

"I mean after that. Well, all the details ain't known yet, but what happened was the Connecticut militia jumped 'em on the return march, took their plunder off of 'em and drove the whole kit and caboodle of 'em into Long Island Sound! That's what!"

There was a flurry of interest.

"Must of took the whole militia of the state to do that," someone suggested skeptically.

Odell shook his head. "Funny part is there was fewer of us than of them. A lot fewer—two thousand British regulars and the pick of the Tory regiments, and far's anybody can figure no more'n twelve hundred militia!" He sensed their interest and hastened on. "Seems there was a Continental general home on leave and he took over command—Benedict Arnold, it was, that fellow did the fighting up north last year. Well, instead of just sniping at 'em from behind and picking up a few stragglers like usually happens, he cut in ahead of 'em, turned the column aside and fell on their flanks. Routed 'em, he did! He'd of taken every mother's son, hadn't the fleet been waiting for 'em with big guns and fresh troops!" He looked about the room triumphantly. "You going to tell me us York State men can't whip regulars and Tories when them lousy Connecticutters can?"

No one replied. With perplexed eyes Odell saw that the interest of an instant before was already fading.

"We might if we had an Arnold," somebody said after a moment. "Only we ain't. We got George Clinton, only most of us ain't never seen him. We got old woman McDougall, afeared to stick his nose outside of Peekskill."

"We got an army been whipped so much it's got the habit," said another. "And a Congress that leaves us to our fate. And officers who send us into traps and run like hell to save their own necks."

"What in God's name do you figure on doing?" Isaac Oakley demanded scornfully. "You going to sit on your arses and see yourselves ruined without lifting a finger?"

"Well, I don't know," said one of the older men. "We got off pretty easy so far. Maybe if we don't irritate 'em no more, they'll leave us be."

"Leave you be? You think men you drove out of their homes—jailed as Tories—tarred and feathered, maybe—you think they're going to leave you be when their chance comes, just as if you ain't done enough already to irritate 'em! There's plenty such among the cowboys. You'll find 'em in Rogers' Rangers, too, and all them other Tory regiments that'll be rampaging up this way any day now the roads are dried out!"

"Wait, Ike," Odell interposed. He looked very tired now. "We come here looking for volunteers," he resumed patiently. "Fellows willing to turn out for a little while to help save our own county from ruination—to help a cause we used to think was pretty fine, to judge by all the shouting some of us did when the going was easy—like Ike and me and Abe here been doing all these months past. Won't none of you join us now when the need's so bad?"

Silence; heavy, sullen, dispirited silence.

Abruptly Oakley's arm shot out, leveled. "How about you, Martin Post?"

He had singled out a young man of about his own age, seated with several others at a table across the room. Abe recognized him as an occupant of an adjoining farm at the crossroads a half mile west of the Oakley place.

"Me? Why, I—I can't, Ike."

"Why can't you? Pa says you folks ain't working only half your farm this year. Can't be you're needed to home."

Post gulped and stared at the table. " 'Tain't that. My pa's declared us neutral. We ain't taking sides no more."

"Neutral! Why, you're both in the militia! You been strong Whigs right along. You can't turn into a neutral all of a sudden like this just by saying you're going to!"

"We're going to try, anyway. We've quit the militia. We ain't going to fight no more. We're—" Post hesitated. "Oh, God!" he cried miserably. "What's the use? We done our share—much as anybody hereabouts. But what's anybody done for us—the Congress, the State Convention, our own County Committee even? All we can do's mind our own business and keep the peace and try to save whatever we can."

Abe turned away abruptly and strode out of the tavern. He felt a qualm of illness, physical illness, as though he were about to vomit. He sat down on the low stoop and held his head in his hands, and after a moment the queasiness passed. He remained seated, however, staring straight ahead with empty eyes. The sun had set only recently, and a fading afterglow still stained the sky, laced with long, milky stratus clouds. The air was mild, balmy. The gentle breeze of afternoon had gone down with the sun. In the hush of early evening the fresh green countryside lay still and peaceful; as remote as another world.

In the tavern behind him the drone of voices continued: Odell's patient, persuasive, baffled, still asking for volunteers; Oakley's sharp, bitter, singling out individuals by name; a mutter of reply, sullen or indifferent or resentful. Abe listened without interest. When the two guides emerged, alone, he fell in beside them and walked in silence to the hitching rail where their horses were tethered. Still silent, they mounted and turned back toward the Oakley farm.

"Well," Odell said at last, "we'll try White Plains tomorrow, and if we don't have no better luck I reckon we'd best be getting back. You in shape to come along, Abe?"

"I—don't know." Abe hesitated. "I still feel kind of funny in the head, John."

"I don't aim to rush you none, but after what you seen just now I guess you can figure for yourself how much we need you."

Abe did not reply at once. He rode on for several minutes, frowning into the gathering dusk.

"John"—he groped for the words uncertainly—"John, you —you think it's worth while—to go on fighting for folks ain't got the gumption to fight for theirselves?"

He was aware of their surprised eyes upon him, but he did not look at them.

Oakley cursed. "These bastards can be stripped clean for all of us! It ain't them we're fighting for!"

"What ails ye, Abe?" Odell demanded sharply.

"I don't know. I been thinking about things lately, or trying to. I ain't never done much thinking, and it don't come easy." Again he groped for words. "What I mean's this, John. I don't know much about this liberty there's so much talk about, and running our own country our own selves, and the like o' that. I don't know nothing about the Congress and the State Convention that are supposed to be running it, only that folks is all the time complaining against 'em. I want to do what's right, and—well, if all these things are right, why is it the folks who're supposed to enjoy 'em won't lift a hand to win 'em?"

"Why, there's a-plenty lifting a hand and doing a whole lot more, too!" Odell rejoined. "The army don't feel like these sniveling cowards, for all the beating they've took. And the Committee of Safety—they may act stupid as hell and be pretty useless most of the time, but they're doing the best they know how!"

"But the Tories think they're right, too," Abe persisted. "Leastwise, there's them among 'em that do. They think they're fighting for their country and that we're a pack of traitors. And from what you say, they feel strong enough about it to come through in hundreds to fight of their own free will, while out of this whole county that's supposed to be all for liberty there's only some forty-odd volunteered for the rangers."

Odell puzzled over that in silence for a moment. "There ain't a lot of us, for a fact," he admitted heavily. "But I reckon that's the way the world goes, Abe: it's the few does all the work to win what the many live to enjoy."

"But it's the many that make up the country, ain't it? Well, if most of 'em don't want liberty and the rest enough to fight for it, is it right for a few of us to keep trying to win it for 'em against a lot of other fellows willing to fight to keep 'em from having it?"

"For Christ's sake!" Oakley exclaimed in disgust. "You

sure are funny in the head! Right, right, right! You need somebody to tell you what's right when there's a pack of the bastards rampaging through your own county, robbing, burning and beating folks up?"

"Looking back to when I was shot," Abe said, "a fellow might think there was them among us tarred with the same brush."

"Them damn skinners ain't none of us!"

"I reckon there's decent Tories might say the same about the cowboys!"

"Decent Tories! Who ever heard of a decent Tory!"

"Oh, have done, Ike," Odell cut in wearily. He turned to Abe. "I don't know no more than you about this here 'glorious cause' Whig orators rant about, but as for what's right and what ain't—well, I reckon that's something a fellow's got to feel inside himself. If I didn't know without having to ask myself that the folks we been born and raised among was worth fighting for, I wouldn't be here. 'Cause I ain't like you and Brom—I don't like fighting. It scares hell out of me."

"But when they won't even—"

"Hell, Abe, our people ain't perfect. There's cowards among 'em, and scoundrels and shirkers. But they ain't all of 'em that, nor even most of 'em. They're scared now and discouraged because they've been beaten and plundered, and nobody's lifted a hand to help 'em. Down underneath they're about like you and me and the rest who've been more lucky maybe." He paused, shrugged. "I ain't going to argue no more," he said wearily. "I'm plum argued out for tonight. If you don't feel in your own heart that what you're doing's right—then maybe you'd better quit right now."

Abe made no reply, and they rode the rest of the way in silence. Absently he watched his horse's head, bobbing in rhythm to its leisurely walk. At the head of the familiar lane, Oakley reined in.

"Home!" he said bitterly. He gestured toward the small

white house a hundred yards away. "Home! How much longer do you reckon it'll be standing there? How much longer will any of us have homes?"

They stabled their horses in silence; a constrained silence in which an invisible wall was rearing itself. Not till they were crossing the yard did Odell break it.

"We'll be leaving at sun-up, Abe. Reckon you'll be with us?"

Abe stumbled, staring at the ground without seeing it. "I don't know," he said miserably, "I don't know."

Chapter 7

MARTIN POST JOINS UP

Martin Post topped the crest of the adjoining pasture and raced down the gentle slope. At sight of him Abe's breath caught sharply. He dropped the horses' bridle. At the same instant Ben Oakley let go the plow handles. Both had seen men running for their lives before. Without a word they dashed toward where their muskets leaned against the stone fence. They were looking to their priming as the breathless youth came up.

"They've took—my pa!"

Oakley snapped the musket pan shut. "Cowboys?"

Post's eyes were dilated. His breath came in gasps. He choked as he tried to speak.

Abe shook him roughly. "Who? How long since?"

"They after you?" Oakley demanded.

"I—don't reckon—"

"Then easy, lad. Take your time."

Post's eyes lost some of their wildness. After a few seconds his breathing began to steady.

"I was in the fields. I started home for dinner. They was herding cattle in the yard. They had my pa trussed up. I run straight here."

"How many of 'em?"

"A powerful lot! They—had green coats."

Abe and Ben Oakley exchanged a grim look.

"They get your brothers, too?" the latter asked.

"I don't know. They was plowing the north twenty acres. When I seen they had Pa, I run straight here."

There was an instant's silence.

"I reckon he forgot to tell 'em he'd turned neutral," Abe said.

Post stared at him without comprehension. "Lend me a musket! We got to do something!"

Abe snorted. "Ain't you afraid you'll irritate 'em?"

"Shut up!" Ben Oakley cut in sharply. He was thinking fast. "Way Marty was running, he'd of made it in five-ten minutes. They'll be busy some time yet. Come on. I got a spare musket over to the house."

He set off toward the house at a lumbering trot. Post, following, was soon staggering from exhaustion. As Abe took hold of his arm to help him, he saw that, for all his winded condition, the terror of a moment before had lessened. Oakley's wife saw them coming. She was in the doorway when they arrived, mouth gaping in apprehension.

"Kate," her husband ordered, "take the girls and get for Acker's ordinary fast's you can. Tell any you meet by the way there's Tory troops on the Post place—troops, mind you, not just cowboys."

She did not stir. "Where—where you going?"

"To have a couple shots at 'em maybe."

"Oh, no!" Her hands flew to her throat.

"Hasten, I say! They're driving off the stock and have took Joe Post prisoner. Bid any men that's willing to grab their muskets and join us."

Abe sneered. "That pack of skulkers!"

Ben Oakley ignored him. He brushed past his nerveless wife into the living room where the extra musket rested on pegs above the fireplace. He thrust it into young Post's hands, snatched down a cartridge box and powder horn and hung them about the youth's neck.

"Better recharge."

Post's fumbling hands got the worm down the barrel somehow, drew out the old load. He clawed a cartridge from the box. Abe watched with detached curiosity as he tore off the

end of the paper cylinder with his teeth. The black powder
made a smear about his mouth, and some grains fell to the
floor as he spilled fresh priming into the pan. He had some
trouble getting the rest of the charge into the muzzle. He
tapped the butt on the floor a couple of times to settle it,
then the ramrod rattled in the barrel as he drove the wadding
home. His hand was already steadying as Abe clapped on
his dragoon helmet and buckled the heavy saber belt about
his waist.

Mrs. Oakley had recovered herself by the time they
emerged from the house. She was running toward the road,
dragging her youngest daughter with one hand and holding
her skirts high with the other while the two older girls raced
ahead. She was a stout woman, and her gait appeared so
grotesque viewed from the rear that Abe burst out laughing.
He had no intention of being rude. It was simply that this
whole scene seemed unreal. It had nothing to do with him.
He could not feel it; he could only see it as though it were
a picture in a book.

"Girls!" Oakley shouted. "Mary! Susan! One of you get a
horse and ride ahead! Don't take time to saddle! Shout the
alarm to everyone you see!"

They saw the oldest girl wave her hand and veer toward
the barn. Then the three men turned and headed for the
Post farm. They took the shortest route, cutting across the
fields, slowing to a walk after a moment to allow Martin
Post to recover his wind. He halted them at length on the
ascending slope of a high, grassy knoll.

" 'Twas from the top of this I seen 'em. There's a fence a
bit beyond. Come easy."

Just short of the crest they threw themselves flat and
wormed forward on their bellies. Not until they were behind the cover of the stone fence did Abe raise his head.
Again he had the curious impression that the scene spread
out so clearly below was a picture from a book. The cattle
had all been collected in the barnyard by now, where a few

green-coated figures were keeping them herded together. The
rest of the soldiers, their main purpose accomplished, were
occupied with the pleasant business of looting the gray clapboard house. Two had posted themselves in the second-
story windows and were throwing out various objects to
their comrades on the ground, who were sorting them criti-
cally and stowing what they wanted in bags or bundles.
Shouts and laughter carried to the men on the knoll, but
actual words were indistinguishable at this distance.

"Say! Ain't that your ma?" Oakley asked suddenly.

He pointed toward the front of the house. A mounted
officer sat there, aloof from his milling men. A woman clung
to his stirrup as though she were pleading with him. As they
watched he pushed her aside. He did it neither roughly nor
gently, but with what appeared to be complete indifference.

Abe grabbed Martin Post's musket. "Don't fire, you fool!"

"Leggo!" Post cried. He struggled furiously, but Abe held
on.

"You can't hit nothing at this range. Must be two hundred
yard. And if you fire on 'em, they're like to burn the place."

"What're we going to do?" Post's voice was a despairing
wail. "We can't just sit here and watch 'em!"

Abe shrugged. "What can we do—three of us?" He peered
over the fence. "There's thirty of 'em if there's a one. Maybe
forty."

"But when the neighbors come—"

"The neighbors are neutrals!" Abe's mouth twisted.
" 'Maybe if we don't irritate 'em, they'll leave us be,' " he
quoted ironically. " 'Militia can't stand up against troops!' "

"Martin Post was neutral, too—till he seen 'em take his
pa and loot his house and drive off the cattle," Oakley said
quietly. "And I reckon there's others seen the like. Joe Post
never owned all them cows down there, so this ain't the first
place they been to today."

"Oh, God!" Post cried. "Can't we even have a shot at 'em?"

"Wait till they leave and we'll trail 'em and see can we get close enough to—" Abe broke off short. A puff of dirty gray smoke blossomed suddenly against the trees that topped a rise to the northwest of the house, and the report of a musket carried to them. A second followed. "Ah! It's too late now!"

"That's Jack and Sam!" Post leaped to his feet excitedly, but Abe pulled him down again as half a dozen more shots sounded in quick succession and a smoke cloud briefly hid the trees.

"What did I tell you?" Oakley cried. "There's more of 'em! The countryside's turning out!"

Abe shook his head. "They're too scared or they wouldn't open at such range."

The men in the farmyard seemed to have reached the same conclusion. For an instant they stood frozen, staring in the direction from which the shots had come. In suspended animation, the scene had the quality of a tableau. Then, as though at a given signal, the tension broke, and the sound of their voices and laughter, contemptuous laughter, carried to the knoll again. There was a difference in their activity now, however. The mounted officer had come to life. He rode among the soldiers, shouting and gesticulating with drawn sword. Other men, non-commissioned officers apparently, added their urging to his. Gradually a purposefulness began to emerge from the aimless milling. Men gathered up their bundles of loot and straggled into a semblance of formation. Those in charge of the cattle herded the beasts into the lane toward the road. A squad moved out without haste toward the trees to the northwest, and the firing ceased abruptly.

"Either they ain't taking no chances or figure they got all they can handle," Abe remarked. He still had that strange feeling of detachment, that all this concerned him in no way, but from sheer force of habit his mind commenced analyzing the picture. From the red facings on their coats, it was evident that these men were not the dreaded Queen's Rangers. From the amount of hubbub required to get them into ranks, it would appear that they were from one of the newly formed regiments. "Raw troops, no better'n militia, hardly." He spoke half aloud, unaware that he was speaking. "If only they'd a-come a week sooner, when Ike and Big John was here!"

"Look!" Ben cried suddenly.

He pointed toward the barn. Two green-coated men had just emerged from it, hustling Martin Post's father between them, his arms bound to his sides. A billow of smoke rolled from the door behind them. A third, bearing a thatch of flaming straw, appeared an instant later and started for the house on the run.

"The bastards! Oh, the dirty bastards!" Young Post's voice was a gasping sob. Before either could stop him, he leaped to his feet and fired blindly.

The concussion of the shot sent Abe staggering. The musket's muzzle had been less than a foot from his head. Deafened, blinded, he lurched against the fence, coughing and sputtering from the reek of gunpowder smoke. Briefly the world swam. Then he was on the ground and Ben Oakley's frightened face was bending over him.

"Leave me be! I'm all right!"

He struggled to his feet. Beside him Martin Post, crying, was trying frantically to reload his musket. Abe ignored him and gazed out over the fence. He must have been stunned for a few seconds, for the scene below had changed. The raiding force, in column now, had turned into the road, driving the cattle before them. Flames from the hot-burning hay had burst through the roof of the barn, and a thin curl of smoke came from a window of the house.

It was a picture; remote, unreal. It concerned him not at all. . . . There was a queer taste in his mouth, biting, acrid; strange and yet familiar. Burnt powder! He felt a sharp tingling along his spine. He closed his eyes for a split second, and when he opened them again the scene below was no longer a picture.

He spun about and caught the whimpering Post a clout

across the face with his open hand. "Get hold of yourself! Come on! We can save the house yet!"

He scrambled over the wall and started across the open ground. He ran clumsily, holding the big saber in one hand to keep it from tripping him, his musket in the other. Halfway there young Post overtook him and raced ahead, then the heavier Oakley.

"The well!" he shouted. "Get water!"

He saw them veer aside but kept on toward the house himself. His ears still rang, but his brain was clear; clear as it had not been these many weeks. Racing blood had washed away the last sick miasmas of uncertainty. He saw that the raiders had sighted them. Several men at the rear of the column turned back as though to thwart them, but at that instant more shots sounded from the woods beyond the road. The officer shouted something, and the column continued its retirement.

The smoke-filled living room was a wreck. Hungry flames licked up the window curtains and a pile of broken furniture and debris still smoldered in one corner. But the man detailed to fire the place had not taken the time to do a thorough job. He had simply thrown his flaming straw on the rubbish heap. Mrs. Post, who had been making butter when the raiders arrived, had contrived to upset the contents of the heavy churn on it before it gained full headway and was now beating at the flaming curtains with a broom. Abe hacked them down with his heavy sword and stamped them out in a few seconds. By the time Post and Oakley arrived from the well, the fire was under control, and their buckets quickly finished it.

They ran out of the house again, ignoring the woman's thanks and protests. The raiders had turned south on the Tuckahoe road. The firing from the woods had ceased. As they paused to take in the situation, they saw several figures slip from among the trees and start gingerly across the open ground toward the crossroads. With one accord the men at the house hurried to meet them.

There were six of them: Martin Post's younger brothers and four men Abe did not know.

"We get any of the bastards?" was their first question.

"Too long range. We got to get closer to 'em."

"Well, come on! We can't do nothing standing here."

"Careful how ye shoot," Oakley cautioned. "Remember, they got Joe Post with 'em."

The raiders had passed from view around a bend a quarter of a mile down the Tuckahoe road. The little knot of armed farmers set off after them at a run.

"Watch out!" Abe cautioned as they approached the turn. "They may—"

A dozen green-coated men were lined up across the road a hundred yards beyond. The instant the pursuers appeared they let go a ragged volley.

"By God!" Abe cried. "They're scared as we are!"

He was talking to himself. The men who had been beside him an instant before had vanished, and he stood alone in the empty road.

"For Christ's sake! Come back, ye goddamn—"

A musket thudded from the stone fence on his right; another; a whole chorus from behind fences and trees on both sides. The farmers had not fled, after all. They had simply obeyed a natural impulse and dived for the nearest cover. He could see their heads popping up now. Someone shouted, pointing down the road. Through the dissipating smoke of the enemy's volley Abe saw the last of their rear guard passing around the next bend.

"After 'em!"

"Wait!" Abe called imperatively. "We can't prove nothing that way."

It was too late. One glimpse of the enemy in apparent retreat was enough to set them off in full cry. Individually, in twos and threes, they raced in pursuit, cutting across the fields, following the fences. Already the little force had ceased to be a unit.

Abe did not follow. He knew what would happen, because the same thing had happened before. The aroused yokels would give the raiders an unpleasant hour or so. More would join them, and they would swarm upon the enemy rear from all sorts of unexpected angles, sniping from cover but always too scattered to come to grips. They might pick off one or two, even gather in a few stragglers; but they would not recover the prisoner or any of the plunder except such less useful items as the raiders might get tired of carrying and discard of their own volition. Pitted against well-managed rear-guard action of disciplined troops, such tactics could never prove more than a transient nuisance.

A patter of musketry sounded from a short distance ahead. He shrugged and turned back the way they had come, only to stop as he rounded the bend again. A compact group of armed men had turned off from the crossroad and were hurrying toward him, not a quarter of a mile away. At their head he recognized Jacob Acker, the taverner, and through his mind flashed remembrance of Ben Oakley's daughter riding to give the alarm. Waving his musket and shouting, he ran to meet them.

"Hey!" cried a startled voice. Several muskets leaped to cover him. A couple of the men ducked for the side of the road.

"What the hell ails ye?" Abe demanded.

"Jesus! It's young Kronkhyte!"

"What in God's name's happened to ye?"

In crested helmet and clanking saber, half his face blackened from Martin Post's discharge, Abe was an apparition that might have startled calmer men than these tavern heroes whose nerves were already on edge. He did not realize that. What he did realize was that these men were scared, and the realization sobered him.

"Listen!" he began incisively. "We got a chance to wipe

out the whole gang of 'em. I'll show you how if you're game."

"What—what's it ye aim to do?"

"The same's that fellow done in Connecticut—cut in ahead of 'em!"

The men exchanged uncertain glances. There were only a dozen of them.

"I don't reckon we'd ought to do that."

"All we figured was to get a few shots at 'em and chase 'em off."

Abe swallowed hard. These, he saw, were mainly the same men to whom John Odell had addressed his futile plea a week before.

"Joe Post had quit the militia and declared neutral, too," he said, controlling his voice with an effort. "But for the grace of God, any one of ye might be in his shoes right now!" He paused. He had no authority to command these men. He had no official status at all. He was not even enrolled in the militia. Some of these men might be officers, for all he knew. He singled out the leader abruptly. "How about you, Jake Acker?"

The taverner was looking back toward the Post farm. Smoke from the doomed barn billowed above the trees, higher and blacker by the moment. When he turned his face was hard.

"Come on," he said shortly.

Abe led them across the fields toward the west. After half a mile they debouched into a narrow back road, running southward roughly parallel to the one the raiders had taken. Here he set the pace at a brisk dogtrot.

A man stepped out of a farmhouse, fumbling with a musket.

"What's happened? Where ye going?"

"Tories—Joe Post's place. Come on!"

There were other men at other houses; men running in from the fields. The raiders had approached swiftly and quietly in order to get their work done before any widespread alarm should be given. The firing and the smoke from the burning barn was the first warning these people had had that anything was amiss. They were frightened and bewildered, helpless because they did not know the nature of the threat or what to do about it. Normally some of them would have followed the sound of the firing and joined the men harassing the raiders' rear. Now the sight of armed men of their own kind trotting purposefully behind a powder-stained young man with a big sword brought them the reassurance they needed. Shouting encouragement to their families, they sprinted to catch up. Abe's little force had more than doubled by the time he turned eastward and struck for the Tuckahoe road again.

He had outstripped the raiders with no difficulty, loaded down as they were with plunder, hampered by the cattle they were driving and the necessity for holding off the snipers swarming on their rear. He could gauge their position with some nicety by the intermittent firing, now petering out into scattered shots, now rising to the crescendo of a volley. He figured he was a good half mile ahead when he halted his small force behind a stone fence on a high bank beside the Tuckahoe road.

He singled out one of the few among them whom he knew. "Nick Banker, go up to yonder bend and give word when they come into view." He turned to the others. "Take post along this here fence. We'll all fire together when I give the word. How many of you got bagnets?"

A few hesitantly held up their muskets. The sun struck sparks from the glinting bayonets. Abe counted nine.

"All right! You fellows stay by me. Do what I do."

He stopped short. Nicholas Banker was racing back from the bend, his eyes bulging.

"They're on us! They're on us!"

"What! Already!"

The firing still sounded a good distance off, but even as Abe looked in that direction, two green-coated men appeared at the bend, a scant two hundred yards away. They were walking without haste, seemingly undisturbed.

"Duck! All of you!"

He snatched off his helmet and crouched behind the fence. Because it was well above the level of the road, it did not lie in the natural focus of anyone passing below. He raised his head cautiously and peeped over.

Behind the two men came the cattle; fifteen or twenty head, a docile sea of rippling bodies and tossing horns. Several more of the raiders were herding them along. Behind them marched a dozen men in a semblance of formation, a sergeant at their head. Behind these—nothing.

Abe's mind worked swiftly. Somehow he had miscalculated. Either the firing of the rear guard was closer than it sounded, or else the Tory commander, assuming all the danger to lie behind, had divided his force, sent this detail ahead to get the cattle away as quickly as possible while he held off their assailants with the remainder.

"Listen!" he said in a low voice, never moving his eyes from the road. "You fellows without bagnets—soon's you've fired, reload quick's ye can and stay right where ye are. There'll be more of 'em coming down the road."

He lowered his head, very cautiously, as the leading Tories came abreast. Now the cattle were passing; trampling, lowing, kicking up a dust cloud. Time seemed to stand still. He glanced over the waiting men. Briefly their frozen stillness brought back his earlier feeling of unreality. Although they were all different individuals, at that instant there was something strangely alike about them. Those white faces, drawn with strain, mouths half open; those wide eyes, dark with terror, uncertainty, fixed on him, waiting. They looked the way he must have looked that night at Mamaroneck just before the Rangers opened fire. Then his eyes had been fixed upon Major Green, cool and poised. Now their eyes were fixed on him, and he felt as cool as the major.

"Jesus!" whispered a man beside him, risking his head above the wall. "That sergeant—he's Mike Hart—Dobbs Ferry. The son of a bitch stole—"

"Shut up!"

It was too late. The sibilance carried. There was an exclamation from the road. Raising his head again, Abe looked squarely into the sergeant's eyes, not twenty yards away.

He jumped to his feet. "Now, boys! Give it to 'em!"

He saw the sergeant's musket half raised. Then the butt of his own kicked against his shoulder. He had a swift impression of green coats milling about on the road. Then a mighty concussion shook the air, and a great cloud of smoke, leaping from the fence, shut out the scene.

He threw down his musket, yanked out his saber.

"Bagnets! Charge!"

He leaped to the top of the fence. Would they come? It did not occur to him that he was doing anything spectacular or courageous. These men had to be shown what to do or it wouldn't be done.

"Bagnets! Bagnets!"

A man was beside him. Another. More were coming. Beyond the smoke cloud several muskets slammed. John Buchanan spun halfway around and clapped a hand to his shoulder. Nicholas Banker's legs gave way under him.

Abe jumped down into the road. From the corner of his eye he saw the sun glint on level bayonets, following. A face leaped at him out of the thinning smoke. The papery face of a youth no older than he, eyes dilated in terror. He made a wild swing with his saber, missed.

"Quarter! Quarter!"

Abe checked a second stroke midway. The youth in green was screaming. He had thrown down his musket and covered his face with both hands to shut out the horror that rushed at him through the smoke.

"Quarter! Quarter!"

As though at a signal, the cry arose from all sides. A tremendous thudding and bellowing drowned it out.

"Look out for them cows!" somebody yelled.

The cattle, milling crazily for an instant, stampeded down the road, bowling over the men who had been herding them and those up ahead, cutting them off from assisting their stricken comrades as effectively as a regiment of Continentals could have done. The fight was over.

Jacob Acker wiped his bayonet on his coat sleeve. "Jesus!" he breathed.

Three wounded raiders lay writhing in the dust. The sergeant was dead as a stone. The rest, their hands in the air, were still yammering. The farmers stared at them and at each other with the surprised bewilderment of men coming out of a trance.

One laughed nervously. "First time ever I heard 'quarter' cried by any but our folks!"

"We whupped 'em! Christ almighty! *We whupped 'em!*"

Realization seemed to dawn on all of them at once. In an instant the road became a bedlam of shouting, laughing men, slapping each other's backs, shaking hands.

"Hey!" Abe yelled. "Get them prisoners back of the fence!"

He looked about. The stone fence was deserted. Carried away by excitement, the men who were supposed to remain posted there had charged after the ones with bayonets.

"Get back!" Abe cried desperately. "Get back and reload! There's more of 'em!"

Again it was just too late. Even as he spoke a massed knot of men in green appeared around the bend, coming at the double behind the mounted officer. The shouting and laughing ceased as abruptly as though invisible hands had gripped each man's windpipe. Frozen, dumb, they gaped at the peril bearing down on them. There was not a loaded musket in the crowd.

As a matter of fact, there were not many loaded muskets among the Tories. But Abe did not know that. Nor could he know that, spurred to frenzy by the firing ahead, the cloud of snipers in the rear had broken cover and were charging in close on the tail of the remaining raiders. All he knew was that if they got by this point they would escape, recapture the prisoners taken in the first brush and thus undo half his efforts. And he sensed that the instant these men got over their first numbing astonishment, they would stampede as wildly as had the cattle.

"Bagnets!" he shouted furiously. "All of ye! Charge the bastards!"

He spun about. Swinging the saber over his head in flaming circles, he raced straight up the road.

For an instant he was alone. Terribly alone. Then a roar welled up behind him. Those farmers had tasted victory for the first time in their harried lives. Yelling, they sprinted after the helmeted figure with the powder-blackened face.

But the effect on the Tories was even more amazing. They might have been so many tomcats, suddenly assailed by a pack of embattled mice. In sheer astonishment they jerked to a halt, staring at the mob of dusty men bearing down on them, without order, but with purpose—very obvious purpose.

The officer waved his sword and shouted orders. A scattering of shots rang out, wild, unaimed shots. The ranks wavered. A couple of men broke, fled up the road. Shots sounded from that direction, too. Blindly they turned and darted back.

The officer rose in his stirrups. "Charge!"

Straight at Abe he rode. His sword swung downward. Abe parried the blow with his heavier saber. Then man and horse hurtled past him, cut a path through the packed throng behind. Teeth bared, Abe whirled to meet the onslaught of the rest.

"Quarter! We surrender! Quarter! Quarter!"

They had not charged at all. Ranks broken, they were throwing down their arms.

The mob surged about them; a fighting mob no longer, but a crowd of what might have been school boys, whooping, delirious.

"We whupped 'em! We whupped 'em!"

"Gather up their muskets!" Abe ordered tersely. "Herd 'em together. Don't let none get away."

Everyone ignored him. Victory had gone to their heads

like rum. More men were coming down the road, the snipers who had been harrying the raiders for the past hour. Abe saw Ben Oakley, grinning through a mask of sweat-streaked dust and powder smudges.

"Where's my pa?" called Martin Post, beside him.

"Here I be, none the worse for wear!"

In the excitement the rest had forgotten the prisoner whose rescue had been one of their principal objects. They had prisoners of their own now: thirty-four of them in all. Five Tories were dead, eight wounded. Only the mounted officer had escaped. They themselves had only three wounded, none seriously. The plunder had been recovered, and most of the cattle would be rounded up eventually.

Abe felt a wave of unfamiliar emotion. Leaning on his sheathed sword, he watched the others. He had no illusions regarding the magnitude of what had been accomplished that day. A badly planned and badly carried out raid had been thwarted. There had been a minor skirmish in which a small detachment of raw troops had been overwhelmed by an aroused yokelry. But he was not thinking of that angle as he stood there a little apart from the men he had led a moment before.

"You fought," he said in a sort of detached astonishment. He spoke aloud, although he was addressing no one in particular. "By God, you fought great!"

" 'Twas you done it, Capt'n!" cried a man near by, a man he did not know. "We'd not of whupped 'em 'thout you!"

A few others heard him and turned toward Abe. They did not cheer him. They did not rush up and slap him on the back, as they did among themselves. They simply stood and looked at him, and their voices fell silent.

"Hell's fire!" Abe began, puzzled and embarrassed. "I ain't no capt'n—"

He saw their faces: flushed, exultant faces, shining eyes. But they were not looking at a nineteen-year-old farm boy, one of their own kind. They were looking at the man who had gathered them, commanded them, led them to the first victory they had ever known: a powder-blackened veteran in a crested helmet. . . . Then, suddenly, his mind's eye saw those same faces as they had appeared behind the fence a few swift minutes before: stiff, white faces, gasping mouths, trust and terror struggling in the dilated eyes that were fixed upon him. . . .

Abruptly he turned away and strode off up the road, alone.

He was perhaps halfway to the crossroads when he heard running footsteps coming up behind. He glanced back and slowed his pace, and presently Martin Post fell in beside him.

"You—going back—to the Guides?" he panted. Although he was no younger than Abe, he spoke with a curious diffidence.

"Aye, Marty. I got a hankering to get back with my own kind."

Post nodded. "I seen that. I seen a lot of things today." He hesitated. "I seen we got to fight—and not just for ourselves, like you made these fellows do, but for the whole county— the whole country, even. Ain't that what Mr. Odell meant when he was recruiting last week?"

Abe's lips twitched. "That'd about cover it."

They walked on in silence for a moment.

"You think Mr. Odell would still take me?" Post blurted finally.

"You mean you want to join up? You want to join up with a side that's been whupped right and left—that's been chased from pillar to post—that's melted away till there ain't nothing left hardly?"

"Yes, sir. We—we whupped 'em today. We can do it again."

Abe looked away. He was thinking of those frightened men leaping into the road with leveled bayonets.

"Come along," he said. "I stand in real strong with 'Mr. Odell,' and I'll see can I say a word for you."

Part 3. Not for Glory

Chapter 1

DOCTOR CORNELIUS

THE column marched at sunset. All night they
plodded southward, a full brigade of veteran Continentals, putting miles behind them tirelessly. They
traveled light, and the big forage wagons that brought up the
rear were empty. A sultry harvest moon lighted their way for
a while. Then a sharp, sudden storm drenched them, left the
air clear and cool. But it was gone as swiftly as it had come,
and the crimson August sunrise promised another scorching
day. Shortly afterward they made their first protracted halt,
cooked breakfast and tried to make up for lost sleep. But
soon the sergeants passed among them, kicking weary men to
their feet while drums beat and fifes shrilled. Midmorning
found them deep in the Neutral Ground where they made
contact with a converging column of Connecticut militia.
The combined force was the largest which had moved down
from above since Heath's ill-fated expedition against Fort
Independence seven months before.

They advanced more cautiously now, with patrols scour-
ing the country ahead and on the flanks. A little after noon
General Varnum halted the main body and sent a picked
company forward. Within an hour Abe, who had accompanied them as guide, rode back to report that they had
occupied the hamlet of Eastchester Church without firing a
shot, taking as prisoners the entire outpost, including two
dazed officers and a miscellaneous assortment of Tory
hangers-on and Negro teamsters.

The general nodded his satisfaction and turned to the

225

anxious man in civilian garb beside him. "I guess it's your party from now on, Doctor."

Drums brought the field and company officers on the run. "You know our object, gentlemen," the general said. "We will advance at once and seize the medical stores at the enemy hospital at Eastchester Church. For this work you will place your men at the disposal of Dr. Tunison here, our Surgeon General. Let me urge upon you the need for haste. We are well within the enemy advance lines here. It is but a question of time before the alarm reaches their main posts, brings overwhelming numbers swarming down on us." He turned to the three guides, standing a little apart. "Tell me from precisely which points the enemy could reach us first in force."

His eyes swept Dyckman and Odell. As though by unspoken consent, each turned to Abe.

"Come! Speak up!" the general said impatiently.

Abe gave his companions a sour look. "Well, sir, they can throw aplenty of regulars and Hessians across Kingsbridge any time, but I reckon we got more to fear from any outposts and patrols they got working to the north of here who could get in rear of us right easy. The closest force of any real size is them Tory Refugees down to Morrisania."

"Very well. We will send covering parties in both directions. Captain Dexter, you will march westward and post your company in the manner best calculated to observe the approaches in that direction. Captain Alden, I'll leave the Tories to you. Take your company southeast as far as seems discreet with the object of intercepting any attempted advance before it can gain momentum. The rest of you will proceed at once to Eastchester and get about our main business with all expedition." The general paused. "Mind you keep your men in hand. No straggling, no shirking—above all, no plundering! Let me repeat: we are not here to forage or to fight—unless we have to. Our sole object is to capture supplies so sorely needed by our army, and to get them safe away. Are there any questions?"

John Odell cleared his throat. "There's a powerful lot of them Refugees, General. Do you think just one company—"

"It's a damn fine company of Continentals!" the general interrupted. "They'll care for any number of such irregulars, never fear! However, as you are noted for your caution, I'll send you along with 'em. Kronkhyte, you will guide Captain Dexter." He smiled faintly. "You, Dyckman. I want you with the main body—where I can keep an eye on you myself!" He turned to his officers. "All clear, gentlemen? Then—posts!"

The officers dispersed, shouting orders to their men.

"Keep an eye on me, huh!" Brom Dyckman muttered indignantly. "No plundering, no fighting! What the hell kind of a raid's this?"

John Odell shook his head. "No good'll come of sending one company against them Refugees. Just irritate 'em, that's what it'll do."

Abe laughed. "Listen to old gloomy-face, will ye! Wouldn't no raid be complete without a sound-off from you, you damn old calamity howler."

"It does sound right natural," Dyckman admitted. He brightened. "Maybe this'll be a real raid, after all. Say, Abe. If you get far as Phillipse's, see can you borrow me a good horse."

Captain Dexter was forming his company as Abe rode up. They were New England men, perhaps fifty altogether.

"Take the Hunt's Bridge Road, Captain—turn right about half a mile down. I'll ride ahead and make sure all's clear."

He turned into the road, but before he had gone ten yards, the captain's voice brought him up short.

"Come back here, you!"

Abe turned in surprise. Dexter's face was flushed and angry.

"I'm giving the orders here! Understand?"

Abe stared at him in surprise. "Why—why, sure—"

"Say 'sir' when you address an officer!"

A mutter rose from the ranks. "Thick-headed Dutch bastard!"

Abe opened his mouth; closed it. "All right, sir," he said.

"That's better! Now get down off that horse and march beside me. You were detailed as a guide, and I'm not going to have you riding off where you can't be of any use."

"Use?" Abe repeated. "If you think it ain't no use scouting the road ahead, then I reckon you ain't been around the Neutral Ground much—sir."

"You're not here to give advice, but information. When I want any, I'll ask for it."

Abe shrugged and dismounted. The company stiffened at the captain's command, swung from line into column. Abe, leading his horse, fell in beside the captain at the head.

"Forward—*march!*"

Almost as soon as they turned off from the main column the road began to descend, a gradual slope to the narrow valley of the Bronx. They crossed the little river at Hunt's Bridge and came into the region known as Mile Square, a section of small freeholds carved from the vast estate of Phillipse Manor which contained all the rest of the land lying between the Bronx and the Hudson, from the Harlem to above Sing Sing. Just beyond the bridge the road forked sharply, and here, after some debate, mostly with himself, the captain posted a small picket. Then he took the column by the north fork toward higher ground, halting them at the top of the first rise. A mile or so to the northwest a dominating elevation made a rugged silhouette against the sky.

"Looks like a right nice vantage point," the captain observed. "We'll make for that."

"If there's enemy patrols out, that's where we're most like to find 'em," Abe said. "That there's Valentine's Hill—sir."

"Well, suppose you ride up there and see."

"Me?"

"Who else? You haven't lost that itch for scouting already, have you?"

"No—but—"

"If you're afraid, give me your horse and I'll go myself."

Abe said nothing. To hide his face he made a pretense of tightening his saddle girth. Then he mounted and loosened the dragoon's saber in its scabbard.

"Go straight up the road, in plain sight," the captain called after him. "If you draw fire we'll know it's occupied."

Abe did not reply. He rode at a trot over the low ground where the road passed out of sight, instinctively slowing as the winding ascent began. He felt very naked, there alone on the slope; and very foolish. By a bypath he knew he could have gained the summit easily, scouted it unobserved. Hot and cold at the same time, he put his reluctant horse to a canter.

No fire came from the hilltop. No men leaped from ambush to overpower him as he passed over the crest out of sight of his own people. The slanting fields lay still in the afternoon sunlight, bare of man or beast. At the Valentine house a woman assured him that no enemy patrols had visited the place for a week. He rode back to the top of the slope where he could be seen against the sky and waved his helmet in great circles until he saw Captain Dexter's company leave cover and start up the road.

When they arrived Abe quickly pointed out the principal features of the terrain the eminence commanded. The rolling nature of the ground, patched as it was with woods, made uninterrupted observation impossible for any distance, but stretches of several roads were clearly visible; stretches long enough so that any considerable body of troops was unlikely to pass undiscovered.

"Where's that Phillipse Manor house I've heard so much about?" the captain demanded.

Abe pointed west. "Over yonder, hard by Hudson's River."

The captain stared in that direction, but another high, irregular ridge about a mile away cut off the view.

"I expected we'd see the river from here. Why didn't you tell me we couldn't?"

"You didn't ask me—sir," Abe said drily.

The captain gave him a sour look. "Well, for God's sake! Have I got to tell you even when to wipe your nose?"

He told his lieutenants to post pickets at the best points of observation, then made a beeline for the farmhouse, from which his voice issued presently demanding something cool to drink. Weary from the night's march, the men not actually on duty sought the nearest patch of shade and were soon fast asleep. Abe, lacking orders to do anything else, tethered his horse in the farmyard and lay down under a convenient tree. The August sun made him drowsy, but sleep evaded him. Flies buzzed about him in swarms, and his sweat-soaked shirt felt clammy on his body.

After a while he put aside thoughts of sleep and sat up. The lazy afternoon was still and calm, broken only by desultory voices from the shady side of the house where the lieutenants had joined the captain and were passing a stone cider jug among themselves. He listened to them for a moment, then rose and made his way restlessly to the western brow of the hill.

The sentry posted there lay sprawled in a small thicket, snoring without inhibition, his musket across his legs. Abe crouched beside him, looking out over the low ground toward the ridge. In the wooded vale at the hill's foot random sunbeams, finding their way through the foliage, refracted a cool sparkle from the rippling surface to Tibbet's Brook. Farther off and a little to the north, the Saw Mill River Road snaked out of sight behind a wooded rise, brown and dusty, shimmering in the heat mirage.

He had watched there for perhaps half an hour when a hail from the sentry posted on the opposite brow of the hill brought him sharply alert. Turning in that direction, he saw a horseman appear on the road the detachment had followed, exchange a few words with the soldier on watch and set off toward the Valentine house.

Abe prodded the sleeping sentry with his foot. "How 'bout you keeping your own watch for a bit."

The man grabbed for his musket with one hand as he rubbed sleep from his eyes with the other. Then he recognized his disturber and his face became sullen.

"I ain't taking no orders from you."

"Ye'll take a striping at the whipping post if I report ye asleep on duty," Abe retorted. He pointed. "That yonder's the Saw Mill River Road. If trouble comes from that way, 'twill be along there."

As he approached the house, he heard the captain's dry laugh. "Out here I got about as much use for a doctor as I got for an extra pair of feet! You mean they didn't send a message or anything—just you?"

The horseman had dismounted before the officers. He was young, scarcely more than Abe's age, with a keen, pleasant face. His clothes were those of a gentleman; civilian clothes, although holstered pistols sagged from his belt.

"To tell the truth," the young man admitted, "nobody sent me." He smiled ingratiatingly. "They had so many doctors over at Eastchester that I was just in the way, so I thought I'd ride out on my own and see if I could find any excitement. We surgeons don't get much chance for this sort of thing, you know." He looked about at the sleeping detachment, at the officers sprawled in the shade. "Perhaps I picked the wrong place."

"Perhaps," the captain agreed. "How are things going over there?"

"Splendidly. We'll be loaded and on the move within the hour, I'd guess."

"Well, you might as well set and have a swig of cider."

Abe turned away and had started back toward his vantage

point when the sentry he had aroused popped suddenly out
of the thicket waving his musket.

"Hey, Dutchy! Thar's something a-coming down that
road!"

Abe reached the thicket on the run, crouched again. Nothing was to be seen on the visible stretch of road, but above
the high ground that hid it to the north a thick dust cloud
was rising. Presently, as he watched, several men came into
view, moving without haste. More followed; armed men,
though in little semblance of military formation. It was a
small column; thirty or forty men, he guessed.

The sentry's voice had carried to the officers behind the
house. They arrived panting and threw themselves down beside Abe.

"They aren't in uniform," the captain observed. "Not even
the officers, if they have officers. But we've got no troops that
far over."

Abe lifted his shoulders. "Might be anybody in the Neutral Ground. The Refugees got no uniform, neither, only the
light horse."

"Well, well? What about it?"

"Is it information you're asking or advice?"

The captain glared at him. "Information, damn you! Go
find out who those men are and report back to me!"

Abe rose without a word and returned to the house for his
horse. He was mounted and waiting to give the strange
column ample time to pass beyond sight when another rider
drew up beside him. It was the young man who had come in
a few moments before.

"Thought I'd go along, if you don't mind. I'm Cornelius,
Elias Cornelius, surgeon's mate in Colonel Webb's Regiment."

Abe eyed him suspiciously. "You don't talk like no New
Englander."

"I'm from Long Island, but there weren't any vacancies in
the New York regiments, so I took what post I could get."

He smiled amiably. "I've seen you often. Aren't you Kronk-hyte, captain of the Westchester Guides?"

"Us guides get along without no captains."

"No offense," Cornelius hastened. "I just gathered from the way—"

"Come on if you want. Stay close and don't make no more noise than you got to."

He led the way down the hill at a brisk trot, passed the intersecting road at the foot and continued westward for a short distance to where a narrow lane angled off to the south into a sizable patch of woodland, roughly paralleling Tibbet's Brook. Here he turned and proceeded more warily, though still at a good pace, halting after they had covered at least a mile.

"If they was our militia on the prowl, they'd a-come this way and we'd of caught up with 'em by now, or leastwise seen some sign of 'em," he explained. "Reckon they was Refugees and turned off to Phillipse's for free drinks. Well, Doc, have you come far enough, or do ye want to keep on with me?"

"Aren't you going back to report?"

"I got nothing to report," Abe replied tartly, "only guess-work that the capt'n would make me get shot before he'd be-lieve. I aim to have a look at what's going on below while I got the chance."

"But weren't you detailed to guide this detachment?"

Abe considered that angle, frowning slightly. "The way I see it's like this. We—me and the captain and the rest—was sent out to cover the general's flank. Well, if the capt'n sees fit to set on that hill swilling cider, maybe he knows what he's doing. It ain't likely no force will get past him so's to fall on our rear, posted like he is. But there's five miles of open country between him and Kingsbridge which he can't see from that hill and he ain't even sent a patrol through."

The young doctor nodded thoughtfully. "From which they could take us in the flank even if not in the rear?"

"Sure. And I figure finding out whether they're getting ready to do so's like to be a whole lot more important to the general than guiding a Yankee captain who just ain't going to be guided by no thick-headed Dutchman from York State."

"By heaven, you're right! Let's go!"

They pushed forward briskly. The woods ended, but Abe continued along the lane without pause. He made no attempt to avoid the occasional farmhouses where ragged children slunk out of sight at their approach, where men and women stared at them with sullenness, curiosity, or indifference. Cornelius, bringing up the rear, noted the peculiar quality of the guide's bearing: that indefinable air of alertness, the constant turning of the head as the eyes swept unceasingly right and left. His own earlier feeling of excited anticipation gave way to inner tension that grew rather than lessened as each successive rise they topped showed only open, empty country without sight of troops or movement of any sort.

He had only the haziest idea of how far they had come, when Abe, without word or sign, turned off the lane to the left. They rode across several fields, then along a narrow trail that ascended a small, tree-crowned hill. At the farther edge of the woods he reined in and motioned his companion to come up beside him. Following his pointing arm, Cornelius caught his breath sharply. Clear against the sky at the top of the next rise sprawled the brown walls of a large earthwork.

"Fort Independence," Abe said. "What the British call Fort Number Eight."

It lay a good half mile away. Beside it a few men in shirt-sleeves were working leisurely, binding sticks into fascines and arranging them in a neat stack at the base of the redoubt. In the open sally port a blue-coated Hessian leaned on his musket.

Cornelius laughed nervously. "Not exactly what one would describe as a hive of warlike activity."

Abe shook his head. " 'Tain't natural, Doc—this quiet. We got a brigade inside the enemy outposts, not counting them militia. Even supposing we caught all of them at Eastchester by surprise—this whole region's crawling with Tories. It just don't seem possible the alarm wouldn't of got somewhere in all this time." He frowned. "I got a mind to scout over to Williamsbridge, though it don't seem like—"

He broke off, raised his hand. "Shhh!"

Cornelius heard it then: a faint grumble, as of thunder very far away. It came from the southeast. The men about the fort heard it, too. Even at this distance he could see that they had stopped work, stiffened.

"There she goes!" Abe cried. "That'll bring 'em swarming!" The anxiety left his face. He spun his horse about. "Come on!"

They cut across the fields to the lane, taking fences at full gallop. Their hoofbeats drowned out the distant firing, but when Abe halted to listen halfway back to Valentine's Hill, they heard it again: not the same low grumble, but a dull, measured thudding.

"Cannon," Abe said. "And we didn't bring no cannon."

He took a short cut eastward where a larger road provided better going, and in what seemed a moment they were racing up the long slope of Valentine's Hill. The sound of the artillery was clearly audible here. The aroused detachment was clustered at the brow gazing off to the southeast through the dancing heat mirage.

"Well, what about those men?" the captain demanded.

"Men?" Abe repeated blankly. "Oh, them! The hell with 'em! The brigade'll be falling back any minute now, and I reckon we'd better be getting over the Bronx right quick!"

"Hold hard, there! I dispatched you on a definite mission. Where have you been all this time?"

"I been to Fort Independence and back. All's clear below, Capt'n. The general's flank's safe's his own barnyard back home. We can—"

"Fort Independence! I sent you to discover the identity of a dangerous force, and you—"

"There were only thirty or forty of them, Captain, and they turned off to Phillipseburgh," Cornelius interposed.

The captain whirled on him. "I'll thank you to stick to your lancet and leave the management of military affairs to officers!"

"Listen here!" Abe cried, his eyes blazing. "There'll be patrols on every road in ten minutes now the fighting's started! If you got the sense God gave a shitepoke, you'll get your men safe out of this useless post before—"

"How many times have I got to remind you that I'm giving the orders here!"

Cornelius laughed. "Then why in hell don't you give some?"

Briefly the captain was speechless. He glared at the excited young doctor, turned to his own officers and men as though to order him under instant arrest. In the brief lull the rumble from the southeast sounded louder. The soldiers were no longer looking in that direction, however. The captain glimpsed their anxious eyes upon him, and for the first time a shadow of uneasiness crossed his face.

"If the general wanted me to fall back on the column, he'd have sent me word," he began as though to himself. There was a good deal of truth in this. His jaw snapped, and he turned on Abe. "So you want orders, eh! Ride as tight as you can for Eastchester Church. If you meet an express on the road, tell him how to find us. Then report to the general and bring his wishes back to me here!"

"But who's going to guide you if—"

"Get going, damn, you!"

As he galloped down the return road, Abe heard the beat of hoofs behind him and slowed to let Cornelius come up alongside. The young doctor's eyes were dancing with pleased excitement.

"I guess we told off that damned martinet!" he laughed.

"Martinet?"

"That means an officer who's too busy acting like an officer to get on with the war. We have more than our share in this man's army."

Abe grunted. "I got to remember that word."

They pounded across Hunt's Bridge where the nervous picket shouted questions to them, and slowed on the upgrade to spare their lathered horses. Half a mile from Eastchester Church Abe called a halt.

"I don't like the look of this," he said uneasily. "We ain't met no express rider and the firing stopped ten minutes ago."

"The messenger might have taken the wrong road, not knowing where we were."

"Brom Dyckman would have found us. I think the general's just went and pulled out, figuring the capt'n'd have sense enough to come in without being told. Remember, he said he wasn't going to fight no more than he had to."

"Well, we won't find out by staying here."

Abe shook his head. "I don't like the look of it, I tell you."

He led the way forward, moving cautiously now, at a slow trot. Just short of the edge of the hamlet he halted again. They could see the church behind its comfortable green, its door and windows gaping emptily. The little cluster of houses about it appeared deserted, too. Of the forage wagons there was no trace.

"There they are!" Cornelius cried. He pointed up the single street where a column of armed men were rounding a curve; ununiformed men, moving alertly, their muskets held at the ready. "Come on!"

"Wait—"

Cornelius turned impatiently. "Hell! We've been six miles closer to the enemy than we are here!"

"That's what you think!"

But the doctor only laughed and put his horse forward at a canter. Cursing softly, Abe spurred after him.

"Halt!" Half a dozen men leaped into the road from behind a shed. One of them seized Cornelius's bridle and in a trice two others had him by the leg and coattail. "Who are you? What's your command?"

Cornelius fought his startled horse. "Let go, you fools! I'm from Colonel Webb's regiment!"

Abe grabbed for his sword. A strong hand caught his wrist. Before he could spin his horse around another man was clinging to its bridle.

"Where's General Varnum?" Cornelius shouted. "W've got to report, I tell you!"

One of the men laughed. "I'm General Varnum. Go ahead and report!"

The doctor's jaw dropped. "You—"

"Take 'em, boys!"

Abe felt himself pulled from his horse, and in an instant he was on the ground with two men on top of him. He made no resistance, let his body go limp. But Cornelius fought like a maniac. They hauled him from his horse, but somehow he managed to get free for an instant, snatched out one of his pistols.

"Surrender, you scoundrels!" he cried.

Abe turned his face away.

But the Tory leader only laughed.

"Give up, you fool, or I'll blow a brace of pistols through you!"

The doctor looked frantically about. As though for the first time he saw the gaping muzzles that covered him from every side. He wavered, and the pistol fell from his nerveless hand. As though this were a prearranged signal, the captors dropped their own weapons and went to work.

This was a type of business at which they were obviously experts. One appropriated the doctor's remaining pistol, holster, belt and all. Another flew like a homing pigeon for his watch, a third for his pocketbook. A fourth spotted his silver shoe buckles and had them off in a jiffy.

"I get his horse," the leader announced. "Which of you fellows wants the harness?"

"I do!" cried one of the men who had been going through Abe in a similar manner. "This bastard ain't got nothing worth taking."

"Hey!" protested the bewildered doctor, finding his voice at last. "I'm an officer! You can't—"

"Shut up and give me that coat you're wearing!"

"His shirt's mine!"

"Aw, hell! Let the son of a bitch keep his shirt!"

"But it's a damn fine shirt!"

"Look at this!" shouted the man who had got the pocket-book, waving his prize excitedly. "Thirty pounds he had! Thirty pounds hard money!"

"You got to split with the rest of us!"

"Like hell I do!"

In an instant they were all shouting at each other, the prisoners forgotten. Cornelius, his shirt providentially saved, leaned weakly against the shed. "You scoundrels!" he panted. "You villains! You dirty, thieving scum!" He looked helplessly at Abe, by now equally disheveled. "What manner of men are these?"

"The Morrisania gang, Doc—Westchester Refugees, they call theirselves."

The dispute over the doctor's money was interrupted by the appearance of three officers. Two of them were British, the commanders of the outpost that had been surprised by the American raiders. The third, a thick-set man of above medium height, wore the short green coat of the Westchester Light Horse.

"I appeal to you, gentlemen!" Cornelius cried. "I demand the honorable treatment accorded prisoners of war! I'm an officer and—"

The Refugee officer ignored him. He was looking at Abe. "Where have I seen you before?"

Abe felt a brief surge of hope. "Lots of times," he declared eagerly. "I used to work for your friend Squire Hilton. You remember me, Mr. Bartlet—Abe Kronkhyte."

Maxwell Bartlet's face remained impassive: a round face with heavy, rough-cut features. "Yes, I remember you." He turned to the captors. "When you're through wrangling, take 'em to Kingsbridge and turn 'em over to the provost."

"One moment, Major," one of the British officers interrupted. "It would be only fair to say that when we ourselves were taken a couple of hours ago the Rebels granted us parole at once."

"Indeed?" said the Loyalist indifferently.

"And if this man can prove that he is an officer, as he claims—"

Bartlet fixed him with a cold eye. "Permit me to remind you, sir, that the Westchester Refugees are not under the orders of the British Army and require no advice on how to deal with prisoners taken by ourselves—least of all from officers who are themselves prisoners on parole."

He turned abruptly and strode away.

Chapter 2

HESSIANS IN HARLEM

Although they tried later on, Abe and Dr. Cornelius were never able to reconstruct any very clear picture of their southward journey. Certain incidents stood out vividly enough and certain details, but chronology remained vague. The first three days following their capture formed a confused blur of weariness, hunger, unceasing abuse; incidents merging into one another until it was impossible to recall definitely whether they were being cursed, kicked and spat upon by Tories, Hessians or British at any given time.

Following his few words with Maxwell Bartlet, Abe kept his mouth firmly closed and took refuge in sullen silence. But not so Cornelius. The young doctor got over his bewilderment quickly enough, but not his indignation, and he continued to demand his rights and express his opinion of their captors with unabated vigor. This did little to ease his lot, but he declared afterward that it did much to ease his mind. And in one or two minor instances it produced results, to his own great surprise.

Their captors did not take them immediately to Kingsbridge as Bartlet had directed, but instead headed for Hunt's Tavern below Westchester Village with the avowed purpose of drinking up the contents of Cornelius's pocketbook. Before they had proceeded half a mile, they took a third prisoner, a bedraggled, powder-grimed man who stumbled into the road ahead of them, too exhausted and nerve-frayed either to fight or flee any longer. He proved to be a sergeant in Captain Alden's company, and from him they

Not for Glory

learned the fate of the detachment which had been supposed to cover the raiders' left.

"The guide—that big fellow—he kept warning the captain 'twas dangerous to push on so far with so few of us. But the captain allowed them Refugees was nothing but irregulars and the hell with 'em. Even when they begun popping up all around us—hundreds of 'em—and brung up cannon, nothing would do but we got to fight. Then pretty soon the captain was killed and that big guide just took charge of things. Reckon he got what was left of us out, since I ain't seen no other prisoners, only me."

"I'd lay to that," Abe declared. "John Odell wouldn't go into a fight with General Washington himself 'less he had his own private plan of retreat all laid out beforehand."

It was easy to understand how the detachment had been overpowered, for by now the countryside was literally swarming with armed men. They popped out of thickets by ones and twos and threes, while larger groups, organized after a fashion, were still hurrying forward from the log village at Morrisania. They reminded Abe of nothing so much as American militia turning out to defend their homes; which, indeed, was exactly what they were, in their own eyes and in the eyes of the British. Only in politics did these men differ from their brethren in the upper county—sometimes literally their brethren. They wore the same sort of clothes, talked the same language, fought the same way. And they committed the same sort of excesses: they had run the Whigs out from their midst as ruthlessly as ever the Whigs in other districts had run out their Tory neighbors; and, thanks to stronger military support, a lot more thoroughly. To Abe and his wretched companions this was enemy territory; yet it was as thoroughly American as any district in the entire country.

Their southward progress was slow, as each new group encountered demanded a look at the prisoners and a chance to curse them a bit. Abe bore the brunt of this as he was recog-

nized by many, and his activities had made him especially
obnoxious to all. Most of them contented themselves with
jeers and went on their way after a few well-chosen jibes. But
more sanguine souls, scenting free drinks, joined the party,
with the result that the original half dozen had swelled to
thirty or forty by the time they finally arrived at the tavern.

Here the baiting of the prisoners reached new heights.
Benjamin Hunt, the taverner, outdid all the others together.
A mean-faced old man with a cast to his eye, he carried
vituperation to such lengths as to appall even the Refugee
leader, who put a stop to the sport at last by ordering the
captives thrown into the cellar. This was their first encounter
with a phenomenon that soon became only too familiar: that
an individual's capacity for vindictiveness seemed in inverse
ratio to his part in the actual fighting.

They spent that night in the tavern cellar under heavy
guard, forbidden to talk among themselves under pain of
being knocked over the head with a musket butt. But by that
time they had reached a state of utter indifference. After an
all-night march topped off with the events of this day, food-
less since early morning, they slept in a stupor where they
fell, until the Refugees booted them out in the morning, still
breakfastless, to resume the march.

They reached Kingsbridge before noon where, after a final
exchange of compliments with their Tory captors, they were
turned over to the provost guard. This detachment consisted
entirely of Hessians. Although they must have been accustomed to the sight of prisoners, they turned out in force to
add their guttural jeers to the chorus of abuse from local resi-
dents. Abe and the sergeant stolidly ignored them all, but
Cornelius strode straight up to the officer who appeared to
be in charge.

"I'm a doctor," he announced. "Doctor—understand. I
rank as an officer—like you." He tapped himself on the
chest, then tapped the German, who stared at him blankly.
He spoke in a loud voice, as though to bridge the language

gap by sheer lung power. "I'm an officer, and I demand that these men be treated humanly, like honorable prisoners of war!"

Comprehension flooded the Hessian's face. *"Ach! Herr Doktor! Ja wohl!"* He bowed deeply. "You come, yess."

With every appearance of deep consideration, he led the way toward a large barn across the road. Over his shoulder he called something to his men who trooped along behind, laughing and jabbering to one another in their outlandish tongue.

Abe nudged the sergeant. "Watch yourself," he warned.

Cornelius, however, appeared oblivious to any possible untoward developments. Striding along beside the German officer, he was a picture of relieved suspense.

"We'd be grateful, sir, for a little food if you can spare it," he explained. "You see, none of us has eaten since breakfast yesterday."

The other nodded brightly, *"Ja, ja, Herr Doktor!"*

He opened the barn door and bowed again as though offering an invitation to enter. As he did so a small spyglass fell from his pocket as though by accident, directly in front of Cornelius who stooped with instinctive politeness to retrieve it for him. Quick as a cat the officer sprang back, and in a split second his polished Hessian boot, swung with all the power of a strong man, thudded against the doctor's upraised posterior, lifted him literally off the ground and flung him sprawling into the barn.

As though by prearranged signal, two soldiers grabbed Abe and the sergeant and booted them through the door with equal neatness while the rest of the crowd laughed so hard they had to hold their sides, and a few of them rolled happily on the ground.

Cornelius scrambled to his feet. His face was white, his eyes blazing.

"You son of a bitch!"

He started for the door, but Abe caught his arm. "Easy, Doc!"

"Sure," added a new voice. "All of us here made our entries the same way. That's the squareheads' idea of a hell of a good joke. Don't seem like they ever get tired of it."

Abe saw then that they were not alone. A dozen-odd bedraggled men stood about observing them incuriously.

"By heaven, I rank as an officer!" Cornelius cried. "They can't—"

"Well, I'm an officer, too," the other returned. "Prichard, lieutenant in the Connecticut Guards. I even had my commission with me to prove it."

"And you still couldn't get parole?"

"Parole, hell! They took my commission away and burned it."

The Hessians were still clustered outside the open door. Cornelius's reaction had not been lost upon them, and they waited eagerly for any attempt at violence which he might undertake. When it became apparent, however, that he had himself in control again, they slammed the door shut. It was several moments before the new arrivals were able to accustom their eyes to the semidarkness.

"When do they feed you fellows?" Abe asked the man nearest him.

"Well, now, that's kind of hard to say. They give us some bread last night, but there wasn't much left when we got done scraping off the mold."

"Ow!" groaned the sergeant. "And my poor belly flatter'n a flounder."

"Lay down and stay quiet, brother, and you won't notice it so much."

Except for Prichard, the rest proved to be enlisted men. A corporal from the light horse, oldest in point of occupancy, had been there a week. The others were victims of yesterday's raid: a sergeant and half a dozen privates from Prichard's company, and a corporal and two men from the company

Abe had guided to Valentine's Hill. This was a small enough price to pay for an operation on such a scale, but none of them was in a mood to appreciate that angle. As soon as the commotion caused by the latest arrivals had died down, they all subsided to conserve what strength they had left and hope for something in the way of food.

Abe stayed beside Cornelius. Their having been taken together formed a tie between them; besides, he sensed that if any of his companions was capable of figuring a way out of their predicament, this would be the man. But the young doctor was too preoccupied with his own troubles to give much thought to anything else at the moment, and after a few fruitless attempts to draw him out. Abe relapsed into brooding silence.

Late in the afternoon an unexpected interruption occurred. The barn door was swung open, but instead of more hapless prisoners being booted into their midst, a portly man in British uniform stepped in and peered uncertainly about.

"I say. Heard one among you's a physician. That true?"

Cornelius hesitated. "I am," he said warily. "But if you want me to administer to any sick Hessians, you can save your breath!"

"Bah! Those swine! Damn filthy swine!" The Englishman held out his hand. "I'm Carter, surgeon of the Seventeenth Foot. Fellowship of Hippocrates and all that sort of thing. Thought I'd see if there was anything I could do."

"Thanks, Doctor." Cornelius introduced himself. "I'd imagined our profession entitled me to parole, but apparently your people feel otherwise."

"Of course you're entitled to parole! I protested to the commanding officer the instant I heard you were taken. Damn filthy swine! No respect for the profession! Not that I can wholly blame them after seeing the wretches that pass for doctors among them. But you'll be granted parole once you're in British hands. Bound to be!"

"I hope you're right, sir," Cornelius said dubiously.

The British surgeon glared about with distaste. "Beastly place! Do what I can to ease your lot."

"You're very kind, Doctor. A little food would go a long way with us right now."

"To be sure! To be sure! I'll see the chief swine at once." He paused. "You haven't a newspaper hidden about you by any chance?"

"Newspaper? Good heavens! They took even my shoe buckles!"

"Just thought you might. Like to see what the Rebels say about the war. Stuff we read's too one-sided—can't be true or the war would have ended a year ago. Here. See for yourself." He drew a folded copy of Rivington's *Gazette* from an inner pocket. "Keep it. Help you while away the time."

When he had gone Cornelius took the paper to a spot where a broken board in the barn wall admitted enough light to read by. The issue was a couple of weeks old, and the first page was devoted mainly to a grandiloquent account of His Excellency Lieutenant General Burgoyne's triumphant advance from the north. He had inflicted crushing defeats on the Rebels at a number of places none of them had ever heard of, and it was a foregone conclusion that the Colonies would be cut neatly in half any day now. Cornelius read the account aloud to the accompaniment of vulgar sounds from his audience. But as unsubstantiated British triumph piled on triumph, as fresh instances of Rebel cowardice and ineffectuality were ranged beside them, the comment subsided into gloomy silence.

At last Cornelius threw the paper aside. "Lies!" he cried. "A pack of damned lies!"

But they were only too easy to believe. Hopeless men who had fought for a hopeless cause avoided each other's eyes, stared at the trampled earthen floor sullenly, silently.

The British surgeon's efforts brought results of a sort, for at sunset half a dozen Hessians appeared with food. One of them carried a bushel basket half filled with apples. He threw a handful through the doorway where they rolled in all directions. The famished prisoners leaped and scrambled for them while the Hessians roared with delighted laughter.

"Like feeding hogs," Cornelius observed. But he was much too hungry to be overnice for long. In another moment he was scrambling on the floor with the rest. The apples were small and sour, but there were enough so that each man contrived to get several. By the time they were gone, the Hessians had tired of their sport and were willing to leave the rest of the food they had brought to their victim's own devices. This consisted of a small basket of sour, moldy bread and a bucket of water into which a little rum had been poured—about a pint, Abe guessed. Poor and scanty as the fare was, it enabled them to sleep that night in a degree of comfort and awaken in the morning with their strength somewhat recruited against the trials of the new day.

At sunrise they were routed out and lined up in front of the barn. Here they were checked over by a couple of noncommissioned officers and forced to remain standing, breakfastless, sniffing appetizing odors from the Hessian cook fires a short distance up the road. After about an hour a fresh detachment arrived from below. It proved to be a relief for the guard detail, which could soon be observed getting into formation. This finally completed, the commander marched a dozen of the huskiest over to the barn where, with the aid of the sentries already posted there, they began to push the baffled prisoners about to the accompaniments of gestures and unintelligible jabbering.

"I guess they mean we're to march with them," Cornelius decided at last. "Get into some sort of column, boys."

Abe fell in beside the doctor and the rest were soon in place behind them, two abreast. With guards posted on both flanks and ahead, and the remainder of the Hessian detachment bringing up the rear, they began their southward journey.

It soon became apparent that keeping pace with their captors was going to prove anything but an exhausting task, even for scantily fed, dispirited men. These Germans were grenadiers, or heavy infantry: "Probably the heaviest damn infantry in the world," Cornelius remarked when, after half an hour of laborious going during which they covered perhaps a mile, the column halted for a ten-minute rest. Everything about them was heavy: their clothing, their arms, their accouterments. Their shoulders sagged under bulging knapsacks and blanket rolls. Clumsy canteens built to hold a gallon bounced on their hips, wide-bladed swords which they had never been known to draw in battle slapped at their thigh-high black gaiters, threatening to trip them at every step. Their blue coats were of thick woolen cloth, padded to military rigidity, and not so much as a single button were they permitted to loosen for relief. Soon they were panting, and for all the comparative cool of the morning, trickles of sweat began to show under the edges of the tall hats whose polished brass front plates glittered in the sunlight.

What was worse in some respects, they moved at stiff attention to the incredibly drawn-out cadence of the slow march, vertical muskets aligned, veritable caricatures of militarism. Even before the second half-hour's halt several men had fallen out, and the number increased rapidly after that. From the lightly clad prisoners, to whom daily marches of thirty miles or more were not unusual, a murmur of derision began to be heard. At first a few sergeants bawled for silence, but soon even this effort ceased. With Teutonic stolidity they plodded on, all taste for Rebel-baiting lost in their own misery.

"I'd feel almost sorry for the bastards if they didn't look so funny," Cornelius remarked.

The humorous aspects wore thin after a while, however, as the ravening of empty bellies began to reassert itself. For several miles their route lay along the main road leading from New York to Kingsbridge, but some distance below what had been Fort Washington the column turned eastward toward the little village of Harlem. Here they began to encounter more Hessians, fresh troops to whom prisoners were a novelty, and the bedevilment began again.

This reached its climax before the brigade's headquarters where what seemed like thousands gathered to put on a special show for the general. This lost much of its effect through the fact that the prisoners were unable to understand the dire threats being shouted at them. A burly corporal contributed a touch of realism by seizing one of them and drawing his sword across his throat while the wretch screamed in terror to the delight of all. However, with German thoroughness, he insisted on repeating the experiment with all sixteen, looking puzzled and a little hurt as the rest, now forewarned, submitted with bored indifference.

An officer who could speak English informed them dramatically that they were all to be hanged forthwith, adding what he imagined was conviction by issuing detailed orders for erection of a gibbet. But when Cornelius, able to make himself understood at last, advised him caustically not to improve on nature by making himself any more of a fool, he was utterly nonplused and withdrew with every appearance of embarrassment. When no one else came forward with an original idea, the show began to peter out.

It was brought to its conclusion by the appearance of a small British detachment: a noncommissioned officer and half a dozen red-coated soldiers who made a path through the throng by pushing Hessians disdainfully aside with their musket butts. The sergeant in charge presented a paper to the officer who had commanded the guard, then turned to the prisoners.

"All right, lads! We're in charge now. Let's get the hell out of this mob of heathen."

He herded them back toward the road. The Hessians, seeing themselves about to be deprived of their prey, raised shouts of protest which the sergeant ignored.

"Now then. Which one of you's ranking man of this crew?" he inquired when he had them more or less clear.

"Mr. Prichard here is a lieutenant," Cornelius said. "I rank as surgeon's mate."

The sergeant looked at them dubiously. Stripped to torn shirts and soiled breeches, there was nothing to distinguish the two officers from the rest of the scarecrow prisoners.

"I'll have to take your word as to that. Anyways, I'm leaving it to you two to see that the rest behave theirselves without our having to make 'em. See?"

"If you mean not attempt to escape, I'll do no such—"

"We'll see you don't do no escaping!" the sergeant interrupted. "What I mean is see they keep pace and keep order and set 'em an example. We got to get clear to the city by nightfall, and it's going to be a hell of a lot easier for all hands if we don't get called on to break a few heads on the way in."

This made good sense, and the two officers agreed. The sergeant posted Prichard at the rear of the column, Cornelius at the head. He stationed two guards on each flank, the remaining two behind with orders to prevent straggling at bayonet's point if necessary, and placed himself in front of Cornelius.

It became apparent in short order that the new escort was a very different kettle of fish from the Hessians in more ways than their attitude toward their charges. These men were light infantry and they proceeded at no such grotesque slow motion as their mercenary allies. The sergeant himself set the pace, and a brisk one it was, slackening for neither heat nor upgrade. When more than an hour passed without a halt being called, they realized that this was a forced march, and a mutter of protest rose from the prisoners.

"Close up, there! Close up! No straggling!"

The sun beat down mercilessly, a copper-colored ball glaring through the humid haze that veiled the upper sky.

The dry August landscape shimmered through the dust kicked up by trudging feet.

"Close up, damn ye! Close up!"

Abe stood the march better than most of the men. His active summer in the open had conditioned him physically, trained all surplus flesh from his light, wiry frame. Never accustomed to overmuch food, he did not suffer from the temporary lack of it. Cornelius, on the other hand, though possessing the same youthful resiliency, had lived a very different life. He weakened steadily as the grind continued. Perhaps it was his feeling of responsibility that kept him going, perhaps sheer nerve. He held his head high, eyes straight ahead, though a glaze was coming over his eyes and his face grew white and peaked.

One of the Connecticut militiamen was the first to go. Prichard steadied him when he began to reel, and an occasional prick from a guard's bayonet kept him up for a while. They had just passed the fourth milestone out of New York when, with no special warning, the man lurched sideways suddenly and sprawled inert in the dusty road. Then and only then did the sergeant call a halt.

"Get him up!" he ordered impatiently. "Couple of you carry him if you got to!"

Cornelius made his way back, turned the unconscious man over. After a quick examination, he looked up.

"Water!" It was the first time he had spoken for over an hour, and his voice emerged as a hoarse croak. He swallowed, licked his dust-caked lips. "I can revive him with a little water, Sergeant," he said more clearly.

"No time. Hist him up, some of ye!"

A woman emerged from a small shop near by on the right. "For the love of heaven, Sergeant, let the poor fellows rest!"

The sergeant fumbled for his hat. "Oh, 'tis you, Mrs. Clemmons." He shook his head. "Sorry, ma'am. I got my orders."

"In the name of humanity!" she cried. "That man's like to die if you force him on! It's not in your orders to kill him!"

The sergeant avoided her eyes. For the first time he appeared uncertain of himself. There was a brief silence. Abe looked expectantly at the two officers. Prichard's face, he saw, had the same waxen, pinched look as Cornelius's. When neither spoke, he stepped forward.

"You'll make better time in the end by letting the Doc bring him around," he said to the sergeant. "Ain't none of us strong enough to carry him fast after being all day with nothing to eat."

"Nothing to eat all day!" the woman cried. "Oh, good heavens!" She started running back toward her shop. "Wait!"

The sergeant gestured helplessly. "All right, Doc," he said gruffly. "Make it fast as you can."

He sent one of the guards to fetch water and ordered the prisoners to fall out at the side of the road. Most of them sprawled at once in the dusty grass. Abe, deciding that the brief rest would not be worth the effort required to get to his feet again, joined Cornelius who was fanning the collapsed man with his hat. When the soldier returned with water, he sluiced half of it on the man's face before taking a drink himself.

The woman called the sergeant over to the shop, from which he followed her presently, carrying two buckets of beer and looking a little sheepish.

"And don't let your redcoats swill none of it till these poor men have had their fill!" she ordered.

Her own arms were filled with bread—fresh, sweet loaves, and half a large cheese. The prisoners set up a hungry clamor which the sergeant silenced harshly.

"I'll ration this out. No fighting, mind ye!"

The beer was cool and bitter. Cornelius forced some of it between his patient's lips, and presently the man stirred and opened his eyes.

"God bless you, ma'am!" Prichard cried devoutly. "Yours is the first human treatment we have received since we were taken."

She smiled. Abe saw that she was still young, perhaps thirty, although gray already streaked her hair.

"I could do no less for fellow Americans in trouble."

"We can only thank you, ma'am." Cornelius rose to his feet, bowed. "I wish we could pay you for what I fear you can ill afford, but those cursed, thieving Tories took everything—"

The sergeant leaped toward him, eyes blazing. "Be still, you fool!"

The woman grasped his arm. "No, no!" Her expression was changing. She turned to the dumbfounded Cornelius, but her eyes were on the ground. "We are refugees from Boston," she said in a low voice. "They drove us out. They burned our home." Her lip quivered. "My husband joined the Provincials. He was killed last spring—in the Neutral Ground—"

She turned away abruptly and started back toward the little shop, running blindly, her face buried in her hands.

Chapter 3

THE SUGAR HOUSE

"Rebels! Rebels!"

"Hang the dirty bastards!"

"Tear 'em to pieces!"

"Set the dogs on 'em!"

The crowd overflowed the pavements along both sides of Broadway. Their shouts brought more running: tavern loafers, women of the streets, a scattering of soldiers off duty, all the riffraff of the city who had nothing better to occupy them. Urchins snapped like a pack of curs at the heels of the disheveled column, adding their shrill voices to the bedlam. Negroes, freed slaves filled with self-importance, swaggered beside it, cursing and striking at weary men who cringed and snarled like cornered animals.

"Make way!" the sergeant bellowed. "Beat 'em back, guards! Use your muskets if you have to!"

"Keep your heads up, lads!" Cornelius called over his shoulder. "Show the scoundrels we still have some spirit left."

But the truth was they had no spirit left. Ragged and dirty, cowed and hopeless, they were a hangdog lot, and looked it. The man who had collapsed was being supported on the shoulders of two comrades, half carried, half dragged, and another a little ahead of him was in nearly as bad condition. Lieutenant Prichard made a weak effort to second the doctor, but a stone flung from somewhere in the mob struck him on the temple, and for several blocks he too had to be half carried.

Cornelius, however, was capable of obeying his own admonition. This crowning abuse, the ferocity of this mob which far exceeded anything they had encountered before, seemed to reach something implacable inside him. Chin up, contemptuous eyes straight ahead, he marched more firmly than he had all day. A screaming slattern pushed past the guard and spat in his face, but he wiped it mechanically on his sleeve without breaking his stride.

At length they turned into a side street and halted presently before a large, imposing house. Sentries posted at the corners before the door indicated the headquarters of a high officer. With the aid of these and his own now weary guard, the sergeant contrived to get the prisoners through the mob into the quiet of the yard behind, where he left them while he went inside to report. Half the men promptly fell exhausted, but pricking bayonets aroused them.

"On your feet, ye bastards! General Jones wants to look ye over!"

Several officers emerged from the house, red-coated officers, looking very clean and cool in their spick-and-span regimentals. They sauntered along in front of the grimy prisoners, viewing them with distaste, commenting among themselves with aloof indifference.

"So these are Rebels, eh!"

"Fancy such scum attempting to fight the regulars."

"Take 'em to Livingston's Sugar House, Sergeant," ordered the one with the most gold lace when they had looked their fill.

The sergeant saluted. "Yes, sir." He hesitated. "With the general's permission, a couple of 'em's officers, and oughtn't they go to the Provost?"

The general shrugged. "All Rebels look the same to me."

A young ensign, a downy-faced boy who appeared about sixteen, strutted up to Cornelius. "Are you one of those calling themselves officers?" he demanded.

"I am an officer."

"Oh, you are an officer! I suppose you're a gentleman, too? An officer and a gentleman!"

Cornelius said nothing. Although he was little more than medium height, his level eyes stared off above the head of this popinjay.

"Speak up when you're spoken to! Do you call yourself a gentleman?"

"Yes. Do you?"

For an instant the boy was speechless. Then his face turned fiery red. "You scoundrel!" he screamed. "You damned Rebel villain!"

His voice had not fully changed, and in his rage it cracked to a high falsetto. Abe felt a sudden impulse to laugh. He yielded to it. The little ensign spun about. With all the strength he could muster, he struck Abe in the face. Abe laughed again. Instantly the boy leaped upon him, clawing, screaming like a girl. When one of the older officers dragged him off by main force, he was crying with impotent fury. Abe laughed again, more loudly.

"You've upheld the dignity of the service enough for the moment, Mr. Henry," the general said caustically. "Go to your quarters, sir! Take 'em out of here, Sergeant. They stink."

Most of the mob had dispersed while they were in the yard, but more gathered upon their reappearance. Once more their progress was the signal for jeers and abuse. After a few blocks they turned west on Crown Street into as dismal a scene as any of them had ever come upon. This section of the city had suffered severely in the fire that had been set following the American evacuation the previous year, and nothing had been done to clear up the wreckage. Here and there chimneys still stood, sometimes a few blackened timbers, frowning above cellar holes clogged with charred debris. Such few houses and shops as had not been wholly destroyed had fallen victim to looters and gaped empty and disconsolate.

But surpassing even the desolation in sinister gloominess was the Sugar House that was the prisoners' destination. A plain, gaunt building, five and a half stories high, it loomed out of the gathering dusk like a spirit of evil brooding over the destruction it might have wrought. It was old and dilapidated, its brick walls faded unevenly, stained by the elements. It lay at right angles to the street, one gabled end flush with the pavement, the rest of the building hidden by a high board fence as the prisoners drew near. In the visible portion not one whole pane of glass was to be seen, and many of the windows were without frame or sash.

Sentries posted outside gave word of their approach, and they had scarcely halted when a gate in the fence opened and several men came out. These, too, wore the red coats of British regulars, but with facings different from those of the prisoners' escort. There was something else different about them, too; something subtle and sinister. The burly non-commissioned officer who headed them carried no side arms, only a stout stick, halfway between a staff and a cane in length, which hung with seeming negligence from a rough, hairy hand.

This man the sergeant addressed. "Sixteen more for ye." He spoke curtly, without friendliness. He turned to Cornelius, and surprisingly his tone softened. "I must leave ye with Sergeant Wally now. God help ye, sir!"

They looked at their new custodian. He was not a tall man, but inordinately broad, with a coarse, wide face that was splotched with small veins which had turned purple. His upper lip was long, his mouth big, with thick lips that twisted upward at one corner. His nose was big, too, and so was his chin. Indeed, everything about him seemed big except his close-set eyes, small, hard agates: a very caricature of a provost sergeant.

"Inside with ye!"

The stout stick, hanging so negligently an instant before, swung with practiced swiftness, thudded across the back of the nearest prisoner. The man gave a startled cry, bolted blindly through the gate.

"Move, ye bastards!"

Thud! Thud! The rest of the soldiers took their chief's cue with right good will, pounding with musket butts, pricking with bayonets, heaping curses and obscenities the while. Like recalcitrant cattle the captives were herded into the prison yard. Half dead with hunger and weariness, inured to abuse as they had become, they sensed a difference here from anything they had met before. The Tories had had cause to hate them. The bullying of the Hessians had been nothing more than the horseplay of rough, unusually stupid soldiers. On the city streets they had encountered the violent, unreasoning spirit of the mob. But brutality with these prison guards was a form of self-expression, its viciousness unmitigated because it was inborn.

Abe had a hazy impression of stumbling into a large, littered quadrangle, walled-in by the fence on two sides, the main building and a large ell on the others; of ragged, sorry figures scuttling out of the way. His back smarted where a blow had struck him, and blood trickled down his right thigh from a bayonet prick. He kept his head up as best he could and managed somehow to stay close to Cornelius as they were driven across the prison yard and through a sagging doorway into the dark, foul interior of the Sugar House itself.

"Break 'em up! Put 'em in different cells!"

Groping in the darkness, they were hustled along a narrow hallway, up a steep staircase. At the top of the first flight a door was opened, admitting a little gray light.

"In there, you!"

Abe impulsively caught Cornelius's arm, clung to it, as a guard seized him. Another guard caught the doctor from the other side, and the two of them were hurled headlong into the room. Behind them the door slammed and a bolt clicked into place.

"Jesus!" groaned a voice from somewhere in the gloom. "Ain't we crowded enough already?"

Abe lay where he had fallen. He had an impulse to get up, but it occurred to him that there was no useful purpose to be served by doing so. There was no use in anything. He felt Cornelius stirring beside him, heard his voice; other voices. But he remained supine.

A year before, when the Rebels had thrown him into White Plains Jail, he had cried with terror, frustration, broken nerves. He did not cry now. Head pillowed on his arm, he stared unseeingly at the worn board floor from dry, hard eyes until the sleep of sheer exhaustion closed them.

Whether it was the stench that awakened him or the rain, Abe was never quite sure. He had been aware of the stench for some time as he drifted slowly out of his deep sleep: the smell of unwashed human beings and a more fetid smell, thick and nauseating. But the rain was a more tangible thing: a steady drip-dripping that soaked his shirt and at length sent a clammy trickle down his back. He sat up and rubbed the sleep from his eyes.

Daylight, shining through a paneless window, revealed a small, narrow room. Gray, cheerless light of a stormy morning, it fell wanly across a more woebegone collection of men than Abe could have conceived. Clothed in filthy rags, many of them half naked, they sat huddled in their crowded quarters trying as best they could to avoid the water that dripped or trickled from a dozen leaks in the sagging ceiling. Matted beards hid their faces, but the emaciation of their bodies was evident enough.

"We got it better here than most," one of them observed, following Abe's glance ceilingward. "The roof of this place ain't been fixed in years, but them above soak up a whole lot of rain that don't never get through to us."

Cornelius rolled over and sat up. With only four days' growth of beard, he looked almost clean-shaven beside the others.

"Phew! What a stink!"

"You'll get used to it, mister," said the man who had addressed Abe. "You see, we ain't got no necessary here."

"No necessary? Then what—" He followed the man's gesture to the room's one empty corner. "Gaah!"

"They lets us clean it out once in a while if we behaves good," the man said wryly.

Cornelius found his voice with an effort. "They must be mad! My God! We'll have a pestilence here in no time!"

"We got a pestilence here, mister. Men are dying off eight to ten a day. We been hoping that when the weather turns cold maybe it won't be so bad."

"No," jeered another. "Come winter, we'll die of lung disease 'stead of pestilence."

Cornelius opened his mouth to speak, closed it. The shock to his professional instincts was visible in his face. Oblivious to the water that dripped ceaselessly from above, he squatted where he was, his brow wrinkled in what appeared to be an effort to grasp this new problem, cope with it. The others soon lost interest in him and turned their attention to Abe. What they craved most was news of the world outside, of the progress of the war. But Abe could tell them little enough beyond describing his own capture and the events leading up to it.

The older inmates numbered eleven all told, an assorted crew. Several of them had been captured at Fort Washington the previous fall. The newest of them had been there three weeks. They came from different parts of the country, from different walks of life, but misery had reduced them to a common level that made individuals all but indistinguishable. Packed in as they were, it was some time before Abe was aware of their number or realized that the two who lay silent by the window were sick of the pestilence to the point of death. About the only hope that sustained any of them stemmed from the persistent rumor that, somehow, an exchange of prisoners would free them. When Abe could not

substantiate such rumors with firsthand evidence from behind their own lines, they lapsed into gloomy silence, lacka-
daisically plucking at the vermin that infested them. When
Cornelius brought up the possibilities of escaping, they only
shook their heads. Those who had tried it had been clapped
into irons and thrown into the dungeon in the cellar. None
of those they knew of personally had been seen or heard of
again.

After a while the bolt was drawn on the outside and a
guard's head appeared.

"Bring out your dead!" he shouted.

"We got none today," one of the men said.

"Ye will have, ye bastards! Ye will have!"

"What do they do with the dead?" Cornelius inquired
when the bolt had been shot again.

"We stack 'em in the yard outside the door. Soon's there's
a cartload, they take 'em off and bury 'em somewhere."

"You'd think they were deliberately trying to kill us!"

"Well, this is cheaper than shooting us, ain't it?"

The doctor subsided, frowning harder than ever. His
revery was interrupted by a sudden din from below. The
other men, so lackadaisical an instant before, sprang to their
feet and fought for places at the window!

"Food! Food, for the love of heaven!"

"Help us, sir! We're starving!"

Peering over and between the crowded heads and shoulders, Abe saw that the window was in the gable end of the
building that faced Crown Street. All the other windows on
that end appeared to be similarly crowded with screaming,
supplicating men. Their object was in the street below, a
small farm cart piled high with cabbages and turnips. The
driver, evidently appalled by the din and the sight of five
stories of windows packed with thin, bearded faces, came to
an uncertain stop, whereupon the shouting was redoubled.

"Keep moving, there!" a guard's voice ordered.

Still the driver hesitated. Impulsively he caught up a cabbage and tossed it to the nearest window where a score of frantic hands tore it to bits. Before he could toss another, a guard ran up and sent the horse bolting down the cobbled street with a blow from the flat side of his musket. The chorus of supplication changed to groans and cursing. The guard looked up at the windows, grinned and thumbed his nose.

"God!" Cornelius was staring at the scene from Abe's side. "Our soldiers—begging food that way, from any passer-by!"

"They're hungry, Doc. Even hungrier than us, I reckon."

Cornelius turned away. "One thing's certain: we must get out of this place before—before we're reduced to that!"

"Fine! But how?"

"Let me think. There must be some way."

He retired to a corner by the door, empty now that the cell's other occupants crowded the window. The working day had begun and more people were passing outside, pedestrians and wheeled traffic on the way to and from market, and the prisoners continued their cries. The sentries posted outside made no effort to check the din, whether because of sadistic enjoyment or realization of the moral effect upon the populace of this Rebel degradation; but they were quick to hurry along any passer-by who exhibited merciful tendencies. Abe watched the scene for a while, then went over and sat beside Cornelius. To his straightforward mind, getting out of this place involved simply figuring a method of escape that had some chance of success, but the doctor silenced his suggestions impatiently.

Their fellow prisoners' state became more comprehensible soon after when rations were issued. This was an event, the others told them, that usually occurred every fourth day. To feed the cell's inmates for that period of time, four pounds of moldy bread was dumped unceremoniously on the floor, together with an equal weight of Irish pork which had been contaminated by bilge water on its way across the Atlantic, and a bucket of drinking water drawn from the pump in the yard outside that was faintly brackish and smelled nearly as bad as the pork.

About midmorning a guard opened the door again and ordered the two newest arrivals to report to the provost sergeant. He escorted them, pushing them forward roughly when they slowed to grope their way down the dark, narrow stairs, and thrust them at length into a small, dingy room on the ground floor. At a paper-littered table Sergeant Wally of His Majesty's Twentieth Line Regiment lolled in a wide chair beside a sour-faced civilian clerk, his ubiquitous stick hanging indolently from his hand.

"Well, my pretties," he greeted them. "And how do yez like the fine, airy quarters his Majesty generously provided for the likes of you?"

The clerk poised a quill above a large ledger. "Give your name, rank and regiment, and be quick about it."

"Elias Cornelius, surgeon's mate, Colonel Webb's Regiment," the doctor returned without hesitation. Then, as the clerk was in the process of writing it down, he added unexpectedly, "And Abraham Kronkhyte here is my assistant."

"Hey!" interjected the sergeant. "Since when has surgeon's mates got assistants?"

Cornelius registered surprise. "Why, they always have in our army."

The sergeant blinked. He glanced doubtfully at Abe, whose mouth was hanging open in astonishment.

"Why should we give a damn what the Rebels want to call themselves?" the clerk said wearily, making another entry in the ledger.

"Look here, Sergeant," Cornelius began. To Abe's surprise, his voice was suave, pleasant. "Let's be reasonable about this. You are burdened with a number of sick here, and I chance to know that all the hospitals in the city are overcrowded and understaffed. Now, if my assistant and I were granted parole, we could be very useful to—"

"You ain't going to get no parole!"

"But why not?"

"Because you ain't, that's why!"

Cornelius swallowed. "That is not your responsibility, of course. If you will allow me pen and paper so that I may write direct to Sir Henry Clinton—subject to your approval, of course—"

"Like hell I will!"

Cornelius's unnatural control cracked. "Then I'll write a letter that you won't see! My father happens to be a Tory and a dear friend of the general—"

The sergeant rose ponderously. "You son of a bitch!" He lurched around the corner of the table. The purple vein-splotches stood out sharp on his dough-colored face as he thrust it within inches of the American's. "You're a Rebel doctor, huh!" The heavy stick flicked upward. "Then dose yourself for that!"

Cornelius reeled a few steps backward from the force of the blow. Instinctively he raised his hands to protect himself. Then the hands dropped to his sides, and he stood quite still. There was not a trace of fear in his face; only icy, unmitigated contempt. It was the sergeant's eyes that wavered. His staff, upraised again, sank slowly.

"Take 'em out of here!" he ordered.

Back in their cell, Abe ministered to his companion as best he could. The blow had taken Cornelius across the side of the face. Blood poured profusely from his nose, and a great black bruise was closing his left eye, but he was laughing.

"By heaven, I think it's going to work!"

"I think he knocked you dizzy," Abe retorted. "Hold still now, while I mop up this mess."

He swabbed the doctor's bloody face and neck with a rag torn from his shirt which he soaked in the stinking water bucket while the cell's other inmates begged him to go easy on their supply.

"I'm not dizzy by a damn sight," Cornelius protested. "He's

scared, I tell you! That dog hasn't the courage to be even a first-rate bully! Mark me: he'll get rid of us just on the off-chance we might make trouble for him."

"Aye! He'll get rid of us by putting us in some worse place!"

"No place could be much worse."

Abe pondered that. Events of the past few days had made him skeptical.

"Is it true your pa's a Tory?" he asked after a moment.

The doctor's expression changed. "Aye, he's a Tory," he said slowly. "He's sworn allegiance to the Crown and lives among them by choice—he and my grandfather and my brothers and sisters. But I doubt if he has any influence with General Clinton."

He paused, and a faraway, bitter look came into his one open eye. "And if he had," he added, "I doubt if he would lift a hand to help me if I were rotting of the plague in the lowest stinking dungeon his dear friends could devise!"

The rest of the day dragged by wearily. During the afternoon the prisoners were allowed to clean their cell, then taken to the enclosed yard for a half hour. To their companions this was a rare treat, but Abe and Cornelius found it depressing. In the cell there had been only a dozen men to see. In the yard there were hundreds: filthy, bearded, emaciated, foul-smelling men who shambled about with lowered heads; whose eyes, when you saw them, were like the eyes of animals—baleful, crafty, miserable by turns, with here and there smoldering sparks of desperation, hatred. More than anything he had seen, felt or thought, the spectacle of this mass of men in the process of being broken focused Abe's determination to escape.

Back in the cell he turned his mind to ways and means. He had little faith in the success of the doctor's expedient, and no great taste for it in any case. He had noticed that the board fence surrounding the yard was not so high but that it might be scaled by two determined men working together; but, of course, the guards would be on the lookout for precisely such a break. Access to the street from the cell's second-story window was ridiculously easy; but there again the means was so obvious that guards had been posted specially to cope with it. And even if, by some miracle, the sentries could be avoided for a moment—what chance had hunger-weakened men at large in a strange city teeming with alert enemies?

How weakened they really were was demonstrated graphically the following morning. One of the sick men died during the night, and the combined strength of four of the older inmates was required to lift the corpse, wasted though it was, until Abe and Cornelius took it from them and carried it easily outside.

" 'Twon't be long before we're like that, too," Abe said grimly. "If we're a-going to get out, it's got to be right quick."

"Never fear! We'll get out."

And Cornelius was right. Before noon they were haled once more to the guardroom where they found another prisoner waiting, a man of superior bearing who wore the dilapidated remnant of a Continental captain's uniform. But Abe did not like the look on Sergeant Wally's face when he addressed them.

"So ye think ye're too good for the Sugar House, huh? Well, I found a place for the likes o' ye!"

Again they were marched through the streets. Their guard set a course toward the Common, then across it to a tall, square building topped by a cupola. Although it was smaller than the Sugar House and much newer, it had the same indefinable aspect, at once dismal and sinister.

"Oh, my God! The Provost Jail!" muttered the man in the captain's uniform.

"Shut up! Inside with ye!"

In a dingy office that might have been Sergeant Wally's they lined up before a man who might have been Wally's own brother, even to the heavy stick he carried. He squinted at a paper the guard from the Sugar House handed him.

"Who of you's the doctors?" he demanded.

Cornelius stepped forward. After a second's hesitation, Abe followed. The sergeant eyed them malevolently, turned to a knot of soldiers lounging behind him.

"Throw the other bastard into Congress Hall," he ordered, "and bring these two along after me."

He led the way down a flight of stone steps that lost themselves to sight in a yawning cavern. Somewhere a bolt grated, and they were pushed in that direction, groping in the murky light along a wall that was clammy with congealed moisture.

"In here!"

They had learned to let themselves fall limply by this time. The stone floor was hard and damp.

"Here's a doctor for ye, ye damn Rebel!"

The sergeant's voice was a senseless jeer. An iron door clanged shut, leaving them in total darkness.

Abe raised himself without haste to a sitting position. "Aye, Doc—that fine plan of yours sure worked to beat hell," he said.

Chapter 4

THE PROVOST

"Is one of you really a doctor?"

Abe and Cornelius started. For an instant they had imagined that they were alone. Now, as their eyes began to adjust themselves to the half-light, they saw that the dungeon was quite large, that the shadows huddled along the walls were the figures of other men. One had risen and was standing before them.

"I'm Travis, late commander of a Continental sloop of war," he said. He spoke in the soft accents of Virginia. "Come over here, if you will be so good. Captain Chatham stands in need of your attentions."

"You're officers? Here!"

"Of course. Don't you know where you are?"

"Someone said the Provost Jail."

"That's right—reserved for what the British consider the most notorious Rebels. You'll find the company very select."

The sick man lay in one corner on a small heap of moldy straw covered with filthy rags. He had been captain of a Pennsylvania privateer, and his claim to being a "notorious Rebel," it appeared, lay in his refusal to pilot the fleet that captured him up the Delaware. Cornelius diagnosed his ailment as a severe case of nervous fever, but, wholly lacking medical supplies, there was little he could do.

Nine of the cell's dozen occupants turned out not to be officers or even soldiers, but forgotten leftovers from the time when the building had been used as a civil prison: a choice collection of cutthroats, cutpurses, thieves and murderers.

269

The only other officer besides Travis and the sick Chatham was John McCalsenden, quartermaster of the First New Jersey Battalion of the Continental Line. He had been accused of deserting from the British army six or seven years before the war began and was under sentence to be hanged.

"I only wish they'd hurry up about it," he declared sardonically. "After six months in this hole, hanging will be welcome!"

"And you said there couldn't no place be worse than the Sugar House!" Abe said to Cornelius.

"Oh, there are worse places than this," Travis assured them. "Chatham and I figure we're right lucky to be here. On those prison ships in the East River, where they put most of the seagoing prisoners, men are packed in so thick they have to take turns lying down. Besides, it isn't so bad up topside. These are punishment cells down here."

"Punishment? What offenses call for punishment here?"

"Well, that depends what sort of mood that son of a bitch Cunningham happens to be in. Chatham and I were so indiscreet as to ask for a drink of cold water when he was still in the throes of a hangover."

"Who's he—the sergeant who brought us down?"

"No—sergeant's name's Keith. Captain Cunningham is his boss—the Provost Marshal. Except that he has more imagination in devising ways to be devilish, there's not much to choose between 'em."

The seriousness of Captain Chatham's condition gave Cornelius genuine concern. His illness had reached the critical stage where it was touch and go whether he lived or died. A little fresh air might save him, a little of the right medicine; even a small store of decent food to strengthen his resistance could well be the deciding factor. But the rations here were about like those in the Sugar House: two pounds of meat and two pounds of bread per week—about one-third the British soldier's ration, Travis said, and more often than not drawn from condemned stores. Although both

he and Chatham had a little money with them, they had been
refused permission to purchase anything for themselves.

"For the love of heaven, Sergeant," Cornelius pleaded
the next time Keith appeared, "take this man upstairs. He'll
die if you keep him here."

Keith laughed. "We won't charge nothing to bury him."

"At least get me some medicine for him."

"Go to hell!"

But Chatham did not die. He turned the corner somehow
and began slowly to become lucid again after days of de-
lirium. He was pitifully weak and gained strength imper-
ceptibly on the miserable food, but Cornelius assured them
all that he was recovering.

"Don't credit me, though," he added. "No doctor or anybody else has any real conception of what the human constitution will stand. Remember that, Abe. Remember it
when you're sick or starving or exhausted to the point where
you feel you can't go on. Because you can go on, long after
your conscious mind has given you up."

Abe did remember that admonition. It was one of the two
things that he did remember clearly from the three dreary
weeks they spent in the dungeon of the Provost.

The other was his first view of the fabulous Captain Cunningham, the night McCalsenden was hanged. Accompanied
by two guards and Keith who was carrying a lantern, he
swaggered into the cell at midnight, took a few random kicks
at such men as lay within reach, and thrust a handful of
ropes under the condemned man's nose.

"Pick your own halter, ye dirty turncoat!"

The lantern rays, shining upward, patched his face with
high light and shadow; a gross face, oddly distorted. Narrow
eyes glittered, thin lips smiled in sheer pleasure. Seen behind prison bars, this might have been the face of a particularly vicious criminal. To see it above the dapper uniform of a British officer was somehow uncanny, intensifying
subtly its aspect of horror.

But McCalsenden was going to give no more sadistic pleasure than he had to. He examined the ropes indifferently, tested them in his hands.

"This one will do nicely, thank you."

Cunningham's smile faded. "Seize him!" He spun about and shook the remaining halters at the cell's other occupants. "I'm saving the rest of these for you!" he snarled.

The guards fell upon the prisoner, bound his arms, gagged him, blindfolded him. Then they thrust him roughly outside, and the door clanged shut. That was all. It was over in a matter of seconds. But the cell's familiar darkness was different.

Abe's sharp intake of breath broke the choked silence. "My God! He—he looked like something out of—out of the infernal regions!"

Travis cursed in a low tone. "If I ever get free again with a gun in my hands . . ."

On his filthy pallet by the wall Chatham stirred faintly. They could not see him, but his voice was clear enough; a weak voice speaking with the detachment which comes to the very ill.

"I wonder," he said thoughtfully, "how long it will be before England harvests the crop of hatred her servants are planting in the hearts of all America."

It was September twentieth when they were removed from the dungeon in the basement of the Provost, though by then they had lost track of dates. At Sergeant Keith's orders they carried Captain Chatham up the stone stairs as gently as they could and from thence up more stairs, wooden this time, to the second floor. The sergeant cursed and taunted them over the entire distance. Abe wondered why he wasted the breath. They had become so inured to abuse long since that even Cornelius paid no more attention than he might have to the scolding of a sparrow.

Their new quarters proved to be a long, cheerless room

that ran the whole depth of the building. It was bare of furniture or floor covering, save for a small iron stove near one end. After the gloom of the dungeon it appeared extraordinarily bright, for there were windows on three sides. On two they looked out into the prison yard, but on the third there was a view of the street and the Common beyond. Men were everywhere: sitting and lying on the floor, striding restlessly up and down. A dozen of them called greetings to Travis and Chatham and, as soon as the sergeant had left, gathered around them. Abe and Cornelius, ignored for the moment, glanced about at their new surroundings.

The occupants of "Congress Hall," as they had ironically christened it, were of many types, from many different walks of life. Some were sick, some were well, but all were lean, emaciated, dirty. Imprisonment had placed a common stamp upon them, as it had upon the wretches in the Sugar House. Yet these men were different from those others. They were officers, and to some extent picked officers. Perhaps their moral fiber was stronger; perhaps they had greater resources within themselves. For some reason, or combination of reasons, prison was not breaking their spirits.

At first Abe was uncomfortably conscious of his own inferior position, and there were those among the officers who showed a tendency to look down upon him. But prison was a great leveler, and most of his new companions accepted him as a matter of course. He was at pains to be as unobtrusive as possible and to maintain a respectful attitude while making himself helpful in any capacity he could.

Cornelius, being younger than most of the others and comparatively low in rank, was in a somewhat similar position. Thus he and Abe were drawn still closer to one another while finding a place for themselves in the curious society to which that crowded room gave birth. Besides Travis and Chatham who had shared the dungeon with them, there were three other officers whom Cornelius had known before their capture and who were glad to resume his acquaintance:

Major Williams and Captains Paine and Wells. Although he did not realize it until much later, this long association on terms of equality with men of superior background and education did much to broaden Abe and to mature him.

All of the prisoners had tales to tell of their capture and its aftermath, some of which, though fairly typical, made the experiences of Abe and Cornelius appear tame. There were cases of men who had been driven at forced march for as long as three days without a scrap of food; of sick men who had been allowed to lie in the filth of dysentery for a week. Four reputable officers taken at Fort Washington had been carried through the city streets for hours in a cart with halters around their necks for the edification of the populace, even brought to the foot of a gibbet. Of some 5,000 captives in the city and on the prison ships, it was reported that 1,500 had already died.

"There's one thing all this has done for us, though," Major Williams observed grimly. "It has shown the meanest spirited wretch in our ranks that is far better to die like a man in battle than surrender himself to the tender mercies of the British."

The ranking officer in Congress Hall was Colonel Ethan Allen of the Hampshire Grants, a burly, surly ruffian who had little to do with the others, but spent most of his time glowering out the window at the Common. One day, by dint of tactful patience, Abe drew out his story; a story that put the worst of the others to shame.

Allen was the man who, at the outset of the war, had captured Fort Ticonderoga by surprise. The following fall, during the first northern campaign, he had been taken prisoner during a rash attempt on Montreal and promptly ironed in the hold of a man-of-war where he was subjected to beatings and all manner of abuse. In a rage he had knocked one of his jailers unconscious with a blow of his manacled hands, after which he had been chained flat on his back. For six months he had been kept that way, save for occasions when he was brought out as an exhibit.

They had taken him to England to show the folks at home what a real Rebel looked like. Twice they had brought him ashore there, marched him through the streets to a gibbet, only to "reprieve" him at the last moment. They had repeated this show in Ireland, then brought him back to Halifax and staged the same show again. Tiring of their sport at last, with outraged Americans threatening reprisals on captured British officers, they had finally brought him to New York where he had been paroled for a short time, only to be thrown into the Provost for no reason he could name.

"I guess they just got an antipathy against me," he concluded.

He told his story with a directness and simplicity that had in it a certain rough eloquence. Others gathered to listen, though most of them had heard the tale before. When he finished there was a moment of silence.

"It seems incredible," someone said, "that the British, from whom most of us are directly descended, should prove to be such a race of monsters."

"That is not quite true," Captain Paine said. "The British are no more a race of monsters than we are. It is simply that the decent men among them draw aside from the unpleasant business of running prisons and leave it to those who have a natural taste for it: the vicious, the depraved, the corrupt—a splendid way of using those bullies who are too cowardly to be relied upon in battle."

"Doesn't that amount to the same thing?"

"I hope not, for if it does I fear we are tarred with the same brush—or will be before the war is much older. Prison guards are much the same in all armies. Decent men gag at such unpleasant but necessary duty and are glad to leave it to those with a taste for it." He looked about. "In all honesty, would any of you gentlemen willingly accept domination over British prisoners such as this brute Cunningham holds over us?"

"I would—and with pleasure!" Allen declared, so grimly that they all laughed.

Several of the occupants of Congress Hall and other rooms in the big building were natives of the city and had relatives still living there. These often made attempts to visit them but were as often refused permission. When women—mothers, sisters, wives, sweethearts—loitered on the street outside in hopes of glimpsing or exchanging signals with inmates, the sentries drove them off mercilessly, beating at them with canes and ramrods. Nevertheless, this gave Cornelius an idea. With money borrowed from Travis, he contrived to bribe one of the guards to smuggle out a letter to his father. The latter's standing as a Loyalist accomplished what the others had failed, and two days later the doctor was summoned down to the barred wicket on the ground floor.

He was gone for only a few minutes, and there was a dazed, stricken look in his eyes when he returned. It was an hour before Abe was able to worm from him what had happened.

"When I first saw my father standing there, I broke down," Cornelius confessed. "For a moment I couldn't speak, just held his hand through the grille and cried like a baby. 'What do you think of yourself now?' says he. 'You, my own son, confined in this hideous place like a common criminal! Why could you not have been forewarned by me where your rebellious course would take you?'"

Cornelius paused and clenched his hands. "My God! Does he imagine that mere willfulness would cause a man to turn his back on home and loved ones—throw himself into the world, so to speak? I didn't have a relative or even an acquaintance in the army when I took service. Indeed, I didn't have a relative in the world who was not openly in sympathy with the enemy. And he treats me like a froward boy who has been led astray!"

"Did he say anything about helping you get out?" Abe inquired practically.

Cornelius raised his hands in a hopeless gesture. "He wanted to know why I hadn't accepted General Howe's offer of amnesty and come in to beg forgiveness like a sniveling coward! I turned my back and walked away."

He choked and tears started to his eyes again.

"I thought I had made the ultimate sacrifice short of my life for the cause," Cornelius continued after a moment. "Well, I guess now I really have. But it's bootless to think of that. Let us draw strength from the thought of how much more others have suffered to the same end. Thousands have died. More thousands have been crippled, that a free nation may arise, with justice for all. We, at least, are still alive and may yet be able to strike another blow for the cause."

"You mean, take it out on these bastards for what they have done to us?" Abe asked doubtfully.

"Well, not exactly." Cornelius paused and his mouth twisted into a wry grin. "Or perhaps that *is* what I mean, at least in part."

In spite of his adamant attitude, however, the elder Cornelius did do a little something to alleviate his son's lot. He made up a bundle of the doctor's clothes, included a sizable sum of money and, partly by political influence and partly by a large bribe, prevailed upon Sergeant Keith to deliver it at Congress Hall. Cornelius's first impulse was to send it back without a word, but the others persuaded him not to be a quixotic fool. The clothes provided him and Abe with the first change of linen they had had in more than a month. The money he used to bribe a guard to get him some medical supplies with which he set about administering to the growing number of sick among them.

He tried to extend this field of operations in mid-October when the officers captured at Fort Montgomery were brought into the Provost. These were quartered in two small rooms directly beneath Congress Hall, packed in so tightly that when they wished to turn over at night while sleeping on the bare board floor, they all had to turn together, at a word of command. Many were seriously wounded, and their groans carried clearly to the men above. Cunningham, in a moment of unprecedented good humor, agreed to permit Cornelius to treat them the following day. But when that day came, his good humor had vanished. He whacked Cornelius across the back with his cane and told him gruffly that he would be put in the dungeon and left there if he mentioned the subject again. The next time they were up on the roof for one of their rare periods of exercise, however, the doctor contrived to drop a package of lint and ointment down the chimney flue to the floor below with directions for its use.

Subsequently they established more direct communications by loosening a board in the floor. Thus they were able to learn the details of the debacle. They knew now that the Hudson was open to the enemy all the way to Albany. There remained nothing to prevent the army in the city from making direct contact with General Burgoyne's force which was coming down from Canada, bowling over opposition like a juggernaut, from all earlier reports. Another of their few lingering hopes was crushed.

Isolated here, they were wholly without news of the outside world; without even the rumors and tavern gossip that flew thicker and wilder as October wore on. It became apparent that, after all, Burgoyne had not yet reached Albany, was long overdue. As days dragged on with no word of any sort from him, tension grew in the city until it penetrated even to the Provost. The guards became taut, jumpy. Cunningham and his alter ego were more surly and abusive than ever. From the windows the prisoners could see people gathering to talk in apprehensive groups. One day a passing woman paused and, before the guards could drive her away, shouted to the watching prisoners: "Burgoyne is taken!" and briefly they were electrified.

Cunningham quickly dashed their hopes, however, by

bringing them the latest issue of Rivington's *Gazette*. Captain Paine read the leading news story aloud.

"Last Thursday the rebels came to Elizabeth-town Point, to enlist recruits for the rebel service, and in order to deceive raised a false report, fired cannon, made fires, and gave away rum without measure, and said that General Burgoyne and his whole army were taken prisoners. But notwithstanding all their efforts they could not get a single man. And the account of General Burgoyne being taken prisoner is too ridiculous to be believed."

They were silent after he had finished. They had all learned better than to take Tory newspapers at anything like face value. But such a rumor was indeed ridiculous. Their earnest efforts to make themselves believe it seemed wishful thinking. When several more days failed to bring an atom of corroboration, they gave up all pretense of believing, clinging to the wishful hope that some small part of the rumor might have foundation.

Most of them had abandoned even that by the time confirmation arrived. It came with dramatic suddenness that was breath-taking. Early in the evening of a day that had been just about like every other, they were passing the time as best they could when, without the slightest warning, pandemonium broke loose in the cell below them. Men screamed, shouted, beat upon the door, smashed out the windows. The concerted din drowned individual voices, made words indistinguishable. Whether it was a riot or an attempted jailbreak, the listeners could not tell. Cornelius, fearing that they had all gone stark raving crazy at once, removed the loose floor board and peered down, to have a folded paper thrust up into his face a moment later.

It was a letter to one of the Fort Montgomery prisoners from his father, which, through some unexplained oversight, had got by the authorities and been delivered. It named names, dates, places. With a matter-of-factness that seemed almost grotesque to these news-avid prisoners it listed the regiments which had surrendered and itemized the spoils. Before the doctor had read a dozen lines, the din in Congress Hall had drowned out that of the cell below.

This was victory! What mattered it that Philadelphia had fallen, that the Congress had fled half across Pennsylvania, that Washington, defeated in two major battles, had been driven into the hills? Burgoyne and his whole army were taken! This was victory—and something more. With the strange intuition of men long detached from the active world, they sensed that the tide of the entire war had turned. For once the guards were powerless to control them. Only as exhaustion overcame weakened bodies did they lie down, one by one, to sleep off their exuberance until another cheerless dawn brought them back to the grim reality of the Provost.

About a month after they had heard the news of Saratoga, Abe was mystified at being summoned down to the first-floor wicket as Cornelius had been before. A visitor awaited him there, an officer in a green coat, silver-laced, his right arm in a sling. Abe needed a second glance at the pale, peaked face, to recognize him.

"Major Bartlet told me you'd been taken," the Young Squire said. "I had some difficulty locating you, or I should have come sooner."

Abe clasped the hand extended to him through the bars. They looked at each other in silence across the year and a half that lay between them.

"What happened to your arm?" Abe asked at last, unable to think of anything else to say.

"I stopped a Rebel bullet at Brandywine—was invalided back here before we took Philadelphia."

"Oh," Abe said.

Again the silence protracted itself, the uneasy silence of men who had become strangers. Hilton broke it with visible effort.

"Well," he said, trying to make his voice brisk and cheerful, "I owe you a debt that I'd like to repay. There's little enough a mere Provincial can do"—his lips twisted ironically—"toward effecting your release or exchange, but perhaps I have the means to make your lot more endurable."

"You owe me a debt, Squire?"

"For that Mamaroneck business, of course." His level eyes were thoughtful. "You risked your life to save me—a man in arms against you. It's the only instance I know of where something fine has risen above the all-pervading hatred this damnable war has engendered."

Abe looked at the floor. "I don't know why I done it, Squire. Seems like I don't know why I done most of the things I done. I'm only just now beginning to find out."

The Young Squire inquired about Abe's family and about Hilton Manor. Abe told him what little he could. Constraint sat heavily upon them. Neither spoke of his war service nor inquired about the other's. The changing months separated them far more effectively than the tangible iron bars through which they faced each other.

"I'll do what I can with the authorities," Hilton said as he prepared to leave, "though I promise you it's likely to be little enough." He drew a bulging purse from his pocket and handed it through the grille. "Here. This ought to help you in the meanwhile."

Abe shook his head. "I don't want your help, Squire."

"What do you mean?"

"I aim to get loose out of this place, and when I do—" Abe hesitated. " 'Twould be only fair to tell you, Squire," he blurted. "If Mamaroneck was to happen over again tomorrow, I—I wouldn't do like I done before."

"Oh," Hilton said slowly. It seemed to Abe that his shoulders slumped a little, that his face looked old and tired and infinitely sad. "So that has gone, too, the way of—so much else." He straightened with an effort. "Well, take the money, lad. Take it and call the debt canceled, if you like."

He turned and strode out of the jail without a backward

glance. Abe looked down at the money in his hand, but he did not see it. He saw instead the Young Squire on his black mare, the long stretches of road they had ridden together during those happy years that now might belong to another lifetime.

Nor was he thinking of what this money might mean to him as he climbed the stairs again, hustled along by a guard. He was remembering how he had stolen away from home nearly a year before and how lonely he had felt, how lost, with the irrevocable severing of those other ties. But he was dry-eyed now, weighted down though he was by depression; dry-eyed, aware for the first time how hard was the core that had formed deep inside of him.

Chapter 5

CRUSTED SNOW

Abe and Cornelius saw their last of the Provost Jail on January 9, 1778. Their old acquaintance, Sergeant Wally, appeared with a squad of guards, collected them and five inmates from other cells, and herded them all back to the Sugar House for no apparent reason.

That place was, if possible, even worse than they remembered it. Neither roof nor windows had been repaired. That had been bad enough in the early fall; now it was the depth of winter, a damp, chilly New York winter. All day half-starved wretches huddled around the small fires their meager fuel allowance permitted them, but all fires had to be extinguished at nine, and for the rest of the night they could only shiver on the bare floor, wrapped in thin, tattered blankets.

The previous guards had been relieved by a detail of Hessians. In addition to the traits that appeared common to all prison guards, these were richly endowed with that rapacity for which their countrymen had become notorious and which the worst of the British were never able quite to equal. Although there was little enough to plunder in that miserable prison, they made the best of what there was. Able-bodied prisoners who had contrived to retain anything that might be salable were starved until they had to trade the very clothes off their backs for barely enough food to keep them alive. Those too sick or weak to protect themselves were stripped at leisure, and there were instances of men unable to rise being virtually kicked to death for the filthy rags that covered them. This mean loot the Hessians traded to Ser-

geant Wally for rum, with the result that many of them were
drunk a good deal of the time.

Cornelius had come down with scurvy before leaving the
Provost, and within two days was seriously ill. Abe stayed
close to him to prevent his being robbed or beaten in his
sleep, but was soon suffering from a severe cough and fever
himself. On the fourth day, as his companion showed no
signs of improving, he took a long chance and offered Wally
what remained of the money the Young Squire had given
him as a bribe to have Cornelius moved to a hospital.

"How in the bloody hell did ye manage to hang on to
that?" the sergeant demanded. He snatched the money and
pocketed it. "Get back to yer sty before one of them squareheads decides he wants that coat you're wearing."

Abe cursed himself for a fool. But that evening, to his
great surprise, Cornelius was taken away. And he was no less
surprised the third morning following when a British guard
appeared with orders for his own removal to the same place.
Cornelius, he discovered on arrival, had contrived this by
playing on his professional ties with the English doctor in
charge.

The hospital was not much better than the Sugar House.
It was an old brick meetinghouse that had been allowed to
fall into disrepair like most of the buildings the British took
over for official use. There were few beds and fewer medicines for the hundreds of sick and wounded who had been
packed into the place; no attendants save the prison guards.

"The surgeon has promised me parole in the morning on
condition that I assist him in ministering to this charnel
house," Cornelius explained. "Well, I'm not going to take
it."

"For God's sake, why? Ain't that what you been wanting
all along?"

"I don't any more. It means giving my word not to escape
but wait for regular exchange—stay here nursing dying men
till the end of the war, most likely, without a chance to strike

another blow." The doctor paused. "If I decline, of course, that will arouse suspicion, make escape all the harder. So what I propose to do is make a break this very day. Are you with me?"

"But how—"

"I've worked that all out. Late every afternoon those of us who are up and about are allowed in the yard for a short time. It's the church yard, you know—the burying ground— and there's one corner where a tombstone lies so close to the wall that I'm convinced that by standing on it we could reach the iron spikes that line the top of the wall and pull ourselves over quite easily. If we made the attempt at nightfall, just before the lamps are lighted, I daresay we wouldn't even be seen."

"Ain't there no sentries?"

"Only one—inside the yard with us. You see, since we're all supposed to be sick, they don't take so many precautions."

Abe shook his head. Although Cornelius was on his feet again, his face was woefully pale, his too-bright eyes bloodshot.

"You ain't just supposed to be sick, Doc—you are sick. Even did we scale the wall safely, you'd not have the strength to get clear of the city—not the shape you're in."

"We won't have to—not right away. I've had word of some friends of liberty hereabouts who have banded together to aid escaping prisoners. There's one I used to know myself: Mrs. Dunn who runs a small coffeehouse on Queen Street. I'm sure she would not only hide us, but arrange some means for getting clear."

Abe laughed in sudden exuberance. But the laugh irritated his throat, set him to coughing again; a hacking cough that left him breathless and red in the face.

"You're not a well man yourself," Cornelius said with concern. "Here. Take off your shirt and let's have a look at that chest of yours."

He tapped and listened; shook his head dubiously. "I

wouldn't be surprised if there's a tumor on your lung. Might have a stoppage any time."

"That ain't real bad, is it?" Abe asked in some alarm. "Not so bad but we can—"

"It's bad enough so that you ought to be in a good, warm bed. Well, perhaps you will be before this night's over."

The day dragged by interminably. In prison time had lost its meaning, with one hopeless, dreary hour about like every other. Now, after nearly five months of that, there was hope again. They forgot how miserable they felt, ignored the trials and dangers that lay before them. Cornelius had already taken certain preliminary steps. Heads together, they went over the entire plan again and again, perfecting the details, ceasing only when they observed that they were attracting the curious attention of others near them.

The British surgeon appeared and sat with Cornelius for some time, eager for the companionship of one of his own kind. He was an earnest man, sincerely distressed by the condition of his charges and the restrictions under which he had to work. These he described at length, bitterly denouncing the corruption which, he declared, permeated not only his department but every department of the army. Cornelius listened politely and managed to make appropriate responses, but Abe, unfamiliar with what they were talking about, had all he could do to keep from biting his nails in impatience. Both were jumpy from the long suspense when at last a guard summoned those well enough for exercise in the yard.

Abe's first glimpse of the yard was not reassuring. It was smaller than he had expected, and the wall was higher; a thick brick wall with a serried row of sharp-looking iron spikes along the top. The ground was level, bare of trees or anything else that might provide temporary cover, save the tombstones, most of which were too small to be of much value in that respect. The enclosure was roughly ell-shaped, flanking the meetinghouse on side and rear, but a sentry posted at the angle would have a clear view of the whole stretch in both directions; clear enough, at any rate, so that he could hardly fail to observe any unwonted activity at such a distance in anything short of total darkness.

For a few moments they strolled aimlessly about with the other prisoners, perhaps a score of them in all. The air, clear and cold, bit their lungs as they breathed it in, quickened their blood even as it chilled their underfed bodies. Overhead the rich colors of sunset were fading slowly in a cloudless sky, tinting the snow underfoot. It was three or four inches deep, this snow. Along the paths it was trampled and discolored by the churning of many feet, but over the low mounds of the graves it was unbroken, and the freeze that had followed yesterday's thaw had formed a smooth, glistening crust across its surface.

With a brief inclination of his head, Cornelius indicated the spot where their attempt was to be made. It lay directly in the rear of the meetinghouse, close to the far corner of the yard. Abe gave it a quick, appraising glance as they sauntered past.

"You ain't had a chance to try whether that tombstone's close enough to the wall?" he asked in a low voice.

Cornelius shook his head. "It's damn well got to be!"

They continued without haste, following the wall where it turned to parallel the side of the hospital. The sentry had posted himself in the angle. He leaned negligently on his musket, stamping his feet now and again to drive out the cold. He made no effort to prevent the prisoners wandering at will within the confined area, only the occasional turning of his head indicating that he was even aware of their existence.

At the front corner of the wall Cornelius turned and led the way for a short distance along the side of the hospital itself. Beside an overturned tombstone he paused. Abe saw that from here the obtruding rear corner of the building shut out any view of the point at which they planned to scale the wall.

Cornelius, after a quick glance toward the sentry, stooped and fumbled under the reclining tombstone. From a recess well hidden by the snow he extracted a large brown bottle, uncorked it and passed it to Abe with a single movement.

"He's watching. Take a good one while you're at it."

Rum, heavy and potent, gurgled into Abe's throat. It was the first liquor he had tasted in months and it set him to coughing. Blindly he passed the bottle back. Cornelius had it tilted to his own mouth when the sentry arrived on the run.

"What the hell's going on here?"

Cornelius made a clumsy effort to hide the bottle. The soldier snatched it from his hand.

"B'Jesus! And where did ye get a-hold of that?"

"It—it's from the medical stores," Cornelius stammered.

The sentry sniffed the open bottle. "Medicine my eye! I'm reporting ye for this!"

"No, no!" Cornelius appeared to be thinking fast. "If you report us, you'll have to turn in the liquor as evidence. You don't want to turn in fine rum like this, do you?" He paused, watching the slow change in the man's expression. "Now let's be sensible. You need a drink on such a cold afternoon as much as we do. Suppose we leave the bottle hidden here where all of us can—"

"The hell ye say! I won't report ye, seeing's ye put it that way, but this here rum's mine—all of it!"

"Then I'll report you! And you know the surgeon will take my word."

"Why, ye son of a—"

"Don't be a fool! There's plenty here for all of us. We'll stop by when nobody's looking and grab a quick one, and you can do the same."

The sentry debated that, recalling himself after a moment to cast a quick glance around the yard. Most of the prisoners continued their lackadaisical plodding, but a few had noticed the scene and paused to stare with the indifference of the sick.

"Keep moving!" he yelled at them. He turned, grinning. "All right, Doc. Every man for himself—and devil take the slowest. Now get the hell out of here. But I'll be watching ye!"

He looked about furtively, raised the bottle. As they walked away, they heard the gurgle of liquid; a long, greedy gurgle.

"God!" Cornelius murmured. "That worked almost too well!"

They continued on their way, trying to look as though nothing had happened. Inside Abe the rum felt warm, potent. It seeped into his veins, driving out the chill that had been numbing him. But when they stopped by the overturned stone on their next trip around, Cornelius warned him not to take more.

"For men in our condition a little goes a long way. But go through the motions—he's got his eye on us."

Gradually the sky darkened. A full moon, hanging like a round white cloud low in the east, grew luminous as the afterglow waned, and star points began to show overhead. Dusk came swiftly in winter, but to the two men biding their time in the hospital yard its approach seemed agonizingly slow that day. Slow, too, seemed the rate at which the level in the bottle lowered.

"He'll never get drunk enough in time," Abe said impatiently. "You'd ought to of give it to him right out 'stead of going through all this hocus-pocus."

"He'd have been suspicious then—kept his eye on us instead of on the bottle."

A few of the other prisoners, aware at long last of what was going on, began sidling toward the overturned stone themselves. The sentry shouted at them, but they still lingered and more began to collect. Not until he transferred his post to the corner of the building in easy reach did the thirsty

wretches slink reluctantly away. After that the liquor disappeared faster.

"You're cheating on us, ye bastard!" Abe whispered as they
passed him at his new stand.

The sentry glared. "Why, ye goddamn Rebel—"

At last his voice sounded thick, slurring. More than half
the rum was gone. But he was steady enough on his feet as
he turned to drive away another prisoner who had sidled up
toward the bottle.

"Aw, just one little drink, mister!" the man pleaded.

"Get along with ye 'less ye want a bagnet up yer arse!"

"He's feeling it, all right," Cornelius said uneasily. "But
those others hanging around will attract attention soon. We'd
better chance it next time he goes for a drink."

They paused at the spot where they proposed to scale the
wall. The dregs of daylight still lingered in the sky, and as
yet no lamps had been lighted anywhere in sight. They could
see the corner of the building and the man standing there
much too plainly to please them.

"We'd best move on," Abe said. The words came indis-
tinctly. His heart seemed to be in his throat, literally choking
him.

They resumed their slow course, parallel to the wall. They
had gone perhaps twenty yards before they saw the sentry
wheel about, start back toward the hidden bottle. With one
accord they, too, wheeled.

"Now!"

"Easy!" Abe cautioned. "Don't run till we're out of sight."

Ten slow steps and the angle of the building hid them.
Another instant and they were at the spot.

Their plan was for Abe, who was stronger, to climb up
first and reach down a hand to help his companion. He
mounted the tombstone at a bound. But it was not close
enough. His groping hands reached the wall, but a good two
feet below the top.

"Jump for it!" Cornelius whispered tensely.

Abe crouched to spring. But the stone's top was rounded. His feet slithered off the sides and he fell sprawling in the ground.

"Oh, Christ!"

"You go first. I'll swing you up!" Abe was on his feet. He braced his back against the wall. "Put your foot here!"

Fingers laced, palms upward, his hands made a stirrup between his straddling knees. Cornelius placed his foot in it. A quick heave sent him sailing upward. His frantic hands clawed at the short iron spikes. In an instant he had pulled himself up.

"Now you!"

Abe reached for the hand held down to him. He had to jump to catch it. The sudden shock of his weight nearly pulled Cornelius off the wall. For what seemed an eternity they tugged futilely.

"Let go! I'll try jumping from the stone again."

This time Abe took greater care. His heart was pumping, but he felt more collected than he had all afternoon. For several seconds he teetered precariously, then steadied himself, crouching, and leaped forward and upward. As his hands clutched for the spikes, Cornelius grasped him by the coat collar and heaved mightily.

The effort upset what little balance he had, tumbled him over the other side into the street. Abe, jerked to the wall top more suddenly than he had counted on, stifled a cry of pain as spikes jabbed into his arm, chest, thigh. Two of them had impaled his coat. He cursed under his breath as he struggled to free it.

"Hey!"

The sentry had reappeared at the corner of the hospital. Abe lay very still. Apparently the liquor had taken effect at long last, for the man just stood there, staring, as though incredulous.

"I see ye! What the hell ye doing on that wall?"

It was the thick voice that reflected a thick, slow mind.

Abe made no reply. With coolness that surprised him, he set systematically about disengaging himself.

"By God, I'll get ye down!"

The befuddled man started toward him. Abe, free of the first spike, tried to get over the wall, but the second held him like an invisible hand.

"Run, Doc!" he called. "Save yourself!"

The sound of his voice brought the sentry up short. Then the full significance of the situation seemed to dawn on him.

"Rouse!" he shouted. "Turn out the guard! Prison break!"

Abe saw his musket come up. Its slamming report reverberated in the walled enclosure. The bullet knocked a spurt of brick dust from the wall. It would be half a minute before he would be able to reload. Calmly Abe sat up and, by using both hands, disentangled the last spike and dropped to the street.

"Rouse! Rouse!"

The drunken sentry was still shouting, and other voices were taking up the cry. The prisoners, suddenly come alive, were running about, yelling, contributing to the confusion in the yard to aid their comrades' escape. But the street outside was silent and empty.

"This way! This way!"

It was Cornelius's voice. Abe descried him now, paused in midflight a block away. He started running in that direction, but before he was halfway there he collided full tilt with a man who popped out of a tavern doorway just ahead of him. The glancing impact knocked him sidewise, sent him caroming off the wall of a building. He had a fleeting vision of the man he had hit sprawled in the roadway. It was a soldier. That was enough for Abe, dazed though he was by the violence of his double collision. A dark aperture gaped a little way ahead. He dodged into it.

He found himself in a narrow alley, gloomily shadowed in the dusk. He tripped over something; lay flat and still as a man ran past the alley's mouth, calling excitedly. Abe breathed easier and got to his feet. Apparently the soldier he had collided with had sighted the fleeing Cornelius and set off in full cry without pausing to scan closer ground. The doctor had a good start and knew the city better than any Englishman. Abe wasted no time worrying about him. His own problem was to put as much distance between himself and the point of alarm as he could.

The alley led through to the next street. There he paused to assure himself no one was near, then sprinted for another alley diagonally across. Behind him he could still hear the shouts of "Rouse!", but less clearly. He was puzzled to find no one abroad with all that din going on, no further sign of pursuit. Events had occurred so swiftly that he found it difficult to realize that probably not more than a minute of actual time had elapsed since he had dropped from the wall. So far he had outdistanced the alarm. Blindly he raced on, from alley to alley, until he could no longer hear the shouts behind him.

At last he lacked the breath to run farther. Pain stabbed his chest like a hot iron. Pounding blood roared in his ears, blurred his vision. He was aware of the bulk of a large building ahead. With a final effort he reached it, threw himself flat on the snow in the deep shadow of its wall.

He had no means of knowing how long he lay there. Returning breath sent him into a paroxysm of coughing which he had neither the strength nor the will to control. It was only as his brain began to clear that full realization of his predicament dawned on him.

He was a fugitive in a city filled with hostile troops, its streets patrolled, its every approach guarded. Worse, he was lost. The only refuge he knew of was the coffeehouse of a Mrs. Dunn, somewhere on Queen Street, and he had no idea where Queen Street might lie. To ask anyone would be tempting fate, now that the alarm had been given; not only for himself, but for his friends.

"Best thing I can do is get out of this damn city fast as ever I can," he decided.

He scrambled to his feet and made an effort to orientate himself. The building beside which he had taken refuge, he discovered, was a church; a church of some importance, to judge from the steeple that soared above him, tall and slender in the moonlight. That was a bit of luck. This, he was sure, was St. Paul's whose spire had been pointed out to him from the front window of the Provost, showing above the housetops on the lower side of the Common. If so, he was in the northwestern part of the city, within a few blocks of the Hudson and not much farther below the city limits.

He debated his course for several minutes. Although unfamiliar with the streets, he had a good general idea of the lie of the land, and the rising moon enabled him to adjust his sense of direction. The most obvious route back to his own people lay straight north; but this meant traversing some ten more miles of hostile York Island, crossing the guarded Harlem somehow and threading his way through the outposts beyond it, after which the entire length of the Neutral Ground would confront him.

The Hudson offered a much quicker way out. If it were frozen solid this far down, getting to the Jersey shore would be simply a matter of walking across a mile or so of ice. What he would do when he arrived at the far bank was another matter, for he knew nothing of the terrain, the people or the enemy dispositions over there. At least, he would be in open country where his highly developed talents as a scout would be of some practical use. Kicking his feet against the wall to restore circulation, he set off westward.

He took a circuitous route, slinking up alleys and through back yards, and he was badly winded from climbing innumerable fences before he caught his first distant glimpse of the river. To his bitter disappointment, it was not frozen. A little way below he could see the riding lights of several warships in midstream. Worse, the shore was ice-locked for fifty to a hundred yards out, which meant that crossing by boat would be virtually impossible, even in the unlikely event that he were able to find a boat.

"Boom!" A column of flame leaped from one of the ships below, and the report of a single gun carried hollowly across the water. Abe jumped as though the shot had been aimed at him.

"Alert gun!" The call came from the shadow of a warehouse not fifty yards from him, was repeated farther off. "Alert gun! Pass the word—halt every person who approaches!"

Abe shrank back, cursing himself. He should have spotted that sentry line minutes before. Dodging about this unfamiliar city was ruining his nerves.

He began working his way inland again, and emerged after a while near a large building which he recognized as King's College. The Young Squire had pointed it out on the occasion of his one previous visit to the city. Here there were more people on the streets; ordinary people proceeding without haste about their ordinary affairs. Thoroughly jumpy by now from alley-skulking, Abe stepped boldly out among them. To his great relief, no one paid him any attention. The clothes Cornelius had given him were shabby and ill-fitting, but far superior to the filthy rags that were the hallmark of the Rebel prisoner, so that he might have passed nearly anywhere as a laborer or artisan.

The houses became less closely crowded against each other as he proceeded northward, and the throngs on the streets began to thin out. He knew that he was approaching the edge of the city and moved with greater caution. He had no idea of the exact location of the outpost line but realized that he must be getting dangerously close to it. His nervousness had subsided as the country became more open, and his mind was functioning alertly once more. Finding no one in sight at last, he hid himself in the shadows beside the road and waited until two other men appeared heading in his di-

rection. He allowed them to pass, then set out after them at
a discreet distance.

Within half a mile they were challenged. Again Abe slunk
into the shadows, listening. All he heard was an indistinct
murmur of voices, but he had accomplished his main object:
he had located the city's northern sentry line. All he had to
do now was figure out a way to run it.

On his right was a large orchard, its well-spaced trees
throwing a dappled pattern on the moonlit snow. Gingerly
he climbed the fence that separated it from the road. A loud
crunching, crackling sound brought every hair on his head
up on end. Aghast, he looked down. He was standing in snow
halfway to his knees; not the hard-packed snow of the streets,
but light and powdery, its crusted surface almost but not
quite strong enough to bear his weight.

For several seconds he stood stock still, listening. When
nothing indicated that he had been heard, he essayed another
step. Again the crust gave way. In the windless night the din
sounded as loud as a pistol shot. Panic seized him and he
began to run. The crackle pursued him like a string of fire-
crackers tied to a dog's tail. The broken crust clutched at his
feet. Finally it tripped him. He made one frenzied effort to
rise. Short breath set him to coughing again. The tumor in
his lung burst, adding its discharge to the phlegm. He let
himself go then, too miserable and spent to care any longer
what became of him.

Finally the paroxysm passed. For several moments longer
he lay limp in the snow while his self-possession returned.
If all the din he had made had failed to attract notice, he
must be well beyond earshot of the picket line or anyone
else. He cursed his panic and sat up. Nothing stirred in the
shadowed orchard. Only his rapid breathing broke the silence
of the night.

He rose and resumed his crunching progress. He took his
time now, both to save his breath and to listen between
steps. When he reached the fence that enclosed the far side

of the orchard, he lowered himself with infinite gentleness until he was stretched full length upon the snow. In this position the crust supported him. Flat on his belly, he began to pull himself forward, sliding easily and silently across the glazed surface. The moon was still low enough to throw the fence's shadow across him.

He proceeded in this manner until he reached the orchard's northern boundary, another stone fence running off at right angles. As well as he could judge by the distance covered, he should be close now to where he had tentatively located the picket line. He lay very still, and after a few moments he was rewarded: his straining ears caught the subdued clatter of a soldier's accouterments.

Inch by inch he raised his head. As his eyes came level with the top of the fence, he caught his breath and had all he could do to check the impulse to duck swiftly. The sentry was so close that Abe could almost make out the insignia on his uniform buttons in the clear moonlight. Even as he stared, unmoving, the man turned without haste and began to retrace his course, his footfalls muffled in the trodden snow of what appeared to be a narrow lane.

Abe watched his receding back for a moment, then turned his attention down the lane in the opposite direction. Sure enough, within half a minute a second soldier appeared, wheeled on approximately the same spot and returned the way he had come. Abe nodded his satisfaction. By great good luck he had struck the guard line at the precise point where two sentry posts joined each other. He began to count to himself at a slow, steady rate, meanwhile scanning the terrain across the lane. There was another stone fence there, but the country beyond was open, a wide, rolling meadow bare of tree, fence or rock for as far as he could see from this vantage point.

His count had reached nearly three hundred when the first sentry hove into view again. At the end of his beat he halted, lowered his musket and blew on his hands to warm them while his mate sauntered up leisurely. Abe heard a low exchange of words, a casual laugh; then they turned simultaneously and started back their respective ways.

Abe began to count again in the same measured cadence. When he reached fifty he raised himself with infinite care and drew himself to the top of the fence. He felt terribly exposed, perched there in the moonlight, but he was at pains to avoid making any swift, sudden movements. At seventy-five he was lying prone beyond the fence. He crept forward until his hands felt the packed snow of the lane. There he drew himself to a crouching position. His eyes swept right and left. The first sentry's receding back was visible, more than a hundred yards away. The second had passed from sight around a curve.

Abe flitted across the lane, fell prone to negotiate another narrow stretch of crusted snow. Then he was in the field, pressed close behind the fence, panting more from excitement than exertion.

He lay there until the sentries had completed their beats again, then resumed that measured counting. This time when it reached fifty, he began sliding eastward along the fence, thus keeping a safe distance behind the sentry going in the same direction. When the count indicated that the soldier had reached the end of his post and would be turning back, he lay motionless until the man had passed, after which he crept forward again until the resumed count told him that he had reached the post of the next sentry.

He continued in this agonizingly slow manner for what seemed hours, fearful of venturing out on the glistening expanse of the endless meadow beyond. Once he crunched through the crust in spite of all his caution. Twice he had to choke himself till his face turned blue to keep from coughing. Not until he emerged at long last in a curving tree-lined lane did he permit himself a deep breath.

He was out of the city. The sense of safety, however ephemeral, affected him like a strong drink of rum. He felt like shouting in exultation. Instead, after putting a good distance behind him, he indulged in the luxury of the cough he had been suppressing for so long.

The lane led northward, toward the Harlem, and he set out briskly along it. Within half a mile, however, it ended in another which ran east and west, and he was obliged to consider. The only route he knew out of the city was the main one: the Kingsbridge Road which he had followed on both of his visits. He decided to chance that in preference to wandering through unfamiliar byways with only his sense of direction to guide him.

Heading eastward, he soon reached the road he sought, a wide, well-traveled highway. There were several houses in sight, more than his memory had led him to expect. But the road itself was empty. Boldly he stepped into it and turned north again.

"Halt! Who goes there?"

Abe stopped short. That the picket line might be placed farther forward here had not entered his hasty calculations.

"Who goes there? Speak up, damn ye!"

The sentry had stepped out of the shadows ten paces away. Abe's rash overconfidence evaporated. In an instant brain and nerves co-ordinated again.

"F-friend," he said in a smothered voice.

"Advance, friend, and give the countersign."

Abe came forward slowly. He kept his knees flexed to spring, his eyes upon the long brown musket. The desperate expedient of overpowering the man was all that occurred to him, so suddenly had this happened.

But once more he reckoned without the snow. As he tried to spring, his feet slipped and he landed sprawling on his knees.

"Ho!" laughed the sentry. "Had a glass too many, eh, friend?"

Without time to think, Abe snapped at the cue. He rolled over and sat up.

"I'm shober's you are!" he declared with dignity.

" 'Course ye are," the soldier assured him. He dropped his musket butt to the ground and helped Abe to his feet. "Now who might ye be and what's yer business?"

"You got no right to shtop me!" Abe protested thickly. His mind was working fast. "I ain't drunk and I'm a good s-shitizen—"

"Sorry, but there was an alert gun and we got to stop everybody. So who are ye and where're ye going?"

"Home—thash where I'm going. I—I'm Mather Hopper." Abe named a man at whose house the Young Squire had stopped on that well-remembered trip two years before. "Live out near the fourth milestone," he added.

The sentry chuckled. "Ye'll have a hell of a time getting there, shape you're in!"

"I will, huh? Jush you wash me!"

Abe lurched past him and took a few stumbling steps.

"Hey! Come back here! I got to hold ye till the sergeant of the guard comes around and dismisses ye from me."

Abe thought of risking a dash for it, but the soldier already had him by the arm.

"Jeesh, capt'n!" he begged. "I jush gotta get home."

" 'Twill be only a few minutes. I'll ask the sergeant to hail the next patrol going yer way and get 'em to help ye home."

"Patrol!" Abe's heart sank. But if the sentry noticed any change in his expression, he gave no sign.

"You ain't by any chance got a bottle on ye to help pass the time waiting?" he inquired hopefully.

Abe belched. "I don't drink, I tell ye." He racked his brain. "Lishen. I'm going to get hell enough 'thout no shoulgers bringing me home. Lemme go, will ye?"

The soldier appeared to consider. "Oh, all right," he said good-humoredly. "Get along with ye! Only don't be telling any patrols ye meet that I let ye go."

"I ain't going to meet no patrols!" Abe declared devoutly. He staggered up the road, hardly daring to believe his luck. It required will power to continue that lurching gait. Once around a curve he began to run; kept running until renewed coughing forced him to halt.

When he had caught his breath again, he continued at a fast walk. For the first time he was beginning to realize how tired he was. His feet felt so heavy that he had to concentrate his strength to lift them from the road. The pain in his chest had increased, and his belly, denied a square meal for five months, rumbled protests. Only his nerves kept him going, and they were getting frayed.

In reaction to his recent overconfidence, he relapsed into extreme wariness. It was fortunate he did so, for, alert though he was for the patrol he had been forewarned was coming up behind him, he almost ran head-on into one approaching from the opposite direction. Once he had to swing wide through the fields, creeping across the crusted snow again, to get around the cantonments of a body of troops. The houses along the road continued much closer together than he liked. He began to despair of ever reaching the Harlem at this rate, even if his doubtful strength held out.

"You can go on," he said aloud. "You can go on long after your con—conscious mind has given you up."

Cornelius had said that in the dungeon of the Provost when they had all marveled over Captain Chatham's miraculous survival. Abe repeated it until the words ran through his head like a chant, in rhythm to the beat of blood against his eardrums. . . .

Three hours later he was still going on, although he was aware of that only occasionally in the intervals after an attack of coughing had cleared phantasms from his brain, left him weak and gasping but briefly lucid.

By then he was completely lost. Abandoning hope of continuing undetected on the Kingsbridge Road, he had decided to try the East River. What he could have done even had he been able to find a boat was problematical, for unfamiliar Long Island was predominantly Tory, with enemy troops in occupation. But by then his mind had become incapable of retaining more than a single thought: to get off this accursed island, no matter how.

Only instinct kept him from capture half a dozen times. He froze rigid when a soldier stepped out of a lighted house not forty paces ahead of him; stayed rigid while the man took his own good time enjoying the night air before going back inside. He reached the East River at a point where a small stream entered it—only to discover a sentry on each bank, calmly conversing across it. He had to crawl for half an hour to get around them—and found still another guard on the shore beyond. As he paused to consider what to do next, the tree limb by which he was holding himself upright snapped off with the noise of a pistol shot, and he tumbled into a deep hole to lie scarcely breathing while the aroused soldier prowled around, muttering.

He gave up the East River then and headed back inland. "You can go on. . . ." But the time came during one of those rare lucid intervals when he knew that he could not go on much longer; that if he collapsed out here in the open, he would surely freeze to death. With his last conscious effort he dragged himself on until he came to a barn, forced the door and buried himself in the friendly hay.

It was broad daylight when he awoke, or when consciousness returned to him. For several moments he lay still, afraid to try to move lest his muscles should refuse. But he was not frozen; not even his feet were frozen. The hay felt pleasant about him, and a rising sun found its warming way through cracks in the barn wall. Gradually his brain began to clear. His first physical sensation, stronger even than the ache in every muscle, was the ravening of his belly.

After a while he rose and crept to the door. There was no one in the barnyard, no one in sight about the near-by house from whose chimney blue wood-smoke curled invitingly.

Furtive again, he slipped out, dodged across the open ground to a lane that ran past the place.

He followed this until it joined a road; followed that in turn, setting his course by the sun in a generally westward direction. He walked erect now, maintaining as good a pace as he was able, making no effort at concealment, pausing only when a fit of coughing obliged him to lie down until it had passed. Thus in half an hour he found himself again on the Kingsbridge Road.

He did not turn north this time, however. Instead he set his course in the opposite direction, toward the city he had spent so much time and effort escaping the previous night. Many others were traveling that way now: on foot, on horseback, in carts and wagons. The normal city-bound traffic of a weekday morning, they moved without haste past the shabby young man who plodded southward on tired feet, looking neither left nor right. A friendly farmer driving a load of wood offered him a lift, but he shook his head. He did not want to answer questions, however kindly intended.

"You can go on . . . you can go on. . . ."

Somehow the milestones fell behind him, one by one. The clear-headedness he had felt upon awakening lost itself in a mist of sickness, hunger, exhaustion. But the destination he had decided upon then remained as firmly fixed in his mind as had a different destination during the night.

He rallied his faculties by dint of colossal effort as he approached the sentry post where he had played drunk, but the man now on duty there gave him no second glance. As he had deduced, the last place the British would look for escaped prisoners was in a throng of market people entering the city. He had a bad moment near the Common when one of the Provost guards who had seen him a hundred times strolled by so close as nearly to brush against him; another when he saw Captain Cunningham himself talking with some officers in front of a tavern. But neither recognized him, if, indeed, they noticed him at all. Heartened, he accosted a prosperous-appearing citizen and inquired the way to Queen Street.

The sound of his voice surprised and shocked him. Although he had been saving his breath for this occasion, the words grated out in a hoarse croak that resembled nothing human, and the effort sent him off into another fit of coughing. This last was providential, however, for the stranger's sympathy quickly overcame any curiosity he might have had. And it cleared Abe's mind sufficiently to grasp the detailed directions that were forthcoming.

"You can go on . . . you can go . . ."

Bustling crowds jostled him on Broadway. He counted the blocks mechanically, eyes searching for landmarks the stranger had described. Thus at last he came to Queen Street.

It was a long street. To him it seemed interminable. He passed several coffeehouses, but on none of their signs did he see the name he sought. Perhaps that was not strange, for his brain was reeling and his eyes focused none too well. At the end he turned and shuffled his leaden feet back the way he had come. He could not ask directions now. Twice he trudged the entire length of that street before he found the place. It swam uncertainly into the range of his blurred vision: a modest, obscure house tucked between two large buildings. He stopped and stared at it for several moments before his mind quite grasped its existence.

The entrance was a little below the level of the street. He descended the steps one at a time, his knees shaking with weakness. He was aware of entering a cozy, dusky room; of a matronly gray-haired woman coming toward him. Whether there was anyone else in the room he did not know. He gripped a chairback to steady himself and drew a tortured breath.

"Mrs.—Dunn—?"

She peered at him for an instant. He sensed rather than saw her expression changing.

"I was expecting you. Come this way, please."

He followed her up a flight of narrow stairs, groping along the wall with his hands. The last step tripped him, and he fell to his knees.

"Get up! Oh, please get up!"

The woman's voice was low, tense with urgency. He crept to the wall and, mustering all his strength, propped himself against it. With her help he managed to get one foot under him, but that was all.

"Doctor! Doctor! Help me!" the low voice called.

A door opened near by. Lifting hands were under his arm-pits. That thin, pale face he had learned to know so well was bending close above him. There was no need to struggle any longer. With a sigh he let himself go and collapsed smiling in Cornelius's arms.

Chapter 6

LETTERS OF MARQUE AND REPRISAL

They stayed at Mrs. Dunn's for three days. Rest and good food quickly restored Cornelius's strength, but Abe presented a problem. Not only was he exhausted, but the stoppage in his chest had become so severe that at first he could neither eat nor sleep, only lie in a delirious coma. Cornelius worked over him with all the skill at his command. He prescribed medicines, which Mrs. Dunn was able to obtain and help him to prepare. By some miracle the dreaded lung fever was averted. The stoppage cleared up, and by the end of the first day Abe fell into a sound sleep that endured for twenty-four hours. He awoke rational and ravenous.

"You have the constitution of a dray horse," Cornelius told him. "You and Captain Chatham. If I could tell how I pulled either of you through, my professional reputation would be made."

If he could have had his own way, he would have kept Abe in bed for a week. Mrs. Dunn, a motherly, efficient soul, was willing, but when he learned of the risk involved he refused to impose on her further. It appeared that, since this group of undercover Rebels had developed their system for spiriting escaped prisoners out of the city, a small epidemic of jail breaks had developed which had at last aroused even the indifferent British authorities. A friend brought word that a program of house-to-house search was being inaugurated. Reluctantly Cornelius told him to arrange their own transportation at once, silencing Mrs. Dunn's protests.

"You are very kind, ma'am, but we cannot permit you to assume further risks. Besides, your value to our country depends upon your remaining undetected."

So she cleaned and mended their clothes and tied up a package of food for them: bread—sweet, white bread—and cooked meat that had never known the taint of bilge water, adding at the last moment a small bottle of brandy to see them through their cold journey. At dusk that afternoon a boatman appeared to guide them, a rough-looking, taciturn man, who led them through byways to the section of the East River waterfront where provision boats from Long Island docked. The guards there seemed to know him, for they passed him and his passengers without question.

"It just goes to show all you got to do is know how," Abe remarked drily, recalling his own attempts at flight in this direction.

Once covered by the gathering darkness, the boatman turned his bow northward and, with Abe and Cornelius each tugging at an oar, rowed in midstream for an hour. Their backs ached from the unaccustomed labor, and they could feel blisters forming on their palms. Beyond occasionally damning them under his breath for clumsy landsmen, their companion had nothing whatever to say. When they landed at last on Long Island, he muttered that they were beyond the area patrolled by the shore guard, but when Cornelius insisted on shaking his hand and delivering a short oration on his service to the noble cause, he only grunted.

The doctor led the way without hesitation. Long Island born and bred, he knew this region as well as Abe knew Westchester, and the friends with whom Mrs. Dunn worked had been at pains to locate every enemy cantonment and picket, plot the customary patrol routes. Even before the British had occupied it, Long Island had been predominantly Tory in sentiment. Such Whigs as had remained had found it expedient to be extremely discreet, but Cornelius had been told just which ones could be depended on. A few of them he had known personally since boyhood.

After a while the moon rose, making the whitened countryside nearly as bright as day. Abe felt the old alertness pulling at his nerves, but there was no creeping along fences over the crusted snow this night. Without perfect unconcern Cornelius stuck to the hard-packed roadway, calling a halt whenever shortness of breath set Abe to coughing again.

Once he paused near a house that was set well back from the road among some tall evergreens; a large house whose candle-lit windows patched the snow where the dark trees shadowed it. For a long moment he stood there looking, and in the moonlight Abe saw bitterness cut through the conflicting emotions that showed on his face.

"My father's house," he said tersely, and set off up the road at a faster pace than ever.

They had covered nine miles by midnight when Cornelius turned off the main road into a lane that led to a small, obscure farm. No light showed from the house, but two quick raps on the door, followed by two slow ones, gained them admittance. The farmer welcomed them cordially, stirred the buried embers on the hearth into a blaze. He recognized Cornelius at once and regaled him with news of the region while the fugitives dug into the food Mrs. Dunn had provided, topping it off with a nightcap of brandy apiece. Ten minutes later they were snoring under warm blankets in a narrow bed whose bumpy corn-husk mattress felt like the finest down.

The farmer let them sleep until seven, and his wife had a piping hot breakfast on the kitchen table by the time they were dressed: eggs, fried salt pork, steaming coffee. She apologized for the lack of fresh milk, explaining that the Hessians had driven off all their cattle the previous fall.

"Then they know you're Whigs?" Cornelius asked.

"Course not—or we wouldn't be here. But Tory or Rebel makes no difference to that thieving gentry!"

"You mean they let their foraging parties strip you bare?"

"I ain't speaking of foraging parties, Doctor. They pays for forage, in hard money, too. It's soldiers on the loose I mean, prowling by night without leave of no one, helping theirselves to whatever ain't nailed down. Hessians is the worst, but there's lobsterbacks not much better. Why, in parts where troops are quartered regular 'tis no uncommon thing to find a farmer sleeping in one room with his wife and children, while his sheep are bleating in the living room, his hogs grunting in the kitchen, and cocks crowing, hens cackling, ducks quacking and geese hissing in the cellar, and any cattle he's got left lowing their heads off behind locked doors in the barn and outhouses. And, mind you, I'm speaking of folks some of them having sons wearing the Tory uniform on active service with the army!"

"How on earth do they dispose of such loot without being detected by their officers?"

"Oh, they got ways. I hear tell of a Hessian who has opened a butcher shop over to Jamaica where he's coining money by selling meat cheaper than other butchers can— stolen meat, of course. As for the officers—why, there's them that's even worse. One captain over to Huntington sells the firewood issued his company at so much a cord, leaving his men to get their own—fence rails, fruit trees or whatever they can lay hands on. The honest ones just shrugs their shoulders. Why should they bother with the troubles of low-born Americans? Whigs are enemies and deserving of nothing better. Tories—well, they ought to be that grateful for having a fine army to protect 'em as to be glad to give the poor soldiers whatever they got!"

She seemed to draw ironic enjoyment in the plight of her Loyalist neighbors and might have gossiped on indefinitely had not her husband intervened. It was time, he declared, for their guests to finish eating and resume their journey if they were to reach their destination by nightfall.

They were on the road again before eight, plodding eastward near the shore of the Sound, which they could glimpse now and again across low-lying stretches of salt marsh. There was little danger of their being stopped now, for this region was too distant from any fields of active operations to be considered worth patrolling. Abe had one bad moment when they encountered a foraging party from one of the regiments in winter quarters a few miles inland, but the officer in command merely returned Cornelius's courteous "good morning" and continued about his business without giving the doctor a chance to test the story he had concocted against such an emergency. The greatest danger, they both realized, lay in Cornelius's being recognized by some former neighbor, and this lessened as they put his home farther behind them.

The country became wilder and more thinly settled as they progressed. To Abe, born and raised among the Westchester hills, it was fascinating, exotic country. The gently rolling terrain of northern Long Island broke the shore line into a series of irregular bays and coves, separated by headlands and long promontories, some of which seemed to stretch miles out into the Sound. Although the day was clear, the mainland was beyond the horizon at this point, so that the expanse of water seemed endless; dark blue water, stippled with small whitecaps by a brisk breeze that was just cold enough to set the blood dancing without numbing the limbs as long as one continued walking. The tonic quality of the salt air continued the reviving effect of plenty of food and a good night's sleep and enabled Abe to maintain so vigorous a pace that they arrived at the designated place by midafternoon.

This was a farmhouse much like the last one at which they had stopped. It lay a mile or so from a broad, shallow bay, near the edge of a deep wood which served to isolate it from the more thickly settled region inland.

" 'Tain't often their forage parties takes the trouble to come this far," the farmer told them. "Still, I don't figure it's worth the risk, keeping escapers here in the house no longer than we can help."

"Have many come through?" Cornelius asked.

"Several, several. And I reckon there'll be more. Tomorrow we'll go out in the woods and help you throw up a hut."

"A hut? You mean it's likely to be some time before we're able to cross the Sound."

"'Fraid so. The British have taken up all the boats hereabouts. Maybe we can steal one if we bide our time. Then again maybe a privateer will put in."

"Privateer?" repeated the puzzled Cornelius. "You mean, our people have privateers operating in the Sound?"

"That's what they call theirselves, anyhow. They come out in whopping big whaleboats and mostly work offshore, preying on sloops carrying provisions to New York. Sometimes, though, they land to raid a farm or two or catch themselves a few prisoners. If I hear of any putting in hereabouts, I'll let you know."

They spent the night at the farmhouse. Early the next morning, loaded with axes and shovels, they followed the farmer and his stout son along an obscure winding path into the woods for about two miles. In a small natural clearing hard by a brook they dug away the snow and built a roaring fire. Then they set about felling trees and stripping them. By sundown they had one side of the hut erected, the gaps between the logs chinked with mud gathered from where the fire had thawed the frozen ground. Again they spent the night at the farm and managed to finish the hut the following day.

It served as their home for more than a month. After prison, they found life there tolerably comfortable. There was wood to be had for the cutting, and they kept the fire going day and night to compensate for their lack of adequate covering. Food was supplied them at eight to ten day intervals, either by the farmer who had taken them in or by other secret friends in the neighborhood who volunteered to share the burden. The greatest drawback was lack of companionship, for they were both gregarious by nature.

There were several other huts occupied by escaped prisoners in these woods, but in order to minimize the risk of wholesale detection they had been planted at wide intervals over a distance of some ten miles. For the first week Abe and Cornelius spent much time getting acquainted with these comrades in adversity, always traveling by circuitous routes over well-trampled roads and lanes to avoid leaving tracks which, as long as the snow remained on the ground, would betray the next hut to any hostile persons who chanced to discover one. On such a trip, however, Cornelius encountered a Tory who recognized him. Fortunately, he was a harmless, noncombatant Tory without ill will, and promised, after some troubled debate with himself, not to report their presence to the military. But the incident threw a bad scare into the fugitives and their friends, and after that all agreed to lie low in their own refuges.

To while away the dragging days, Cornelius prevailed upon one of the more literate of the friendly farmers to loan them such books as he had; but Abe, who had never read an entire book in his life, found little relief from that source at first. He kept at it, however, mainly because there was nothing else to do once the simple chores of their life had been finished. Cornelius encouraged him, helped him interpret puzzling words and passages; and almost before he knew it, reading was providing him real enjoyment.

"What does a fellow have to do to get so's he can write?" he asked one day.

Cornelius smiled. "Thinking of taking it up?"

"No, no. It ain't that." Abe looked at the ground, frowning. "There's times, though, when I kind of wish I could say things so's to make folks see 'em like I see 'em."

"What sort of things do you mean?"

"I don't know," Abe repeated. "About the Sugar House maybe, or about the way they hung Mr. McCalsenden. Or about what them devils has done— Oh, hell! I don't know."

"You needn't worry," Cornelius said grimly. "Things like

that are being engraved on the minds of men more elo-
quently than any book could tell them."

March had arrived before the first opportunity to reach
the mainland presented itself. Early one evening a friendly
farmer brought word that two mysterious whaleboats had
stolen at dusk into an obscure cove a few miles eastward and
were still standing by when he had left. Eagerly they followed him to the spot, sloshing through the slush and mud
of the first big thaw. At the edge of a narrow beach he
stopped.

"They got the boats drawn up down that way a piece," he
said. "Reckon I'll leave you here. I don't want to get mixed
up with these gentry no more'n I got to."

Cornelius hesitated, staring into the blackness in the direction indicated. Abe touched his arm.

"This is more in my line than yours, Doc. Stay close, and
for God's sake, don't make no sudden movements."

He started down the beach, walking slowly. By straining
their eyes, they sighted the boats at last—huge shadows
blacker than the night.

"Ho! Friends approaching!" Abe called in a low voice.

There was no sound save their own footfalls, muffled by
the sand. After a few strides he repeated the hail.

There was a faint rustling in the underbrush that rimmed
the beach. Several shadows detached themselves, flitted like
smoke across the open strip.

"Stand! Up with your arms! Quick, now!"

"We're friends!" Cornelius cried nervously. "Prisoners
escaping from New York!"

"Bring a light, boys, and let's have a look."

A man brought up a shrouded lantern, drew aside a corner
of the covering. Yellow light flickered over the faces of the
two captives and their captors, perhaps a half dozen of them.
That Abe and Cornelius were both unarmed appeared to
reassure them, and the tension slackened.

"All we require is passage to the mainland," Cornelius
said. "You will take us, I trust."

"Well, now, that depends. It depends on how much room
we got when the rest gets back, and how much money you
got."

"Money?" Cornelius repeated. "Do you mean that Patriot
seamen require pay to carry Patriot soldiers to safety?"

"We ain't in the passenger-carrying business, mister!"

"Why—why, we—you— Have you no—"

Abe had lowered his arms. He jabbed Cornelius with an
elbow.

"Who's commanding this gang of pirates?" he demanded
harshly.

The man who had been doing the talking blinked. "I am,
I reckon. And don't you go calling us no—"

"You're just the fellow left to guard the boats," Abe interrupted contemptuously. "I mean the real boss."

"Hey, listen! Who the hell might you be?"

"If you don't know who I am, General Putnam can tell
you!"

The man hesitated. "We got no truck with no generals.
We got letters of marque straight from the Governor!"

"Well, you ain't going to have 'em much longer if ye try
leaving us in the lurch!"

There was a mutter from the others, angry but at the same
time uncertain. In the lantern light Cornelius's face was a
picture of dismay, but no one was looking at him any longer.

"Let's shoot the bastards and have done with it," someone
suggested.

Abe laughed grimly. "Save your breath, brother! We been
bullied by experts!" His eyes ranged the circle of faces, returned to the self-announced leader. "Who's your boss?" he
demanded again.

The man's eyes shifted. "Captain Tenny," he said crossly.

"Never heard of him! Well, we'll wait around till he gets
back. Come along, Doc."

He led the way to the edge of the underbrush where he seated himself on a large, flat rock. The boat guard, as though dumfounded, stood in the middle of the beach where he had left them. It was several seconds before one of them thought to re-cover the lantern.

Cornelius wiped cold sweat from his forehead. "You better let me pay them," he whispered. "I've some money left."

"Aye! And they'd take it and leave us stranded, most like!"

"Imagine the like of them masquerading under the name of 'Patriots.'"

Abe shrugged. "It takes all kinds of folks to make a war, seems like."

"For the love of heaven, have a care! These are desperados if I ever saw any."

Abe spat contemptuously. "Desperados, hell! If I had Brom Dyckman and big John here, we'd mop up the pack of 'em and take the boats for ourselves." He smiled into the darkness. "By God, it's going to be good to be with Brom and John again!"

They sat in silence for several minutes. Now and again they heard stirrings of the guard hidden in the brush near at hand. Tiny waves lapped faintly against the beach of the cove, splashed on the sides of the whaleboats, prodigious craft forty to fifty feet long, black against the gray sand.

"You know, Doc," Abe said thoughtfully, "last spring after I'd helped mop up a cow raid, Old Putt—General Putnam, that is—wanted I should organize the Guides and some others into a company of volunteer light horse—me to be captain. I just laughed at him."

"Why?"

"Hell! Me an officer? I ain't gentry like you and most of them at the Provost. And them other fellows are older than me, too."

Cornelius tried to see his face in the darkness. "I noticed that most of them looked to you for leadership just the same."

"Aye. That's what the general said. I been thinking about it. Funny. Everything looks different now."

They lapsed into silence again, each busy with his own thoughts. They had not exchanged another dozen words when, shortly before midnight, the rest of the raiding party returned to the boats. The leader of the guard that had been left behind uncovered the lantern to guide them. Abe watched them as they came into the ring of yellow light, fifteen or twenty nondescript fellows, loaded down with sacks evidently containing loot. They had a prisoner with them, too; a portly, middle-aged civilian, arms bound to his sides, his fine clothing soiled and torn.

Cornelius grasped Abe's arm. "My God! That's Judge Wilson! What the devil do you suppose they want with him?"

"If he's rich, I'd guess ransom."

"The scoundrels! They're as bad as the Tories! I hope to heaven the judge doesn't take me for one of 'em."

Abe shrugged. He saw the leader of the boat guard reporting to the man apparently in command, gesticulating in their direction. He rose and walked over without haste.

"You Capt'n Tenny? Me and my friend wants passage back with ye."

The man's teeth showed in a wide grin. "You got your nerve with ye, son!" He peered at Abe more closely. "Say! Ain't I seen you somewheres before?"

"If it had been in the Sugar House or the Provost, there wouldn't be no argument about your taking us across."

"Huh! Me in a British prison?" The man named Tenny laughed scornfully. "I ain't a damn fool!" He turned to the others. "Throw that old goat aboard and let's get the hell out of here."

A couple of them seized the stout prisoner and pushed him over the gunwales of the nearest whaleboat. He fell across a thwart like a clumsy oversized meal sack, but beyond a puffing grunt he disdained to make a sound. The rest of the men

set about stowing the sacks of loot into both boats, then laid
hold of bows and sides and ran them out into the water with
quick efficiency.

"You two jailbirds can come with me," Tenny said indifferently to Abe. "Hang on tight and keep out of the crew's
way."

They had to wade out in the icy water. The boat listed
precariously as they scrambled in, and the crew piled in after
them.

"Shove off!" Tenny called softly. "Man the oars, lads.
Now—give way!"

Water plashed under the prow as the oars dug in. The
sudden forward jerk threw the unprepared passengers flat on
the bottom. Tenny, manning the long steering sweep in the
stern, began calling the beat.

"And don't none of ye go broaching that liquor till we got
the mast stepped!" he added.

Whatever else might be said of them, these privateersmen
knew how to handle their boats. Rowing evenly, without apparent effort, they pulled their swift, high-sided craft across
the placid, sheltered water. Tenny seemed entirely familiar
with the lie of the land and set his course unerringly for the
cove's narrow mouth. They passed between brush-covered
points and in a few moments were jouncing in a choppy
cross-sea in the open Sound. The dark mass of the shore line
sank behind them, and presently Tenny ordered the oars
shipped, the masts stepped.

"Sheet home, lads, and rest easy. We got all night."

He was in high good humor now that vigilance could be
relaxed. The boats heeled to a fresh easterly breeze. A half-
moon, pushing its edge above the low horizon, laid a long
track of light across the dancing water and picked out the
pattern of a mackerel sky through which scattered star points
showed remotely. Seated side by side on the aftermost thwart,
Abe and Cornelius looked at each other. Simultaneously the
tension snapped in them: that keyed-up alertness, that never-

ceasing strain of being perpetually on their guard that had
been with them so long that it had become almost a part of
their make-up. With one accord they burst out laughing from
the sheer joy of being alive and free.

The tension had broken among the others, too. Men called
back and forth between the two boats. There was a stir of
new activity as others prowled among the sacks of loot. In
the stern sheets Tenny, the steering sweep hooked under one
elbow, was worrying at the cork of a bottle with a thin-
bladed knife. Presently the bottle gave forth a pleasant
gurgling sound, and he smacked his lips. They saw his teeth
flash white in the light of the rising moon.

"Something to warm you, lads!"

Cornelius took the proffered bottle. Fine brandy, old and
mellow, warmed his throat. The unfortunate Tory prisoner
was one of the largest landowners on Long Island's North
Shore and had kept a cellar suitable to his means and taste.

"I know where I seen ye now," Tenny said suddenly, looking closely at Abe. "You was one of them brung in that Tory
recruiter Old Putt hanged over to Peekskill last summer."

"Oh. Was you there?"

"Sure. Doing my turn with the militia." He laughed. "I've
sure learned a lot since them days. You'll not be seeing me
there again!"

Abe said nothing. He took another deep drag from the
bottle and handed it back.

"Hey, Capt'n!" an excited voice shouted from the bow.
"There's a sloop bearing down off to starboard!"

Tenny glanced in that direction, leaped to his feet. "Pass
me that lantern, one of ye!" He tore off the cloth that
shrouded the lantern and waved it in circles around his head.
"Sheer off, goddamn ye!" he yelled. "Can't you see it's us!"

The sloop was coming down wind and coming fast, her
boom swung wide, her mainsail arched like a great black
wing, silhouetted by the moonlight. For an instant she

seemed to hesitate, then swerved to port and rushed past astern.

Tenny subsided and swung the boat back on its course. "There's the damn British for ye!" he said disgustedly. "Supposed to be patrolling, and they can't keep a lookout for theirselves."

"The British!" Cornelius gasped.

Tenny laughed at his expression. "Ye needn't look so almighty scared. We paid our respects to that there sloop on our way over—and respects ain't all we paid, neither!" He winked broadly. "Now do ye begin to see why I ain't likely to end up in no New York prison?"

Abe swallowed. "You've sure found a way to make war safe," he said drily.

"And profitable, too," Tenny agreed. He prodded a sack on the boat's bottom with his foot, brought forth a ringing metallic sound. "Silver—solid silver—four sacks of it! And there was jewels, too, not even hid away. Here, boys, have another drink."

Abe accepted the bottle. As he passed it along, he glimpsed Cornelius's face.

"Guess you were pretty lucky this trip," he suggested quickly.

"Sure we was. But this stuff—that's so much gravy. What we really come for's that old fellow tied up in t'other boat. That's where the profit is—prisoners for exchange."

"You—you mean Judge Wilson?" Cornelius's voice was choked. "What on earth has he—"

"Yeah, Wilson—that's the name, I reckon." Tenny leaned forward, beaming. He was in fine fettle after the success of the venture. "Ye see, it works thisaway," he confided. " 'Bout a mouth ago some Tory privateers come across from Long Island and captured old man Barr, over to Fairfield. He's in the state legislature, a real important fellow, but somehow—I ain't saying how, mind ye—them Tories found out he was home and come and took him. Well, naturally, his

folks is pretty concerned over him—an old man and sickly—
being a prisoner. Well, we got letters of marque and reprisal.
I ain't sure what the hell 'marque' means, but 'reprisal'
means do to others like they done to you. So we goes around
to see Barr's folks and offers to go over to Long Island and
catch 'em a Tory fit to be exchanged for him. Only we're
taking a big risk—our boats and our lives and all—so we got
to be paid real well. So how it works?"

Abe gave a low whistle of what might have been admiration. Tenny beamed at him amiably.

"Well, sir, when they finally got enough money raised, we
gets word—again I ain't saying how—about this here Wilson
or whatever ye call him, so after fixing a few things up we
comes over tonight and takes him away. His folks are going
to be right worried, too, of course, so pretty soon a swap'll
be fixed up and everybody'll be happy. Only," he added,
"seeing as how this here Wilson's richer than old man Barr,
it looks like some more money'll have to change hands."

There was an instant's silence.

"In other words," Cornelius began, "you and those Tory
scoundrels are working hand in glove in this—this—"

Abe shut him off with a sharp jab of the elbow into his
ribs, but Tenny's smile broadened.

"Heaven forbid!" he declared piously. "It so happens—
just by luck, of course—we caught one of 'em lurking on
the beach near where we landed, so we put a gun on him
and made him lead us right to this here judge's house. We'd
have brought him back a prisoner, only he got away. And
what do ye know—the bastard took a whole sack of our best
plunder with him!"

Tenny slapped his thigh and roared with laughter, rock-
ing back and forth on his seat while the boat yawed crazily.

"Easy, Doc!" Abe whispered to the apopleptic Cornelius.
"Hold it till we're safe ashore."

Tenny wiped tears from his eyes. "By God, I'll be a rich

man if only this here war lasts long enough! Drink up, lads!
The bottle's half full yet."

A man in the other boat began to sing, and a dozen voices
quickly joined him. The lilting tune rolled out over the
moonlit waves where the fresh breeze swept it away.

"Yankee Doodle went to town
A-riding on a pony . . ."

"I've marched to that a hundred times," Cornelius said in
a low voice. "With the fifes shrilling up ahead and the drums
pounding out the beat, and men going out to fight for something bigger than themselves. To hear these blackguards
sing it—"

His voice trailed off. Black water hissed along the boat's
careening gunwale, and stars, dim in the gaps of the mackerel
sky, danced above the peak of the triangular sail. In the
stern sheets Captain Tenny beat time with his sweep handle
—beat the time of the Patriot marching song for a crew of
half-drunken pirates in the middle of Long Island Sound.

But his two passengers, for the moment, had all but forgotten his existence.

Chapter 7

THE BOSTON POST ROAD

The wind, which had held strong and steady throughout
the night, brought them into Norwalk, the privateers' home
port, not long after sunrise. The boats were run up on the
beach near an old mill, and as they stepped ashore Abe and
Cornelius heard for the first time in months the challenge
of a Patriot sentry. He was one of a local militia guard posted
along the shore to give warning of enemy raiders, and he
was properly dumfounded when these two nondescript
strangers brushed his musket aside and embraced him like
a couple of crazy men. When he recovered his breath, he
yelled until his captain arrived on the run and took charge
of the situation. This provided the escapers with an excellent
excuse for getting away from Tenny and his crew with no
more ceremony than perfunctory thanks.

The militia captain took them to his own home where his
wife soon had a hearty breakfast laid for them. Then there
was a bed apiece; fine, wide beds with clean linen. Lulled by
the novel sense of entire security, they slept like children
until past noon when their host aroused them for another
hot, filling meal.

He could tell them little of the military situation beyond
the general reports which were public property. But even
these were news to them. The main American army was said
to be in winter field quarters at a place called Valley Forge,
down near Philadelphia somewhere. An outpost line of sorts
had been established in Westchester, based on Tarrytown at
last accounts, but there were rumors that advance posts had

been pushed into the old Neutral Ground nearly as far as Phillipse's. Sporadic cowboy activities had continued throughout the winter, but nothing of great moment had taken place since the previous autumn in that region, or was likely to until the roads dried out, which would be another month, at least.

"Still and all, I'd not let night catch me in the Neutral Ground if I was you fellows," he added. "There's dark and bloody doings there, even in the quietest of times."

"So I've heard tell," Abe said innocently.

Cornelius was impatient to rejoin his regiment and announced his intention of getting to Valley Forge by the shortest route possible. The militia captain found them a couple of old muskets and some ammunition, and on his advice they set out as soon as they had finished eating, reaching Greenwich shortly after nightfall by dint of hard tramping. There they put up at a tavern, rising at dawn in order to avail themselves of every hour of daylight for the most difficult and dangerous leg of their journey.

Abe set their course along the Boston Post Road, his idea being to reach familiar territory as quickly as possible, then attempt to locate one of the rumored advanced American posts where they would be able to obtain accurate information regarding the enemy dispositions before making plans for Cornelius to cross the Hudson. At the Byram River, marking the state line, they were halted by a bridge guard of New York militia, but these showed neither knowledge of nor interest in conditions beyond their own sector, so the wayfarers pushed on no wiser.

The nature of the countryside began to change almost at once, but so subtle was this change that it was some time impinging upon their consciousness. The region they had passed through the previous afternoon had been peaceful and prosperous, where people went unconcernedly about their everyday business. Once beyond that militia outpost, however, they began to enter the sphere of cowboy operations. The first time they came upon a farmhouse that had burned down, Cornelius gave it scarcely a second glance; fire was a common peril to wooden houses that relied for heat and cooking entirely on open hearths. But Abe noticed, and the high spirits that stemmed from his new-found freedom gave way to that old alert awareness that tingled the nerves, sharpened the senses.

His eyes began their restless sweeping, left and right, ahead, now and again quickly backward over his shoulder. On either side of the road the dun March fields lay bleak and empty. Here and there a close-cropped pasture showed, or the moldering furrows of a plowed field, or the bristling stumps of last year's corn. But more often waist-high weeds ruled the land, rank and brown against thawing patches of the winter's snow. On the Boston Post Road, principal thoroughfare of a normally populous rural region, not a wheel turned. In Rye a few early risers stared at them suspiciously, but Mamaroneck might have been a village of the dead when they passed through, though Abe's attuned senses felt the weightless impact of unseen eyes.

It was this pervading emptiness that finally got through to Cornelius. "There's something uncanny about it," he said, shivering a little. "All these farms, these villages—why, we haven't seen another human being in an hour."

"Nor beast, neither," Abe added. "We're in the Neutral Ground now, Doc."

Cornelius glanced about. Up a short lane to the right a cellar hole choked with charred debris showed where a house had stood. Across from it a short distance farther on was a small abandoned cottage. The windows had been boarded up, but looters had crashed in the door which hung crazily from one hinge to reveal the dismal, desolated interior. A plume of wood smoke rose from the chimney of the next house they came to, and a curtain in one of the windows fluttered as they passed as though a hand had let it fall back, but there was no other sign of life about the place.

"I've been in the Neutral Ground before," Cornelius said. A troubled frown creased his forehead. "But I don't remember its being like—this."

"I been thinking just about the same, Doc. I've scouted this whole section—this very road even. There can't such a hell of a change have come over it since August. But somehow it seems like I'm seeing things here for the first time."

"I suppose the change is within ourselves, Abe."

"In us? Why—I reckon maybe it is."

The implications of this new thought engrossed him so that for a moment he lost his alertness.

"Look there!" Cornelius gripped his arm suddenly.

"Huh?" Abe followed the doctor's gaze down the empty road.

"That's funny. I'd swear I saw a man there. He just came around that curve—then all at once he wasn't there."

Abe was himself again. "Act like you didn't see him."

They continued down the road. Once they rounded the curve, a glance showed Abe that no one was in sight beyond. He wheeled swiftly and vaulted the stone fence on the right before the startled Cornelius realized what he was up to.

"Get up! What the hell ye hiding for?"

The man was crouching in the mud, pressed close against the stones. Abe caught him by the collar and pulled him erect. "What ye hiding for?" he repeated.

The man cringed. "Leave me be. I ain't done nothing."

He was unarmed, a shabby farmer in leather breeches and torn stockings. Abe released his grip and shifted the musket back to his right hand. "Honest folk don't go ducking behind fences for no good reason," he said more quietly. "Speak up—what ails ye?"

The man stared at the ground. "I was just going to my neighbor's," he mumbled. "I don't want no trouble."

"He's frightened, that's all that's the matter with him," Cornelius said. "Good heavens! We're not going to hurt you!"

The man did not look up. His abject, hangdog expression changed not a shade.

"You know of any Rebel outposts hereabouts?" Abe demanded.

"I ain't a Rebel."

"Nobody said ye was. All we want is to know where's their nearest outpost."

"I—I don't know."

"How about the Refugees—they been prowling this way lately?"

"I don't know."

"Listen," Cornelius interposed. "You've nothing to fear from us, even if you're a Tory. All we want is information."

"I ain't a Tory."

"Oh, come on!" Abe said impatiently. "He ain't got the guts of a louse. Might as well save our breath."

They were silent for some time as they walked on, occupied with their own troubled thoughts.

"Did you notice his eyes?" Cornelius asked after a while. "More like an animal's than a man's—like a slinking dog with his tail between his legs. I suppose the poor devil has been kicked around so much that he's afraid to say anything for fear we'd turn out to be enemies." He breathed deeply. "By heaven! One might think the British were deliberately trying to break the spirits of our whole nation. Their prisons were bad enough, God knows! And now—this!"

Abe said nothing. His lips, Cornelius saw, were tight and grim, and there was a hard line along his lean jaw.

The deeper they progressed into the Neutral Ground, the more urgent it became for them to locate friendly troops. When, after another half hour, they had encountered no one else abroad, Abe decided they would have to begin inquiring at houses. So the next time they sighted a smoking chimney, he turned up the lane and approached with ostentatious deliberation. Even so, it was several minutes before his knock was answered, then by a woman who opened the door a mere crack.

"We want to speak with your husband, ma'am," Abe told her.

Frightened eyes dilated. "He—ain't here."

"We mean you no harm, I swear." He hesitated. "We're prisoners escaped from New York trying to get back to our own people," he added boldly.

He saw a flicker of expression cross her face and vanish. "He ain't here," she repeated stolidly.

With a swift movement Abe thrust his foot between the door and the jamb. The woman let go of the latch and fell back, mouth open, eyes pitiful.

"Please, mister. We got so little—"

Abe's glance darted about the small room. It was dusty and shabby, and two broken chairs had not been repaired: telltale signs of the apathy, shiftlessness of people who had been beaten down.

"We won't take nothing, ma'am." He crossed the room and opened a door in the opposite wall. "Please tell your husband to come out from under that bed yonder where we can talk to him."

The man scrambled from his hiding place. He made a perfunctory brushing gesture at the dust and cobwebs that covered him and faced Abe with a sort of sheepish defiance.

"What ye want with me?"

"Only to find out where's the nearest Rebel outpost."

The man hesitated. "Be ye Rebel escapers, for a fact?"

"Aye, for a fact."

The man struggled visibly with his indecision. "I can't take ye to 'em, mister. They'd burn the house if they found out. The house's all we got left, and they'd burn it for certain."

Abe snorted. "I don't need no guide in Westchester! Just tell me where they're at."

The woman found her voice. "Don't ye tell 'em, Hiram!

They may be Tories for aught we know. We'll get in trouble either way—"

Abe turned on her. "We don't aim to make no trouble, ma'am," he said harshly. "But we'll make a-plenty of it right now if we have to. Now, mister! Tell us what ye know and be quick about it!"

"They're at the Glebe house over to Phillipse's," the man said hastily. "There's three hundred of 'em camped in Widow Babcock's meadow."

"You swear to that? You send us into a trap, and by God, I'll flay ye alive!"

"I swear it, mister! I swear! They was there last week, anyhow."

Abe looked at him hard for a long moment, then turned on his heel. "Let's go, Doc."

Cornelius, however, did not follow at once. "I'd like to ask you people a question, if I may," he said. "You've been robbed and bullied by British, Hessians and Tories. If that's not enough to make a man a Rebel, what in heaven's name is?"

A shadow of bitterness darkened the man's face. "The Rebels ain't saved my stock for me. We pleaded to 'em in vain, our committees and all. If we counted on them for protection, we'd be a sight worse off than we are."

"We haven't men enough to patrol the whole county. But hundreds in your position have found safe protection behind our lines. Why do you remain here in this miserable state?"

"Ye mean I should abandon my land? Not me, mister! I worked twenty years to get this here ninety acre freehold, and I'm hanging onto it, come hell or high water."

Half through the door, Abe turned. "Ninety acres, you say? Why, that's just the size of my pa's freehold. Up Bedford way, it is."

He paused, and Cornelius saw his expression change. His gaze swept the weed-grown fields, the empty barn, the forlorn little house that was falling into disrepair; then came to rest on the abject, broken-spirited man, the cringing woman with the frightened eyes. Once more his mouth thinned, and that hardness showed along his jaw.

"Come on, Doc," he said abruptly, and strode down the lane without looking back.

Chapter 8

MY COUNTRY AND MY PEOPLE

The war had touched northern Westchester lightly as yet. In contrast to the universal devastation in the Neutral Ground, the hilly Bedford countryside reflected rural prosperity: fields well cared for, buildings in repair. Yet, like the Neutral Ground, it appeared subtly different than Abe remembered it. ("The change," Cornelius had said, "is within ourselves.")

His family was at supper when he reached home. Uncertain of his reception, he went around to the kitchen door and let himself in quietly. For a long moment he stood framed in the doorway without speaking.

The homey, familiar scene, movement arrested, made a tableau on the retina of his brain. At the kitchen table his father, mouth open, a forkful of food half raised; his brother Jack with startled eyes. His mother, bending over a pot on the open hearth, straightened with a small scream, her face red and moist.

"Why—it's me. It's Abe! Don't ye know me?"

His mother was the first to speak. "Abe! My son! What have they done to thee?"

She ran to him and gathered him into her arms, oblivious to the tough stubble of beard that accentuated the gauntness of his face. Later, when he studied himself dispassionately in the mirror, he could understand better why they had been slow to recognize him.

George Kronkhyte rose deliberately. His face was stern, but it looked tired and old. After an instant's hesitation he grasped his son's hand. "Give him a chance to set, Ma," he said. "From the lad's looks, he's had little enough to eat these past months."

He had plenty to eat that night, and he gorged himself to repletion. Between mouthfuls he tried to describe what had happened to him, tried to answer the puzzled questions with which they interrupted him. As though by tacit consent, perhaps out of consideration for what he had been through, none of them mentioned his last visit, more than a year before, with its abrupt termination. Their affection poured over him like a warming flood, brought a poignant happiness to his heart such as he had not imagined himself capable of feeling. He had all but ceased to think of home after that dismal Christmas Eve. Now he had come, and it was good to be there; to sense that, in spite of all that had happened, this was still a part of him, and he of it.

But after supper, full of food, the keen edge of contentment dulled, he was aware of a feeling of detachment growing upon him; of that old aloneness.

"Have any folks been around asking word of me?" he inquired abruptly. "Folks you don't know?"

"There was the two young fellows come to tell us thee'd been taken," his mother recalled. "One great hulk of a lad and t'other dark and always laughing."

"Big John and Brom Dyckman!"

He could see them as clearly as though it were yesterday; could hear hoofbeats on a lonely road, the tread of marching men. He became aware of a pain in his right hand, clenched so tightly that the nails were biting into the palm. In the silence that came upon them then, the others were watching him uneasily.

George Kronkhyte cleared his throat. "Thee's had a terrible experience, Abe," he began, "but that was for thy own asking. Perhaps it is as well. The best lessons are ever the hardest learned. If this has taught thee what I have held from

the first, I shall be content—that war is not a game for boys
to play at, but a fearsome and evil thing."

Abe looked at him across an unmeasurable gulf. Somberly
he nodded. "I found that out, Pa."

"Then it is in my heart to forgive thee for running
counter to my will. We shall count on thy staying hence-
forth like a dutiful son. Soon there will be planting, haying,
harvest. In honest service to the soil there is penance for the
sin that has stained thee."

Abe shook his head. "I reckon not, Pa. I'm off for the
army, come morning."

His mother gave a strangled cry. "Oh, no—no—"

"I got to go, Ma. I'm sorry, but I got to." He saw their
confounded expressions and essayed an explanation. "I
couldn't stay safe at home—not now. I'd feel like I was going
back on 'em—on Doc Cornelius and Brom and John and the
rest—on them poor devils rotting in the prisons, and on them
freezing and starving in the field, sticking to their guns.
Don't you see? We all been fighting together for the same
thing. I couldn't never look myself in the face again if I
skulked off home and left them to fight on alone."

His father expelled his breath in a great gust. "Thou'lt
persist in the vain pursuit of glory at the cost of mortal sin?"

"Glory?" Abe repeated. "I ain't never been sure what it
is, this thing folks call 'glory.' Only I don't reckon it's what's
fell our lot—defeat, humiliation, filth, disease. No, Pa.
'Twasn't for glory me and Doc took our lives in our hands
so's we could get loose to risk them lives again."

"For shame! Could not even prison teach thee the evil
folly of thy course?"

Abe rose to his feet. "Well may you talk of evil and folly,
safe beyond the scoundrels' reach!" he said bitterly. "I just
come up through the Neutral Ground, no better'n a wilder-
ness hardly, where folks slink out of sight when ye come by
—folks like animals, with fear in their eyes. Folks of our own
kind, or who used to be. Folks who might be us today, but

for the grace of God—you and Ma and Jack—and this freehold you worked for all your life growing up to weeds and woods, the stock driven off, everything we own plundered, and the house a heap of charred rubbish in the cellar hole!"

In a small mirror above the mantelpiece he glimpsed his face; a face that might have been thirty rather than not yet twenty-one. He tried to remember what he had looked like the last time he had peered into that mirror, but without much success. There was some change there greater than mere maturity would effect. It showed sharpest around the hard, narrow mouth, the level eyes. He turned again to the confused, conflicting expressions of his audience.

"I don't want to be ungrateful, Pa, nor a disobedient son," he said more quietly. "And you, Ma—I don't want to do nothing to make you feel bad. Only I seen things you folks ain't never dreamed of. And I reckon they've done something to me."

"What thee's seen is war, lad," his father said heavily after a moment. "War—man's greatest crime against Almighty God!"

"It ain't the war, Pa—not what I mean. It—it's them!" His hands clenched and unclenched. To organize his thoughts he commenced pacing restlessly up and down before the hearth. The firelight, flickering upward, made a moving pattern on his gaunt, tense face. "It ain't our army they're making war on. It's the helpless among us—poor folks who've done 'em no harm, beaten and robbed and their houses burnt—prisoners who can't defend theirselves starved and tortured and left to die in their own filth. It's like Doc Cornelius says: having failed to whip our soldiers by right or even might, they're trying to break the spirits of our whole people till we're no better than beaten curs, fit only to be kicked around, without the gumption to resist, only whine for mercy.

"And they're in a fair way to do it, too! But they ain't a-going to, because there's them among us who'd rather be dead than like that! And if we got to die, we aim to take a-plenty of the scoundrels along with us where they can't do our people no more harm, and where they can roast in hell for what they done already!"

His father paled. "Hast forgot thy Bible, son? ' "Vengeance is mine," saith the Lord!' ' "

Abe made a helpless gesture. "If only I could make you see!"

"If only I could make thee see! This senseless, cruel and bloody war has deprived men of their reason, turned innocent boys into savage brutes! Would thee protract it now that the King has offered peace; peace that gives in to all the Rebel demands short only of liberty?"

"The offer comes too late. Too many of us have learned what justice and mercy honest men can look for under the yoke of such masters!"

"Is not peace—any peace—better than piling more misery on what we have already, breeding more hatred in men's souls? And to what purpose? Can even a headstrong boy like thee still hope for victory after the past two futile years?"

"Victory?" Abe repeated. "Maybe you're right about that, Pa. Maybe we can't win—not with all we got arrayed against us. Regulars and Hessians and Indians and Tory traitors— men and guns and money and food. No, I reckon there ain't much hope we can win. But hope or no hope, we're going to keep a-trying!"

He stopped speaking but did not look at the others. One elbow on the mantelpiece, he stared down at the fire, watching the draught form pictures of light and shadow across the bed of glowing coals. He could not make these others see the pictures that he saw there. He could not make them understand what he felt, for they spoke a different language.

Slowly he raised his head. "I ain't never known much about this here 'liberty' folks orate about," he began. "Time was when that used to bother me some. Now I just don't give a damn. 'Cause I know what I'm fighting for, and whatever others want to call it don't make a whole lot of difference."

He paused, groping for words. "Maybe the war's made a savage brute out of me, like Pa says. But there's one thing I've learned out of all the hell I been through: this here is my country, and the people in it are my people. If my heart's full of hatred and vengeance, it's on account of what's been done to them. And those that done it's the ones that's going to pay, whether we whip 'em in the end or not!"

He saw their faces, shocked, uncomprehending, and all at once he realized that it was a matter of complete unimportance whether they comprehended or not. They seemed infinitely far away. He wondered whether he could ever feel toward them again as he had felt as a boy, and once more only a short time before at the supper table: warmed by their affection, by the illusory ties that made them seem part of him. . . . He wondered whether he would live to enjoy the vaguely defined blessings of liberty.

Then he realized that that, too, was unimportant.

THE END

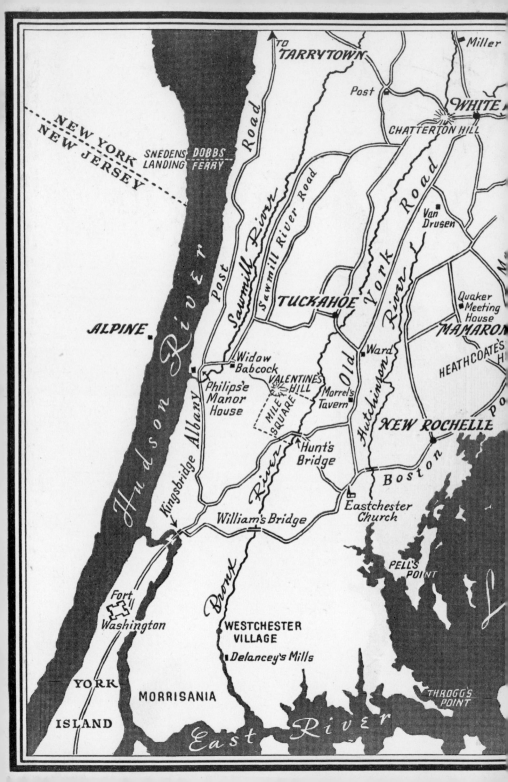